Leap of Hope

Chance at an Austen Kind of Life

Crossroads Collection, Book 2

Shannon Winslow

PRELUDE

Hope O'Neil – recent orphan, college student, and Jane Austen devotee – awoke completely uninjured but mystified to find herself in unfamiliar surroundings.

The last thing she remembered, she had been minding her own business, just walking down one of the many tree-lined sidewalks on campus on the way from her freshman English class to a ten o'clock appointment with someone by the name of Mrs. Tanaka, a guidance counselor.

It was a beautiful spring morning – deliciously cool but already hinting at the balmy South Carolina summer ahead. The air smelled of fresh-cut lawns. Larks and wrens were singing. Pink magnolia trees had begun bursting into bloom all over campus. Long-legged youths in khakis and polo shirts played Frisbee on the quad. In short, it was the sort of day that made a person glad to be alive.

And Hope was... glad to be alive, that is.

No, her life wasn't perfect. For one thing, she was pretty much alone in the world. She'd never had any siblings. Now her mother and father were gone. And she still hadn't stumbled across the hunky-but-sensitive man of her dreams that the Regency era novels she read inspired her to expect. Yet her native optimism, which had allowed her to move beyond the tragedy of her parents' deaths, also told her Mr. Wonderful was bound to turn up at any moment. She was sure some romantic adventure lay in store for her too; at least she dearly hoped it did.

In the meantime, she planned to focus on finding her calling. The fact that she didn't know exactly where she was headed, career-wise, wasn't at all unusual. Less than half of the kids on campus had decided on their major by the end of their first year. Most of the others had changed their minds at least once.

It wasn't so much that nothing interested her. Quite the opposite; nearly *everything* did. College was a glorious buffet to Hope, with a hundred tantalizing entrees to pick from. English literature had the upper hand at the moment, but social work, environmental science, art history, and even paleontology had all been contenders at one time or another. Making a definite choice was the challenge, and, even more difficult, sticking to it. But that's what guidance counselors were for, right? – to help students who lacked clear direction get things sorted out? Even though she had never met the woman, Hope placed the utmost confidence in Mrs. Tanaka's ability to do just that.

And there was plenty of time to get herself sorted, have adventures, and fall in love, she reasoned. After all, she was only nineteen.

Yes, plenty of time.

Ironically, that's what Hope O'Neil was thinking that March morning as she made her way toward Grady Hall. Then suddenly she heard a roaring noise overhead and time ran out.

Part One:

Hope's Second Chance

Shocking as was the idea, it was at least better than a death un-fairly hastened... (Northanger Abby, chapter 23)

Chapter 1
Light Dawns

Clueless.

There's no doubt about it. That was me: plumb clueless.

I usually get a sort of early warning when something big is about to happen. You know, sort of a premonition a few seconds in advance. A jolt of adrenaline hits my brain, and my skin breaks out in a whole flock of little goose bumps. That sort of thing. Like last year when I found out I'd been elected homecoming queen. Half a minute before the phone rang, the little hairs at the back of my neck started to prickle for no apparent reason, standing straight up like a company of tiny toy soldiers fixin' to march off in a dress parade.

This time, though? Nothin'. Not even an itch in my baby toe to alert me. Then it was all over before I knew what had hit me. And I *do* mean hit me... literally. Now I'm about to start my new life in 1809 as a proper English gentleman's daughter. Is that awesome or what? It's going to be like somethin' straight out of a Jane Austen novel. I just have this feeling.

But I'm getting ahead of myself. I should explain what came in between.

"There's been a little accident," I was told when I opened my eyes.

I gingerly sat up, blinked twice, and stared at the lady who brought this surprising news. She had a kind face and a soothing voice, but at first it was hard to hear what she was saying at all on account of the distraction of her loud outfit – a noisy hot pink number with enormous polka dots everywhere. Not a nurse, then, I guessed, even though the room had the scrubbed-clean look of a hospital.

"Where am I?" I asked, looking around myself. It seemed a reasonable question, all things considered.

"Unfortunately, there isn't an easy answer to that..." the older woman replied. She looked about forty to me, with dark, reddish brown hair and a very curvy figure. "...but I'll try to explain," she continued. "My name's Cora, by the way. May I sit down?"

My good manners kicked in, despite the strange situation. *Southern hospitality knows no borders,* as Momma always said. So I motioned to the space at the other end of the sofa – the only piece of furniture in the room – saying, "Of course. Be my guest."

Cora seated herself and then began with an unexpected topic. "Have you ever heard of blue ice?"

Baffled, I shook my head. "What?"

"Blue ice," Cora repeated. "It's water that somehow leaks out of an airliner in flight – lavatory water, actually. It's extremely rare, but when it happens, the water freezes at that altitude, and they call it blue ice because of the color."

She paused for my response. I drew my brows together in a frown. "Yes, ma'am, but pardon me. What has that got to do with why I'm here, wherever 'here' is?"

"I'm coming to that. This place is called Crossroads, and you were brought here after the accident. You see, the other thing you need to know about blue ice is that when it builds up and gets heavy enough, it's likely to break free and fall back to earth, crash landing who-knows-where."

My hand unconsciously went to the back of my head.

"That's right," said Cora, nodding meaningfully. "Do you remember?"

"Not really. I think I heard something and then..."

"Yes," she said slowly, allowing that much to sink in. "I know it's hard to understand, but your life, as you knew it, ended at that moment. Try not to be too upset, though. The good news is you've been given a second chance. That's what we do here at Crossroads..."

Bless my soul! Cora probably kept right on a'talkin. All I know is I didn't hear another word. I'd never fainted in my whole life – a life that was, apparently, now prematurely over – but the fact that I was basically dead was certainly worthy of a serious swoon. Not that I keeled over on the floor or anything. I just mentally checked out for a bit in a panic over the things that seemed to have slipped away from me.

Images from the past scrolled before my eyes: my parents, our green and white clapboard house in Baton Rouge, Louisiana, and Sheila Brown, my best friend from grade school. I felt a fresh pang of loss over each one. Then I reminded myself that those things were gone long before this accident. I'd lost track of Sheila ages ago, and the house – the only one we'd ever stayed in longer than three years – was sold after my parents died when I was a senior in high school.

"Hope? Hope, are you all right?" I heard Cora asking.

Her question, along with my own urgent curiosity, brought me back to my senses. "Oh, yes. A second chance, you said. What does that mean exactly?"

Before Cora could answer, though, I heard a sort of swooshing sound and turned to see a man coming in through a sliding door, one I hadn't even noticed was there. He put me in mind of a smaller, wiry cousin to Colonel Sanders, dressed in a white suit, the way he was, and with the same style mustache and goatee.

"This is Mr. Poindexter," Cora said, rising. "He's the director of Crossroads."

"Co-director," he amended, gently. "Good day, Miss O'Neil," Mr. Poindexter continued in his cool, British-sounding accent. (Or was it Australian? Maybe South African. I can't always tell them apart.) "No ill-effects from the recent unpleasantness, I trust?"

I paused to take stock. My skin looked a little pale, but that was about it. "No, I seem to be just fine."

"Good. Good. Has Cora explained the situation to you yet?"

"We were just comin' to that, I think."

"Very well. Then I shall leave you to it. I just wanted to look in and say hello. We'll talk more later. Be sure to let me know if there's anything I can do to make your stay with us more comfortable. Meanwhile, you are in very good hands," he said with a glance and nod to Cora.

Although their behavior was entirely business-like, I thought I saw some more-than-business-like affection between them. Of course, I knew it was probably too soon to tell.

"Thank you, Mr. Poindexter, sir," I said, smiling at him. "I'll do that." He gave me a formal little bow before going out the way he'd come in. I turned my attention back to Cora, who was still looking after Poindexter. "What an interesting man," I remarked, "and so polite!"

"I'm glad you like him," she answered, turning back to me and sitting down again. "Not everybody does, you know. His manner can put people off sometimes – men, mostly. They sort of lock horns. You know. But I'm sure you'll get along fine with him. Dex can be very charming when he tries, and he tends to make more of an effort with the women."

This time I was sure. By the way Cora defended her co-director, I knew there was something going on between these two, something beyond a work relationship. I can spot romantic attraction a country mile away.

I couldn't help myself; I blurted out the question on my mind. "Are you two a couple?" You don't often see a middle-aged woman blush, but I swear this one did. Then I felt bad for putting her on the spot. "Excuse me for being so forward," I added quickly. "It's certainly none of my nevermind."

Cora looked away and cleared her throat before continuing. "Yes, well, shall we get back to the business at hand? You must be in a state of shock and full of questions."

I had a whole boatload of questions; that was for sure. But I didn't feel like I was in shock, although I knew I probably should be. After that first moment of panic passed, I felt more excited than terrified. I couldn't wait to find out what might happen next. Was that proof of shock in itself, I wondered? Or maybe the whole thing was only some kind of incredibly convincing dream.

Before I could decide, Cora went on.

"Now, here's the situation in a nutshell. You have been selected to receive a second chance at life, which is really quite a rare honor. Crossroads is what you might call a holding area, a way station of sorts between your former life and the next. There are many pathways that lead from here, but you have three main options to choose from. Number one is to skip directly to the afterlife, if you have no desire to return to the world under any circumstances. Secondly, if you're the adventurous sort, you can start over in a totally different existence – as a different person, in a different place or even a different time period. The possibilities are endless. Your third option is returning to your old life, but with a chance to make

11

some kind of change for the better – to avoid a costly mistake or make a different choice at a critical point in your past, for example. Or you could simply avoid the accident that ended your life and go on from there. It's completely up to you."

I just sat there as still as a stump while she rattled off all this information, fascinated and overwhelmed by what I heard. It was too much for my puny little brain to take in all at once. I couldn't believe what Cora was telling me, and I said so.

She leaned forward and patted my hand, saying, "That's only natural, Hope. All our clients feel some disorientation in the beginning. You can take as much time as you need to decide what you want to do, though, so try to relax and just get used to the idea first."

Suddenly, I was struck by a bolt of inspiration. "Cora! You said I could go back and make a change to my old life, right? Well, if that's true, could I change what happened to my parents? Could I save them from gettin' into that awful wreck?" It had been a car accident on highway 61. They were returning home from New Orleans – a special night out to celebrate their anniversary – when a truck driver, who'd apparently fallen asleep, crossed over the centerline. The driver survived to face charges, but Momma and Daddy were killed instantly. "Maybe I could convince them to stay home that night instead."

I saw by Cora's sympathetic expression what her answer would be.

"No," she said, "I'm sorry, but that's not possible. Your second chance is authorized to make a different outcome for yourself, not for anybody else. You can't prevent your parents' deaths, but you can your own. You could arrange to leave your English class five minutes earlier or five minutes later, for example, or take a different route to Grady Hall. Then the blue ice would hit an empty sidewalk instead. Something to consider, anyway." Cora moved toward the door. "And we'll get some more furniture brought in for you soon to make your room a little homier. Do you want anything in particular? You'll be here several days."

"Gosh! I don't know," I said, getting to my feet. "A bed, maybe?"

"Of course. You'll find that you won't actually need to sleep while you're here, or eat either, since your body is in what you might call a state of suspended animation, but we do simulate cycles of night and day to maintain some sense of normalcy for our clients. A bed is as good a place as any to relax and think. You'll be doing a lot of that here – thinking, I mean. One more thing before I go. Do you like gizmos and gadgets? What I mean is, are you good with technology – computers, video games, and so forth? You'll need to research your alternatives before you make any decisions. I just want to be sure you're able to access our data banks in a way that suits you."

What could I say? I knew how to word process, but otherwise, I treated computers like outhouses – necessary for gettin' your business done, but not a place to hang around any longer than you have to. As for video games, I never could understand what all the fuss was about. I preferred books myself. So I said, "Better give me the low-tech option, if you have one."

"Not a problem. We'll get you started on that soon. In the meantime, just settle in and try to get comfortable with what's happened."

I thanked her and promised I would try.

When she left, I started pacing my room. It was only about sixteen feet wide, so there wasn't far to go, but I just couldn't imagine sittin' still when there were so many bees buzzing around inside my head. Eventually, though, I did calm down enough to consider my options in a more organized manner.

The afterlife? Well, I knew what the Bible said, and I did look forward to living in heaven one day, seeing God and Jesus and all the folks I loved who had passed on before me. I didn't really feel like my time had come just yet, though. So much for option one.

What about option two, then? A brand new life in a different place and time. Did that mean I could choose something in the future? Hmm, I'd have to ask Cora. Although the past was actually more intriguing to me. It always had been. I knew many things had changed for the better over time, but it also seemed to me that some of the best of civilized life had been lost along the way. People didn't bother to dress up anymore, and they had forgotten their manners. "Please" was no longer the magic word, and you almost never heard a "no-thank-you" nowadays, especially from anybody under fifty. Everything had become so careless, so casual – "coarse," as my Aunt Connie was fond of saying. And I had to agree. It would be refreshing to return to a slightly more formal, gracious time.

Then it dawned on me. Of course! Regency England.

Catharine had the misfortune, as many heroines have had be-fore her, of losing her parents… (Catharine, by Jane Austen)

Chapter 2
Making Jambalaya

"The second option's the one for me!"

I burst out with it as soon as Cora came in the door the next morning. Of course, there weren't any actual nights or mornings at Crossroads, as had been explained to me. Still, when the lights had gone low, I figured it was time to try out the comfy-looking bed that had been brought in for me, along with a few pillows and other things. Somebody understood my tastes in books; that's for sure. There was a neat little stack of Jane Austen on the side table, with my absolute favorite, *Pride and Prejudice*, right on top. Also a Georgette Heyer novel and a couple of romances written by more modern authors.

But who could read at such a time? I tried and gave it up in five minutes when I couldn't get my mind to hang on to even one of the sentences right there in black and white, plain as day. So I set the book aside and just rested with my eyes closed for what seemed like hours, thinkin' and thinkin' about what I should do with my second chance.

Despite my immediate inclination towards choosing an alto-gether different life, I resolved to at least consider option three. It had suddenly struck me as kind of disloyal to dismiss my old life without a second thought, as if I hadn't appreciated what I'd been given the first time, which certainly wasn't true.

I had loved my parents with all my heart, and I never doubted – not for one minute – that they loved me just as much. Nothin' could be more important to a girl growing up than that.

I'm also smart enough to see that they did their best to provide me a normal, healthy childhood. They were both caught up in their careers, it's true, but I was proud of how successful they were. And so what if that meant we had to move around a lot? I'm sure it made me a better person – more flexible, well-adjusted, and quicker to make new friends too. Those skills would always come in handy. The only thing I really regretted about my childhood was not having at least one brother or sister: a friend I could have taken with me wherever we went. But the glass-is-half-full side of being an only child is I didn't have to share my parents' attention with anybody else.

They meant the world to me, and it left an awful hole in my life when they passed, both of them so suddenly and without warning.

"What will you do now?" my friend Julie had asked me at the reception after the funeral.

I shrugged and sighed. "I don't know exactly. Aunt Connie says I can stay on with her as long as I want."

Julie followed my gaze across the room to the gray-haired lady in the severe, navy blue dress. "Are the two of you close?"

"Not really. I mean she's nice enough and all, but she's so much older. I think she was like eleven or twelve when my daddy was born, and she's never been married or had any kids of her own. To tell you the truth, I don't think she has the faintest idea what to do with me. But it's kind of her to offer, and it would only be for a few months until I graduate. I'm sure it'll be fine."

So that's what I did, stayed with Aunt Connie in Baton Rouge until I graduated high school and through the summer afterward. Then in September, I packed up my things, kissed her, Julie, and all my other friends good-bye, and I moved a hundred miles east into a college dorm to start all over again. I was used to doing that – starting over in a new place every few years. Maybe that's why I wasn't all that shocked to find myself at Crossroads, facing the need to do it one more time.

Of course, I technically didn't have to start a new life. I could go back to my old one and see what I could make of it. If I couldn't save my parents, though, there didn't seem much to gain by it. Besides, this was a huge opportunity I'd been given – a rare honor, Cora had called it. It seemed only right I should make the most of it by undertaking something big, something brave.

And so, I thought of Regency England. I could go back to the world Jane Austen had written about, the world of graceful ladies wearing long gloves and handsome gentlemen in cravats and cut-away coats. If I did, would I be swept off my feet like Lizzy Bennet by another Mr. Darcy? No, that would be too much to expect. I'd be more than happy to settle for a man like Jane's loyal but slightly-less-handsome and slightly-less-rich Mr. Bingley. What I really envied about that pair of Bennet sisters was the fact that they always had each other. No matter how bleak things became, they never needed to go through it alone. Jane had Elizabeth and Elizabeth had Jane: best friends forever.

By contrast, I'd spent far too much time on my own, suffering through grief and loss by myself. I had lots of friends, but no one as close as a sister – something I could attempt to fix with this second chance.

It seemed a little risky to charge ahead into the unknown – a different era and country – rather than choosing something familiar like most people probably would. I wasn't the least bit timid, though, and hadn't I been longing for an adventure? Well, sure as shootin', I'd never be given a better chance for one than this!

The more I thought about it, the more enthusiastic I became. By the time Cora came in that morning (this time wearing a crazy hat that looked like a bowl of fruit balanced on top of her head), I was nearly beside myself with anticipation. That's why I blurted it out so quickly.

"The second option?" Cora repeated after my declaration.

"That's right. I'm not ready for the afterlife just yet, and I've got nothin' to go back to in my own. But trying something altogether new? Well, that idea gets me real excited! What are my choices?"

"Too many to list. It's up to you to narrow things down and make the final selection from positions available. There's an entire menu."

"A menu? You mean I can pick out a new life the same as ordering lunch at Denny's? 'I'll take a cheeseburger with a side of 1973, please.' That easy?"

Cora smiled. "Not exactly, Hope. You log in your preferences over a range of variables – time period, age, sex, occupation, geographical location, family situation, etc. – and you'll be presented with a slate of options that meet those criteria. There are stock positions available at most time and location coordinates that will allow you to enter the scene unobtrusively. No one will think twice about another coed on campus, for example, or someone new coming to the big city looking for a job. We'd give you a cover story, and you could slip right in. But if you prefer a more intimate society, such as a small town, or being part of a family…"

I interrupted. "Oh, yes! I must have a big family this time, or there's no reason for goin'. A family is what I long for most!"

"In that case, the options are a little more limited. You can't just show up at the dinner table one day, out of the blue and fully grown, and expect people not to wonder where you came from, can you?"

"No, I reckon not. How is it done, then? You must have your ways."

"Of course, or we could never offer that option. If you wish to travel into the past, it's a case where you would have the chance to assume the life of someone who has died, or I should say someone about to die. You step into their place just before the end, avoiding whatever calamity originally took that person's life and then living it out in their stead. It's done all the time, more often than you might guess. Perhaps you've even encountered a 'transplant' before without knowing it – a man who seems to miraculously recover from an illness that was expected to be terminal or a woman who missed certain death in a car accident because the brakes inexplicably engaged on their own. That sort of thing."

"I *did* hear of a gal once – her name was Sandi Baker – who everybody said had no right to survive this terrible kind of food poisoning she got from eating some bad sushi. But then she did survive after all. And what's more, she bounced back, right as rain. Although people said she was never quite herself afterward, which was put down to the fact of her brain having nearly been fried by the high fever. Do you think Sandi was one of your transplants?"

"I'm really not at liberty to say."

"Oh, I get it," I said with a wink. "Top secret stuff."

Cora nodded. "Our whole operation must be kept strictly confidential. You can imagine what would happen if word ever got out to the general population. People would begin imagining Crossroads clients wherever they turned, stirring up trouble, making accusations, or worse still, pinning all their hopes on the remote possibility of getting a second chance of their own. Life is difficult enough without adding those types of distractions."

"Hey, Cora, I just had a thought. Do you suppose someday my spot might be offered in your catalog of options? Like you said, all a body'd have to do is walk a little faster or stop in their tracks a second, and then that big ol' ball of ice would crash onto the sidewalk with no harm done. My replacement could go merrily on her way. No, I suppose not. Why would anybody choose my boring life instead of somethin' more exciting? Even *I'm* not going to do that! Forget I mentioned it."

"No, it could happen. You never can tell what will appeal to people when they're craving something different from what they had before. The question is what do *you* want? Give it some serious thought, and the next time I see you we'll get started. In the meantime, you can feel free to roam about the complex and meet the other residents. They're here for the same reason you are; they're all deciding where to go next – which option to take."

"I'd like that. I'm a real 'people person.' Everybody says so."

"I'm sure you are, Hope. Let me show you how to activate the door, then."

There was a place on the wall that you had to pass your hand in front of and the door would swoosh right open. Pretty cool.

"Are you coming?" Cora asked when I didn't follow her into the hallway.

"In a minute," I said, hesitating.

"Of course."

I'm sure she understood what I was feeling. She'd probably seen hundreds of people pass through Crossroads ahead of me, some more bewildered than others, I expect.

"Whenever you're ready," she said before leaving me, "turn left down the hall and you'll come to the commons. A group of clients is already collecting there. I think you'll find them very friendly."

I did want to meet the others, but first I needed to absorb what I'd learned. Certain things take time, and there's no way around it.

It's like making jambalaya. If you just throw everything in the pot and don't let it simmer, all you've got is water, boring rice that's like to break your teeth, and a bunch of other separate flavors that don't make any sense at all. Give it another half hour on the stove, though, and it starts comin' together. The spiciness of the sausage and peppers rubs off on the shrimp and melts into the chicken. The rice turns chewy soft from soaking up all that tasty goodness. With a little patience, you end up with somethin' a person's taste buds can really appreciate. The jumble settles into jambalaya.

That day, I was plain white rice thrown into a pot with a bunch of foreign and unfamiliar ideas. It was going to turn out yummy in the end, I expected. I just needed to sit and let things simmer a while.

One new question did occur to me while I was stewing, though. I wondered if anybody knew how to cook real Cajun in Regency England.

"I have traveled so little that every fresh place would be interesting to me..." (Persuasion, chapter 20)

Chapter 3
A Day at Disneyland

When I had benefited all I could from mulling over my situation, I did venture out to the commons. It felt like Crossroads was the gateway to the most awesome theme park ever invented, and I was eager to begin exploring all it had to offer, to find out what the attractions were and make a plan for covering as much ground as possible. I didn't want to miss a thing.

Mr. Poindexter was there at the doorway as if he had been expecting me. "Ah, Miss O'Neil," he said, "how are things progressing? Have you been able to come to terms with the new state of affairs?"

"I think so, Mr. Poindexter, sir. It's a lot to take in at first, but I've pondered it awhile, and I'd say I'm getting used to the idea. I'll tell you this much; I can hardly wait to see what comes next!"

"Excellent," he said, making some kind of note on a clipboard he seemed always to carry with him. "A positive attitude is very helpful in the process. I felt certain you would adjust quickly, once everything was explained. Now, I've told the others to expect you, so you can go right in. Be sure to let me know if there's anything I can do for you."

I thanked him and then turned toward the dozen or so folks gathered in the commons in a rough circle of colorful chairs. They were all looking my way, I noticed, and all dressed in white tee shirts and sweat pants, same as me. That was the standard Crossroads' uniform, apparently, which made Cora's flamboyant wardrobe stand out all the more.

"Hi, y'all," I said as I approached. "I'm Hope."

"Welcome, Hope. Have a seat," said a middle-aged man whose name was Jeff, as I learned a minute later.

I took the only empty chair in the circle, which happened to be right beside this dreamy looking guy, who was probably about twenty-five.

"Thanks!" I said looking around at all the new faces. I must have been sort of nervous, because I gushed even more than usual. "This is so exciting! Isn't Mr. Poindexter super? And I just adore Cora. I can hardly believe this place is for real and that I'm actually here. What happens next?"

"Well," began the elderly gentleman on my other side, "we normally start with introductions when someone new arrives. My name's Joseph Rutland."

"Pleased to meet you, Mr. Rutland," I said.

He was headed for the afterlife he then informed me, the same as Mrs. Cuthbert on his right, who was of a similar age. One by one, following around the circle, they each gave their names, a little about themselves, and which options they were considering. Most were leaning towards returning to improve on their former lives, I discovered.

It was quite an eclectic mix of people. After Mr. Rutland and Mrs. Cuthbert came a life insurance agent named Ken Fielding, a former professional wrestler who went by "Bruiser," Karen, a thirty-something dental hygienist, Jeff Kendall, who had been a plastic surgeon in his first life, and a handful of others.

The last to speak was the good-looking young man on my left.

"My name's Ben Lewis," he said. "I'm going back to my old life, to a point before an illness sidetracked my plans to play professional baseball. This time, thanks to my second chance, I won't get sick. The tricky part is I'll need to be sure I still find a way to meet and marry Abby. I don't want to end up gaining the career I always dreamed of and losing my wife instead. She's the best thing that ever happened to me."

"That's very sweet, Ben. You're lucky to have each other," I responded, meaning every word.

"We are," he agreed. "Now it's your turn, Hope."

I had seen how open and supportive everyone had been with each other, so I didn't hesitate to tell my story, such as it was. "Well, as I was saying, I'm Hope. I'm nineteen, and I was brought here just as I was about to die anyway. Apparently, in another millisecond I would have been clunked on the head with a chunk of blue ice the size of a picnic ham."

This seemed to take everybody by surprise.

"It's true," I assured them.

"Yes, it is possible," said Ken. "Things like that happen. A gasket on an airliner leaks toilet water, which freezes at altitude, busts loose, and plummets to earth like a meteorite. In my business, you hear of every possible way there is to die, but the odds on that one are incredibly long, Hope."

"Leave it to me to find the most ridiculous way to expire known to man. My gym teachers always did say I was accident prone."

"I don't know how you can joke about it," Karen said. "It sounds awful, and you're so young."

"I didn't feel a thing. Besides, now that I'm here, I plan to cash in on option two – a completely new life. I don't have any family, or much else to go back to. Plus, I've always felt like I was born in the wrong place and time. So, here's my big chance to fix up the mix-up. Is that great or what?"

"What kind of new life do you have in mind?" Ben asked.

"I haven't worked out the details yet. But I might try England – say around 1800 – you know, because I'm such a huge Jane Austen fan and all. The main thing is I want to finally be part of a real family. You're so lucky to have that, Ben. If I had family of my own, I wouldn't dream of leaving them behind. Both my parents died, though, and I don't have any siblings, a boyfriend, or even a flea-bitten hound dog to miss me."

Lots of questions followed. What had happened to my parents? Where had I lived, and what had I been intending to do with my life before the accident? Why was I so interested in the Regency period?

I had to explain the Jane Austen reference for the benefit of a few people who had never heard of her, let alone read any of her books. Imagine! But I found a kindred spirit in Karen Altman. Turned out she was a big fan too.

"Which Austen book is your favorite?" she asked me later, when the larger group had broken up. "Mine's *Persuasion*."

I recognized the hushed excitement in her voice. It was the same enthusiasm I felt whenever I found a person who spoke my language, who understood and shared my obsession, who knew that real men wore cravats and that a lady couldn't possibly talk to a gentleman without a proper introduction, someone else who involuntarily sighed upon hearing the name Pemberley pronounced.

"Oh, I do adore *Persuasion*," I said. "I'm sure I've read it a dozen times. But *Pride and Prejudice* is my absolute favorite. I guess you could say it was my first love, and you never quite get over your first love, do you?"

Karen *did* sigh then. "Sounds like you know a little something about that, Hope. Who was your first love, besides *Pride and Prejudice*, that is?"

Daniel. I hadn't thought about him in a long time, which was just as well. When I was sixteen, I had signed up for tennis lessons during the summer, and Daniel was one of the instructors. He was older – all of eighteen – handsome in a suntanned, athletic sort of way, and smart too. We had a lot of fun together, but it only lasted a few months. He abandoned me for someone else at the first bump in the road. I cried for weeks.

"His name was Daniel," I told Karen. "Ben Lewis over there," I said, nodding to where he was talking to Jeff across the room, "reminds me a little of him, although the comparison is probably not fair to Ben. I already think better of him than I do of Daniel. I expected Daniel to be faithful like Colonel Brandon, but he turned out to be a Willoughby instead, if you know what I mean."

"I do, totally. I've run across one or two Willoughbys in my day."

"To them, the grass always looks greener in somebody else's backyard, so they hop the fence first chance they get."

"Well, your Daniel obviously didn't measure up to Austen-hero standards. I suppose you're hoping to find your very own Mr. Darcy in your second chance. Do you fancy yourself another Lizzy Bennet?"

I laughed. "Oh, no. I haven't deluded myself into believing I could get that lucky. I'm an optimist, but I don't have my head completely in the clouds. Actually, maybe we all do. Nobody's explained exactly where this place is, have they? And there aren't any windows, I've noticed." Then, to be polite, I thought I should ask my new friend more about herself instead of talking only about me. Besides, I really was interested. "What about you, Karen? You didn't say much during introductions. Any Mr. Darcys in your life? Or maybe you'd prefer a Captain Wentworth."

To my dismay, Karen's smile crumbled, and she drew in a long shuddering breath.

"Oh! I'm so sorry," I said, feeling terrible that I'd apparently brought this woman to the brink of tears with my nosiness. "I didn't mean to pry. Just forget I asked."

"That's all right," she said, clearing her throat and stabbing at a tear that had spilled onto her cheek. "I've had to face facts since I arrived here at Crossroads. The right guy for me did come along, once. But I... I... Well, I made a complete mess of it. I didn't appreciate him like I should have. That's what it amounts to. Now, though, I've got the opportunity to go back and correct my mistakes, thank God." After another deep breath, Karen recovered her smile and sense of humor. "Even Lizzy Bennet had to admit she'd misjudged her Mr. Darcy, didn't she?"

"That's right, and Anne and Captain Wentworth got a second chance too! I just love that about Austen's stories. No matter what problems her heroines come across, you can count on a happy ending when all is said and done."

Whew! We had just barely escaped that pit of nasty quicksand to plant our feet firmly back onto solid ground again. Talking about our mutual interest in Jane Austen's books and characters was a whole lot safer than baring our souls. I felt compassion for Karen, yes, but I didn't think we had been acquainted long enough yet for me to act as her true confessor and confidante. After all, we had just met, and these things take time.

Although that rule would have applied under ordinary conditions, I was starting to discover that time didn't mean much at Crossroads, and ordinary rules weren't always relevant. People had too much at stake, and some of them had arrived through desperate circumstances. This was no day at Disneyland for them.

...the past and the future... must be before her, must force her attention, and engross her memory, her reflection, and her fancy. (Sense and Sensibility, chapter 19)

Chapter 4
Possibilities and Perplexities

When the lights dimmed for my simulated night number two, everybody in the commons began drifting away to their own rooms. I gathered that was the routine, but I was a little disappointed, to tell you the truth. I wasn't ready to be alone again yet. And despite my hesitation with Karen, I really did have a powerful hankering for getting to know what made these folks tick. Each one had a fascinating tale to tell, I was pretty sure, or at least they would have after things played out. Of course, not one of our stories was finished being written yet – that was kind of the point – and they wouldn't be so long as we stayed at Crossroads.

I also had to warn myself not to get too attached to anybody in the group. On any given day, one or two might leave and another arrive. It wasn't as though we had much chance of staying in touch after we went our separate ways either. *Well, golly. I think I'll drop dear Mr. Rutland a line. What was his address again? Oh, that's right; it's Heaven, in care of... Who? God?* Would I have any better luck posting a letter from 1800 to Ben Lewis in 1995 or wherever he ended up?

No, it was more like striking up an interesting conversation with somebody at an airport or bus station. You could enjoy the moment for what it was, but odds were you'd never see each other again. That didn't make it any less worthwhile, just different.

With that thought in mind, I returned to my room when the rest did. But I wasn't by myself after all. I found Cora there.

"Hi, Hope," she said when I came through the door. "How did you get along with the others?"

"Great," I answered, "except I think I made Karen Altman cry. I didn't mean to, mind you, but I guess I said the wrong thing. I seem to have a talent for that."

"Probably not your fault. Many of our clients come to us as the result of very tragic situations, some even suicidal. They have a lot of emotional baggage to sort through before they can move on. Now, come over here," she said with an abrupt change of subject. "I want to show you how to get started researching your options."

Cora had it all set up. There was a video monitor on the wall and a very basic, user-friendly keyboard for me. One button turned the system on, and then all I had to do was click or fill in blanks for what I wanted to see.

"It'll take you anywhere you want to go," Cora explained, "and show you all the positions available to choose from. That's primarily what you'll need it for – to help you in selecting a new life – but you're welcome to use our data banks to revisit events from your former life too, before you leave it behind."

Leave it behind? I didn't like the sound of that one bit. "I *will* still remember my parents and everything after I move on, won't I?"

"At first, yes. But those memories will naturally fade, and after you're fully assimilated into your new life, they probably won't seem real to you anymore. More like a dream you once had. It's for your protection, so that you won't continue missing things or be tempted to regret your decision. Once you make the leap, there's no undoing it, you understand."

"Yes, I see, but..." I trailed off, feeling a sudden ache in my heart. Not remember Momma and Daddy? I could hardly bear the thought.

Cora, who didn't seem to notice my distress, continued. "Oh, and if you're going into the past, you must agree that you won't use your knowledge of the future to change things. We can't have you inventing the light bulb before its time or taking it upon yourself to revise history. Understand? Your progress will be monitored to mitigate any possibility of that. Everything will be explained in your contract when you get to that point."

No chance of me inventing the light bulb, I was thinking. I wouldn't know the first step for how to go about it! The real question was could I learn to get along without *using* light bulbs? Or electricity of any kind. And although it wasn't a subject Jane Austen wrote about one way or the other, I supposed indoor plumbing hadn't been invented by the early nineteenth century either. Hmm. That would call for some adjustments. I'd been camping as a kid, though, plenty of times. How different could this be? I was confident that I could adapt. After all, people had by necessity found a way to live without our modern conveniences for thousands of years.

So, when Cora had gone, I determinedly plopped the keyboard on my lap and pushed the "on" button. This question appeared:

Do you want to A) see past events from your previous life, or B) view possibilities in another place and time?

Although I was excited to research my options for the future – my future in the past, that is – I couldn't resist a detour to my own history first.

I had arrived at Crossroads completely empty handed, with no mementos whatsoever – not the backpack I carried that last day, not my wallet, not even the clothes I had been wearing. I didn't have a single, solitary shred of my past with me except my memories. It hadn't occurred to me that I would eventually lose those too, which made me want to dive in for a long wallow in a big tub of nostalgia. Maybe if I reinforced those memories while I still could, caked and plastered them into every spare corner of my brain, they might be strong enough to stick around a little longer.

I clicked on "A."

What first showed up on the screen were pages I remembered from an old family scrapbook my mother had spent hours and hours putting together – pictures of me, of her and of Daddy, of the places we had lived and traveled. Mixed in with the photographs, there were other little souvenirs: a lock of my baby hair, a program from a play the three of us had attended in Chattanooga, a ribbon I had won in a fifth-grade talent contest for convincingly imitating and identifying the calls of my favorite birds. It was wonderful to see those things again, but, oh, what I would have given to have that album actually in my hands and to be able to take it with me when I left!

After an hour or so of reminiscing, I knew I had better move on. A body can only wallow so long before getting permanently stuck. Even the pigs on my granddaddy's farm had known when it was time to get out of the mud.

So I started over, this time selecting option "B," which brought up a whole laundry list of variables to choose from next. Even though the system was easy to use, I felt kind of stressed out right away, starting with the very first question.

Are you looking for a position as a female or as a male?

Oh, my! It never occurred to me I might have a choice. Then I realized that it probably just meant I should identify which one I was, so that turned out to be the easiest question of all. I checked "female" and moved on. Although I hadn't definitely decided what I was going to do, I went with my original idea, coming up with this profile in answer to the categories given:

Sex: Female
Age: 16 - 20
Time period: 1800 - 1825 AD
Geographic location: England, small town
Occupation: none
Socio-economic class: upper middle, gentry
Domestic unit: large family
Marital status: single

Most of this was pretty obvious, especially the gender part, as I said, and choosing AD over BC. I might be brave, but not *that* brave! I was tempted to see what would happen if I requested a place in royalty or at least nobility, but I wasn't sure I'd know how to behave. Jane Austen's novels, which I expected to be my best guide, didn't really cover that territory, except if you consider Lady Catherine de Bourgh a good role model. Also, I did waver on the age range, shifting the lower end up by a couple of years and then back down to sixteen, where I had begun. A wider sample would give me more options, I figured.

Finally, when I was satisfied, I took a deep breath and gave the command to search.

Results started popping up one after the other, like a row of sunflower seedlings in the garden after a spring rain. A baker's dozen in all: thirteen young women who had died too young, each represented on the screen by a short bio and a picture. It hit me then for the first time that this was for real, not just some hypothetical exercise for my entertainment. These were young women who had actually lived – lived lives cut short by some disaster or another – and I could step into the place of any one of them.

Camilla Harrington of Derbyshire had died at seventeen of influenza. Elizabeth Fogerty, who had resided in Kent, was killed along with her younger brother when the carriage in which they were riding overturned. Appendicitis had claimed the life of nineteen-year-old Amanda Haines from Bath – something a simple, twentieth-century operation could have corrected. Mary Talbot had been carried off by a smallpox epidemic and Kathleen Barrett, when she struck her head falling from a horse. The other eight girls fared no better, or they wouldn't have wound up on my list.

I started to cry as I read through them. I couldn't help it; I always cried at unhappy endings – books, movies, or real life. (Happy endings too, to tell the truth, although that was different.)

Their sad stories made me want to do something for those girls who had lived and died so long ago, but at most, I could help only one. At least it seemed like a sort of tribute to pick up somebody's life and carry it forward. If not a kindness to the girl herself, then to her family, who had loved her. I could make her alive again and spare them that grief.

Or could I? Hadn't they already suffered and then died themselves? If I went back in time now, did any of that really change? Did those people get a second chance right along with me? But I would be dead by now, too, if I chose a life in the 1800s, wouldn't I?

The whole time-travel, alternate-reality business was so confusing. I always got bogged down with unanswerable questions when I read a book like that. Now I was about to become that kind of story. Hard to believe. And another thing, how could I possibly choose one girl's life over all the rest, even looking no further than the small sample I already had? Then doing her justice would be a huge responsibility.

Feeling myself beginning to sink under a weight of perplexity, I immediately pushed the "off" button, setting the keyboard aside. I needed to give myself a mental health break. So I flopped down on my bed and, as I picked up the copy of *Pride and Prejudice* from the side table, recited one of my favorite lines from it.

"Elizabeth was not formed for ill humor." And neither was I.

The honour was readily granted, and he then departed, to make himself still more interesting, in the midst of a heavy rain. (Sense and Sensibility, chapter 9)

Chapter 5
The Dearly Departing

"Mr. Lewis," Poindexter called from the doorway after we had all been mingling in the commons for a while the next day. "A moment of your time, if you please."

Ben jumped up from his chair like he'd been shot out of a cannon. Everybody else suddenly hushed and watched him follow Mr. Poindexter from the room.

"What's going on?" I whispered to Karen, who was sitting beside me.

"I'm guessing Ben is about to leave us," she answered, returning our conversation to a more normal volume. "He's already stayed the minimum five days that's required, so he can go anytime he wants now. He didn't tell us he'd definitely decided, but he must have said something to Poindexter. They're probably doing the paperwork now, and then we'll no doubt hear what the scoop is."

Everybody was talking about it in the meantime, chattering away like a flock of jays settled in a chestnut tree, nonstop. I was just as curious as the rest. Like Ben had said during introductions, he planned to go back to his old life and try again for a career in professional baseball. I knew that much from the start. As we talked more, though, I learned he had a real dilemma as to what date to pick for his new start. If he went back far enough to have the best chance with baseball, there was a real possibility he might never get together with his wife on this second go-round. On the other hand, if he went later on, after he'd already met Abby, his chances of resurrecting his career were slim. Two things that meant so much to him – two goals that didn't necessarily both exist in the same universe, or at least in the same timeline.

So when Ben finally returned, we all formed our chairs into a circle to hear what he had decided to do.

"I'm going back to my college days, to before I got sick... and before I met Abby," he announced.

He let that set a spell. I knew – and of course, so did he – some in the group would think that was the wrong choice. Although driven career types (and probably die-hard sports fans, too) might applaud a man putting major league ambitions before love, the romantics in the crowd wouldn't. Still, everybody was polite and outwardly supportive when Ben went on to explain his reasons.

"Make no mistake; I dearly love my wife," he said, "and I'll do everything in my power to make sure we hook up again. But she deserves so much more than I was able to give her before. I don't mean just material things either. She deserves a man who is successful and living up to his full potential, not the disappointed, broken-down shell I had become. If I have my health back, I feel like I'll be able to do anything I set my mind to, making it to the majors and winning Abby back too. I don't care how long it takes or how hard I have to work; I intend to build a better life for us both. That's what we're here for, right? And that's what my decision came down to in the end: what's best for me *and* for Abby."

"It's what I would have done in your shoes," said Ken Fielding.

"Right on, brother," Richard Fegals agreed. "Don't give up the dream."

Jeff gave Ben a thoughtful nod. Mrs. Cuthbert wished him well, and the rest of us threw in our encouragement. Whether we agreed with his decision or not, we all hoped things turned out for the best. He really did seem like a good guy.

I could tell by the way he was squirming in his chair, though, that unlike me, Ben was uncomfortable being the center of attention so long. Funny how a guy might think playing a super competitive sport in front of a few million strangers on TV is no big deal, and yet he can't bear to talk about his personal feelings in front of a handful of acquaintances he'd never have to see again.

Anyway, I did what I could to rescue him, saying "I'm totally impressed, Ben, that you could put together such a logical plan for yourself." Then, turning to the group as a whole, I went on. "Me?

Well, I'm so gosh darn dazzled by all the possibilities, I can't think straight. You know how I was saying yesterday that I was considering starting my new life in Regency England? Well, I got a list of potential openings with Cora's help. Isn't she just as cute as the knees on a honeybee, by the way? Now, tell me what y'all think about this idea…"

I went on to fill everybody in on a few of the options I'd looked at so far – just thinking aloud, really. I wasn't anywhere near making up my mind. I had been told I could take as much time as I wanted, and I was in no particular hurry. I intended to enjoy the ride. It's like when you're traveling. You have a definite destination in mind and a whole slate of exciting activities you're looking forward to when you arrive, but that's no reason to shut your eyes to the sights along the way.

Same thing with my stay at Crossroads. It was only a brief stopover, and yet I might as well enjoy it all I could while I was there. One thing was for sure; I'd never pass that way again.

When the lights dimmed, signaling the start of our recommended hours of retirement, people began saying their good-nights. For me, it was the first of a series of good-byes too. Ben would be leaving us that night, followed shortly by two of the others. I didn't worry about Mr. Rutland and Mrs. Cuthbert, but I couldn't help wondering what would become of Ben and if he'd be happy in his new life, or actually, the new version of his old life.

I stopped to talk to Mr. Poindexter on my way out.

"Ah, Miss O'Neil," he said with a polite smile when I approached. "Is there something I can do for you?"

"I just have a couple of teensy questions."

"I am at your service."

"Well, Karen mentioned something about waiting a minimum of five days?"

"Yes, every Crossroads client is required to remain here at least five days before choosing a destination and making the leap. It's to guarantee he or she has thoroughly considered the options and made an informed decision. I'm sure you can appreciate the wisdom in that, especially considering that once you embark on your new life, your choice cannot be undone."

"I understand, but is that all? Do you just drop each of us like a sack of sweet potatoes off the back of a pickup and drive away? I'm thinking of Ben Lewis, and I guess I'm kind of hoping you'll keep an eye on him to be sure things work out okay."

"Oh, we'll keep an eye on him, Miss O'Neil, to be sure, but not in the way you mean. Mr. Lewis, as you may have noticed," Poindexter went on, a smidgen of disdain creeping in his voice, "is supremely confident in his own abilities. I doubt he would admit to needing any help from us. He will pretty much have to sink or swim on his own. His progress will be monitored, though, mostly to be sure he complies with the terms of his contract – not violating the clause about using his knowledge of the future for personal gain or to deliberately change history, for example. If he should do so – and I would not put it past him – swift disciplinary measures will follow. Cora did explain that clause to you, I believe."

"She did, yes," I confirmed

"And I know we needn't worry about you in that regard, Miss O'Neil. You have my complete confidence."

His tone had returned to the gracious one Mr. Poindexter always used with me. He clearly didn't like Ben Lewis as well as I did, though, which was interesting.

Cora came in not long after I returned to my room. "I brought you another book," she said, handing it to me.

"The Mysteries of Udolpho! Do you mean the book everybody's reading in *Northanger Abbey* is a real book?"

"Yup, and I thought you might want to read it too so that you'll be up to speed for Regency life. How are you getting on with the data system?" she asked.

"Fine, although I've barely gotten started," I told her. "Nice outfit," I added, acknowledging the authentic, original Star Trek series uniform she was wearing this time, making her look like a middle-aged, white version of Uhura.

"Thanks. It's in Ben's honor, since he's leaving tonight. Did you know he's a huge Star Trek buff? All things sci-fi, actually."

"Let me ask you something, Cora. Poindexter says Ben, which means the rest of us too, I suppose... Well, that Ben will have to 'sink or swim' on his own. Is that true? Isn't there anything you can do if he gets into real trouble? Like what if he misses his chance to meet Abby again?"

"Well," she said, glancing side to side. Even though we were alone and the door was closed, she dropped her voice to a near whisper. "I probably shouldn't be telling you this, because we don't want our clients expecting to be bailed out of every scrape they get into, but we can sometimes help matters along a bit. Nothing major, you understand, but maybe a little nudge in the right direction here and there. That sort of thing. Although Poindexter didn't hit it off with Ben, *I* did, and I'll do what I can for him if he gets into trouble. I promise."

"You're like a fairy godmother, then, or a guardian angel."

She chuckled. "I suppose. Hmm. There's a thought. I'll have to work up an outfit for that."

I did feel a lot more comfortable about Ben after Cora's visit. I imagined him going on to a very good life with the help of an occasional 'nudge in the right direction.' And if he and Abby were meant to be together, which I was pretty sure they were, they would find each other again. I chose to think so, anyway, although I would never really know.

...in the course of the sleepless night... she found one or two such very serious points to consider... (Emma, chapter 50)

Chapter 6
A Two-Horse Race

The commons was a little more subdued after Ben and the others left and before any new faces arrived. It was like everybody had agreed it was time to get down to business. Dr. Jeff Kendal said he was closing in on a decision, and Richard Fegals sounded almost ready to go too. Not me, though. I still had a lot of research to do. Even after I decided whose life I wanted to assume, I would need to make myself familiar with her past, her family, her community, and her culture before I could hope to blend in, to convincingly take her place.

Early on, I narrowed my choices down to the two that appealed to me most, the ones that fit my wish list best: Elizabeth Fogerty and Kathleen Barrett. I trust I wasn't overly influenced by the names themselves, which both had a certain ring to them, reminding me of my ideal heroine Elizabeth Bennet. And let's be honest; that was my dream. I could deny it till I was blue in the face, but it was the God's honest truth. I was secretly hoping to slip into Elizabeth Bennet's shoes, or at least shoes that bore a striking resemblance. What I really desired to get for myself was a quality knockoff of her life and a ticket to Pemberley.

I wanted the noisy chaos of a big, affectionate family, where something interesting is always happening. I wanted sisters who were also my best friends. I wanted to dress up in fancy clothes, ride in horse-drawn carriages, and go to candlelit balls. I wanted the genteel language and manners I had read so much about. And most of all, I wanted to be properly courted by an Austen-worthy hero, a genuine gentleman, and to find my *happily ever after*. So what if I had to give up a few modern conveniences to get it? That seemed like a fair tradeoff.

But would I have a better chance at the fairy tale as Elizabeth Fogerty or as Kathleen Barrett? That was the question.

Added to the ideal name (I really was thrilled by the thought of becoming an Elizabeth!), Miss Fogerty had a lot going for her. She lived in the south of England, in Kent, and I was a southern girl through and through. She had two parents, three sisters, and two brothers, meeting the 'large family' requirement more than adequately, although the younger of her brothers was killed in the carriage accident when Elizabeth originally died. If I survived as Elizabeth, would I be able to save him too? Otherwise, I'd be plunged directly into a family in mourning. I could see to it that Mr. and Mrs. Fogerty lost only one child instead of two, though. That would be worth something.

On second thought, they might have preferred to save their son (the spare to their heir) instead of only one of four useless girls. If I had learned anything from all those Regency novels, it was that unmarried daughters were often considered a curse and not a blessing, especially where there wasn't enough dowry money to go around, enough to reel in good husbands for them all.

The Barretts were equally cursed, however, also having four daughters, with Kathleen being, appropriately enough, the second oldest. But unfortunately for them, they were not equally blessed with sons. No, the Barrett estate, I soon discovered in my research, was entailed away for lack of a male heir, just like Longbourn in *Pride and Prejudice*. Gracious! Not another cousin like Mr. Collins, I hoped.

As far as my choice, though, I couldn't decide if the Barrett entail was a good thing or not. On one hand, the more closely the circumstances matched my favorite novel, the more perfectly the situation fit what I had imagined. On the other, it might be smart to take practical matters, such as financial security, into *some* consideration rather than being completely swept away by my romantic notions. That would require more thought.

I could hardly wait to see Karen in the commons the next day, to tell her what I'd learned so far about the leading candidates in my search and get her opinion.

"I don't know," she said as we were taking a turn about the room, in the style of Lizzy Bennet with Caroline Bingley. "I think you have to go where your heart leads you, even if it doesn't seem like the most *practical* choice as to money. That's where I made most of my mistakes the first time around. I was too busy chasing the lifestyle I thought I wanted to notice when something really worthwhile came along."

"Do you want to talk about it?" I asked. Then, remembering what had happened the last time, I hurried to add, "You don't have to, of course. I just wouldn't want you to think I don't care."

"Thanks, but I'd much rather think about *your* life right now. It's less stressful and more interesting besides. Didn't you say that these Barretts lived in Hampshire? That seems like a real plus. Hampshire is where Jane Austen grew up, you know."

"And where she lived later on too, when she did most of her important work, at Chawton Cottage."

"That's right! I'd forgotten. When would you arrive on the scene?"

"Kathleen Barrett died in 1809, so that's where I'd step in."

"I'd have to double check, but I think the Austen ladies would have been at Chawton by then. If you lived nearby, you could happen to meet Jane on the street one day. Imagine! You could buy first editions of all her books as they came out!"

"Why, Karen Altman, if I didn't know better, I'd swear you were considering taking the spot yourself."

"Believe me, if I could go just temporarily, I would! But not forever. I have too much unfinished business in my own life to tend to."

Mr. Poindexter interrupted before we could carry these interesting ideas any further.

"Your attention, please, everyone," he said in a loud voice to be heard above the buzz of conversation in the commons. When the noise died down, he continued. "I wish to inform you that we have a new arrival here at Crossroads. I expect she will be joining you shortly. Her name is Amy Nichols."

"What's her story?" asked Ken Fielding, who happened to be standing closest to Poindexter.

It's what I wanted to know, too. I was pretty well acquainted with all the others by then. I'd heard as much of their stories as they were willing to tell, and it was time for fresh material. I can't speak for anybody else, but it really helped me that I could be around other people at that time – to learn about their lives and their plans, to hear their opinions on my own situation or to take a break from it entirely for a while. It warded off feelings of isolation and kept things in better perspective. Whoever had set up this program had been smart to allow for that kind of social interaction instead of keeping us all boxed up in separate cages like so many lab rats.

"Come on, Poindexter," Ken added. "Give us a hint."

"I am no gossip, Mr. Fielding," he answered crisply. "You should know that by now. You have also been here long enough to be aware of Crossroads' strict confidentiality policy, by which all our personnel are bound. What Amy Nichols chooses to divulge to you is entirely her own business. You will not hear any of it from my lips. I will only remind you all to welcome her warmly."

Joining us later that day, Amy herself was not very forthcoming either. Not at first, anyway. When the standard introductions made their way around to her, she choked out, "I'm... I'm Amy Nichols," then covered her face with her hands, and promptly burst into tears.

Karen, who sat to her left, immediately wrapped an arm around Amy's shoulders. "You poor thing!" she soothed. "Here you are, hijacked away from your regular life and dropped down in the middle of a bunch of strangers. I know it's pretty overwhelming at first, but this really isn't such a bad place once you get used to it."

"It's not that," Amy managed after a few awkward moments. "Everyone's been extremely kind, and it's a relief to be away... away from my past."

I felt like it was my turn to do something, since I happened to be on Amy's other side. "There, there, honey," I said, patting her hand. "You don't owe us any explanations. Some of us are just fine with hanging our dirty drawers right out there for everybody to gawk at. But this is mighty new to you. You take your time and get comfortable before you go baring your soul."

With another sob and a face like to crack clean in half for grief, Amy got up and hurried out of the commons.

"Did I say something wrong?" I asked the others in dismay. "My shoes may be only size five but my mouth must be at least a ten 'cause I never seem to have any trouble fittin' both feet all the way into it."

The next day, Amy Nichols braved a return to our group.

"I'm sorry for falling apart like that yesterday," she began. "I'm doing better today, though, and I'm very grateful to have been chosen for a second chance. You see, I made a disaster of my life. I did some terrible things, things I desperately want to undo."

We all leaned forward ever so slightly, and Amy rewarded our rapt attention with a brief account of her sad history, how her disillusionment with her husband and an extramarital affair had drawn her progressively deeper into a tangle of lies, eventually leading to the worst possible outcome.

"I swear I had no idea it would end so badly," she said by way of wrapping things up. "It seemed so harmless in the beginning. Still, I know a lot of it was my fault, so I try not to feel sorry for myself. What I can't get over is what it did to my family, especially to my kids. My husband has to take his share of the blame, but my children were innocent. They didn't deserve to have their world ripped out from under them. I want so much to make things right for their sake."

"And now you'll have your chance to do just that, Amy," concluded Jeff.

"Yes, thank God. It doesn't matter what happens to me as long as my kids are okay this time."

"Ain't one of us that don't have regrets," said Richard Fegals. "I sure 'nough do. What counts is you want to change. That's why we were all brought here, I believe."

Was Richard right? Did we all have regrets?

I thought about that later, when I was by myself again. I spent very little time looking backward, and I had never been one to constantly repine over what I should have done differently. Not that I had fooled myself into thinking I'd been Little Miss Perfect. I hadn't been! Not by a long shot. I'd made plenty of mistakes, but no really big ones I could think of. Was I living in denial, or was it just because my life had been cut so short, before I'd had time to majorly bungle it?

I suppose it makes me some kind of Pollyanna, but I always feel like things happen for a reason, and difficulties that come along give a person the chance to grow. I think the harder a circumstance is, the more you tend to learn from it. Although I would have given anything to prevent my parents from dying, it had been the single event in my life that had taught me the most. It taught me I was stronger than I thought. It taught me never to take anything for granted, especially a person I loved. Life is precious. It must never be wasted but lived to the fullest. My parents had done that, and I intended to as well.

I learned so much from people, whether they were characters in Jane Austen's novels or in real life. And now I had the chance to continue my education through the pool of experience shared by the clients of Crossroads. So I listened carefully, filing away bits of wisdom from each one, lessons learned the hard way, in many cases. They hoped to avoid those mistakes in the future, and so did I. Maybe I'd have enough to write a whole book about it when I was done. But not yet. My adventure had just barely gotten started.

"You promised to take a family dinner with us, as soon as you returned. I have not forgot you see..." (Pride and Prejudice, chapter 53)

Chapter 7
Tiebreaker

The tiebreaker came when I found out I couldn't save Elizabeth Fogerty's brother along with myself. If I chose to take Elizabeth's place, I would survive the carriage accident, but that was the only change I could expect. Apparently, this fell under the same general rule that would have kept me from preventing my parents' deaths. The second chance was for me and nobody else.

With that in mind, I researched exactly how long and how unpleasant the mourning period would be, discovering that it primarily affected what a person could wear and whether or not they were allowed to have any fun. Men had it pretty easy, required only to wear armbands. But the women of the day were plunged into a sea of inky black right up to their Regency chins – a year's worth for a mother mourning a child and six months for siblings. As for fun of any kind, that was a big no-no.

Pretending to be sad for a whole half a year over losing somebody I'd never even known seemed like an arduous task. I wasn't heartless, but I also wasn't that good an actress. Besides, I had spent quite enough time genuinely grieving recently, thank you very much. I didn't cotton to the idea of voluntarily doing it all over again so soon.

"Not exactly how I had pictured starting my exciting new life," I told Karen the next time I saw her, "sittin' home every night, drowned in black bombazine!"

"What's bombazine?" asked Amy Nichols, joining our conversation.

"It's a very dull fabric," I explained with a sigh, "designed to be sure those who wear it are equally dull. It was preferred for mourning clothes back then because it had no sheen to it whatsoever. Apparently, you weren't considered properly somber if your clothes reflected a single speck of light. A person must have positively disappeared after dark in that kind of getup, except maybe her disembodied head and hands, floating in mid air."

Amy laughed, which pleased me. It was the first time I'd seen her so much as smile since she arrived.

"Still," Karen said, more seriously, "six months of mourning would be worth it if everything else about the situation was what you wanted. It might even help you make a more gradual transition, since nothing much would be expected of you at first."

She had a point, although I thought as Kathleen Barrett I would have the same advantages without wearing widow's weeds. When I survived Kathleen's riding accident, I could ease back into an active life at my own pace, blaming everything from slips of the tongue to forgetting how to dance a quadrille on the blow to my head. It was the perfect cover story.

Of course, I hoped not to need excuses. I hoped to arrive on the scene up to speed on Regency life, so I could hit the ground running.

I wasn't completely ignorant, fortunately. I was glad now that I'd elected to take that English history class my very first semester in college – my only complete semester, as it turned out. I had also collected quite a bit of knowledge of social customs along the way from what I'd read and seen in period movies. Cora had brought in a couple of other books for me to help fill in the blanks about that place and time period too – things I'd need to know regardless whose life I chose to step into.

"Whatever person you choose, some of her memories will carry over," she told me. "I can't explain how it happens, but you will know a lot of things she knew, remember things she remembered. Still, you'll want to learn as much as possible ahead of time and not leave anything to chance. With the video system, you can view all the events in your candidate's life up to the point when you would come on the scene. You can get to know the family and their circle of friends as well. Preparation is key to successful integration, so don't neglect your studies."

Cora didn't have to tell me twice. I dove right in and had more fun than a hungry raccoon up a tree full of ripe plums.

The world was at my fingertips for the picking!

It was incredible that, just by typing in a few instructions, I could watch things that had happened two hundred years ago and thousands of miles away as if it were here and now. I couldn't begin to understand how it was possible, but I guess that was about the least of the miracles they were in the business of performing at Crossroads.

To be thorough, I did first explore Elizabeth Fogerty's life a little further. Other than the disadvantage of upcoming mourning, I didn't find anything particularly *wrong* with the situation. What's more important, it didn't feel quite *right* to me either. It was just like watching a show on TV – a detached look at episodes in the lives of people I didn't know and had no particular connection to.

By contrast, when I watched my very first segment of Kathleen Barrett's life – an ordinary family dinner – I felt at home almost immediately. Within five minutes, I was longing to pull up a chair, pass the peas, and jump into the lively conversation. By then, I had sorted out the cast of characters.

Mr. and Mrs. Barrett were the easiest to identify, of course, sitting at opposite ends of the table. Mrs. Barrett would have been in her mid-forties at that time, according to the information I'd been given about the family. She appeared very well preserved, though, unless she was hiding a mass of gray hair under the mobcap she wore. As for personality, she reminded me a little of Mrs. Bennet, the way she carried on and on about how she'd been slighted by another lady in town the day before.

"...She gives herself such superior airs, just because she has got her two daughters disposed of already. To my mind, there is no very great credit in having only a curate for one son-in-law and a complete dunderhead for the other. So what if he will inherit an estate in Yorkshire one day! I should think it more a punishment than a reward to be sent to live so far away from all good society. I hope I know how to do better than *that* for my four girls!"

"My dear Mrs. Barrett," said her husband, who was many years her senior. No hiding *his* gray hair, what was left of it. "Do not exasperate yourself with these trivialities, I beg you. You know your nerves will not bear such histrionics... and nor will mine."

"Trivialities? How can you be so unfeeling, Mr. Barrett? Surely, there can be no more important and sacred duty for any mother than to see her daughters well provided for in marriage. After that is done, I care not if I am put out to starve in the hedgerows."

"Mama! Please do not speak so! You know your family will never allow such a thing to happen." This heartfelt protest came from a very pretty young woman sitting next to her father – the oldest, Lucy, I concluded.

"I hope it may not be so," said Mrs. Barrett, calmer now. "If only one of you can marry very well, that will be the saving of all the rest."

"Lucy's job," said the girl next to her.

This was Kathleen! This was the girl I had the opportunity to become! It was a thrill to get my first look at her in action, to hear her voice for the first time.

"She is the prettiest as well as the oldest," Kathleen continued, "and so it is clearly her job to raise our fortunes."

"Be fair, Kate! Why may not the job be mine?" said one of the others. "I may be the youngest," (ah, so this was Carmen), "but I think my chances of marrying a duke or a marquise are as good as anybody else's. If Papa will only agree to take me to London for a season, then perhaps it will be I who saves the family when he is dead."

Mr. Barrett continued at his supper, apparently unperturbed.

"The chance of any one of us marrying a duke or marquise is exceedingly remote," added the last and most serious of the sisters, which would make her the third in order of age: Matilda. "It is absurd to even propose such an idea, Carmen. Nobility marries nobility, as you should know. They have no need to explore the lower orders looking for wives."

"We are not the lower orders!" Carmen declared. "We are a gentleman's daughters."

"So you are," Mr. Barrett cut in, stridently. "Quite right. You should all make free to marry dukes and lords if you please, but not, I trust, for the purpose of 'saving the family.' For your information, I have every intention of living on to a ripe old age. I'm sorry if that fouls any of your fine plans…"

By this time, I was nearly in stitches! I swear I fell in love with the Barretts – all of them – that very minute. They were exactly what I had imagined: noisy and real and full of genuine affection for each other. That's the way they seemed to me, and the more I observed them, the more that first impression was confirmed.

How could I resist the chance to be a part of them? To be Kathleen Barrett, who was apparently called 'Kate' within the family; to have an older sister like Lucy for my best friend; two younger sisters with distinct, colorful personalities; and two parents, both alive and watching over us all. The striking resemblance to the Bennets of *Pride and Prejudice,* although one daughter short, did not escape my notice either. Was it possible Jane Austen had known this family and based the characters of her book at least partially on them?

I couldn't help feeling it was a sign. Hadn't I wanted Lizzy Bennet's life? Hadn't I asked for a shot at finding my Mr. Darcy and winding up in some version of Pemberley? No way I'd find anything closer than this setup for it, not in a million years.

"Indeed you should take care of yourself as well as of your friend. Let me entreat you to run no risks." (Emma, chapter 13)

Chapter 8
Going for Broke

"It's a sign," I told Karen the next day.

"What is?" she asked, very reasonably.

"How much the Barretts are like the Bennets! Plus, I've watched Lucy, the oldest, how she is with Kate – so loving and kind. I can hardly wait to have a sister like that."

"You sound as if you'd already made up your mind."

"Golly. I guess I have at that."

"Weren't you wondering about the family's finances? You don't want to step into a situation where you could end up penniless, even homeless. Remember, as neurotic as Mrs. Bennet seemed in *Pride and Prejudice* – scheming to get her daughters married and wailing, 'What is to become of us?' – her fears were entirely legitimate. She and her girls could have been put out onto the street when her husband died."

"I don't understand the complete financial picture since I only have access to whatever Kathleen would have known. There isn't much money for big dowries, that's for sure, and then there's the business with the entail, same as with the Bennets. But look how well that came out in the end."

"Hope, that was fiction! This is real life! There is a difference, you know."

"Yes, I do. I'm not a complete goose. Still, I can't help feeling this is the answer I've been looking for. Maybe the same force that brought me here – God, I suppose, although nobody will say – has been guiding me into making the right decision too. I'd like to think so. Anyway, weren't you the one who said I had to follow my heart?"

"I just want you to be sure. It seems like such a gamble. At least I know what I'm going back to, more or less."

"*Life* is a gamble, Karen, and I'd rather go for broke than play it safe. If things don't work out exactly as I planned, I'll just have to make the best of it. But I really believe it will be fine."

It was true. I'm not sure where it came from, that strong conviction, but at that moment, I felt like I could conquer the world, like I could take on dragons or even Lady Catherine, like I could deal with a creepy cousin such as Mr. Collins, if he existed. Nothing would stand in my way.

Hmm. Thinking of Mr. Collins and all, I wondered how far the parallel to *Pride and Prejudice* would go. Would there be a rich Mr. Bingley soon moving in next door, who happened to have a handsome friend visiting? How about a wicked Mr. Wickham in a dashing red coat? None of their counterparts – if they existed – had arrived on the scene yet, so far as I could discover. But then things were just getting started, the Barrett sisters just coming of age. Lucy was nineteen, almost twenty, with Kathleen and Matilda following close behind at eighteen and seventeen. Then there was a little gap before Carmen, not quite fifteen, brought up the rear. They were all on the threshold. Yes, the fun was about to begin, and I couldn't wait to be part of it.

More research first, though.

It was a little like being back at college, doing a term paper on a favorite topic, but this time I not only had a huge stake in the outcome, I had the most amazing library imaginable to help me.

Through the video system, I took a virtual tour of the Barrett estate called Laurelwood. I snooped down hallways and poked my nose into every room of the house. I supposed it would have been considered modestly sized and furnished as manor houses go, but it was a lot grander than any place *I* had ever lived. More like a plantation house in Charlotte, North Carolina, I had once toured. One thing missing, though; not a single bathroom of any kind in the place. No toilet, shower, or running water to be found. Darn! That's what I'd expected but hoped I was wrong about.

When I had seen everything there was to see, when I had memorized the layout and the contents, when I figured I could find my way around the house, even blindfolded, I moved on to the gardens with Lady Catherine's words ringing in my ears.

You have a very small park here… There seemed to be a pretty-ish kind of a little wilderness on one side of your lawn. I should be glad to take a turn in it…

So take a turn I did.

It was hard for me to judge whether what I saw on the screen was large or small by the standards of the day, but there certainly was a nice lawn out front. From there, walks and paths took me off in all directions – to a garden, an orchard, a definite kind of wilderness, outbuildings, and farmland. I explored them all to my heart's content. There was one rather private spot with moss-covered stone walls that reminded me of when I'd read *The Secret Garden* – all lush and green and separate from the rest of the world, although not locked away in this case. I could see myself strolling there some sunny day on the arm of a fine gentleman. I couldn't help thinking it would be the perfect place for a proposal.

When the time came, would he be shy and tentative, doubting his right to approach me? Or would he be over confident, like Mr. Darcy when he first asked for Elizabeth's hand? Maybe he would invite me to sit on one of the stone benches, and then he would drop to one knee before me…

But I'm getting off track.

Back down to business, I decided to examine the stables more thoroughly. Even though I knew that's how Kathleen had died, I looked forward to continuing to ride in her place. I'd begged and begged my parents for a horse throughout my growing-up years. Never got one, of course. It would have been completely impractical, as they patiently explained each time, considering the places we lived and how much we moved around. So I'd picked other sports instead, and music lessons (piano and voice) had been substituted for riding lessons.

About my only contact with actual, live horses had been at carnivals and county fairs atop one of those poor ponies, tethered and endlessly plodding in circles. That hardly counted as experience. But there had been that one glorious year at summer camp – full-sized horses and instruction on how to ride them! I think my parents hoped I would finally get all that 'horsy nonsense' out of my system, that I'd discover riding wasn't so special after all. Instead, I was as happy as a dead pig in the sunshine. I couldn't get enough.

Surely I must still retain *some* of what I'd learned in those two wonderful weeks. It was probably like riding a bike; you never forgot how.

The Barretts' small stables contained four horses altogether – a matched pair of sturdy looking beasts, which I took for carriage and work horses, and two sleek, lighter-weight creatures. These had to be saddle horses. Yahoo! I could picture myself atop one of them, galloping across rolling hills, wind in my face and my billowy skirts flowing gracefully behind me, preferably all of it in slow motion. Yes, I could see it clear as anything.

Skirts. Oh, that's right. I guessed I'd not only have to relearn to ride but to ride sidesaddle, like a proper lady.

With that thought in mind, I went in search of the room where they kept the bridles and harnesses and so forth. I'd never actually seen a sidesaddle up close, and I thought I'd better have some idea what to expect before I attempted to take my first ride in one.

A strange looking contraption for sure, with only one stirrup and a couple of curvy paddle-shaped things (pommels, I think?) sprouting out of the front of it like a pair of rabbit ears. I studied it from every angle – I could only look and not touch, unfortunately – until I thought I had figured out how it worked. Somebody must have to boost you up there, backside first. Then you hook your right leg around the top paddle thingy, being careful to arrange your skirt so it won't be damaged. Your left foot would go into the stirrup with your knee snugged up into the curve of the other paddle. After that, it's squeeze and hold on tight, I suppose. Not a very practical way to go about things, but it looked elegant and ladylike. That's what was important. I could hardly wait to give it a try for real.

Once I was pretty familiar with Laurelwood, I was ready to expand my ramblings further into Kathleen Barrett's world. So I hunted around until I found a way to zoom out for a bird's eye look at the surrounding countryside, just to get my bearings. I was happy to see a few other substantial houses in the vicinity, which improved the chances that there would be fine, eligible gentlemen living in or at least visiting the neighborhood *à la* Darcy and Bingley at Netherfield. Most of the houses were occupied by settled families, according to the information provided, but the nearest to Laurelwood – an estate called Coleswold – stood vacant in want of a new owner. That had definite possibilities.

I knew the nearest town was called Carding, and I wondered if it would be anything like the Meryton of my imagination. So I tagged along (virtually, that is) when the four sisters were headed that way one day a few months before Kathleen died.

"Here is what I need from Grimstock's," said Mrs. Barrett, handing a hastily scribbled list to Lucy. "And be sure to call on Mrs. Abernathy as you pass by. You know how she loves company, and she thinks of you girls quite as her own daughters, or nieces at the very least."

"Yes, Mama," Lucy replied for all of them.

"A visit of fifteen or twenty minutes should suffice. No need to wear out your welcome. And mind your time so that you will not come home late for dinner. Cook will complain for a week if the lamb dries out waiting to be served."

Then at last the girls were on their way with me right after them, my view as if I were flying just above and little behind and close enough to hear their conversation. Although it felt a little impolite eavesdropping, it was in a good cause – part of my education, so that I'd be able to pass myself off as Kathleen later. I needed to get a feel for her personality and mannerisms, to see how she related to her family members and others.

The girls had gotten no more than a hundred feet down the long gravel driveway when Kathleen suggested, "Let us take this way instead." Not waiting for the others to answer, she scampered off across the lawn.

Carmen didn't hesitate; she hightailed it right after her big sister.

"Your shoes, Kate!" cried Lucy from the driveway. "You two will ruin them in all that dirt."

"Nonsense," Kathleen called back, stopping to wait. "It is perfectly safe and dry and shorter this way besides. Come along, now. There is no reason we may not add a little adventure to our errand. Mama will not mind, so long as we are home in good time."

Lucy and Matilda did give in then and follow, which made me happy because I was excited to get off the beaten path too. I'd already seen all there was to see along the driveway.

There wasn't any trail, so I wasn't sure where exactly we were headed. But Kathleen seemed to know; she made straight for a rock poking up at the far edge of the lawn like some sort of obelisk.

Just before we got there, I could see that the ground didn't gradually slope away at that point and then back up as I had thought. It actually dropped six or seven feet almost straight down, like it had broke off and sunk along that line in an earthquake. But I knew it was on purpose. It was a *ha-ha*!

I was pretty impressed with myself for remembering what the thing was called, especially since I'd never actually seen one before. I'd come across the word somewhere reading Jane Austen and been curious enough to look it up. Turned out a ha-ha was sometimes used back then in England instead of a fence or a wall to keep farm animals out of the garden. It worked just as well, and I guess it was supposed to look more natural or something, since you couldn't see it from the house. It just looked like the garden rolled right on into the pasture beyond.

The rock sticking up marked the place where a narrow set of stone steps had been built into the side to let people, but not cows and sheep, up and down. Kathleen, still leading the way, marched right down the steps as if they were nothing. Lucy and Matilda picked their way more cautiously. Carmen was last, and she must have decided to show off a little because when she got almost to the bottom, she gathered up her skirts and jumped the rest of the way with a shriek and a laugh.

When I saw it, I couldn't help thinking of Louisa's accident at Lyme in *Persuasion*, but in this case, no harm was done. Carmen was fine, and they all continued on their merry way across the pastureland and through a patch of scattered deciduous trees.

"I do so hope we shall see officers today," Carmen said a little further on. "Do you think we shall, Lucy?"

"It is not very likely, Carmen. You know the militia has moved on. They are needed mostly along the coast and have no further business in Carding, so far as I am aware."

"What you say is not strictly true, my dear sister," said Kathleen in a teasing way. "When they were encamped here, they made it their business to keep all the young ladies within five miles entertained. I believe that is a job that still needs doing. Do not you think so?"

Lucy laughed. "The sight of a red coat does tend to stir the imagination, I will admit."

"Such imaginings are pointless, however," Matilda contributed, "for none of them, even the officers, has any fortune to speak of. One would be foolish indeed to pin one's hopes on the idea of marrying a soldier."

"No doubt you speak the truth," said Kathleen. "From what you say, I apprehend that you are become quite an expert on the matter. Have you made a *very* thorough study of our military men, then?"

Matilda blushed and stammered.

"Never mind," Kathleen continued, laughing and giving Matilda an affectionate sideways hug as they walked on. "I should be the last person to fault you for doing so. But since the militia are now gone, we shall not need to trouble you with any more questions on that subject, I fear."

By this time, the girls had cut their corner and reached the road, where they turned left and continued on another half-mile or so to the village. Carding looked just like I had expected. In fact, I could have sworn I'd seen it before as one of the movie representations of Meryton or Highbury.

I was eager to peek into the shop windows as we worked our way toward Grimstock's, which was the general store, I found out. I had to be satisfied with looking in the windows there too, because I discovered that for some reason I was unable to follow my future sisters and self inside with my video tour.

So I looked around while I waited. The main street, or "high" street, was crowded on the left and the right side with a hodgepodge of picturesque little buildings – some houses, some businesses, and some both – not all lined up straight, but a little cattywampus for added quaintness. Grimstock's and what I took to be a hotel were both charming, two-story stone buildings. Others were framed in dark timbers with some kind of white stucco or plaster filling in between in a Tudor style. That's as much as I know about medieval architecture.

For a small town, there were sure a ton of people parading up and down the street – on foot, on horseback and in a variety of carts and carriages. Once again, it was hard to believe I wasn't watching a movie with these the extras in perfect period costume. Good thing I was having a chance to get my first look at all this in advance, because I couldn't stop staring. At least this way I could gawk as much as I liked without anybody seeing me do it.

While I was still getting my eyeballs full, the Barrett girls emerged and began retracing their steps toward home. I would have to view more of Carding later – perhaps next time in person!

Just outside of town, a lady poked her head out the window of a fine-looking house and waved enthusiastically. "Hey ho, girls," she called. "Do come in."

"Good day, Mrs. Abernathy," Lucy answered back. "Yes, we were about to call on you, although we may not stay long."

In they went, and once again I found the door slammed in my face. I have to say it was a little frustrating – agonizing, really – to get so far and no further.

"Am I a vampire or something?" I asked Cora when she checked in on me later. "I can't go inside unless I'm invited? Is that the way it works?"

Cora laughed. "Not exactly. There are limits to what our technology will allow. That's all. You have full access to your primary subject's residence, but not necessarily everywhere else she goes. Think how much fun you'll have exploring those places once you're there."

I *was* thinking about it, and it all looked pretty idyllic to me: the time, the setting, and the people. The only thing missing from the picture was me – me carrying on as Kathleen Barrett, that is.

"In a country neighbourhood you move in a very confined and unvarying society." (Pride and Prejudice, chapter 9)

Chapter 9
Speaking of Departures

I'd made up my mind what I wanted. I wanted to live out the rest of my life in Kathleen Barrett's shoes, where I would have a big family and a permanent home like I'd always wished for. No more moving around every few years. No more making friends only to leave them behind again. The Barretts were firmly planted in one small, country corner of England, and I actually liked the idea that their society (and soon mine, too) would be somewhat *confined and unvarying.* It meant I would finally be able to put down some permanent roots too. I could hardly wait.

But I still had things to do first and about a million questions. For starters, who would I look like in my new life – like me or like Kate or some combination? I thought of those computer animations where they say, for instance, "If Paul McCartney and the Mona Lisa had a baby together, what would it look like?" Is that what would happen? Would Kathleen and I morph together into one person, someone not entirely like either one of us? I tried to imagine it. One blue eye and one brown? I had known a girl in grade school who had a mismatched set like that.

No, probably not. It would have to be one or the other of us. And if I looked like me, that could get complicated. Everybody else would have to be under a kind of mass hypnotic suggestion or something, so they wouldn't notice Kathleen Barrett had suddenly changed from a petite dark-eyed brunette to a blonde four inches taller. Plus, there might be awkward questions about why suddenly none of my clothes fit anymore.

Cora straightened me out. This time she had on a getup that appeared to be straight out of the roaring 20s, but by now I was used to her eccentric taste in clothes, and I never batted an eye.

"No," she said, "you won't look or sound like Hope anymore. That's part of what you agree to leave behind by making this choice. That's part of integrating fully into your new identity. You will look and sound like Kathleen, Kate, to everyone around you, and that's who you'll see in the mirror too. Will that be a problem for you?"

I had wondered how it worked, but I really hadn't worried about it one way or the other. "I don't think so, as long as I feel like me inside. Otherwise, what's the point?"

"Then don't worry. You'll still be you inside – your mind, your soul, your personality – in every way that matters. Only the outside changes to fit your new surroundings. Think of it like a caterpillar becoming a butterfly. It's the same organism, just modified externally to move into the next stage of its life."

Cora's analogy helped some, although I had a hard time thinking of my current self as an unappealing caterpillar. If I was going to be an animal of any kind, I much preferred the picture of a flamingo or baby giraffe.

I never consider myself vain. I had always been pretty satisfied with my looks, but I didn't spend a lot of time thinking about them. And as far as losing the advantages they had brought me… Well, Kate was equally blessed, if I was any judge. Still, it would be odd to catch my reflection and see her face instead, to open my mouth and hear someone else's voice come out, to get used to moving around in a smaller body. Part of the bargain I was making, though, as Cora said, the cost of the pass to my Regency life.

I intended to think of this transition not so much as losing who I was but finding the new me. Besides, I liked Kathleen, and I saw a lot of myself in her already, personality wise, so it didn't seem like it would be too much of a shock when I made the switch.

But what did I know? I'd never done anything remotely like this before! The closest I'd ever come was when I'd tried to reinvent myself on our move to Phoenix – the brief stop before Baton Rouge. At fourteen, I thought I was pretty mature and that it was about time people started treating me accordingly. So I planned how I was going to behave when I got to my new school. I started dressing differently, wore my hair pulled back tight in a neat ponytail or a bun, and tried to lose my southern accent. I even wore a pair of glasses I didn't need, trying to look more intellectual. But it didn't work out. I kept bumping into things because of the glasses, making me look clumsy instead of smart. And it was just too much work pretending all the time; within a week, I was worn slap out and had to give up the idea in favor of being myself again.

That's why it seemed so important that I picked someone like Kathleen, someone who was more like me than not. I'd have enough to do adjusting to a new culture without trying to fake a completely different personality at the same time.

~~*~~

Dr. Jeff Kendal was the next to leave Crossroads.

"I finally decided to devote myself to medical research this time around," he announced when the group gathered in the commons the next day. "I'll be leaving tonight."

I knew his whole story by then. He'd become a doctor with the high ideals of helping people and saving lives, and then he'd gotten sidetracked into doing nonessential cosmetic surgery instead. He planned to turn back the clock and choose a different path after medical school this time, to put his education to "better use." But he had been stuck at Crossroads for ages, trying to decide between going back as the doctor at an orphanage in Africa during the AIDS epidemic and going into medical research in hopes of speeding progress towards a cure for one of the deadly diseases.

"What made up your mind?" I asked him. I found this part of the process fascinating. For me, it had been a gut feeling, but I suspected it would be something more concrete for a doctor, a man of science.

"You remember that orphanage post I had been considering?" Jeff asked. Everybody nodded. "Well, it's the strangest thing. They didn't have a doctor and wouldn't for years to come unless I took the spot, or so I had been told. And then suddenly, out of the blue, Cora says the position has been filled. Just like that."

"No explanations?" asked Karen.

"Nope, but that's okay. As a matter of fact, I'm relieved. I took it as a definite sign, especially since it was so unexpected. With that door closed, I'm free to go with what really would have been my first choice anyway. I can pick research without feeling selfish, without worrying about those sick kids needing my help. I was so determined to do the right thing this time that it paralyzed me. I needed a good boot in the right direction to get me moving again."

So Dr. Jeff believed in signs after all. I never would have thought it. Although he did try to make it sound like a completely logical decision. I suppose in a way it was. When you're left with only one of your two former options, it would be illogical not to take it. Anyway, I was happy for Jeff that he finally had an answer for what to do with his second chance. He'd always been nice to me – to everybody as far as I could tell – quick with an encouraging word or something helpful to say. He would be missed.

But I meant to be right behind him out the door... or whatever the exit from Crossroads was. Something else I hadn't found out about yet. I really had no clue how the departure process worked. So, when I saw Poindexter free, I went over to ask him.

He answered my question with another question. "Are you quite certain you know what you want to do, Miss O'Neil? There is absolutely no rush. You can stay as long as you like, within reason. Look at Dr. Kendall. He must have been here for the equivalent of three months or more."

"I appreciate that, Mr. Poindexter. I really do. And this is a nice place you've got here and all. But I'm excited to get where I'm going and start my new life. Once I've decided something, I never second guess myself."

"Very well. I can see that you are a young lady who knows her own mind. And the departure process is very straightforward. You simply notify us which opening you have chosen to take, assuming you are still planning for option three – a completely new life."

"That's right. I have one all picked out and everything. I just want to study up a little more before I go."

"Very prudent. I can prepare your contract in the meantime so that there will be no unnecessary delays when you *are* ready." He paused. "Why, Miss O'Neil, you look a little uneasy. Was it my mention of contracts? That's nothing to be anxious about. Just a formality, really, to be sure you understand what to expect and what is expected of you. We run a tight ship here at Crossroads, and we do everything we can to avoid unpleasantness."

"What kind of unpleasantness do you mean?"

"Oh, I was referring to what we spoke of before when you asked if we monitor our clients after they leave us. Occasionally, disciplinary action is required to limit the damage when a former client runs amok. Not something we shall have to worry about with you, I trust."

"I don't think so. I'm usually pretty good about followin' rules."

"It has never been more important than now that you do. The rest of your life hangs in the balance."

"Gosh," I said, walking away in a sort of daze.

I wandered back into the commons feeling about as lost as last year's Easter eggs, with Poindexter's words echoing in my head. *Contracts... disciplinary action... the rest of your life in the balance.* I guess it was true; it always had been. I'd just been so blindly optimistic that I hadn't really admitted to myself how much was at stake.

Karen came over to me and she asked, "What's the matter, Hope? You look a little shaken up."

"Oh, it's nothin', really. Mr. Poindexter was just telling me about how the departure process works, and for the first time I got a little nervous about what's ahead – the business of no turning back and the rest of my life hanging on this one decision. Crazy, right? I mean I wasn't scared before and nothing's changed."

"Not crazy. Why do you think I'm still here?"

"You're scared too?"

"In a way."

I waited for her to go on, but she didn't. This was practically my last chance, though, so I pushed for more information. "Please tell me what's going on with you, Karen. You know everything there is to know about me, and I feel like we've become really good friends. Yet I still have no idea where you came from or what you plan to do, except that you hope to correct some mistakes you made in the past. Won't you tell me your story before I leave? You can trust me."

"You're right," she said, lightly resting her hand on my arm for a moment. "We are good friends and you deserve to know. We may as well get comfortable first, though. This may take a while."

We found a couple of chairs off by ourselves and sat down. Then Karen took an enormously deep breath before starting her story.

"I met Kenny my senior year in high school. We were both in band, but we hadn't even talked until we were all on this trip to a jazz festival near Portland. On the bus ride home, my best friend ditched me to sit with a guy she'd been flirting with, and I ended up sitting with Kenny. Believe me; you can really get to know someone on a three-hour bus ride in the dark. Anyway, we were pretty much inseparable after that. He was a great guy – nice, honest, hard-working, and he could always make me laugh. It didn't take long before he was telling me he loved me and talking about a future together."

Karen had a far away look in her eyes, and I wasn't sure she even remembered I was there. "Did you love him too?" I asked, hoping to encourage her.

She sighed. "I did, and I told him so, but part of me was still holding back. I had grand plans in my head, plans for more than just settling down and having babies with a hometown boy whose biggest ambition was to open a car repair shop. First of all, I wanted to get out of our small town in eastern Oregon and never come back. I intended to go to college, have a career and a metropolitan life-style. And when I got married, it was supposed to be to someone with an impressive degree and lots of money. Some great plan, huh?"

"I don't know. There's nothing wrong with having goals, I guess, and getting an education is a good thing. So did you break up with Kenny when you graduated? A lot of high school couples do. I had a teacher my senior year who actually recommended it. He said no way would any couple who went to separate colleges ever stay together, so we might as well all get our breakups over with before-hand. I still felt like he had no right telling us that, though."

"I think your teacher was way out of line, but I did kind of break up with Kenny before I left for college."

"How do you 'kind of' break up with somebody?"

"Well, I didn't say it in so many words. I told him I thought that, since we were going to be apart so much of the time, we ought to both be free to go out with other people. Not on serious 'dates' necessarily, but for fun. There wasn't any point in us both sitting home every night because we had an exclusive arrangement with a person who was a couple hundred miles away. I rationalized that we should be able to go out as one of a group of friends and not feel

59

guilty about it. But what I was really thinking was that I might meet somebody else that fit my long-range plans better."

"Let me guess; Kenny didn't take kindly to your free-to-date-other-people policy."

"That's putting it mildly. He was pretty hurt. We stayed in touch for a while – phone calls, and I'd see him whenever I came home. But he finally got tired of waiting for me to commit, and he walked away for good. The thing is, I've regretted letting him go ever since. And even with all the guys I dated afterwards, I never did find anyone I could care about half as much."

"Is that why you like *Persuasion* – because you want a second chance with Kenny like Anne got with Captain Wentworth?"

"Something like that, although it's more complicated for us than just turning the clock back to high school. Although I never married, Kenny did. The marriage didn't last, but they had a child. I can't undo a little boy's existence by preventing his parents from ever getting together."

"Oh, I see what you mean. It *is* complicated."

"So until I figure out how to fix my life without hurting anyone else, here I sit. Maybe I'll just stay at Crossroads forever. Honestly, sometimes I think that might be better all the way around."

"Don't say that, Karen! You wouldn't have been brought here if there wasn't something good you could make out of it. I'm sure you'll figure out what that is real soon."

"I hope so."

I do not pretend to regret anything I shall leave in Hertford-shire, except your society, my dearest friend... (Pride and Pre-judice, chapter 21)

Chapter 10
Last Look Before Leaping

Two days later, I finally felt ready to make my leap. I'd prepared as much as I possibly could, so there didn't seem any point in sticking around longer. Seeing Poindexter to complete the departure paper-work came next, and it went off without a hitch.

"See, that wasn't so terrible, was it?" he said after I'd signed the last form.

"Not at all. What do I do now?"

"I imagine you'll want to say your farewells, and then Cora will come to your room later and get you sent on your way. It's been a pleasure having you here at Crossroads, Miss O'Neil, and I wish you all the best in your new life. I'm sure you will do very well in Hampshire. It's lovely country. I grew up not far from there, as a matter of fact, although during a different time period from the one you've selected, of course."

"Really? You know, I did wonder where you were from with that darling accent of yours. Mine still needs work, I'm afraid."

"You'll find that it begins to come more easily once you get where you're going and settle in. Well, I'll take my leave of you now, if you don't mind," he said, extending his hand.

I shook it and thanked him for all his help. I could tell Poindexter was not one for long, sentimental partings. So I returned to the commons for the tougher part: saying goodbye to the other Crossroads clients – my "fellow travelers" as Cora liked to call them.

I'd only recently met some of the newest residents, but a few had been there as long as or longer than I had. They were the ones

I'd gotten to know best and the ones I would miss most. But my excitement about starting my new life had piled up so high by then that it pretty near drowned out my nerves and prevented me from becoming too sad about what (and whom) I'd be leaving behind. That is, until I came to Karen. In no time at all, we were both wailing and blubbering like a couple of widows at a wake, competing to see who could grieve the loudest as we gave each other one final hug.

None of the usual reassuring words applied either. *It won't be forever. We'll stay in touch.* Not true in this case. It *would* be forever, and there wasn't any possible way of staying in touch. I wanted to at least promise my friend I'd never forget her, but I couldn't even do that, since we'd been told our memories of Crossroads and of our former lives would fade.

But as difficult as parting with Karen had turned out to be, one goodbye was even harder.

After leaving the commons for the final time, I sat alone in my room, spending every single minute I had left looking at pictures and video of my parents, trying to etch the lines of their faces a little deeper into my brain. It seemed impossible that I could forget the two most important people in my life. But I told myself that if I did, it would only be temporary. I had to believe that when we all met up in heaven, everything I had lost, including my memory, would be restored and I would recognize my original set of parents again. What a reunion that would be! Hanging on to that picture helped a whole bunch.

I also felt like I had their blessing for the decision I'd made. Momma certainly would have approved; after all, she was the one who had introduced me to Jane Austen in the first place. I pulled up the scene on the video system to relive it.

It was a Saturday afternoon, and I was fifteen.

Momma told me, "There's something I want you to watch with me tonight."

It must be something 'educational,' I thought, which in my mind at the time meant it was going to be deadly dull. "Do I have to?" I whined.

"Yes, you do," she said firmly. "It's the 1995 mini-series of *Pride and Prejudice.* I remember watching it when it first aired, and it was wonderful. So when I spotted it at Costco today, I picked it up."

I silently groaned and rolled my eyes. My mother was a bit of a fanatic on the subject of *Pride and Prejudice*. She had been trying to get me to read the darn book since I was twelve. I still hadn't because I already knew enough about it to be sure I wasn't interested – a bunch of people who lived eons ago, sitting around in old-fashioned clothes and talking in old-fashioned language about nothing at all important. That was my opinion.

"Give it a chance," she said. "It won't kill you, and who knows? You might even like it."

"Doesn't sound like I have any choice."

"That's right. I want you to watch at least the first episode with me before you make up your mind."

So when the time came, I sat down on the couch, crossed my arms, blew out an exaggerated sigh, and waited to be bored.

I was *not* bored.

The music came up. The opening credits started to run. And then there were horses – something I liked. Horses galloping with handsome men riding them – even better. Then a family full of sisters and dancing and more men. Some of the old-fashioned clothes were wonderfully elegant, I discovered, especially Miss Bingley's and Mrs. Hurst's. And did I mention the men? I liked the way their clothes looked on them too. About an hour in, Momma paused the DVD and told me, "That's the end of episode one. If you don't want to watch anymore, you can go now."

I started to get up and then stopped. "But what happens? Does Jane marry Mr. Bingley in the end?" I demanded. "And what about Elizabeth?"

"I can't give the ending away! That would spoil it for you if you decide to read the book or watch this video later." She waited a bit, then suggested, "If you're not sure if you like it yet, you could always watch a little longer."

"Okay," I agreed, "because I'm not really sure yet."

I settled back into my spot, and Momma pushed the play button. She knew what she was doing. She had given me a graceful way to stay, where I didn't have to admit I'd been totally wrong, at least not yet. Because I *did* know already. I was completely hooked in the first ten minutes. Jane Austen had set the barb in my mouth herself, and she had let Mr. Darcy reel me in like a big ol' catfish. I was a goner, stuffed and roasted and fit to be served up on a platter.

Two hours later, after Mr. Darcy's botched proposal to Elizabeth, the credits rolled again.

"That's not the end, is it?" I asked, feeling a little panicky at the thought. "That can't be the end."

"No. It's only halfway through. The rest is on the second disc." Momma glanced at her watch. "My goodness, look at the time! I guess I'll have to watch it tomorrow. It's almost midnight."

"Would... Would it be all right if I watched it with you?"

"Of course, as long as your homework's done first."

"I'll do it as soon as we get home from church, I promise."

"And we'll need to get going right after dinner so you won't be up too late on a school night. Maybe you could help me in the kitchen to speed things up a little."

"Okay."

My mother smiled at me. "I'm so glad you're enjoying it, honey. We'll have one thing more in common from now on. If only we could get your father on board," she added pointedly as he came into the room.

"I see how it is," he said, leaning over to kiss my mother on the top of her head and then me. "I'm going to be outnumbered and outvoted on everything from here on, aren't I?"

"I'm afraid so, Daddy."

I paused the display at that spot to soak up the happy family scene. It was a lovely memory... and an appropriate place to leave off since it represented a big part of why I was about to do what I was about to do – to get myself a new life in Regency England.

Cora came in right on cue and dressed to match the theme, wearing a pale green, empire-waist gown, topped with a coordinating spencer and bonnet. "It's in your honor," she said, indicating her Regency outfit. "Do you like it?"

I was delighted. "Very much, Cora. Are you sure you don't want to come with me? You'd fit right in."

"It would be tempting except I could never leave Poindexter."

"I understand."

"Plus I've gotten very used to the comforts of Crossroads. Well," she said after taking a deep breath. "Are you ready to go?"

"As ready as I ever will be. I'm all studied up, and I can't wait to get started!"

"Take it easy, Hope. Be patient. You'll arrive exactly the same time whether you leave now or in another hour. You're going to have a straight shot – no detours or traffic jams. Just one minute." Cora took the controls of the video system and began typing in commands. When she was finished, she said, "Now stand about here and relax." She positioned me in front of the screen and gave my shoulders a quick rub down.

"In a second I'll start up the program, and this is what you'll see. First, events of your original life will play backwards to the beginning and then Kathleen's life will start and go forwards to the point where you arrive on the scene. Try to keep your mind blank, just letting the images flow past you like a warm summer breeze. Don't try to focus on any one of them, and don't fight it when you feel yourself getting sleepy. That's what's supposed to happen. It's kind of like hypnosis and makes the transition more comfortable. I'll stay with you and monitor every part of the process. It's entirely safe, I promise. When you wake up, it will be 1809 and you'll be Kathleen Barrett. Understand?"

Understand? How could I possibly understand something completely beyond comprehension?

"Not really. I'll just have to take it on faith. Thank you, Cora. I'll never forget everything you've done for me!" I said, giving her a quick hug. "Well, I suppose I will forget, won't I? That doesn't mean I'm any less grateful for your kindness, though. And I'll think of you watching over me like my guardian angel."

"I'll keep an eye out, but I'm sure you'll do just fine. Enjoy your second chance, Hope, and make the most of it. Are you ready, then?"

I nodded. Then I took a deep breath, exhaled, and stared straight ahead at the screen, trying to keep my eyes and my thoughts unfocussed as the lights went out and the display began to play just the way Cora had said.

Starting with the image I had left on the screen, events unwound backwards, and I saw myself and my parents in different circumstances and different places we had been. The layers time had added peeled away one by one, like the skin of an onion. We all became younger until I was just a newborn. Then it was a different newborn

– Kathleen – growing up. The images seemed to come faster and faster, until it was all a blur and I blacked out.

That's how it happened, this second chance of mine. At least that's what I remember. But sometimes I wonder if it could be true... any of it.

FIRST INTERMISSION

After Hope O'Neil's successful departure, Cora found Poindexter in their shared office. "Well, she's on her way," she told him. "Off to Regency England, just like she wanted."

"Excellent. New outfit?" he asked, giving Cora an appraising look.

"It is! I've never had call for anything from this time period before, so I couldn't pass up the chance. Do you like it?"

"Oh, very much indeed. You look simply fetching, my dear."

"Thank you," she said smiling warmly at him and beginning to untie her bonnet. "I wanted Hope to see the entire ensemble, but I really don't need this anymore. Could you help me off with the jacket too, Dex? It's called a spencer, you know, but it fits so tightly that I can't manage by myself. Now I understand why everybody needed servants to help dress and undress them."

"I am more than happy to oblige. Extra layers of clothing are superfluous in our climate-controlled environment. Besides," he added, catching sight of her emerging *décolletage*, "I think I prefer the dress without the spencer."

Cora laughed. "I could be wrong, but I don't think it's my dress you're admiring at the moment."

"Do you mind?"

"Not at all, although we should keep our thoughts on business for at least a little longer. Don't you want to update your notes on Hope's status?"

Poindexter sighed wistfully and picked up his ever-present clipboard. "Very well. Hope O'Neil successfully transported. Check." He paused and began tapping his pen on his chin. "I will miss her more than most of the others, I think. Such a pleasant, cheerful sort of young person."

"Pretty too."

"Oh, do you think so? I really hadn't noticed."

"I find that hard to believe, Dex. But if you wish to pretend you only have eyes for me, I won't complain. Anyway, I do hope she will be happy in her new life. She doesn't know what lies ahead, of course."

"The same can be said for every person on the face of the earth."

"True. It's just that I can't help wondering what Hope would have decided if she'd been given all the facts, if she had known what we know. Would she still have gone ahead with her plans or made a different choice?"

"It is impossible to say. But try not to worry, my dear." Poindexter gathered Cora into a gentle embrace. "The girl is strong and resilient. Look what she's come through already."

"Yes, look what she's come through already! It seems a little cruel to expect it of her again."

"*We* are not expecting it of her. We cannot blame ourselves for things over which we have no control. Now, will you allow me to take your mind off your worries with a gourmet dinner? Just a little something I whipped up in my spare time. All you need to do is choose the wine to go with it. What do you say?"

"How can I resist?"

"Why should you try?"

"Well, for one thing, I always feel like we're eating and drinking behind our clients' backs, since they are not invited to join us."

"They are not *able* to join us in their current state of being; think of it that way. Our clients may resume the pleasures of food and drink when they take up a life on earth again. Excellent motivation for not remaining here indefinitely, I should think."

The two adjourned, hand in hand, to their private quarters, the smell of something roasting in the oven drawing them in. The table was already set and the view of the stars was spectacular, as always.

Part Two

Awakening in Austen

His person and air were equal to what her fancy had ever drawn for the hero of a favourite story... (Sense and Sensibility, chapter 9)

Chapter 11
No More Hope

"Kate! Kate, can you hear me?"

I *could* hear the voice, but I couldn't answer right away. Even though I remembered where I was supposed to be, I still didn't quite believe it.

I must have viewed the scene a hundred times at the Center, forwards, backwards, and crossways: Lucy and Kathleen out for a sedate horseback ride on that fateful day. Then, Kathleen had suddenly taken it into her head to race away at top speed. I could see how exhilarated she was – laughing, with the wind blowing in her face – and I could relate.

It seemed a lot like something I might have done in her place. I always headed straight for the more extreme rides at any amusement park or county fair, and I admit to driving a little too fast with the windows rolled all the way down. So I could just as easily have been the one who met with disaster. Well... actually, I did meet with disaster; it just didn't happen to be on account of my taking risks.

Anyway, Kathleen ignored the warnings her sister called after her and rode even faster. That's when, as I saw it, she made her fatal mistake. Nearly at the last moment, she turned Horatio's head to the left, steering him onto a trail that would take them through the woods. The gelding made the corner but Kathleen didn't. It was horrible to watch. For a moment, she seemed to hang there in midair, half in and half out of the saddle. But gravity won out, like it always does. Over she went, tumbling toes over teakettle to the ground, landing on her behind and knocking her head.

That's when the exchange was supposed to take place, with me slipping in just as Kathleen slipped away. I could swear we passed practically right through each other and that, just for a moment, she saw me. Maybe I only imagined it, but it seemed like she understood. I like to think so, anyhow.

"Kate! Kate, please wake up!"

This time I opened my eyes. There was the sky directly overhead where it should be – a puffy patchwork quilt of clouds in different shapes and shades – and to one side, a shadowy face hovering. The face gradually came into focus and connected to a body.

"Lucy?" I said. "Is that really you?" At least that's what I tried to say. What actually came out of my mouth sounded like total gibberish, and then I guess I went unconscious again.

The next thing I knew, I was waking up in a very old-fashioned looking room, like something somebody's great-grandmother might have thought was stylish back in the day. There was brown paisley print wallpaper, a picture rail all around, and no overhead light fixture where you'd expect to find one. It all seemed both familiar and unfamiliar at the same time.

I was flat on my back again like before, but this time at least, it was in a comfortable bed instead of on the hard ground. And now I had six worried faces staring at me instead of only one. The closest person was a youngish man, who I remember thinking was criminally handsome. He kept waving something nasty-smelling in front of my nose, though.

"She is coming round," he said as he finally put that foul vial away. "How do you feel, Miss Barrett? Can you speak?"

I could not, not as Hope O'Neil or Kate Barrett either one. I had to get a firmer grip on reality before daring to open my mouth.

It seemed to be true, though. Everything had happened just as Cora and Poindexter had told me it would. I was alive as promised and presumably in 1809. This was Kathleen's house, Kathleen's room, and Kathleen's family gathered around the bed, looking at me and seeing their beloved Kathleen. I recognized them all from my research. And the young man must be a doctor, I decided… or surgeon or apothecary or whatever the period-correct term might be.

I shouldn't have been surprised. This is what I'd planned, after all, what I had asked for. But somehow I don't think I had understood (not deep down, anyway) that it would actually come to pass.

"Kate, say something," pleaded Lucy from the other side of the bed. "How are you?"

"I'm okay," I managed before my hand flew up to cover my lips. Cora had warned me, but it had still been a shock to hear Kate's voice coming out of *my* mouth!

"I'm okay?" repeated Mrs. Barrett as if the words were a foreign language to her. "How very odd. What can she mean by it? Mr. Cavanaugh, why is my daughter talking nonsense? Has she gone completely off her head?"

Darn! A mistake already! Ditch the contractions and no 'okay' either – too contemporary.

"It should not amaze me if your daughter were to say and do many odd things, Mrs. Barrett," Mr. Cavanaugh replied, beginning to pack away his instruments in a small black case. "At least in the beginning. It is to be expected in cases of head injury. Not to worry."

I exhaled a small sigh of relief, silently blessing the good doctor for his explanation. I didn't necessarily like his tone – which immediately struck me as condescending, possibly bordering on contempt – but he had neatly excused my first error and conveniently established my alibi for all the others that would surely follow. Still, the sooner I got my head in the Regency game, the better. Time to break out that British accent I'd been secretly cultivating too. Choosing my words more carefully and preparing myself for the strange sound of my new voice, I tried again.

"I am well," I said. "I have a little pain in my head; that is all." Much better. I could do this. It would just take a little focus and a little practice.

I gazed around the circle at the Barretts, my eyes hungry to take them in for real this time. They were all there – Mr. and Mrs., Lucy, Carmen, and Matilda – in 3-D flesh, not just virtual on a screen anymore. This was my new family!... for better or worse, for richer or for poorer, forever and ever. And it *was* sort of like a marriage in that there was no going back. The strangest thing was my growing sensation that I had known them all a long time, much longer than the period of my research at Crossroads. Bits of brand new memory began popping into my head too. Looking at Matilda, I had a vivid impression of more than once watching her carefully choose a long, flat blade of grass from the garden to use as a bookmark. Where had that image come from? And Papa Barrett winking at me across the dinner table after a remark that amounted to a private joke between us.

These must be some of the 'carryover' memories Cora had talked about, things I inexplicably now knew just because Kathleen had known them before me. Perhaps she had handed them off to me as I slid past her on the exchange, like the baton in the relay races I used to run on the high school track team.

It was a little creepy on one level, considering that I was, more or less, inhabiting the skin of another person, the skin of a dead person at that. Probably better not to think about it too much, I decided. It was just one of those mysteries of life we weren't meant to understand, like how the universe is infinite or why some women can wear hats and others just look ridiculous.

The more of Kathleen's memories I recovered, the better; that was the practical point. There would be less groping around in the dark that way, and a lot less stumbling into gopher holes.

Even the stern but distinguished-looking doctor in front of me began to seem familiar, although I couldn't imagine why. I was sure I'd never run across him in my research. Not even once. That particular flavor of sweetmeat I would have remembered. He was still staring at me, now with one eyebrow lifted, like he was challenging me to say something.

Then he turned to speak to the others. "I believe Miss Kathleen is out of danger," he said. "Rest is the best thing for her, so if you would be so kind..." He stood, towering over the bed, and began ushering Barrett after Barrett towards the door with a definite air of authority.

I *did* say something then. "I desire that Lucy should stay with me for a while," I declared, proud of how I had phrased it. It sounded very Regency-ish to me. At the same time, I reached for my new sister's hand, thinking it's what Kathleen would have done.

Lucy smiled tenderly down at me. "May I, Mr. Cavanaugh?" she asked.

"By all means. Someone should probably sit with the patient for the first four-and-twenty hours or so, just to watch for any sign of trouble. I myself had best be getting on, but I will return first thing tomorrow. Sooner if I am needed. Will that be acceptable to you?"

He directed this last bit at me, that is to say Kathleen, with a serious look. I hardly knew how to respond, so I just nodded. Apparently satisfied, the doctor went away, leaving Lucy and me alone.

"Oh, Kate," Lucy began, still holding my hand, "what a fright you have given us! When I saw you slip from Horatio's back, I thought for sure I had lost you forever."

"Did I strike my head?"

"Oh, yes! There happened to be this great stone exactly where you fell. There was so much blood, and then you lay still for the longest time. I hardly knew what to do. I thought perhaps I should ride for help, but I could not bear to leave you. So I screamed at the top of my lungs, hoping against hope that someone would hear and come to my aid."

"And did someone?"

"He did! A stranger, although I daresay he will be a stranger no longer. It was Mr. Sotheby, the new owner of Coleswold. Just think, Kate! It was only this morning we were discussing how we could contrive a way to meet our neighbor, and now he has been introduced to our family in such an unexpected fashion!" She then hastened to add, "Of course I should have much preferred it had been by ordinary means. Surely Papa would have eventually relented and done what was required, or we might easily have been introduced at a ball."

"But wasn't it clever of me to expedite matters by throwing myself from my horse?" I suggested, trying out my best British accent. "Now you must tell me all about this Mr. Sotheby, for I was quite unconscious, you will recall."

Although I believe Lucy Barrett was as solicitous for my health as any sister could possibly be, she was equally enthusiastic for the subject I had suggested. Once I had assured her I was not too tired to hear it, she launched into an animated recital of Mr. Sotheby's merits in impressive detail. He was rumored to be rich. Most importantly, though, he was definitely single. Lucy had cleverly induced him to give up this information. He must also be handsome, I suspected, judging from the way she was blushing as she talked about him. His gallantry could not be doubted, considering how he had managed to be around just when help was needed.

"And he is so strong!" Lucy continued, breathlessly.

"A definite virtue in a man."

"He lifted you so easily, as if… as if…"

I could not resist filling in the blank from my own frame of reference. "As if I weighed no more than a dried leaf?"

"Yes, it was exactly so! How well you have captured the idea! And then he carried you all the way home without becoming the least bit tired. It is unfortunate that you were deprived of seeing it for yourself."

"Unfortunate, yes, but if I had been awake, there may have been no need."

Lucy laughed. "I suppose you are right."

"I can imagine, though. I have witnessed such things before," I added, thinking of that rain-drenched scene in my favorite film version of *Sense and Sensibility*.

"Have you? When?"

"Oh, never mind about that now. Tell me more of Mr. Sotheby. And what of this Mr. Cavanaugh? His manner implied some level of acquaintance, but I really cannot at this moment remember." Here, I closed my eyes and reached one hand to the back of my bandage-wreathed head to reestablish the reason for my lack of recollection.

"You poor darling!" Lucy cooed. "I suppose it will come back to you in time, but let me help you along a little. You met Mr. Cavanaugh at the most recent assembly, where you refused to dance with him, I might add."

No wonder, then, that he seemed none too friendly. "But why would I refuse such a reasonable request? Did I say? I love to dance, after all, and there is nothing objectionable in his looks."

"Nothing whatever! He is such a fine figure of a man. No, you told me it was something else that did not suit you. Something you overheard him say, although I cannot now recall what it was."

But suddenly I *did* recall – another carryover memory. Mr. Cavanaugh had been speaking to some gentleman or other when Kathleen happened to be passing unnoticed behind them.

"In truth, I find these country assemblies more punishment than pleasure," he had declared, clear as anything. "One feels obligated to dance with every mother's daughter sitting down in want of a partner, no matter how undesirable. Really, I sometimes think these affairs are more irksome than even the 'marriage market' balls of the London season. It is the same everywhere; if one has a tolerable fortune, one is considered fair game for every husband-hunting miss in the country."

How rude! How very Mr. Darcy-ish of him (the Darcy before Lizzy taught him the error of his ways, that is). No one could blame Kathleen for refusing to dance with the man after that!

And then I remembered something else I (Kathleen) had heard at the same assembly. "You were quite right to cut the man, deary," an older lady standing nearby told me. "I wonder that the man has the nerve to show his face among us after what he did to poor Mrs. Conner, may she rest in peace. Imagine, refusing to come when she sent for him, all because she had no money to pay."

Kathleen had seen Mr. Cavanaugh for what he was that night. Now it was my clear duty to go on disliking him in Kathleen's place, out of loyalty to her and on principle. He probably only bothered to attend *me* because my father had enough money to pay him well.

With this new information in mind, I announced to Lucy, "He's a conceited snob, stuck up higher than a light pole."

"A what?" she asked.

"Oh… I mean… I mean that he gives himself airs," I corrected. "He thinks too well of himself, above his company. And who is he, after all? Only a doctor." My outburst had been another mistake, but at least I had remembered that doctors had no special status here.

"Now, Kate," Lucy chided, "Mr. Cavanaugh is a gentleman from a very good family, we are told. I hope you do not intend holding the fact that he also has a profession against him. Really, I think it quite commendable that he should want to do something useful with his time. There are far too many idle young men about as it is. So I said before and you agreed with me. Do you really not remember, dearest?"

"It's coming back to me, little by little. So you have a high opinion of this Mr. Cavanaugh as well as the handsome Mr. Sotheby." This reminding me of another Austen reference, I asked, "Do you never see a fault in anybody, Jane? *All the world are good and agreeable in your eyes*, I suppose."

"Jane?" Lucy repeated, her brows drawn together with confusion. "You know my name as well as your own, Kate. You had better rest, as Mr. Cavanaugh recommended. That will no doubt set your brain to rights. I will sit with you a while, but you must close your eyes now."

I humbly obeyed, relieved to have an excuse to shut my big, fat mouth too. I had begun feeling at home in my new role, to enjoy being *in character*, so much so that I let down my guard. And look what happened!

When Lucy described our handsome new neighbor coming to rescue ladies in distress, I had pictured Willoughby sweeping Marianne up into his arms. And when Lucy spoke so favorably of Mr. Cavanaugh and Mr. Sotheby both, I had heard Jane Bennet's voice.

Although I was tickled beyond anything to finally be a living, breathing part of the culture that had inspired the Regency stories I loved so much, ideas like this were bound to keep popping into my head. How was I supposed to stop them popping out of my mouth? That was the question. It seemed like this was going to be harder than I'd expected since everywhere I turned I was sure to see something that would remind me of Austen – her books and the movies made from them. My mistakes might be blamed on my accident for a while, but not forever.

Keep your head in the game, Hope, I coached. Then I reminded myself of one more very important fact. There was no more Hope; I was Kathleen now.

"My mind was more agreeably engaged. I have been meditating on the very great pleasure which a pair of fine eyes in the face of a pretty woman can bestow." (Pride and Prejudice, chapter 6)

Chapter 12
A Mother's Duty

No more Hope. I sighed a little at the thought when I woke up the next morning. But it was only a play on words, not a comment about my future. Not at all. It was a bright, shiny new day, and I was starting my new Austen-style life!

What to do first; that was the only question… a question quickly answered by the growing pressure in my bladder, which was probably what woke me up in the first place. Now my eyeballs were floatin', and there wasn't a moment to lose.

Like other families of the era, the Barretts had a privy out back for most ordinary occasions as well as chamber pots available for convenience or emergency. I knew that much from my research. Did this qualify as an emergency? Possibly, but I hated to make peeing in a pot (especially one somebody else would have to clean up later) my first official Regency act. To the outhouse, then. The pain in my head wasn't too bad when I sat up, but a stern voice stopped me before I could get any further.

"Kathleen, where do you think you are going?" It was Mrs. Barrett.

"Oh," I said, a little startled. "I did not notice you there. Have you been sitting in that rocking chair all night long, Mama?"

I had a hard time calling her that in the beginning, but I couldn't go on thinking of her as only Kathleen's mother forever. Besides, I *was* Kathleen now, and I was pretty excited to have a mom again.

"Where else should I be, I should like to know? Mr. Cavanaugh said somebody should stay with you at all times. Is that not a mother's job, to sit with her sick child through the night?"

"How kind you are, Mama, but I am feeling much better this morning. I was just going to the... uh..." I searched my brain for the correct term. "...the necessary."

"Down a flight of stairs and across the yard in your condition? I should think not! Use the pot, child. Use the pot and have done. I am sure Mr. Cavanaugh would be very severe upon me if I were to allow you to take another fall, and *I* would not have it for the world. We nearly lost you yesterday, my dear. I shudder to think of it."

When I made no move to get on with the business, she came to my side. "Here, I will assist you; you are still weak and it is a mother's duty. No need to be shy about it either, child. It is nothing that I have not done for you or your sisters a thousand times."

It was a good thing my new mom was there to help me, or I might still be fumbling around for how to undo my Regency drawers and where to go. I'm sure I blushed and blushed, though, especially when Flossie, one of the maids, appeared to carry the covered pot away. I felt like I should apologize to her for being the cause of what had to be an unpleasant task. To her credit, though, she didn't make any kind of face about it, at least not in my sight. I suppose it must have been very routine for her, but I was certainly glad I had been able to choose a new life that did not include emptying other people's chamber pots.

With the most urgent feat accomplished, I had no sooner gotten myself sat back into bed when Mr. Cavanaugh arrived. After what Lucy had told me and what I had 'remembered,' I was anxious to get another look at him, to have a chance to observe and evaluate him more thoroughly. Of course, he was there to evaluate *me*, that is, my health, but I could tell at once he had not forgotten the incident at the assembly or his pompous attitude either.

"Good morning, Miss Barrett," he said to me after Mama let him in. "And how are we feeling today?"

We? Was he kidding? Or was his use of the royal 'we' another sign of his presumed superiority? Being a gentleman wasn't good enough for him? He had skipped right over nobility to imagine himself a prince or something equally grand. That sort of arrogance really rubbed me the wrong way. I wanted to zing him, but what I actually said wasn't all that clever.

"I don't know about you, Mr. Cavanaugh, but *I* am feeling much better than yesterday, thank you very much."

Although I suspect he noticed my sarcasm, he maintained his business-like expression. "Excellent. Not too much pain in your head or... or otherwise, then?" he said, making a vague gesture to regions somewhat lower.

"No, sir. My head is improving and my *otherwise* is none of your business."

"Kathleen!" interrupted Mama. "Remember your manners. There is no need for impertinence, I am sure."

Mr. Cavanaugh gave a nod of acknowledgement to Mama and then returned his attention to me. "Perhaps you find my inquiries indelicate, Miss Barrett. I *am* a qualified physician, however, and you *did* fall rather violently on your..."

I watched him struggling for the right word again. I could think of so many options – butt, heinie, derriere, posterior, backside, gluteus maximus, caboose – and no one would have batted an eye at saying or hearing any one of them (or worse) where I'd come from. But this was a more genteel society requiring more genteel language – one of the reasons I admired it so much, I reminded myself. So I also had to admire Mr. Cavanaugh's restraint, I supposed.

"You are quite right, of course," I said, "but I believe no lasting damage has been done there either."

"Very good. I am pleased to hear it. Have you been up yet this morning?"

"Yes, I needed to..." Now *I* was the one unable to finish my sentence, but apparently he caught my drift.

"Of course. And that went... went well? No difficulties in any respect?"

"Only a little throbbing in my temples when I moved about, but less than yesterday."

"It appears that your recovery is progressing as well as we... as well as *I* could expect. I just have one or two more things, and then I will leave you in peace. Could you turn toward the light, please, Miss Barrett?"

He came around to the window side of my bed and tipped my chin up so that we were looking straight into each other's eyes. I probably should have questioned what he meant by being so forward. Wouldn't it have been more proper to ask permission or at least give me fair warning before touching me? Although I admit what I actually wondered at the time was if his hands were always so warm and if he found my eyes as "fine" as Mr. Darcy had thought Lizzy's. I couldn't help noticing that *his* were an unusual heathery green, like the subtle tapestry of different shades you might see deep in a forest – ferns and moss all woven together. I don't think I'd ever seen eyes quite like that before.

It's lucky he spoke up right then, before I completely lost my grip on reality and forgot who he was.

"Mrs. Barrett, would you be so good as to assist me?" he asked without looking away from me. "At my word, will you quickly draw back the draperies, please? And Miss Barrett, continue to look straight ahead with eyes wide open, if you would."

While Mama got into place, he leaned in even closer until I could feel his breath on my face. I believe I was holding mine.

"Ready?" he said. "Now."

Mama did as instructed, throwing back the curtains with a dramatic swoosh. Bright sunlight suddenly flooded the room and my eyes. For a few seconds, Mr. Cavanaugh held his position only inches from me, still gazing at me and supporting my chin with his hand. Then he abruptly let go and pulled away, all business again.

"I am done here, Miss Barrett. I needed to confirm that your pupils reacted properly to the change in brightness. That required the close contact. I am sorry if it has discomforted you in any way."

Was he speaking for himself or for me? He looked uncomfortable enough. And I was too. Still, I didn't want *him* to know it. I needed a sharp comeback so he would see I was unaffected – something witty and possibly cutting, to put him in his place.

"I...uh... Not at all."

Well *that* was brilliant.

Lizzy never seemed to have this problem. In fact, she considered her dislike of Mr. Darcy a big help, inspiring all kinds of clever remarks. The situation reminded me of a line in *Pride and Prejudice* that goes something like this:

One can continually be abusive without saying anything just, but one cannot always be laughing at a man without occasionally stumbling across something witty.

That could be my new strategy. I wouldn't abuse Mr. Cavanaugh, at least not to his face; I would laugh at him instead. Maybe then I would eventually stumble across something witty to say.

"What do you think of Mr. Cavanaugh, Mama?" I asked when he had gone. "I cannot quite make him out."

"A fine gentleman, to be sure, even if perhaps he is a little proud. And I do not understand this business of taking up a profession when there is no need. He is the eldest son, you know. Or was it the only? I forget, but they say he will inherit a very pretty property in Derbyshire when his father dies…"

Derbyshire! My heart did an involuntary back flip at the word, and my head instantly conjured up images of Pemberley.

"…although the father is reportedly in very robust health at the moment. Too bad. Still, I daresay it would be well worth the wait to be mistress of such a fine estate. One thing is certain; Mr. Cavanaugh would make an excellent catch for you or for any of your sisters. So I will give you this little hint, Kate. Mind your tongue when he is about. Sharpen that troublesome instrument on somebody else if you must, but not on a man of his consequence. You know I never criticize, but it is a mother's responsibility to improve her children's characters if she can."

"What of *his* character, Mama? Is that of no account? It seems that if a man is wealthy enough he may have as many faults as he likes without suffering anybody's censure. But I would not want to be married to such a man. All his wealth and consequence could never make up for bad behavior and disposition." (I was really getting the hang of this Regency language!)

"And a *good* disposition will never make up for being poor." Mama reminded me. "Mark my words. You must marry, Kate, and with some eye to fortune. With your father's estate subject to entailment, you cannot afford to do otherwise. As your mother, it is my duty to make you understand that much. Therefore, you should at least *try* to like Mr. Cavanaugh. It is improbable you will ever do any better."

Lucy liked him and now Mama. Wasn't that enough? Did he really need my approval too?

Nevertheless, I smiled and said, "I will try to like him, Mama, just to please you. But do not announce our engagement quite yet. I doubt that Mr. Cavanaugh has the least intention of liking me in return. Have you considered that?"

"Well, I cannot see where that is any of his concern. It is his clear duty to society to marry, and there is no earthly reason it should not be one of my girls that he settles on in the end."

But despite what I had said to appease Mama, I really was determined to go on disliking Mr. Cavanaugh. I only hoped I could do it with Lizzy Bennet's flair.

His manners gave a disgust which turned the tide of popularity, for he was discovered to be proud, to be above his company, above being pleased; and not all his large estate in Derbyshire could then save him from having a most forbidding, disagreeable countenance... (Pride and Prejudice, chapter 3)

Chapter 13
Doctor's Orders

I didn't want to think about Mr. Cavanaugh anymore. He had come and gone, and I had listened to Mama's opinion of him. That was enough for one day.

But it turned out I was not allowed to get rid of him so easily, or at least not his lingering effects. It was as if he had conspired with my new family against me to be sure that, despite his absence, I would feel his presence, that I would be constantly reminded of his power over me. And not in a good way. Was it his means of getting back at me for refusing to dance with him? If so, he certainly had his revenge.

Even though I wasn't the least bit unwell, I was forced to stay in bed the whole day by Mr. Cavanaugh's decree. It was particularly aggravating since I was anxious to get on with things, excited to get out and explore my new world... or at least as far as the sofa in the drawing room downstairs where I could have rested quite comfortably while still keeping an eye on everything going on in the house, including any visitors who might come to call.

Here again I was thinking of the model of Mr. Willoughby in *Sense and Sensibility*. After rescuing the fair maiden Marianne, he had returned to Barton Cottage the next day to check on her recovery. Would Mr. Sotheby do the same for me, I wondered? This time I would presumably be conscious and able to make a somewhat better impression.

He did come, and I missed it.

"He stayed for a full hour, and said he was very glad to hear you were out of danger," Lucy reported when she came upstairs to me afterward, "and that he would call again in a day or two. Then you will finally have the chance to meet him for yourself."

"Yes, finally," I said with a sigh. "Did you like your Mr. Sotheby just as well this time, with him sitting quietly in a drawing room rather than racing about the countryside rescuing damsels in distress? I suppose a hero is a hero, regardless."

"Now you are teasing me, Kate. In the first place, he is not *my* Mr. Sotheby. And I am certain he would be dismayed to hear you speak of him as a hero, for he continues to say that he is simply grateful to have been of service." The door opened. "Ah, here is Flossie with your breakfast. I will leave you now. We were told to keep our visits short so as not to tire you: Mr. Cavanaugh's orders."

I was sorry to part with Lucy, but at least I had something else to look forward to. Food! Finally! I was so hungry by then that I reckon I could have eaten the north end of a southbound goat. But I admit that what first popped into my brain when I saw the maid carrying my breakfast tray in was the image of her earlier carrying the chamber pot out with those very same hands. Had she washed in between? What was the current understanding of hygiene and germs, I wondered? There was nothing I could do about it at that moment, however, so I tried to dismiss the thought from my head.

Flossie deposited her burden on the small table by the door, helped me arrange the pillows so I could sit up straighter, and then brought the tray over to me. "Here you are, Miss," she said, "a nice basin of gruel."

I'd heard of gruel, of course, but I didn't know exactly what it was, only that Mr. Woodhouse had set great store by it. In *Emma*, I remembered, he recommended it as the cure for whatever ailed a body and protection against any other danger that might happen to come along in the future. I didn't recall anyone else being as enthusiastic, though, and I soon found out why. With my first bite, I discovered that gruel was basically a thin, runny version of oatmeal – an unappealing, bland kind of drivel, not at all the oatmeal my mother had made for me when I was a kid. Where was the brown sugar? Where were the cream and the dollop of melting butter? From the way it tasted, I don't think any salt had even been used to cook it.

I didn't want to complain, and yet I was SO HUNGRY! A little tact and diplomacy might serve my purposes best, I decided.

"Mmm," I murmured. "Did you make this yourself, Flossie?"

She smiled and blushed. "Yes, Miss. I am glad you like it."

"I *do*, but I was wondering if you might bring me something else too. Perhaps some toast with jam and a nice slice of ham. I must keep up my strength, you know."

"Oh, dear," she said, twisting her apron nervously. "I'm sorry, but I may not do as you ask, Miss. Mr. Cavanaugh left very precise instructions. You are to have nothing but gruel for now."

Of course. Mr. Cavanaugh strikes again. He had sealed my fate and then gone merrily on his way. Did he know what I was suffering on his account? Was he laughing to himself as he thought of my misery? For now, I could only grin and bear it, but at some point, I'd need to find a way to make him pay.

"I see," I told Flossie. Then I tried a new strategy. "Did Mr. Cavanaugh give any orders restricting amounts?"

"I don't believe so, Miss."

"Then will you kindly bring me another basin of this delightful gruel, perhaps this time with just a pinch of salt added? I will have this first one finished off in no time."

She seemed pleased to be able to do that much for me. And I discovered that if a person is hungry enough, almost anything becomes palatable, even gruel.

Mr. Barrett arrived in my room next. (I really must learn to call him "Papa" from here on.) He came to my bedside, hesitated, and then took my hand, holding it limply for a moment before letting it go again. "How is my girl?" he asked with a somewhat pained expression on his face, as if he had just discovered he'd stepped in something unmentionable. He was obviously embarrassed, or at least ill at ease.

"I am pretty well, I think, Papa, except that I am sure I would feel a good deal better if only I were allowed to get out of this bed and come downstairs."

"Now, now, child. Doctor's orders, you know." He pulled up a chair and gingerly perched on the front edge of it. "Mustn't complain. Lucky to be doing so well, I should say. You took a nasty tumble."

"Which reminds me, Papa, how is Horatio? He didn't go down too, did he?"

"No, no. He is as right as rain. Think he felt bad for what happened, though. Followed you all the way home like a stray dog afterward – you and your sister and Mr. Sotheby, that is."

"I'm glad he came to no harm. And how do you like this Mr. Sotheby, Father? Lucy seems to approve of him. Do you?"

"How could I not approve? Had he been introduced to my notice in a more customary way, I think I should have liked him well enough. Considering the service he rendered you, however, at the very outset of our acquaintance too, he has earned my special esteem and gratitude."

"Naturally. What sort of man is he, though? Until I am allowed to meet him for myself, I must rely on the reports of others."

"Upon my soul, if I had known I would be required to render a detailed report, I might have paid more particular attention. He seems a pleasant, good-humored sort of fellow. That is all I can say for him at present. I am certain that in good time we shall learn all the rest. Rest, yes." He seemed happy to catch on that idea. "That is the very thing. I will leave you now so you might rest as Mr. Cavanaugh prescribed."

"But, Papa, I am not the least bit tired…"

It wasn't any use; he was on his feet before I could get the words out, holding his finger to his lips and silently slinking from the room as if I were already asleep. How vexing! – to use one of my favorite Regency words. I thought that if I had to be stuck in bed, away from outside visitors, at least I could get to know my own family members better. Perhaps I would have more luck with Matilda and Carmen when they came, which undoubtedly they would.

No one else arrived right away, though, probably because I was supposed to be asleep. Then nearly an hour later, I heard a light tap, tap, tap at the door.

"Come in," I said eagerly, thrilled I would have somebody to talk to again. "Ah, Matilda, you cannot know how delighted I am to see you."

"As am I to see you, Kate," she said in that rat-a-tat-tat cadence I had noticed in her voice from my 'virtual' time spent with the Barretts at Crossroads. "How are you feeling? I could get little information from Papa."

"I am very well now, but no one seems to believe me. I suppose I shall just have to be patient a little longer and hope for more freedom tomorrow. The quiet is nearly more than I can endure, however. Where is the cheerful noise I have become used to in this house? I have not even heard you practicing at the pianoforte today, and you almost never miss."

"Unfortunately, I must make an exception this one time. Mama has said I may not play."

"Wait. Let me guess. Mr. Cavanaugh's orders. Am I right?"

"I'm afraid so. We are all under his strict injunctions against excessive noise of any kind, so that you may get proper rest."

Oh, for heaven's sake! "I thought it was only I who was suffering. I did not realize my whole family had fallen under that gentleman's cloud of gloom."

"I am sure he means well, Kate. Perhaps you should have more respect for his medical opinion. In any case, I brought you a book of verse for when you cannot sleep. I consider reading – at least the reading of poetry – very soothing, so I hope you will find it appropriately restful."

I thanked Matilda, and she stayed a few more minutes before I was left to "rest" some more.

I couldn't bear it. I was perfectly well. Even the pain in my head had faded completely away by this time. So, while no one was there to see, I crept out from under the covers and wandered the confines of my bedroom, hoping that no creaky floorboards would give me away. If I had known that I would be held a virtual prisoner in this room my first full day in Regency England, I would have left some of my exploring until now instead of being so thorough about it before I came. But I poked through a few drawers and cupboards anyway, just for something to do, and then ended up at the window, staring out at the fine weather, wishing I could be strolling in the gardens below.

It was June, I knew, and everything was green and growing. My window looked out over the front lawn and driveway with the road and rolling hills beyond. *A fine prospect.* In the distance, I could just make out the roof of another house. Was it Coleswold, I wondered? It seemed to be about the right place in relation to Laurelwood, according to what I could remember of the bird's-eye view I'd studied. In which case, it couldn't be more than a mile or two away, further up the road from town. *An easy distance* for walking. It seemed I couldn't see this or hear that without such familiar phrases popping into my head. Thankfully, I had avoided making any more major mistakes because of it, though… for the moment at least.

Suddenly, a noise in the hall brought me back to the present, and I had to make a dash to reach my bed before the door opened. It was only Carmen, though, as I could have guessed it would be.

"I have been waiting and waiting!" she exclaimed when she came in. "I thought it should never be my turn. Why must the youngest always be last? It is *so* unfair," she concluded, dropping dramatically into the chair next to me.

"You could have come in earlier with one of the others. I would not have minded."

"But Mr. Cavanaugh would have," she said rolling her eyes. "One visitor at a time, he said, lest the patient should become 'over-excited.' Honestly, I cannot help wondering if he is only making up these rules to be as tiresome as possible."

My thoughts exactly. But that isn't what I said. "I trust there is more to it than that, Carmen. He *is* a qualified physician, as he took pains to remind me. But I have heard quite enough about *that* gentleman today. Let us speak of something more pleasant."

"Very well. What say you to Mr. Sotheby? Is not that subject more agreeable?"

"Indeed, but you will need to do most of the talking since I have yet to set eyes on him."

"He is very well *worth* setting eyes on! That is the first thing I can tell you. And they say he is ever so rich. I think Papa should give a dinner for him, as a kind of thank-you and by way of welcoming him to the neighborhood. We could introduce him to all the prominent families. And then I'm hoping Mr. Sotheby will decide to return the favor by giving a dinner at Coleswold. Or better still, a ball. For I am dying to get a look inside the place, and I should love a ball above all things."

"But do you think Papa will allow you to dance at such a ball? You are only fourteen, after all."

"My birthday will be here soon, and when I am fifteen, he shall not stop me going to a private ball given by a gentleman he knows."

"Then we had better hope Mr. Sotheby is not *too* prompt with his invitations.

Marianne's illness, though weakening in its kind, had not been long enough to make her recovery slow... (Sense and Sensibility, chapter 46)

Chapter 14
Liberated

However frustrated I was by my temporary confinement (and however annoyed with Mr. Cavanaugh for imposing it on me), I did feel a little ashamed of myself later for my bad attitude. After all, I was the lucky one; I had been given a second chance.

The original Kathleen had not... so far as I knew, although it was interesting to think about the possibility. Hmm. What if she *had* been given a second chance, and she chose to take the spot I'd vacated, just as I had chosen to take hers? We would simply have traded places! I wondered how she would adapt to living in the future. What would she think of cars and computers, of television and telephones? Although it would be even stranger if she decided on Crossroads option three, to return to her old life. Could we end up with the two of us both trying to be Kathleen Barrett at the same time? No, if Kathleen decided to return to her original life, I'm sure it would be to avoid the accident that had ended it in the first place. Then, where would that leave me? Would I be kicked back to Crossroads to try again?

Good lord! If anything could make my head spin and start it hurting all over again, it would be trying to sort out all the possible implications this crazy form of time travel created. Better to leave it to the professionals – to Cora and Poindexter. They had the knowledge and experience. Like Poindexter said, they ran a tight ship and no doubt kept everything under control... except, of course, when one of their clients ran amok.

I didn't intend to make any trouble, though, at least not that kind. I couldn't necessarily promise for my behavior in every case.

Although I didn't fly off the handle easily, when severely provoked, I had occasionally lost my temper. So far, only Mr. Cavanaugh had come close to getting me that riled. But, when he came that next morning, removed my bandages, and granted his permission for me to freely move around the house and to begin eating normally again, I was soon *in charity* even with him.

Freedom! And one step closer to taking up my new life in full.

Flossie, whom it seemed I shared with Lucy, came in to help me dress as soon as Mr. Cavanaugh had given his instructions and gone. I certainly couldn't have managed without her. She fastened the framework of stays over my chemise and laced them up tight before slipping a muslin frock dress on me and buttoning up the back. I felt like a trussed Thanksgiving turkey by the time she had finished, and it didn't take much longer for me to understand why Regency ladies always sat so primly and were prone to swooning at the drop of a hat. Slouching was impossible and breathing deeply nearly so.

When I was a child, my mother, who was appalled by my lazy posture, reminded me constantly to sit up straight. If only she'd known about the corset, she could have had me whipped into shape in no time.

Although the clothing *was* restrictive, it was also an instant help in making me feel like I really was Kathleen Barrett. Hope O'Neil had worn denim, spandex, and cotton. But that girl and that wardrobe were gone. If I'd had any doubt, all I had to do was look in the mirror.

I was used to my new voice by then, but not my new face. I actually gasped when Flossie sat me down at the dressing table and I caught my first glimpse of my reflection.

"Don't worry, Miss," she said. "That bruise on your cheek will be gone in another day or two."

Of course it wasn't the bruise that had shocked me; it was the stranger in the mirror! No, not a stranger exactly. I knew that was Kathleen Barrett's face; I'd seen it plenty of times before. And once I got over that first shock, I really was okay with its new location. In fact, I was completely fascinated. I'm sure Flossie thought I'd lost every last one of my marbles, but I just couldn't stop staring.

Turning first one way and then the other, I examined the face peering back at me. All the features were regular and acceptable, but I liked my nose especially. I'd always thought my old one the tiniest bit too long. This new model was small and perky. My teeth were reasonably straight, which was lucky because there wouldn't have been a darn thing I could have done about it anyway. Besides, I'd already put in my time with braces, and once was enough. I leaned in still closer to the mirror and ran my fingers over my clear skin. The complexion was a little darker than I was used to, but I didn't think it could be considered unfashionably swarthy. And it was in keeping with the dark eyes and chestnut brown hair. Flossie was attempting to pile and pin up all that hair in some sort of style for me. No doubt she would have made more progress if only I had held still for her.

I'd thought Kathleen was pretty from the first time I'd seen her. Not truly beautiful, perhaps, but close enough. Now – now that she was me – it was much more difficult to be objective about it.

"Do you think I'm pretty, Flossie?" I asked her.

The question didn't seem to surprise her. Maybe Kathleen had asked it before. "Oh, yes, Miss," she said.

Of course, what else *could* she say?

When Flossie had finished with my hair, I turned my head from side to side to admire the result. She did nice work. I had always worn my hair short and simple as Hope, so this too would be different for me. But different is what I'd asked for, right?

"It looks very nice, Flossie," I told her. "Thank you. And now I suppose I had better go down to breakfast before it is too late."

"Yes, Miss, but I am to take your arm and see you safely down the stairs. Madam's orders."

I didn't argue. I was so thrilled to be leaving my room at last that I would have gladly put up with the escort of a pair of Sumo wrestlers if necessary... although, come to think of it, we'd never have fit down that narrow back stairway together!

I'm sure I wasn't the only one who was happy to have yesterday's restrictions lifted and things returning to normal. The house was busy and alive with noise again. I could hear Matilda at the pianoforte, catching up on her practicing; Mama was somewhere down the hall, raising her voice to one of the servants; and there was a rustle and clatter from the direction of the kitchen.

"I am sorry, Kate, but I'm afraid everybody else has already finished and gone," Lucy told me when I reached the dining parlor. "Come sit down by me and I will serve you a plate."

"That is very kind of you, but I'm sure I can manage."

"Nonsense," she said, going to the sideboard where what remained of the food was spread. "I would like to do it. What do you want?"

"It all smells wonderful and I am powerfully hungry, so some of everything, I guess. Just no more gruel."

Real food! It tasted as good as it smelled: farm-fresh eggs, ham, warm homemade rolls with butter, fruit, and tea. Lucy kept me company while I ate two helpings, and Mama poked her head in partway through.

"Nothing too strenuous today," she told me. "Mr. Cavanaugh is pleased with your progress but warns against risking a relapse. So, mind you, keep to reading and your needlework. There are those things to be mended for the poor. I daresay that will keep you and your sister busy for most of the afternoon, Kate."

"Yes, Mama," I said, and Lucy echoed.

Needlework! I wasn't equipped for that. When it came to sewing, I was about as useless as a screen door on a submarine. While I was so conscientiously preparing myself to assume Kathleen's life, why hadn't I thought to work on improving my skills in that area too? Every proper Regency lady knew how to handle a needle!

I lingered over breakfast as long as I could and then only very slowly made my way to the drawing room, where I knew Kathleen's workbasket awaited me. Lucy sat down on one of the sofa and set to it, but I detoured to the pianoforte. Matilda had finished and gone by then, so I slipped into the seat behind the keyboard, relieved to have a way of stalling off the inevitable disaster I would make of my sewing. Also, it seemed like a long time since I'd had a chance to play, and my fingers were purely itching to try out a genuine period instrument.

I meant to start out with a piece I knew by memory, but fortunately, I caught myself just in time. I was thinking of *Phantom of the Opera* and I'd never have been able to explain that. Close call. I would have to stick to the old masters, pieces composed before the nineteenth century. So I looked through the sheet music Matilda had left out until I found something I recognized – a Beethoven sonata I had played before. I charged into it with great enthusiasm, quickly adjusting to the feel of the new instrument. Well, old really, just new to me.

It felt wonderful to be producing music again; it fed something deep inside my soul. And I had never been shy about performing. How lucky for me that this was something else valued in a Regency lady. I could play and sing to my heart's content, and that was likely to result in more male admirers than a crocheted doily or a neatly stitched sampler ever would. After hearing me, would some young gentleman decide he would like to ask me to try the instrument in *his* drawing room, to entertain him and his guests with my musical accomplishments?

I was so caught up in these kinds of thoughts and with the music itself that I didn't notice a crowd had begun to gather. When I finished the first movement of the piece, though, I glanced up to find my entire family gaping at me in some sort of mass stupefaction. I would have been pleased with a little polite applause, but their silent stares made me uneasy. "What's the matter?" I finally asked, looking from one to the other to the other.

Matilda was the first to regain her powers of speech. "Where... where did you learn to play like that?" she asked, although the question sounded more like an accusation.

Then it started to dawn on me what the problem might be. From my research, I knew Kathleen played the pianoforte, but I hadn't actually heard her or taken the time to find out how skilled (or possibly unskilled?) she really was. Had I played much too well for her? Too late now.

"I have been practicing a great deal," I said, hoping for the best.

Matilda turned without another word and stalked off.

Carmen watched her go and then said, "I thought it was very good, Kate."

"Thank you."

"Yes, *very* good!" Papa agreed. "No one can contest that it was an accomplished performance. However, you will forgive me for pointing out that you have not shown much promise in this area before, my child, so I am at a loss to explain the transformation."

"Never mind what has brought this miracle about, Mr. Barrett," said Mama. "Just thank God for it. Kate, my dear, you must learn to put yourself forward more from now on, learn to display to advantage. Talent like yours must not be hid under a bushel basket any longer."

One by one, they wandered off again, leaving me alone except for Lucy. She came over to the pianoforte then.

I idly tinkled an elementary little tune with my right hand. "Did I really do something as shocking as all that?" I asked without looking up at my sister.

"You honestly do not know?"

"Perhaps I play a little better than before. Is that it? As I said, I have been practicing – more than any of you may have realized."

"Your improvement is far beyond that, Kate. You saw Matilda's reaction; she has been used to being the most accomplished musician in the neighborhood, or at least in her own family. That is no longer the case."

"It was not intentional, besting her performance, that is. I just sat down at the instrument and the music began to flow. Poor Matilda. Do you think she is very angry with me?"

"More hurt, I suspect, but I trust it is nothing that cannot be overcome. If your new ability has been given by God, which is the only thing that it can be, who are we to question it?"

"Or perhaps it is another effect of hitting my head. Some things seem to have changed for the worse. I believe I have forgot nearly everything I ever knew about needlework, for example. Does it not seem only right and fair that at least one other thing should have improved by way of compensation?"

It was generally evident whenever they met, that he did admire her; and to her it was equally evident that Jane was yielding to the preference which she had begun to entertain for him from the first... (Pride and Prejudice, chapter 6)

Chapter 15
Mr. Sotheby

I made up the best I could with Matilda, telling her I couldn't explain why my playing had improved so much, that I was just as surprised by it as she was. "...but I think it very likely my new ability may be only temporary. If it has come to me somehow by the blow to my head, all may return to normal in time."

This seemed to cheer her, and it was something within my control. I didn't intend to stop playing altogether; music was too important to me for that. To quote Mrs. Elton, "...without music, life would be a blank to me." Well, that might be overstating the case. There were lots of other things I enjoyed, but I would hate to give up music entirely. Instead, I would tone things down, especially when Matilda was present, to be sure I didn't show her up at what she seemed to consider her one claim to fame, her main source of pride. I personally thought she had many other fine traits.

Mr. Cavanaugh came one more time – completely unnecessarily, I thought – to check on my progress. I kept a civil tongue in my head, and he didn't stay long.

Later that day, Mr. Sotheby called again, and Mama, Lucy, Carmen, and I received him in the drawing room. He was just as I imagined he would be and just as the others had described him: good-looking, in a blondish sort of way, and amiable. I thanked him as warmly as I dared for carrying me home after my accident. "You may very well have saved my life, Mr. Sotheby," I concluded.

"No, no, I will never allow that," he said in response, dropping his eyes and trying to fend off the compliment with his upheld hand.

"It was your sister who did it all. It was her cry that alerted me to the crisis. She knew what to do and where to send for Mr. Cavanaugh. She stayed faithfully by your side every minute. I was simply fortunate enough to have been of some small service."

"You are too modest, sir, and I shall never forget your kindness," I assured him.

"Nor shall I," added Lucy.

By the way they looked at each other, Lucy and Mr. Sotheby, I knew I had been right. These two had really hit it off and were possibly on their way to being in love already. All they needed was more time and opportunity. This matched up nicely with my dream that I would land in my very own version of *Pride and Prejudice*. Lucy was obviously the Jane Bennet character in this scenario and Mr. Sotheby, her Mr. Bingley. But would the parallel go far enough to benefit me? So far, there had been no hint of an attractive and available friend staying with him, which would have been far more interesting to me than what he did have: a sister.

"My younger sister Dorothy is staying with me to keep my house, Miss Kathleen," Mr. Sotheby explained when I asked how he was settling in at Coleswold. "She had the servants organized within a few days of our arrival and has the most creative ideas for improvements. I need not worry for anything while she is acting lady of the house. That is very well for me. But I have stolen Dorothy away from her usual society in London, and I must find a way to make her some amends."

With this opening, I couldn't help tossing a line into the pond and fishing for a little more information. "Surely you will often have friends visiting to expand your society," I suggested. "That would be pleasant for you as well as a kindness to your sister."

"From time to time, perhaps," he replied, "but I've no desire to have my house always filled with people. I retired to the country to escape the noise and strain of town. No, the company of good, honest country folk is all I require, and it shall have to do for my sister as well. Miss Barrett," he continued, turning to Lucy. "I hope I might soon have the opportunity to introduce Dorothy to you and to all your family."

"I would be delighted to meet Miss Sotheby as soon it may be arranged," Lucy answered.

He smiled. "And once we are fully settled, perhaps I should give a dinner to meet the rest of our neighbors. What would you advise me, Mrs. Barrett?" he asked. "Do you think a dinner at Coleswold would be well received?"

Carmen opened her mouth (presumably to suggest to our new neighbor that it should be a ball instead), but a sharp look from me closed it again.

"No doubt it would be," said Mama. "However, that is for Mr. Barrett to do, sir. We shall see that you and your sister are properly introduced to all the best families. Indeed, we were only waiting for Kathleen to be entirely recovered before fixing a date. Perhaps sometime next week?"

"You are extremely kind, Mrs. Barrett. My sister and I shall be delighted. You have only to name the day."

This was very promising – a dinner at Laurelwood to acquaint Mr. Sotheby with all his new neighbors! It would serve the exact same purpose for me, of course, as well as being my first Regency social event. Is this where I would discover my Mr. Darcy, I wondered? So what if he wasn't Mr. Sotheby's houseguest. I had to accept that some things would be arranged a little differently. What I refused to accept was that Mr. Cavanaugh might be as close as I would come. He might share a few traits with my all-time favorite literary hero, but it would take more than a house in Derbyshire to tempt me.

~~*~~

The minute I'd been released from my sickbed, everything started going more as I had hoped, and I was sure I'd made the right decision by coming here. The Barretts were all I could have asked for in a family. They weren't perfect; they were real. Papa was benevolent, if a little detached. Mama was as goodhearted as they come but sometimes flighty. I liked Matilda's serious streak, although I thought it probably would hold her back socially. And Carmen? Well, Carmen was a typical fourteen-year-old learning to spread her wings – full of energy and scatterbrained ideas. Lucy had been the biggest influence in my choosing this family, and I couldn't find any flaw in her. She was exactly the kind of sister and best friend I'd always wanted.

Once the date was set for the Sothebys' dinner, Mama began cackling and flapping about the house like a nervous hen. She got the invitations ready, made and then remade the menu, and browbeat the servants to get the house into company-worthy condition by the big day. I had the impression that she really loved all the fuss and activity but that she also expected sympathy for how much work she had to do. My guess was that everything would turn out fine, despite her fretting, and she would be glad to accept the credit for it in the end.

Since I was clearly well now, I was soon allowed to resume normal activities and to not be bothered by any more visits from Mr. Cavanaugh. I explored all over the estate and then finally got the chance to walk into Carding with my sisters, this time making it *inside* Grimstock's and Mrs. Abernathy's house, where I had been kept out on my earlier, virtual visit.

Grimstock's was a great curiosity to me. I had almost no idea what to expect and wondered how Carding's general store would compare to its modern counterpart, which I suppose would be the local Walmart. At both you could buy most everything from flour to pitch forks, from pickles to shoes. But that's where the similarity ended. Instead of a high-ceilinged, brightly lit warehouse that sprawled over the equivalent of a city block, Grimstock's was no bigger than an average schoolroom times two, with staples and hardware on the ground floor, fabric and sundries above.

While Lucy and Matilda made purchases for Mama, Carmen and I poked around upstairs. One of the displays there put me in mind of Frank Churchill. Since he considered that buying a pair of gloves at Ford's made him a true citizen of Highbury, I had to do the same at Grimstock's. I wanted to truly belong to Carding as soon as possible.

Next stop was Mrs. Abernathy's. From what I had gathered, she was a well-to-do widow who had known the Barretts pretty much forever. It seems her only daughter had married advantageously and then moved away to Devon, leaving Mrs. Abernathy no one to lavish with her maternal attentions. Consequently, she had adopted us – the Barrett girls – as her own, which seemed to suit everybody just fine.

In my mind, I saw her as sort of a triple cross between Mrs. Jennings, Mrs. Phillips, and Miss Bates. She was the cheerful, doting aunt who liked gossip and company pretty equally. She kept a sharp eye on everything that happened in the Carding vicinity too. I swear, nothing got past her drawing room windows without being noticed. Good luck to anyone trying to sneak into or out of the village without drawing her attention. In that case, a body'd be better off detouring ten full miles out of his way than to pass within a hundred yards of Mrs. Abernathy's front door.

Of course, we had nothing to fear.

"Girls, girls, do come in!" she called from the doorway as we approached. "Kate, I am pleased to see you looking so well. And how fortunate that you have all come by today, for I want your opinions on my plans for refurnishing the back sitting room. Plus, Cook has just this minute taken a tray of fresh biscuits from the oven. But first you must tell me all your news."

"We are to give a dinner on Tuesday at Laurelwood for Mr. Sotheby and his sister," Carmen announced before we were even inside. "And you are invited."

"This is excellent news indeed! Do sit down and tell me more."

Lucy handed Mrs. Abernathy her invitation – the official reason for our visit.

She broke the seal and opened it at once. "Oh, I do love an invitation. 'The honor of your presence,' etc, etc. I suppose all the usual people will be there. Your mother and father certainly know how this sort of thing should be done. And all for Mr. and Miss Sotheby, too! How I long to meet them. I have only seen them passing by – him on his horse once and them both together in a very fine carriage another time – but I have heard all that can be known about them by report, I am sure. He is a fine gentleman, they say, and she a very stylish lady. Of course, the principal thing is how Mr. Sotheby came to your rescue, Kate."

"How did you hear that story, Mrs. Abernathy?" I asked her, for I wasn't aware that it was common knowledge.

"Why, the information was all over the village, if not the county, in a matter of hours, my dear. You must know that such a thing cannot be bottled up for long, nor should it be. Mr. Sotheby has earned everybody's gratitude and admiration by it, I daresay. His reputation has been secured before he has even had time to make the acquaintance of most of Carding's citizens. But what are your own opinions of him, girls? I trust you have all met him by now."

"Yes, indeed," Carmen answered eagerly. "He has come to call on us twice besides the day he brought Kate home. He is very handsome, and he wears a green coat."

"That is a good start. What about you, Matilda? You think serious thoughts. What do you have to say about this Mr. Sotheby?"

Matilda looked unsure. "I... I would prefer to withhold any judgment until I have more complete information."

"Very sensible, Matilda. Then I will look forward to having benefit of your considered opinion at a later date. Kate, I will hear from you next."

How could I resist? I said what first came to mind. "He is just what a young man ought to be – sensible, lively..."

"And what happy manners!" Lucy added on cue, just as if she had read the script. "You are sure to like him, Mrs. Abernathy. I do not see how anybody could not like Mr. Sotheby, as amiable as he is."

"It is unanimous, then, except for Matilda's reservations. What about your other gentleman caller? Do you have as high an opinion of him? After all, I suppose he must also have a share of the credit for returning our dear Kate to health."

"Mr. Cavanaugh?" guessed Matilda.

"Yes. Mr. Cavanaugh, to be sure," our hostess confirmed.

"You misled us by the term 'caller,' dear Mrs. Abernathy," Lucy explained. "His visits were not social calls; he only came to attend Kate through her illness. Although I liked him well enough, his manners are certainly not so easy and engaging as Mr. Sotheby's."

"And Kate, I have heard you did not find Mr. Cavanaugh even appealing enough to dance with before. Has his service to you improved your opinion of him?"

No, it had not; it only confirmed my dislike of him. But instead, I said, "He may be a worthy sort of gentleman in his own way, but too aloof for my taste. I did not care for him at all, and I was never more relieved than when I was well enough to escape the sickbed and any more of Mr. Cavanaugh's visits."

Mrs. Abernathy laughed. "Well, that is not a very positive endorsement, I must say! It may not keep me from summoning him for medical advice, but I shall think twice before adding him to my guest list for one of my card parties."

"Oh, he may do very well at cards, Mrs. Abernathy," I said, adding sarcastically, "Card games are governed by rules, and Mr. Cavanaugh is very fond of those."

Finally! I had managed to produce something mildly witty at Mr. Cavanaugh's expense at last, lines I could imagine Lizzy Bennet herself saying. It wasn't nearly as satisfying as I had expected, although that was probably only because *he* hadn't been around to hear it.

The Dashwoods were so prodigiously delighted with the Middletons, that, though not much in the habit of giving anything, they determined to give them a dinner… (Sense and Sensibility, chapter 34)

Chapter 16
Invited Guests

"Must we have Mr. Cavanaugh, Mama?"

I asked the question two days before the dinner party, when I examined the guest list. I thought I should at least familiarize myself with the names of the people (which I hoped would also conjure up some of Kathleen's relevant memories). Since I was sure she would have known them, I would be expected to know them too.

At the top of the list: the guests of honor, Mr. Sotheby and Miss Sotheby.

Reverend and Mrs. Bell: rector of the parish and his wife. I'd heard him preach that morning and had spoken to her briefly after the service, so I would certainly recognize them again.

Mrs. Abernathy: no problem there.

The Galloways: close friends who lived on the other side of Carding, in the next parish. If Kathleen's memories served, they had a grown son and daughter. George and… oh, what was her name? I could picture her clearly enough – pretty, petite, reddish blonde hair, freckles – but the name would not come. I'd have to work on that before Tuesday.

And Mr. and Mrs. Edgewood: another blank.

The Kingsleys: here I did a little better. Sir John was the nearest thing we had to nobility in the area – a newly created baronet. Lady Kingsley – a dull but attractive woman, now about forty. Their son… I shook my head. No, there were two of them, I was pretty sure. So, their sons, who would presumably be coming too.

Then there was Mr. Cavanaugh.

I didn't want him there. I'd hoped for a clean slate at this dinner, to put my rocky beginning behind me and start fresh without any past taint to spoil it. That would be difficult, knowing Mr. Cavanaugh was there and that we each already had a negative opinion of the other. He could turn out to be the wet blanket that smothered my good mood and drowned my parade.

"He's not even a close friend," I pointed out to Mama.

"It was perfectly right that he should have been included, Kate. You know that. And moreover, the invitations have gone out," Mama explained matter-of-factly.

"Perhaps he will not accept."

"He already has, thank the Lord. It would have put my table completely out had he declined. When one has unmarried daughters, it is so challenging to round up enough unattached men to balance things properly."

"We will have Mr. Sotheby, George Galloway, and the two Kingsley brothers as it is. That is four, and there are only three of us without Carmen attending."

"Two, actually. I gave Matilda the choice, and she said she would just as soon be excused. You know her views on such matters. She cannot be bothered with catering to society or with sparing a thought for finding a husband yet. But still, there is a problem since we must have even numbers at the table. Mr. Sotheby and young George Galloway are cancelled out by their sisters, and then there is Mrs. Abernathy on her own. So you see my dilemma."

"Then pair Mr. Cavanaugh with Mrs. Abernathy," I said mischievously. "She will not mind, for she was asking about the man only the other day."

Mama was not amused.

"Now, Kate, I expect you to behave very civilly to Mr. Cavanaugh, as you would to any of our other guests. You promised you would try to like him. Remember?"

I remembered.

Very well, then. I would have my fresh start despite Mr. Cavanaugh. And instead of allowing him to drown my new and improved attitude, I would make him the test of it. I would be so *nice* to him that it would leave him scratching his head, wondering why.

~~*~~

104

The house had been bustling with activity for the better part of a week, and by the time Tuesday finally arrived, I was as twitchy as a long-tailed cat in a roomful of rocking chairs. Nervous *and* excited. My first Regency dinner party!

It wasn't Lucy's first, I was pretty sure, but she was nervous too. Although she probably wouldn't have admitted it, I knew it was on account of Mr. Sotheby. "How do I look, Kate?" she asked as she came into my room. "I want your honest opinion. I'm not sure I quite like the color of this gown after all," she fretted.

Sitting at my dressing table, with Flossie working on my hair, I reached out and took my sister's hand. "The color is perfect. *That* is my honest opinion. *You* are perfect, dearest. I may as well stay away; none of the men will notice anyone but you."

"Oh, thank you, Kate!" she said in one big exhale. She squeezed my hand. "I know you exaggerate, but if you think I am in tolerable good looks, I must believe you and have confidence."

I laughed. "I said you were perfect, not only tolerably good."

And it was true; Lucy was a picture, with her wispy fawn-colored hair framing her pretty face and in her pale green gown, which brought out her eyes. I would certainly have bet on her to win any beauty contest, although I was pretty sure the only contest she cared about was the *Mr. Sotheby Sweepstakes*.

"Mama has you seated next to Mr. Sotheby," I told her.

"Thanks to you, I understand."

"Well, I did put in a word with her. My little present to you... and to him."

"Meanwhile, you have Mr. Cavanaugh. That cannot be very much to your liking."

"Dinner will not last forever, and I intend to be absolutely charming to him," I said, deliberately applying my new attitude to the situation. "And I must give George Galloway on my other side his share of attention. To own the truth, though, I think Mama would be best pleased if either you or I were to attach the eldest Kingsley brother's affection. She has him on your right, you know, and directly across from me. Since he will be a baronet one day, I suppose he must be considered the biggest catch – the most eligible, that is."

"Frederick? I suppose so. You may have him if you like, Kate, but he seems a bit of a coxcomb to me. I've always preferred Edward for his steadiness of character. At least I did when we were younger. They both seem like such boys to me now, when compared next to a more experienced man."

"Like Mr. Sotheby? Yes, I see what you mean."

Lucy left me, but with a few more of my blanks filled in.

I had continued to recall bits and pieces about the people on the guest list, and now I had both the Kingsley boys' first names and my sister's opinion of them. Also, the information that even the eldest was apparently at least a few years younger than Mr. Sotheby, whom I estimated to be nearly thirty. I didn't think I would mind a man somewhat younger than that, though. After all, I was used to dating guys closer to my own age. And George Galloway was an interesting possibility too. I seem to remember that he had shown signs of liking me – that is, Kathleen – before. A long-time crush, maybe? That was worth looking into.

If I ceded Mr. Sotheby to Lucy, which I was happy to do, that still left three eligible young men for me at the dinner, without even needing to count Mr. Cavanaugh. Of course I realized I wouldn't have them all to myself. Miss Galloway (whose first name, maddeningly, still escaped me!) was pretty enough to catch a man's eye. And then there would be the wild card: Miss Sotheby. "Very stylish," according to Mrs. Abernathy's report, but that wasn't much to go on. No, the proof would be in the pudding, meaning I'd need to see her for myself before forming an opinion.

When I referred back to my *Pride and Prejudice* model, if Mr. Sotheby was Mr. Bingley, then that made Miss Sotheby... Oh, dear; that made her Miss Bingley. In that case, I'd have to watch my back when she was around. Until we had a Mr. Darcy to fight over, though, maybe there wouldn't be much of a problem.

After Flossie had finished putting me together and gone, I just sat there at my dressing table, kind of hypnotized, thinking about what was ahead and waiting. It really did feel as if I were on the verge of something big – perhaps the biggest night of my entire life, or at least of my *new* life. This would be my official launch into Regency society, after all (although nobody would know it but me). It was the sort of thing I'd been dreaming about ever since I'd discovered Jane Austen. Not so good as a full ball, maybe, but a giant step forward – a chance to test my fledgling wings. The question was, would I soar to new heights or crash and burn?

I was mostly excited, not scared. The thing I *was* nervous about, though, was that I might make another one of my mistakes, and this time in front of a larger audience. I might commit some dreadful *faux pas* by forgetting my Regency manners, or what seemed more likely, I would embarrass myself by not remembering something about one of our guests that I should know. I thought I'd been so thorough in my research while I was at Crossroads, but it was turning out that I'd missed a lot of details. I sure hoped Kathleen's memories kicked in when I really needed them.

With my fever-pitch of anticipation, it seemed like *something* momentous was about to happen, and I had to believe it would be something wonderful. I held my breath, figuratively speaking, in a state of delicious yet excruciating suspense. It reminded me of one of my high school track meets, the feeling of waiting in the blocks, muscles tensed and ready to explode into action when the starter's gun fired. So when my door cracked open, the sound made me jump straight up out of my seat, like I'd been jolted with a cattle prod.

Lucy poked her head in. "It is time to go down. Are you ready?"

"Coming," I said.

I took a deep breath and turned around, pausing to get Lucy's reaction, now that I was all dressed and groomed.

I was wearing a pale coral, almost peach, gown – not a color I would have chosen when I was my former, blonde self, but it seemed to go with my new look well enough. When I checked in the mirror, I'd been almost satisfied. Almost. I felt a powerful need to add at least a bit of lipstick and mascara to the picture; I don't think I had ever faced an important occasion like this without them, not since I turned sixteen. But of course, they weren't available, so I had to get used to the natural look.

"Oh, Kate," Lucy said with an affectionate smile. "You are simply lovely."

It was all I needed to hear. With that, we went downstairs, hand in hand.

Mama was so busy fussing over last-minute details that she didn't notice us at first. "Now, Hawthorn," she was saying to the middle-aged man who served as our butler. "I need not tell you how important tonight is to us all. I am depending on you to do everything right and proper. Yours is the first face our guests will see, and so you will represent the family in making a good first impression."

Mr. Hawthorn looked unperturbed and only answered with the standard, "Yes, Madam." All the same, I'm sure he was relieved when Mama turned her attentions away from him to us.

"Girls, girls," she began, "I thought you would never come down, and I did not have time to hurry you along myself. I was about to send Mrs. Brant to check on you but... well, here you are." She scrutinized us up and down and asked us to spin around once. "Well, Lucy, you look very well indeed. Kate, I'm not sure I approve of what Flossie has done with your hair, but it will have to do, I suppose. There is no time to make a change now. Into the drawing room with you both. Our guests will be arriving at any moment. Remember to smile and mind your manners tonight; much may hang in the balance regarding your futures."

Mr. Barrett was in the drawing room already, looking very grim. "Well, girls, are you prepared to suffer the strain of this night's required exertions?" he asked. "We are forced to make ourselves agreeable for an entire evening. Your mama has decreed it to be so, and who are we to argue?"

"Yes, Papa," I said, going over to kiss him on the cheek. "In fact, I am very much looking forward to the 'exertions' the evening requires, as you have put it."

"That is where we differ in our views, my child. But then not much exertion will be required of you and your sister; you need only smile and perhaps sing a little later to be thought everything beautiful and charming. An ugly old man, like myself, must work much harder to be judged even moderately agreeable."

Lucy and I laughed, as he intended we should, and then reassured him that he wasn't old or ugly either – also as I'm sure he intended.

Hearing the crunch of gravel outside and the hoof beats of approaching horses, I rushed to the window to see who had arrived. This was it! It was finally time to make my Regency debut!

She had dressed with more than usual care, and prepared in the highest spirits for the conquest of all that remained unsubdued of his heart, trusting that it was not more than might be won in the course of the evening. (Pride and Prejudice, chapter 18)

Chapter 17
The Dinner

"Come away from the window, Kate!" said Mama, who had just entered the room. "For heaven's sake, you must not be observed gawking as if you had never seen people getting out of fine carriages before."

I hadn't, of course, but Mama was right; I didn't want anybody to suspect what a novice I was at all of this.

The Galloways were shown in, so my first challenge of the evening was upon me right away. I had to either remember their daughter's name or fake my way through. Thankfully, she headed towards Lucy first. And then, just as my sister opened her mouth, the proper name popped out of mine.

"Charlotte!" *Of course. Mercy!* These crazy carryover memories seemed to come on a when-you-need-to-know basis, but that was cutting it mighty fine. "Charlotte, how lovely to see you again."

It was pretty smooth sailing after that. Along with Charlotte's name, I remembered a lot of other things about our history together, how we had often visited back and forth, either just we girls or the whole families. I also remembered some of George's attentions to me but not necessarily how I had felt about them. (I guess I was getting used to the fact that I was Kathleen Barrett for real, because I noticed I'd stopped always making the distinction between the two of us in my mind.)

The Bells arrived next, bringing Mrs. Abernathy, and then the Edgewoods. When I saw Mr. and Mrs. Edgewood, the same thing happened as with Charlotte. Suddenly, a lot of blanks about them began to fill in. I remembered they were a childless couple, around my parents' ages, who lived in the nearest town of any size beyond Carding. He owned the bank there... and nearly everything else, too, it seemed.

By the time Mr. Cavanaugh arrived, there were enough people around for him to talk to that I didn't feel like it was my sole responsibility to entertain him. Which was good, because I was completely distracted with waiting to get my first look at the Kingsley brothers. And presumably more background information about them would automatically fill in at the same time. Now that I knew how it worked, I didn't have to sweat that part.

Mr. and Miss Sotheby came before them, though, and that was just as exciting. I watched for Lucy to light up like a firefly when he came into the room, which she totally did. And then we got our first look at Miss Sotheby. My, she was tall – probably at least five foot eight, like I used to be – very elegant as we had heard, and quite beautiful. Everybody turned to look, and then, since none of the others had met our guests of honor before, a full round of introductions took place.

There were more introductions and greetings when the Kingsleys finally arrived just before dinner was announced. My goodness! I expect the curtsey muscles in my legs were close to cramping up by the time we were finished with all that bobbing up and down, bowing, and how-do-you-do-ing.

But I came through without any major mistakes, at least none that I was aware of. And I was pretty pleased with the crop of eligible bachelors I'd be dining with too. They all looked good to me, dressed up in their fancy duds: white shirts and cravats, waistcoats, breeches, and tailcoats. *Be still my heart!* It seems a shame the tradition of dressing for dinner ever died out. I'm convinced that if modern men knew how good they look to women in formal clothes like tuxedos, they'd wear them much more often.

Other than Mr. Cavanaugh, who wasn't in the running in my book, Frederick Kingsley was probably the best looking of the bunch, which made him the complete Regency bachelor package: looks, money, and future title. But I had a feeling Lucy was right about him being a coxcomb. He did seem to preen and strut a bit like a peacock showing off his fine feathers. Too soon to write him off, though.

110

I thought his brother Edward was nearly as handsome. Taller besides – something I'd always been drawn to. But he was a second son, and I knew what that meant: no money and no title. I wasn't sure I cared about a title, but having some money would come in handy. As Lizzy B. reminds us, *handsome young men must have something to live on as well as the plain.* That's especially true if they plan to marry.

Then there was George Galloway. I had nothing but positive impressions when I first laid eyes on him – my current observations as well as the store of memories that came cascading back to me. I wouldn't call him exactly handsome or tall, but I liked his face. It seemed open and honest, like a person you could count on. He was his father's heir too, which was a plus, although the estate was probably no larger than Laurelwood. That would be enough for me.

So far, so good, but I wasn't sure there existed a single Mr. Darcy in the bunch. And if there was, I'd probably have some stiff competition from Miss Sotheby.

~~*~~

Considering that my first few Regency meals were gruel, the food had been on a sharp upward curve from there, with this company dinner at the definite peak. If I hadn't had to pay such close attention to correct etiquette – how to sit, what to say and not say, which fork or spoon to use for what dish – I could have appreciated the food itself even more. But I'm not complaining. It was loads of fun putting my research to good use. And whenever I was unsure of myself, I just followed Lucy's example. She was sitting caddy-wonked across from me, between Mr. Sotheby (who was next to Papa at the head of the table) and Frederick Kingsley, so it was easy to keep one eye on her at all times.

I think the whole conversational arrangement had been sort of orchestrated. When Papa began by talking to Mr. Sotheby during the soup, everybody else (except me) knew that was their cue and what to do about it. Lucy turned towards Frederick Kingsley. Next to him, Charlotte Galloway turned to talk to Edward Kingsley, and everybody else paired off from there. All of which meant I had George Galloway to begin with, and that was perfectly fine with me. We had plenty to talk about.

"How very relieved I am to see you so well recovered, Miss Kathleen. You cannot imagine how horrified I was, we *all* were at Grambling House, when we heard of your accident. You might have broken your neck or something worse."

"I thank you for your concern, Mr. Galloway," I said. "I'm not sure there is something worse than a broken neck, though." I said. Then, thinking of my less fortunate predecessor, I added, "I was very lucky to come away with only a few minor memory lapses, which I trust are temporary. Otherwise, I am entirely unharmed."

"Thank God."

"Yes, thank God."

"Will you ride again? It would take particular courage to climb back onto a horse after being thrown by him."

"You mustn't suppose it was anyone's fault but my own. I was going too fast and tried to turn too abruptly. I was not thrown off; I lost my balance. That is what happened. I would trust Horatio with my life, and I shall begin riding again as soon as I am allowed, only much less recklessly in the future."

"I admire your spirit, Miss Kathleen."

The roasted pheasant was served after the soup, interrupting our conversation. Then George began again.

"Will your younger sister be joining us later?"

"Matilda? I do not think so. Why do you ask?"

"I only wondered who would play for us if she did not."

"Well, perhaps I will. What do you say to that?"

"Oh, Miss Kathleen, that would please me more than I can say. But it surprises me as well. How many times have you been asked before and refused, saying your paltry talents would not withstand the test of an audience?"

"I have been practicing, Mr. Galloway, and now I hope I may not disgrace myself as I might have done before."

"I am quite sure you could never do anything to disgrace yourself, Miss Kathleen. I will look forward to hearing you play later with great anticipation."

George was very earnest and very pleasant, and I enjoyed our conversation immensely. I also enjoyed taking in the scene in general, so much like I had imagined it would be. Candles blazed everywhere; the best china was in use; and four servants hovered unobtrusively in the background, watching in case anybody should need anything. Mama had hired a couple of extra footmen for the night, to wait on the table so the maids wouldn't have to, which I gather would have been considered bad form. She had everything running smoothly, just as I predicted.

Catching my eye, Mama smiled and nodded at me encouragingly from the far end of the table. She had the older generation collected there – Sir John and Lady Kingsley, the Bells, Edgewoods, and senior Galloways – and she looked to be having a wonderful time. Despite how flighty and flustered she seemed sometimes, Mrs. Barrett was really quite a competent hostess. I would be smart to pay attention and learn as much as I could from her.

About halfway through the pheasant, Papa left off with Mr. Sotheby to talk to his sister on his other side instead, and that was apparently the signal for everybody else to change partners too. I had to give up the pleasant company of George Galloway for Mr. Cavanaugh. I sighed, and I reminded myself of my resolution to torture him by being nauseatingly nice. Aiming for a genuine smile, I turned his way.

"Miss Kathleen," he said.

I responded in kind. "Mr. Cavanaugh?"

"You are looking well."

"I am feeling very well, thank you."

"Are you enjoying the dinner?"

"Exceedingly. Roast pheasant is so much to be preferred over gruel, do not you think? I hope you are enjoying yourself as well. I am somewhat envious of your opportunity to speak so long to Miss Sotheby." I had heard the lady laughing and wondered what she found so entertaining in Mr. Cavanaugh.

"She is a very charming young woman, Miss Kathleen, and so exceptionally accomplished. I am sure you will be great friends when once you have had a chance to become acquainted. It seems as if she reads a great deal. Perhaps you will have that in common."

"I do like to read; that is true. And you, Mr. Cavanaugh?"

"Yes, I read a great deal. Mostly medical journals and the papers, I'm afraid. I have very little time for light reading."

"No novels, then? What a pity. Novels are my favorites." I could have guessed he would think novels were beneath his notice, but I didn't let that negative thought show in what I said next. "I just recently finished *The Mysteries of Udolpho*. Perhaps you have heard of it."

I didn't think I'd said this particularly loudly, but Frederick Kingsley, across from me, happened to hear.

"*Udolpho*! By Mrs. Radcliffe?" he exclaimed.

"Why, yes," I answered. "Have you read it too, Mr. Kingsley?"

"Read it? I locked myself in my room and raced through it all in one sitting, refusing to go out or come down for meals until I had finished. Wasn't it splendid?"

Here, some of the others within his reach – Miss Galloway and even Mrs. Abernathy – joined in with their eager opinions. Meanwhile, I bowed out of the conversation and returned my attention to Mr. Cavanaugh with a calm smile.

He looked a little surprised by this. "You do not share their enthusiasm for this book?"

"I am glad to have read it, but I really did not care much for it myself. I thought it overly melodramatic and tediously long."

"Other things are more to your taste."

"Exactly." I was thinking of Jane Austen's novels, but I didn't elaborate for obvious reasons.

"Such as…" he then said, leadingly.

He was waiting for my answer. I panicked. I couldn't say *Pride and Prejudice* or *Anne of Green Gables* or any of my other favorites that came to mind, since none of them had been published yet. And after *The Mysteries of Udolpho*, which I'd read only thanks to Cora, I was fresh out of novels that had been!

"Oh, nothing that would interest you, I'm sure," I mumbled at last. "They are only novels, after all."

"You might be surprised what interests me, Miss Kathleen. I told you I had not much *time* for light reading, not that I was disinterested. Perhaps another time you will tell me more."

Another time? That was odd. I had been convinced Mr. Cavanaugh was only being polite out of good manners, trying to get through an awkward situation as painlessly as possible, same as I was. But his last comment made it sound as if he would willingly spend more time with me. No, that couldn't be true, for I knew he disliked me as much as I did him. It was just one of those things you said, like asking "how are you?" when you met some slight acquaintance on the street, even though you had absolutely no interest in

114

hearing a blow-by-blow report of her bad breakup or recent bout of stomach flu. Still, I supposed I should appreciate that he had taken the trouble to be pleasant, which must have been a real effort for someone like him. Being pleasant wasn't something Mr. Cavanaugh was naturally good at, according to my observations.

Bingley, from this time, was of course a daily visitor at Long-bourn; coming frequently before breakfast, and always remaining till after supper... (Pride and Prejudice, chapter 55)

Chapter 18
The Dessert

At the end of the meal, Mama stood and simply said, "Ladies," and every last female present followed her out, leaving the men to do whatever men did when ladies 'withdrew' – presumably smoke cigars and drink strong drink considered unfit for their wives and daughters.

I laced my arm through Lucy's as we moved back to the drawing room. Confident I already knew the answer, I asked her, "Which of your dinner partners did you enjoy more – Mr. Frederick Kingsley or Mr. Sotheby?"

She blushed but very diplomatically answered that she had enjoyed them both equally.

"I should say the same, I suppose, but I cannot," I whispered.

"We will speak more of this later, dearest," she said with a twinkle in her eye. "For now, our responsibility is to our guests."

So we separated again. Lucy went to speak to Mrs. Bell, and I looked around to see who else needed someone to talk to. Noticing a chance to kill two birds with one conversation, I collected Charlotte and proceeded to where Miss Sotheby was standing over near the pianoforte.

"Miss Sotheby, I am so pleased you and your brother have come into the neighborhood," I said. "Have you met my dear friend Miss Charlotte Galloway?"

With that we were off and running. Charlotte was a gentle sort of person and a very valuable asset for keeping the flow of conversation going. This was all still pretty new to me, and I sometimes worried I'd run out of appropriate topics. Some of my old standbys

– sports, movies, modern fashions – didn't work here, and I'd already discovered my limitations in what books I'd read.

Despite my expectation that Miss Sotheby would turn out another Miss Bingley, I really couldn't see any of Caroline in her. She was obviously well born and bred and elegant, but not the least bit snooty. In fact, she struck me more as a Georgiana type – more shy than proud.

When the men rejoined us about half an hour later, it looked as if Mr. Cavanaugh intended to come in my direction. Thankfully, George got there first and Mr. Cavanaugh veered off again. What made me even happier, though, was seeing Mr. Sotheby taking a determined beeline to my sister's side. Things were going very well there, and I hoped I wasn't counting my chickens too soon to think there might be a wedding before long.

After coffee and a plate of confections had been served, I knew there would be a call for some entertainment. George wasted no time collecting on my promise to play, asking me to go first and escorting me to the instrument. I wasn't particularly nervous about it other than wanting to be loyal to Matilda, who I figured would be listening from upstairs, by not playing too well. I had to balance that against my natural instinct of not wanting to embarrass myself. I think my performance landed somewhere in the middle. George, at least, was delighted.

"I do not know when I had heard anything I liked better," he told me when I returned to my seat beside him.

Miss Sotheby was just beginning, playing something far more difficult than I had and very skillfully too.

"It is lucky that you convinced me to go first," I whispered to George. "I would not want to have to follow Miss Sotheby's performance." Charlotte had that dubious honor, and she carried it off with some style.

A couple of card tables were set out when the music was finished, but I did not want to show my ignorance by attempting that. Instead, I circulated as best I could among the people who were leftover. At one point – it was unavoidable – Mr. Cavanaugh pulled me aside.

"I hope you will not find my questions officious, Miss Barrett," he began. "I mention this only out of a sincere desire to be of use. Is anything the matter with your father? Is he quite well?"

This got my attention. "Why do you ask, Mr. Cavanaugh?"

"I do not wish to alarm you, Miss Barrett, but I had opportunity to observe Mr. Barrett fairly narrowly during dinner and again afterward. His color seems a little off to me, and his aspect is so grim. Would you say that is usual for him? You know him far better than I do."

My eyes flew across the room to my newly acquired father, who was just sinking down into a chair next to Mrs. Abernathy. He was new to me yet already much loved. He did look tired, though, now that I stopped to notice. But then, it had been a long day, and he wasn't a young man anymore.

"I trust you are wrong, Mr. Cavanaugh. I notice no great difference in him. He did speak earlier of such an evening as this being a strain, requiring extra exertion. I thought at the time he was only joking, but perhaps he was in earnest. Perhaps he does find entertaining taxing."

"Yes, as you say, it is probably only that having a house full of people tires him. Still, please send for me at once if any concern should arise. Will you do that?"

"Of course."

He walked away then without another word.

Once again, Mr. Cavanaugh had surprised me by saying the last thing I had expected.

~~*~~

"All in all, I thought the dinner was a great success," Mama said at the breakfast table the next morning. "In fact, the whole evening came off very well. Do not you agree, Lucy?"

"Yes, very well, indeed, Mama."

"Everybody seemed to enjoy themselves, and they were all very complimentary to me as hostess when they took leave, especially Miss Sotheby. My goodness, she is quite an elegant creature, is she not?"

"I wish I could have got a better view of her," Carmen said. "Not much can be seen from the landing, unfortunately, although I did try my best."

Mama continued as if she hadn't heard. "So well-mannered too. I take a compliment from her as really being worth something."

"She plays the pianoforte beautifully," I added. "I will say that for her. Were you able to hear, Matilda? She performed that Handel piece you do so well. You know the one I mean: the largo."

"Yes, I did hear it, although not clearly enough to judge."

"Well, I daresay Miss Sotheby will have her share of admirers," Mama said, "but her handsome brother is the one who interests me. I noticed that Mr. Sotheby was very attentive to you, Lucy. That is a good sign. Although with a little effort I think you could get Frederick Kingsley, I shall not complain if Mr. Sotheby should make you an offer and you were inclined to accept. You could do much worse, and it would be a relief to see you so well settled."

"Mama, you are embarrassing Lucy," I protested, for I had noticed my sister looking down at her plate to try hiding the fact that she was pinking up pretty close to the color of a radish.

"Very well. I shall say no more about it for now, only that I shouldn't be surprised if we were to hear something more from that quarter before long."

Lucy and I had talked late into the night on that very subject. It took some coaxing on my part, but she finally admitted that she was in love with Mr. Sotheby and that she had reason to believe he felt much the same. I was simply thrilled for her. Even though *Pride and Prejudice* was my ideal, I truly hoped Lucy wouldn't have to suffer what Jane Bennet had, that she would not have to endure a long and painful separation before being reunited with her Mr. Bingley. There was no Mr. Darcy to split the happy couple up, and, after meeting her, I couldn't imagine Miss Sotheby malevolent enough to do the job on her own. All my fingers and toes were crossed for Lucy and Arthur (for that was his given name, as it turns out), that they would marry and live happily ever after.

"And as for you, Kate," Mama was saying now. "You did fairly well for yourself too, I should say, splitting your time evenly between Mr. Cavanaugh and George Galloway. A girl does not want to put all her eggs in one basket too soon. Weigh your options. There will be time enough to make a definite choice later. George is a sweet boy, and I should not deprecate a nearer connection to a family we hold in such high esteem, but I think I must give my nod to Mr. Cavanaugh in this case."

"I hate to disappoint you, Mama, but Mr. Cavanaugh did not say anything to me that could be considered even remotely romantic all evening long. I think you are barking down the wrong road there. By the way, where is Papa?"

"Oh, he was up early and eager to meet with the bailiff. Something to do with one of the tenants."

"So he was feeling well?"

"Right as rain, I should say, and happy to have his household returning to normal after all the extra fuss these few days past."

This was very good news, since I hadn't been completely easy about Papa's health since Mr. Cavanaugh's comments the night before. It just proves that no one is right all the time – not even, it seems, highfalutin' *fully qualified* physicians.

~~*~~

Things moved along rapidly after that. Mr. Sotheby came to call at Laurelwood every day on some excuse or other. The first day it was to thank my mother for her "extreme kindness and gracious hospitality" in throwing the dinner party for him and his sister. This apparently took three hours, for that is how long he stayed. The second day, his stated reason for coming was to beg a brief consultation with my father over a farming matter, after which he remained the entire afternoon and through dinner. By the third day, Mr. Sotheby had given up all pretenses. He was there to court Lucy, and everybody knew it. There wasn't any point in pretending otherwise. Mama suggested a walk into Carding "for the fresh air," sending Matilda and me with the lovers to keep it respectable. On the forth day, he took Lucy for a private walk in the garden, and all was settled by the time they returned.

I kept watch from the window, and when I saw Lucy's radiant face, I knew what had happened out there amongst the rose bushes. Mr. Sotheby went to seek out Papa at once, and Lucy came straight to me. We threw ourselves into each other's arms, laughing and sobbing at the same time.

"I am so happy!" Lucy finally said when she could speak again.

"And I am so happy *for* you."

"Can you believe it, Kate? I am soon to be a married woman! Mr. Sotheby, Arthur, he is the best man I have ever known. I shall never be good enough to deserve him, but I shall spend the rest of my life trying."

"Mr. Sotheby is the lucky one," I said through my tears. "Oh, Lucy, how shall I ever do without you?"

And then it hit me. I had wished with all my might for this very event without thinking how Lucy's marriage would change everything. I would no longer live under the same roof with the best friend and sister I now loved and had longed for all my life. She had been mine only for a short time, and I was not prepared to give her up, not yet.

"You will not have to do without me, Kate," Lucy said, laughing. "I will only be a mile away at Coleswold. We shall see each other nearly every day; depend upon it."

This was looking on the bright side. How lucky that Lucy would be settled close by. I gave her one more enthusiastic hug and suggested, "Let us go to Mama! I can hardly wait to see the look on her face when you tell her. She will be so delighted."

If there had not been a Netherfield ball to prepare for and talk of, the younger Miss Bennets would have been in a pitiable state...
(Pride and Prejudice, chapter 17)

Chapter 19
Preparation and Practice

That night, I lay in bed thinking about how well my second chance was turning out. My life with the Barretts... Correction. My life *as* a Barrett was all I'd hoped it would be and more.

It had only been a couple of weeks, but I felt like I was already pretty well adjusted to my new persona and my new Regency lifestyle. I'd gotten the hang of the language pretty quickly, and my authentic British accent had sort of come along with my new voice – another hangover gift from Kathleen, I expect. The weird part was that I sometimes heard *her* voice with *my* old southern drawl in my head, in my thoughts.

Except for a few hygiene issues (I would have given a lot to have smuggled a crate of fray-resistant dental floss and my battery-operated toothbrush along with me, to name two), I didn't miss the modern conveniences all that much. Of course, I suppose it helped that I wasn't the one who had to wash the clothes without a washing machine or cook the meals without electricity. If I'd come back as a servant of some sort, I might have thought very differently.

I didn't personally, as a female, have as many rights and options as I'd had in my own time. But I'd known and reconciled myself to that before I made this choice. I didn't mind not having a career, especially since I hadn't felt a burning passion for any one thing before. This way, I could continue my education by reading as much as I wanted, and I would have the time and freedom to pursue drawing and music too – things I was interested in anyway. I was even improving at sewing. I still didn't love it, but I didn't hate it either.

I pined a little over the thought of never driving a car again. I would soon have my riding privileges back, though, and I had the idea that I'd like to learn to drive a carriage. A gig, maybe. Only one horsepower instead of hundreds, but at least that horse could love me back.

The tradeoff was more than worth it. I had my first choice of place and time, and I was part of a big, loving family, just as I had wanted. Although I still thought about my original parents every day, I had stopped thinking of them as my "real" parents, since Mr. and Mrs. Barrett were now every bit as real to me. And my new sisters were my *real* sisters too. If anybody had tried to say otherwise, I would have been prepared to tan his hide.

To top it all off, we were going to have a wedding in September! Not a double wedding like at the end of *Pride and Prejudice*. For that, we would have needed two grooms, and we were one short. Still, Lucy had found her Mr. Bingley; that was the important thing. And I believed my Mr. Darcy would come along eventually. He was just a little late, that's all. Maybe he was a time traveler too, like me, and he had taken a wrong turn somewhere. Most likely he'd be popping in at any moment now. I smiled to myself at that thought, rolled over, and went to sleep.

~~*~~

Mr. Sotheby was so overflowing with joy and goodwill at having his offer of marriage accepted by Lucy and approved by her father that he decided to throw a ball at Coleswold in celebration. The date he named for the grand event happened to be one day after Carmen's birthday, and she wasted no time securing Papa's promise that she could dance at it. I'm sure I was nearly as happy at the news as she was, because attending a proper ball was a major item on my Regency checklist that still needed ticking off.

Our house was in an uproar from that moment on. The contents of all closets were evaluated and plans made for how to fill in the deficits. Necessary accessories – everything from hair ribbons to shoe roses – had to be purchased locally or, failing that, ordered from further afield.

Both Lucy and Carmen got new gowns for the occasion. Lucy's came as part of the larger purchase of her "wedding clothes" – an entire new wardrobe – and Carmen because she'd grown out of whatever she had that would have been appropriate. Everything in my closet was new to me and everything still fit, so I was happy enough with what I had. Mama allowed that I should at least have a new pair of shoes, though. Matilda was the only one not excited about the prospect of a ball, and she would probably have ducked out of going altogether if she could, just like she'd done with the dinner party.

"I will go out of courtesy to Lucy," she finally agreed, "but I certainly do not need to be bought new clothes just to sit and watch the dancing."

"If you would only make an effort with your appearance and be a bit more agreeable, Matilda, you might have your share of attention," Mama told her. "At any rate, you must be ready if someone should ask you to dance. You must *all* be ready to make the most of this opportunity. Dancing is the best way to forming a productive attachment I ever heard of."

I was eager to follow Mama's advice to dance the night away, but my skills were pretty rusty. I had taken a Regency dance class once – a special treat from my Aunt Connie, which I absolutely ate up with a spoon – but that was about the limit of my actual experience. Beyond that, I only had what I'd learned by studying educational videos at Crossroads and whatever of Kathleen's carryover memories might kick in on the spot. I hated to leave something so important to that chance, though.

Lucky for me, I wasn't the only one feeling the need for a refresher course before the big event. One evening when Mrs. Abernathy, Mr. Sotheby, and the Galloway family were with us for a little after-dinner card party, Mr. Sotheby himself suggested the idea. We had just finished a game of Speculation at our table, where we spent more time talking about the upcoming ball than paying attention to our cards.

"Here are enough people for a dance, surely," said Mr. Sotheby gesturing to the room as a whole. "Why should not we take the opportunity to polish our skills before the ball? I am very much out of practice, and I would not wish to embarrass Lucy or myself by my clumsiness that night."

"I shall play for you, if you like," Matilda volunteered.

"Oh, no," said Mama. "There will be no hiding behind the instrument for you this time, Matilda. You need to practice your dancing too. Mrs. Galloway will play for us, I am sure."

Mrs. Galloway, hearing this from her place at the other table, enthusiastically agreed to do so. Carmen, who was at the same table, was practically bouncing up and down, clapping her hands with glee. By this time their card play had stopped also, and everybody was united in this one conversation.

"But we have not enough young men," Charlotte Galloway pointed out. "Perhaps it had best not be attempted."

"Your father and Mr. Barrett are not too old to dance, Miss Galloway," said Mama, clearly determined to see the idea through. "Either that or you girls can take turns at the men's parts this once. We have no need to be too particular in this informal setting."

Everyone seemed satisfied with the plan and sprang into action. Mrs. Galloway took her place at the pianoforte and began warming up her fingers with some scales. After the men had rearranged the drawing room furniture to make enough space, those interested in dancing began pairing off to form a set. Mr. Sotheby took Lucy, of course. Carmen swooped in on George Galloway before he could get to me. Since the senior Mr. Galloway flatly refused to dance, Charlotte looked at Matilda. They both shrugged and took their places across from each other. That left only me without a partner until Papa took pity and relented at his wife's urging.

"This is proof that for you, Kate, I would do anything," he told me.

Just then, Hawthorn stepped into the room and announced Mr. Cavanaugh. Mama hurried to welcome him.

"Please pardon the intrusion, Ma'am," Mr. Cavanaugh said before she could get a word out. "I have obviously come at an inopportune moment. I will not stay; I only wished to return this book."

"Sir, you could not be more mistaken," she assured him. "This is no inconvenience. Come in, come in."

By this time, my father had joined his wife in welcoming the new arrival. "Mr. Cavanaugh, your coming just at this moment could not be more fortuitous. As you see, a little dancing has been proposed despite a shortage of gentlemen. If I can convince you to take my place, standing opposite my daughter, I daresay she and I will both be much better off for it. I am sure you cannot refuse to dance with such an inducement."

Embarrassed, I began to protest. "Papa, I am perfectly happy with you as my partner. We need not impose on Mr. Cavanaugh. He must have better things to do."

I was ignored, however.

Instead, Mr. Cavanaugh answered my father. "I am at your service, sir. I would be very happy to dance with Miss Kathleen or any of the young ladies." He had already been making preparations to join in, setting down the book he carried and dispensing with his overcoat.

"Good man!" Papa said, patting Mr. Cavanaugh's back.

Mr. Cavanaugh moved into place across from me, and Mrs. Galloway began to play the lively music of a jig. I really would have preferred my father's company, and so I couldn't help being annoyed with Mr. C. for his bad timing in showing up just when he did. But I bit my tongue and tried to concentrate on the steps.

It could have been worse, I reminded myself. I could have had a different Mr. C. (Mr. Collins) instead. At least Mr. Cavanaugh was a good dancer – confident, and moving sort of smooth and graceful like – which meant I didn't have to worry about him going wrong, only me.

When we had repeated the whole sequence a couple of times, I felt secure enough to attempt some conversation. After all, that was part of dancing Regency style also, and I thought I might as well practice the two together while I had the chance.

"Do you like to dance, Mr. Cavanaugh?" I asked. A harmless enough question to open with, I thought.

"Not particularly," he answered.

That was it. No explanation. Not even a question for me in return. I couldn't help being a little offended. Shouldn't he, just to be polite, have added that in this case he didn't mind, that present company made the exercise entirely agreeable? Something like that, anyway. Honesty was a virtue, but a little diplomatic embellishment of the truth had its place too.

Not able to let the point go, I retorted, "Then I am terribly sorry to be putting you through this odious ordeal, sir. Perhaps you should have left it to my father after all."

126

"That is the last thing I would have wished to do. And, for the record, I said nothing about its being odious to dance with you, Miss Barrett. You put those words in my mouth."

Technically, he was correct. *Oh, bother!* It was way too much work to talk to this man, I decided. Let him be the one to make the effort to speak next if he cared to. I would pay attention to my dancing so that I wouldn't make a mess of it. I didn't shy away from looking Mr. C. in the eye, though, when we stepped toward or crossed by each other. I still couldn't be sure I understood what made him tick. Whatever else I could say about him, he was an interesting if irritating subject to study.

Then something he'd said niggled at my brain a little and I broke my own resolution. "What did you mean – that leaving the dancing to my father is the last thing you would want?"

He hesitated before answering. "Only that dancing is rightly a young man's occupation. There is something rather dismal and unbecoming in an old gentleman pretending to be something he is not. I am very glad to have prevented your father making such a spectacle of himself."

Oh! I couldn't believe the nerve of the man! He was saying that the picture of my father wanting to dance with me was somehow pathetic. I could have creamed his corn right then and there! And to think, I had lately begun to wonder if I might have judged him too harshly. No, he was every bit as arrogant as I had originally believed! He probably thought the sun came up every morning just to hear him crow.

I'd put up with enough from Mr. Cavanaugh; I couldn't let him get away with insulting my father on top of everything else. Hadn't I promised myself I'd make him pay someday? Well, *this* was the moment. I suddenly knew what I had to do. It wouldn't be as clever a revenge as I had hoped. In fact, I couldn't quite picture Lizzy Bennet doing such a thing. She might think of it and laugh, but probably not act on the impulse. I didn't care. Maybe crude but effective was more my style.

So I bided my time in silence until the very end of the dance. That's when I made my move. Smiling sweetly up at him, I said, "Mr. Cavanaugh, my father is twice the man you will ever be." And then I stomped on his foot as hard as I could.

She grew absolutely ashamed of herself. Of neither Darcy nor Wickham could she think without feeling that she had been blind, partial, prejudiced, absurd. (Pride and Prejudice, chapter 36)

Chapter 20
Back in the Saddle

I made an enormous show of apologizing.

"Oh, I am SO very sorry, Mr. Cavanaugh! How could I have been that clumsy? Please, do forgive me," etc., etc. Not that I expected (or even wanted) Mr. Cavanaugh to believe me, but I hoped everybody else would. Dear George Galloway was on my side, at least. He bravely insisted on being my partner for the next dance and came through without injury. And Mr. Cavanaugh, who was not actually crippled by my assault, soldiered on with Charlotte Galloway and then Matilda afterward. Not surprisingly, he didn't speak to me again that evening or offer to dance with me a second time; but I was pretty sure I caught a few murderous glares from his direction, which only added to my satisfaction.

It was late that night when the light about what had happened began to dawn on me. And then, of course, I felt terrible.

On purpose, I was again thinking over what Mr. Cavanaugh had said and done, so that I could keep my temper and the justification for my actions going. Even the hottest anger will begin to fade if starved of further fuel, and that would never do in this case, because I intended to go on hating Mr. Cavanaugh forever. Carrying grudges didn't come all that easily to me, so I suspected I'd have to work at it.

Mr. Cavanaugh's reason for dropping by seemed perfectly plausible since I knew he had indeed borrowed a book from my father a few days earlier. Papa had specifically mentioned it. And a few days before that, Mr. Cavanaugh had also shown up at our door uninvited, asking to see Papa on some other excuse. Since this pattern mirrored what Mr. Sotheby had done while courting Lucy, I admit that I first wondered, in horror, if it might be *me* he was really coming to see. But fortunately, he met with Papa and then went away again, making no effort to linger with the ladies.

So, that made three unsolicited visits since the night of the dinner party, each time with the purpose of seeing my father alone. Hmm. Three unsolicited visits by a doctor since the night he had told me he was concerned for my father's health. Either the two men were forging a strong new friendship, or Mr. Cavanaugh had another, perhaps highly commendable, motive for coming so often.

It was a devastating blow to realize what he might really have been up to, that it might have been his way of covertly keeping an eye on my father's health. Not only did it mean I'd accosted a man without good cause, it meant Papa might be seriously ill. Perhaps the reason Mr. Cavanaugh couldn't bear to see him dancing was that he knew my father's heart couldn't take it. That didn't explain the rest of what he'd said – the insulting part – but it meant it was possible to see things in a much different light, a light where Papa was sick and Mr. Cavanaugh had done nothing wrong.

For nearly the first time, I was frustrated by the limitations of my chosen time period. I wanted to know the truth about Papa's health. Immediately! I needed to communicate with Mr. Cavanaugh (and probably apologize, for real this time), but I couldn't send a text or an email, or call Mr. Cavanaugh on the phone, or hop in my car and drive over to his place. As a single woman, I knew I couldn't even write him a letter, according to the rules of propriety. What I *could* have done was send him a message through my father, that is if it weren't for the fact that I didn't want my father to know anything about it!

But maybe Papa *did* already know. Had Mr. Cavanaugh spoken to him, expressed his concerns, even examined him and given him medical advice? That made a lot of sense, and then probably it was Papa who didn't want the rest of us, his family, to know anything about it; he wouldn't want to worry us. It was reassuring to know Mr. Cavanaugh was on the case. I didn't have to like the man, I told myself. What counted was his medical training.

I couldn't help keeping a watchful eye on Papa after that and hoping Mr. Cavanaugh would come again, so I'd have the chance to speak to him. But when he did come, I was out.

I'd decided that morning it was time for me to get back in the saddle again, literally, and I wanted as few witnesses as possible. So I didn't even tell Lucy where I was going. I just quietly slipped out of the house and went to the stables on my own.

I expected I'd find Smitty there to assist me. Mr. Smith was Laurelwood's all-purpose stable hand and carriage man. He looked after the horses, kept the stables clean and orderly, drove the carriages, and maintained them as well. Larger estates would have employed separate people for each job, but with only two carriages and four horses, Mr. Smith could handle it on his own with the assistance of his teenage son Roger. All this I knew from my research at Crossroads, which gave me more confidence when I poked my head inside the open door of the stable block and called out his name.

A minute later, Smitty appeared, wearing a heavy work apron and wiping his hands on a rag. "Yes, Miss?" he said.

"Would you saddle Horatio for me, please?" I immediately saw his hesitation. "You need not look so worried, Smitty. You know I have my father's permission to begin riding, and besides, I am not even planning on leaving the yard. I just need to get used to being in the saddle again. If it will make you feel better, I will promise not to take Horatio above a walking pace this first time."

"Very well, Miss," he said and then left to do what I'd asked.

My belly filled with a whole passel of butterflies as the moment of truth approached. I was more nervous than I had expected, although I wasn't sure where to place the blame for it. Was it because I, the new Kate, had so little experience, or had I inherited some fear from the original Kathleen for how badly her last ride had gone? Whatever the case, I set all those thoughts aside when Smitty came back with Horatio.

"Good boy," I said to Horatio, looking him over like a long-lost friend and stroking his sleek neck. "I have missed you."

He sniffed and looked sideways at me with one eye, the way that horses can. I had the feeling he knew that something about me was different, although he wasn't sure what. But then he nickered softly and gave me an affectionate nudge with his velvety gray muzzle. So I figured we were on good terms again.

Smitty took Horatio to the mounting block and then boosted me backwards from it into the sidesaddle, not releasing me until I had my balance. Then I maneuvered to lift my right leg over the pommel and slip my left foot into the stirrup. It was more difficult than I expected, but then it *was* my first time.

"Strange," I said, trying to cover for my awkwardness. "After so long, it feels like starting all over again."

When I was finally settled, with the reins in my hand, I couldn't seem to find the courage to set out on my own.

"Would you mind leading Horatio out and round the yard once or twice?" I asked the stableman. "That will make me more comfortable."

Mr. Smith obeyed without comment, although he must have been thinking it was an odd request. It's what I needed, though, to be able to focus on one thing at a time. I had to get used to balancing in a sidesaddle without worrying about how to steer too. By the time we'd made a full circuit of the open dirt yard in front of the stables, I felt confident enough to strike out on my own.

Horatio was as docile as a lamb with me that day. He must have understood that I wasn't up to frisking about as he had probably been used to in the past. I would be again, I hoped, but not right away. I sedately walked him back and forth and around the immediate area for fifteen or twenty minutes, all under Mr. Smith's watchful eye. When I felt comfortable, I headed out a little further, toward the front of the house. I still didn't intend to go close enough where anybody might notice me, but then I saw Mr. Cavanaugh, getting on his own horse to ride away. He'd apparently finished what he'd come for – probably seeing Papa again – and I had missed him. Now he was leaving before I had a chance to speak to him. He would be gone in another minute if I didn't do something quickly. My choices were to holler (not very ladylike, besides attracting too much attention) or ride ahead and intercept him.

I didn't have to ask Horatio twice. I merely tapped my boot into his side and made a clucking sound, and he broke into an easy canter, which was so much smoother than a ragged trot would have been. Once again, I had the feeling he was taking care of me.

Mr. Cavanaugh spotted us as soon as we came out of the trees, and he immediately detoured in our direction. When he drew close enough, he tipped his hat and said, "Miss Barrett, it is good to see you are riding again."

"I thought it was time," I answered, but then I hurried on. "Mr. Cavanaugh, how fortunate I have caught you. I have been watching for an opportunity to speak to you."

"If it is about the other night, there is no need."

"Oh, but there is! I'm afraid there has been a misunderstanding, which I am anxious to clear up."

"You have, repeatedly, made your sentiments quite clear to me, but now I will incommode you no longer. In fact, I was just to see your father and take leave of your family."

"Take leave? You are going away?"

"Yes, I return home to Derbyshire almost immediately."

"Derbyshire? But I thought you were settled here."

"Just temporarily. You must know that I only came to take Mr. Fitch's place while he was away on family business. He is returned now and ready to resume looking after the people of Carding as before."

"But my father... Does Mr. Fitch know about your concerns?"

"Yes, I have fully apprised him, and he will know what to do. Now you really must excuse me, Miss Barrett. I am terribly pressed for time, unfortunately. Here," he said, suddenly sticking out his hand with a piece of folded paper in it. "This will explain everything."

I automatically took the note he handed me. And while I was puzzling over what it might mean, Mr. Cavanaugh said goodbye and rode away at a gallop.

I had a peculiar feeling in my belly, watching him go and realizing that this view of his retreating backside rhythmically bouncing up and down was probably going to be my last sight of him. The peculiar feeling was at least partially regret, I knew. It was rare that I met someone like Mr. Cavanaugh, someone I simply couldn't get along with. I should probably have been glad that such a person was leaving my life again so quickly and so thoroughly. And yet, strangely enough, I wasn't. I regretted not having discovered a way to overcome our differences – not making more of an effort, perhaps, or not having more time. It felt like a first-class failure on my part, and I didn't much like to fail.

But he was gone and there wasn't anything I could do about it. I looked down at the note in my hand: another surprise, surely the last Mr. Cavanaugh would have the power to drop into my life. I was desperately curious. What had been important enough that he had taken time to write it out in advance, just on the chance he could slip it to me on this visit? If I hadn't seen him at the very last minute, would I ever have found out?

With no expectation of pleasure, but with the strongest curiosity, Elizabeth opened the letter... (Pride and Prejudice, chapter 35)

Chapter 21
Not in a Million Years

I couldn't wait to read Mr. Cavanaugh's note, so I returned Horatio to Mr. Smith's care and made my way to the walled garden, which was by then one of my very favorite spots. There I sat down on a stone bench in the warm sunshine and opened the letter.

Dear Miss Barrett,

Please pardon the liberty I take in writing to you. There are, however, two things of very different natures I feel compelled to address, and I will therefore hope for some opportunity of placing this missive into your hand.

First, I am sure you will be wondering about your father's health. By my information to you at the dinner party, you inadvertently became aware of my concerns. Since then, perhaps you have noticed my frequent visits to Laurelwood, most recently the evening you so graciously bestowed a dance on me...

Oh, yes, so graciously! I bestowed a dance on him and a little something extra to top it off. Not my finest moment.

...At one of these subsequent visits, I did persuade your father to allow me to make a cursory examination of his person and give him my opinion. I cannot be certain, but I believe your father's heart is not strong...

I gasped. That's what I had been afraid of. *Oh, Papa!* I couldn't bear to think he was sick... or worse.

...If he is careful, however, he may yet have many more years with his family and friends. He should by no means be doing anything strenuous, like lifting heavy objects or partaking of vigorous dancing. This I told him, to little effect, apparently.

Your father did not wish his family worried, and at first, I intended to abide by those wishes (thus my obscure answer to your question as we were dancing). But I finally concluded it would be wise for someone close to him to be aware of his frailty, in part because he seems so little inclined to heed my warnings on his own. You, Miss Barrett, seemed to me to be by far the properest person I could charge with this task. Unlike your sister, who is soon to leave the household, you can remain to keep watch over him. You also have, according to my certain proof, strong protective feelings towards your father...

Another stab of guilt. Yes, I'd given him proof of that; he probably still had a limp and a purple bruise on his foot to remind him. And yet Mr. Cavanaugh had somehow managed to turn what I'd done into a virtue.

...I know you will do what you can yourself and, if the need should arise, be ready to call on Mr. Fitch, whom I have apprised of my findings. I hope I do right by telling you these things and that you will not find it too great a burden to bear.

I will not dwell long on my second point, and you will likely say it would have been better left unmentioned. But I find that my character and my conscience demand it be addressed.

Please understand that I hold you, personally, as well as all your family, in high esteem. It grieves me, therefore, Madam, that your opinion of me is so obviously the reverse. I know not how I might have offended you in the very beginning, but I can only conclude this must be the unhappy case. I therefore beg to apologize and to assure you that any insult was wholly unintentional. It matters little now, I suppose, since we will probably never meet again. Still, I regret not being on better terms with you through our brief acquaintance. Whatever you may think of me, please accept my best wishes for your future health and happiness.

Fitzwilliam Cavanaugh

Fitzwilliam? No way!

I couldn't believe my eyes when I saw the signature. Although I had wondered about his first name, I would never have imagined it could be Fitzwilliam! Not in a million years.

~~*~~

I felt sick to my stomach. Had I really missed all the signs? Had Mr. Cavanaugh been my Mr. Darcy all along – the one I'd come all this way to find – and I'd spoiled it? Maybe I'd been so busy playing Lizzy Bennet that I'd unknowingly copied her biggest fault as well. I had taken offense at the very beginning – and it wasn't even my feelings that had been offended but Kathleen's before me – and I had adopted a prejudice that I refused to let go.

And really, what were Mr. Cavanaugh's awful crimes?

He disliked being pursued by fortune-hunting females. Understandable. He was indifferent to dancing and said so. Inconvenient, but not illegal. He took the care of his patients seriously, enough so that he was willing to be disliked for giving unpopular but prudent orders. If I actually had struck my head falling off a horse, an extra day's rest and bland diet didn't seem like such cruel precautions now. And taking the dancing duty to preserve my father's health (as well as the blame to preserve his privacy) looked almost heroic in hindsight.

I was shocked to find how easily I had managed to explain away nearly all the things I'd held against Mr. Cavanaugh for the weeks I had known him. Only one remained, and it was the most damning: the accusation that he'd refused to care for a patient who couldn't pay, *which, if true, would be grievous indeed.* But was it true? I had taken a rumor as fact, the whispered word of a woman I didn't even know.

I wished I could recall all the words and phrases Lizzy had used to punish herself in her *mea culpa* moment after reading Mr.

Darcy's letter, when she realized how wrong she'd been about him. But all I could think of was 'alas.'

"Alas, alas, alas!" I said aloud, and then looked around me to be sure no one else was in the garden to have heard. I wasn't certain I even knew exactly what 'alas' meant, but I felt a little calmer after getting it out of my system.

I did remember something else from the book – a passage further on that seemed to apply. I'd memorized it because it was so beautifully poignant, so exquisitely expressed:

As he quitted the room, Elizabeth felt how improbable it was that they should ever see each other again on such terms of cordiality as had marked their several meetings in Derbyshire; and as she threw a retrospective glance over the whole of their acquaintance, so full of contradictions and varieties, sighed at the perverseness of those feelings which would now have promoted its continuance, and would formerly have rejoiced in its termination.

It was true. Before, I never wanted to see Mr. Cavanaugh again. But now, now that he was gone forever, I would have given a lot to have him back, especially if he was really supposed to have been my Mr. Darcy.

Only... (reality check time). Only, we'd never actually had any meetings in Derbyshire, cordial or otherwise. There had never been a proposal. In fact, I had no reason to think Mr. Cavanaugh cherished any special feelings for me at all; his letter said "high esteem," the same as for the rest of my family.

As for my own feelings... Well, I certainly felt bad that I'd misjudged the man and then had no opportunity to properly apologize. I regretted never giving him a chance, especially since I now believed he was someone I probably could have liked. In fact, I wondered if he might not be exactly the sort of man who would have suited me best. But I certainly wasn't in love with him! So what if his name *was* Fitzwilliam and he had an estate in Derbyshire? That wasn't proof of anything, probably only a crazy coincidence.

All I could say, really, is that it's possible I could have fallen in love with Mr. Cavanaugh if I had another chance, if we could have spent more time together, now that my initial prejudice had been mostly done away with. But unlike Lizzy, I had no aunt and uncle to take me to Derbyshire so I could tour Fitzwilliam Cavanaugh's estate and accidentally run into him again, in a wet shirt or a dry one.

When I returned to the house, Carmen, bubbling with excitement, hurried to meet me just inside the front door. "Kate, you have missed Mr. Cavanaugh," she announced, obviously pleased to be the first to give me the news. "He came to take leave. I hope you were not *very* much in love with him, for he is gone off to Derbyshire forever."

Before I could say anything, Mama jumped in. "It is all too true, my dear, and I am so distressed. We can ill afford to lose such an eligible gentleman from the neighborhood, especially one who has shown such promising signs. Not that I blame Mr. Cavanaugh. The one I am really vexed with is Mr. Fitch! He told everybody he would be gone for six months to bury his father and settle the estate, and instead he comes back after only three. If I had known, I would have advised you to move more quickly, Kate, to give Mr. Cavanaugh more encouragement. Then you might have already secured him. But now it is all too late; it has come to nothing in the end. At least I do not suppose he left you with any assurances of your seeing him again."

"No, Mama, he did not."

There wasn't much I could say to console my mother, so I got away as soon as I could and went upstairs to look for Lucy. She was the only one I was willing to talk with about Mr. Cavanaugh. I found her in her bedroom and closed the door behind me.

"So, Mr. Cavanaugh is gone back to Derbyshire, from whence he came," I stated, being a little proud of myself for slipping a good Regency word like 'whence' into the conversation. "I saw him outside as he was leaving."

"I trust this does not much affect you, Kate," Lucy said, "since you never liked him."

"I admit, I am sorry to see him go, more so than I would have expected. I wish I at least had the chance to properly apologize for hurting his foot when we danced."

"You *did* apologize, over and over again!"

"But I did not mean it at the time, and Mr. Cavanaugh knows it. Oh, Lucy, I believe I misjudged him terribly. And although I have no reason why I should now care for his good opinion when I never did before, somehow I cannot bear to know he is alive in the world and thinking ill of me." I couldn't help borrowing another one of Lizzy's lines; the words so perfectly described what I was feeling.

My sister listened patiently to my confession – how I'd been prejudiced against Mr. Cavanaugh from the beginning and used every circumstance after that to justify my disliking him, and finally how I'd tromped on his foot on purpose. I'm sure that action came across as completely indefensible, since I didn't want to mention anything about Mr. Cavanaugh's concerns for Papa's health to Lucy. No need for her to worry; I would do enough of that for the both of us.

I felt a little better after unburdening my conscience to my sister and receiving her absolution, which was the next best thing to being forgiven by Mr. Cavanaugh himself. Lucy was sure he wasn't the sort of man to carry a grudge, and I hoped she was right. There wasn't anything else I could do about the mess I'd made of things; it was simply time to close that distressing chapter and move on.

The prospect of the Netherfield ball was extremely agreeable to every female of the family. Mrs. Bennet chose to consider it as given in compliment to her eldest daughter, and was particularly flattered... (Pride and Prejudice, chapter 17)

Chapter 22
The Ball

Avoiding the temptation to look back with regret was a whole lot easier since I had something thrilling to look forward to. That was the Coleswold ball!

By the time the big night arrived, we were ready. Our wardrobe issues had been resolved, and we four girls had practiced again, as best we could, all the dances we might run into. The more we worked on them, the more came back to me from Kathleen's experience. And so I was feeling pretty confident in my abilities and very excited to finally put them to good use. I even had a partner secured for the first two dances, since George Galloway had ridden over the day before specifically to ask me to reserve them for him.

We were kind of squashed up in the carriage on the way over, all six of us together, but it was only a short drive to Mr. Sotheby's fine house, soon to be my sister's as well. Although I had by this time seen the place once, I knew it would be done up special for the ball. This wouldn't be just any ball. Not only was it Mr. Sotheby's first at Coleswold, it was also given in celebration of his engagement to Lucy.

Mr. Sotheby had gone all out. Everything sparkled and shined. There were probably enough flowers strewn about the place to fill up a swimming pool – baskets and vases full of them everywhere I looked. And the candles! I'd never seen so many in my life. I was a little afraid they'd set off the smoke detectors until I remembered that there weren't any.

This was literally a dream come true for me. I had pictured scenes like this a thousand times, waking and sleeping, reading and watching movies. So even though I'd had a couple of months to get used to my new Regency life, it was still hard for me to believe this was real and not some super cool movie set tour.

I had to keep reminding myself that I shouldn't be gawking at everything and everybody. It wasn't easy, though, because I'd never been in a situation quite like this before. I felt like rushing up to some of the ladies to get a closer look at their gowns or ask them about how they'd done their hair. And the men looked just as good. I'd become completely fascinated with cravats, and I would have given a lot to know how to tie all the fancy styles I noticed the gentlemen wearing that night.

Lucy had taken her place between Arthur Sotheby and his sister as they received their guests. I stuck pretty close to the rest of my family while we mingled around, waiting for the dancing to start. Mama made sure to point out to me any man in the crowd she wanted me to be particularly nice to. Now that Lucy was engaged, I was clearly the next one on her list to get married off, and Frederick Kingsley was at the top of her eligibility chart.

An alarming thought occurred to me about then. "Papa, you do not mean to dance tonight, do you?" I hurriedly asked him.

"I? Certainly not, my dear. I understand some card tables will be made up in the other room before too long. So, after I enjoy the spectacle of the ballroom for a little while, that is where you will find me."

A lot of the guests were people I already knew, but there were a few strangers too, who turned out to be London friends of Mr. and Miss Sotheby. I was glad for Miss Sotheby, and she did look as if she were having the time of her life, meeting and greeting and playing hostess to such a fine looking bunch of people.

One person I didn't see, of course, was Mr. Cavanaugh. It's funny, but when I first heard there was going to be a ball, I'd pictured him here and wondered if he would ask me to dance. Not that I wanted him to back then, but I knew if he asked I'd have to say yes. It wasn't polite to refuse just because you didn't like somebody. You could only get away with doing that if you were prepared to sit out the rest of the night because you were "too tired to dance anymore." A high price to pay, and I hadn't hated Mr. Cavanaugh *that* much.

Of course, now with my sentiments so changed, I wouldn't have minded dancing with him one bit. And if he'd been brave enough to ask me, I would have made darn sure not to step on his foot again.

But it was probably just as well that I had George Galloway to start with instead. I couldn't help suffering a few nerves, it being my first formal Regency ball and all, so it was a blessing to have someone I was at ease with as my first partner. Hard enough to focus on my dance steps with so many distractions. It would have been worse having to make small talk with a total stranger (or an uncomfortable acquaintance) at the same time.

When the small orchestra that Mr. Sotheby had hired struck up the lively introduction to the first dance, my heart did a little skip-to-my-lou too. George was at my side in a flash.

"Good evening, Miss Kathleen," he said. "It is time for our dance."

He led me out onto the floor where the set was forming up. There must have been about twenty couples altogether, the men in their fine evening clothes on one side and the ladies on the other, all gussied up in long gowns of white or pale pastels. What an enchanting sight it was too, like something out of a fairy tale, that still moment just before we began to move into the dance. I took a mental snap shot so I would never forget.

And then we were underway.

George was a good dancer, which I already knew from the impromptu dance at our house. Maybe he didn't move with quite the same confident ease of Mr. Cavanaugh, but I certainly couldn't complain. I thought of poor Lizzy, who had to put up with the mortifying Mr. Collins as her first partner at the Netherfield ball. How lucky I was to have George Galloway instead!

I soon stopped worrying that I might forget the steps and started really enjoyed myself. Dancing was just plain fun, and I couldn't quit smiling, especially when we met Lucy and Mr. Sotheby. They were coming down the set and we were moving up, so we danced with them for one sequence, which was simply delightful, before going our separate ways again. I could surmise from the giddy looks on their faces that they were having just as good a time as I was.

It took ten or fifteen minutes for the dance to finish, for each couple to go up and down the set and get back to where they started. Then everybody clapped and the second of the first pair of dances began.

George and I fit little snippets of conversation in here and there along the way – nothing very consequential, just your typical good-natured small talk. Then, when we were standing at the bottom of the set, waiting our turn to resume, we had a minute for something a little more substantial.

"I enjoy dancing with you more than I can say, Miss Kathleen. Thank you."

"It is my pleasure, Mr. Galloway."

"Very good. Then, if you are not otherwise engaged, would you consider reserving the quadrille just before supper for me as well?"

I recognized this as a high compliment, not only because being asked twice by someone meant he was more than casually interested. It also meant that George wanted to be my companion at supper too. But that was out of my power.

"Thank you for asking, Mr. Galloway, and I would accept if I were free, but I have already agreed to dance that one with somebody else."

He looked quite put out to hear this. "With whom, if you do not mind my asking?"

I didn't mind telling him it was Frederick Kingsley who had asked me shortly after I arrived.

"With Mr. Frederick Kingsley? I am definitely too late, then."

"It would seem so."

George settled for my promise of another dance after the supper break, which I was happy to give him. I felt like his kind attentiveness should be rewarded.

I danced the next two with Edward Kingsley, who was very pleasant to me. Then I was obliged to sit down for half an hour without a partner before another young man came along to ask me, and another after that until Frederick Kingsley's dance came up. He bowed and smiled and did everything right. Except it seemed to me that he exaggerated the moves of the dance in kind of an affected way, as if he were showing off or something. I didn't care much for that, and I couldn't help thinking Frederick could have learned something from Mr. Cavanaugh's understated grace on the dance floor.

When supper was announced at the end of my two dances with Frederick Kingsley, I was *so* relieved. Not because I was tired of dancing or even of my partner, but because I was starving! It was almost midnight by then – hours since dinner, and I'd been working up an appetite ever since. Plus, I was curious to see what would be served. Would I get to taste the delicious white soup I'd read about? And would there be negus to drink, I wondered?

"May I take you in to supper, Miss Barrett?" Frederick asked me, as a mere formality. He offered me his arm, and we joined the others moving out of the ballroom to where the supper had been prepared. Yes, there was white soup! …and roast beef, and oysters, and boiled eggs, and asparagus, and cheese, and bread – plenty of good things to restore us and make us ready to dance some more afterward. To drink, we had wine, including the spicy negus, which I didn't like very much, although I thought I might have if it had been cold instead of hot.

Once Frederick and I were seated, I got the conversational ball rolling by asking him what other books he liked besides *Udolpho*. Lucky he didn't ask me back, or I would have been in the same fix I'd been in before with Mr. Cavanaugh. But Frederick seemed perfectly happy simply to make recommendations to me from his favorites. After exhausting this topic, he asked me if I intended to ride again.

"…It must be a harrowing prospect," he continued, "but then there is never any definite need for a lady to ride if she would rather not."

"Oh, but I want to, Mr. Kingsley! In fact, I already have. Life is full of risks, but I do not believe in letting fear for what could happen hold me back from something I enjoy so much."

"I honor you for that, Miss Barrett. Yes, there is even enjoyment in risk itself, I believe. The chance of disaster heightens the pleasure when one succeeds. This is something I cannot make my father understand. He would have it that one must always be dull and take the safe road, but where is the satisfaction in that?"

"Refusing to be fearful as one goes about one's daily business is different from deliberately inviting danger, sir. I hope you are not placing yourself at unnecessary risk."

"Not at all, I assure you. It is only the contents of my purse that I occasionally wager."

"You are a gambler, sir?"

He laughed. "Only in the most trivial way, Miss Barrett. Do not be alarmed. And after all, a young man must have *some* occupation, mustn't he?"

"Could you not be doing some sort of work, Mr. Kingsley?" This was the wrong question, though, and he looked puzzled.

"Work, Miss Barrett? What do you mean?"

"Well, as your father's heir, you will one day be responsible for managing his estate. Should you not be helping him, or training under him, or perhaps finding some other useful project or pursuit?"

"What queer ideas you have, Miss Barrett! It is true that some-day it will be my turn to shoulder the burden of responsibility. But my father has everything well in hand at the moment, I assure you, and I should only get underfoot by involving myself prematurely. No, I am certainly not needed at present. That being the situation, my attitude is that I have the right to do as I like for now, so long as I am no bother to anybody."

"I see," I said, although I really didn't. "So you do as you like, Mr. Kingsley. And what is it that, then."

"Oh, anything to do with horses, dogs, guns, or sport, much the same as with the friends from my college. They are excellent fel-lows, and one or the other of them is always coming up with some capital scheme for amusement. The shame of it is that our numbers have sadly diminished of late."

From his mournful expression, I imagined the worst. "I hope you do not mean that some of your friends have lost their lives!"

"Worse than that, in my view, Miss Barrett. They have had to surrender their freedom. One has gone into the army, which is not so bad, I suppose. But two others have actually taken orders and entered the church. No choice, apparently. The sad lot of younger sons, you know. Poor Edward, there," he said, nodding in the direc-tion of his own brother, who sat at the next table eating his supper with Matilda, "may have to do the same. Worse than death, as I was saying."

"Perhaps your brother and your two friends do not share your dismal view of the clerical profession, sir. One must hope for their sakes as well as their parishioners that is the case."

"I daresay it is possible, Miss Barrett, but hardly likely."

Frederick Kingsley continued to talk of his ideas and views while we finished our meal, but it was difficult for me to give him my full attention anymore. There was so much else to look at. I located all my family members, here and there throughout the room, and I was pleased as punch to see them all behaving themselves, even Carmen. They were *not* having a contest over exposing themselves to the most ridicule possible, like Lizzy Bennet's family had done at the Netherfield ball. Although I did get a little nervous when Mr. Sotheby asked for some music after supper was mostly over.

Matilda didn't hesitate for a second. She shot out of her chair toward the pianoforte in the corner. I wasn't worried for her playing, which was accomplished enough, only that she might also try to sing – something she didn't do nearly as well. It wasn't too bad, though, and nobody seemed to find fault. Miss Sotheby played next, and another young lady that I didn't know. Then George Galloway turned up at my side to convince me to play as well. I had been practicing – singing too – so I didn't mind. I played something relatively simple but that I thought complimented my voice. Still, I was glad when I finished and it was time to move back to the ballroom.

My duty to Frederick Kingsley was done, but George Galloway had fastened himself to me as surely as a sidecar to a Suzuki. He was there to claim the second dance I'd promised him, which was perfectly fine with me. George had been my favorite partner so far, just because of his pleasant good nature.

It felt invigorating to be moving again after sitting still for an hour, and our conversation was comfortable, if a little disjointed due to the demands of the dance. George asked me how I liked the supper.

"Oh, very well, thank you. I believe I have never tasted better white soup," which was true, since of course I'd never tasted any at all before.

"I, too, thought it was very good. I would have enjoyed it more, though, if you had been beside me..."

Here, I almost forgot where I was in the dance and what to do next. What had distracted me and nearly made me lose my place was the astonishing sight of Mr. Cavanaugh in the ballroom.

She found herself suddenly addressed by Mr. Darcy, who took her so much by surprise in his application for her hand, that, without knowing what she did, she accepted him. (Pride and Prejudice, chapter 18)

Chapter 23
The Last Dance

Mr. Cavanaugh stood on the sidelines, watching the dancing and looking very distinguished. He smiled slightly and gave a little bow when our eyes met.

"Miss Barrett?" George was saying.

I brought my attention back to my partner. "Yes, Mr. Galloway?"

"You did not seem to be listening, and you nearly missed your step. Are you well?"

"Oh, yes. Forgive me. I was momentarily distracted. What were you saying?"

"Only that I would have enjoyed your company more than the supper companion that I *did* have."

"That is a fine compliment to me, sir, but at the expense of Miss Glover, I think. I hope you will be careful not to say anything of the sort within her hearing."

"Of course. She is a very good sort of girl, just not someone I can particularly admire myself. Not like you, Miss Kathleen."

"I respect you too, George, but you must be careful not to fall into the habit of giving excess flattery. You will make me think better of myself than I ought!" I finished, laughing.

The dance was finished too, and when I looked up, there was Mr. Cavanaugh again, waiting right in front of me.

"Mr. Cavanaugh!" I exclaimed. "It is quite an unexpected pleasure to see you here." I *was* pleased to see him, actually. The ball had seemed somehow incomplete before, with him absent.

"Good evening, Miss Barrett, Mr. Galloway," he said.

With the interruption, I had almost forgotten George again. So I thanked him sincerely for the dance. Somewhat reluctantly, I thought, he bowed and left me to talk to Mr. Cavanaugh.

"So you have returned to Carding, Mr. Cavanaugh."

"Only for tonight. I had unexpected business that brought me close enough that I decided it might be possible to accept Mr. Sotheby's kind invitation after all. But I was detained at the last minute and so have arrived shamefully late. I do not intend to miss out entirely, however. Will you do me the honor of dancing with me, Miss Barrett?"

I looked at him wide-eyed. "You wish to dance with me, sir? After what happened the last time?" I asked in surprise. "You *are* a courageous man if you are willing to risk more punishment at my hands... or, more accurately, my feet."

"Perhaps I am looking for revenge, and it is *you* who must be brave."

His expression was unreadable, so I couldn't be sure if he was joking or not. "I had not considered that," I said, "but you should know that *my courage always rises with every attempt to intimidate me*." (I couldn't resist this, and no one would know except me.)

"Think of it more as a challenge," he said. "Will you accept it? Will you dance the next with me?"

"I would but I am engaged."

"Engaged?"

"Engaged for the next dance, Mr. Cavanaugh. And all the others too, except the last. I will reserve that one for you, though, if you like."

"Thank you. Perhaps I will pay my respects to your parents in the meantime. Your mother I saw sitting over there, but where is your father? Did he come with you?"

"I believe you will find him in the card room, sir."

"Ah." He reached for my hand and bowed over it, saying, "Until later, then, Miss Barrett."

Apparently, I had been wrong to think this man was done surprising me, and I went on to dance with my other partners in good spirits.

It must have been nearly three in the morning when the last dance was called, so it was a good thing I'd had a rest before leaving home. I didn't want to miss a single minute of my first ball. The night had turned out to be everything I had hoped, and now I would have Mr. Cavanaugh to finish it.

We took our places on the floor, the music began, and we got moving.

My partner had a very serious look on his face as we went through the first set of figures. "Did you speak to my father," I asked him, thinking that might be the reason for his somber expression.

"I did," he said at the next opportunity.

"Did he not seem well to you, Mr. Cavanaugh?"

"Well enough, I think. I certainly saw nothing to alarm me tonight."

"Then why do you look so grave? Dancing is supposed to be fun, you know, and this time you are doing it by your own choice."

"I *am* enjoying it, Miss Barrett."

I felt like telling him that he should notify his face, but I bit my tongue instead, considering he might be one of those guys who simply couldn't bear to talk while dancing. Okay, then, I could play that game too. I could keep my mouth shut. I could stare soulfully into his eyes if he wanted to stare into mine. He *did* have beautiful eyes, which I'd noticed even when I didn't like anything else about him. But now I had to admit the rest of him wasn't bad to look at either, and his white cravat was tied in such an interesting way. Yes, I thought, smiling, there was something to be said for just shutting up and enjoying the view.

He was the one who broke our silence. "You smile, Miss Barrett."

"Like you, I am enjoying myself," I said. "Only one thing would make me happier, Mr. Cavanaugh, and that is to know you have forgiven me. I misjudged you from the beginning, I believe. I treated you badly, and I am sorry for it. And although I still cannot quite make out your character, I no longer have a bad opinion of you and probably never should have."

He seemed moved by my confession. When he replied, I could hear emotion in his voice. "We did not start well, Miss Barrett, but we shall end well. That is what I hoped for in seeing you tonight."

My smile faded. "End well? Do you mean this will be our last dance together, Mr. Cavanaugh?"

149

"I am afraid so. My obligations take me elsewhere, and I have no idea of returning into Hampshire immediately."

We were separated for a few moments, crossing back and forth in the pattern, before circling around to face each other again. This fortunately spared me having to make any immediate response, for I felt curiously deflated by what he'd just said. Even though he told me earlier he was back in Carding for that one night only, I think I had unconsciously read more into his presence and the fact that he sought me out than I should have.

Finally, I said, "Your father and mother will be pleased to have you home in Derbyshire again."

"I believe so, Miss Barrett."

"Have you any brothers or sisters also there?"

"Like you, I have three sisters and no brothers. Two of my sisters are married, however, so only the youngest, who is more than ten years my junior, is still at Pellencourt."

"Pellencourt?"

"My home, yes."

Thoughts of Pemberley rushed into my head and immediately out my mouth. "Is it very charming, Mr. Cavanaugh? Are there fine wooded hills, a stream widening into a lake, and an old stone house happily situated on rising ground beside it? I hope it is all very gracefully done, that everything was designed to enhance the natural beauty of the place rather than counteract it with an awkwardly artificial taste."

He looked at me oddly. And no wonder. I had been running off at the mouth again. Then, at his next opportunity he said, "Strangely enough, it is just as you have described it, Miss Barrett. Is it possible you have seen the place before?"

"Pellencourt? No, for I have never been so far north as Derbyshire in my life. But somehow, I felt sure it would be exactly so. I can picture it quite clearly in my mind," I said, still thinking of Pemberley – the way it is described in the book and the film representations I had seen.

"Can you?"

"Yes, and I must tell you that I have often imagined myself living there. It has always been my absolute ideal."

"You have imagined yourself living at Pellencourt?"

I felt myself blushing and hurried to correct my mistake. "Oh, no, sir. Pardon me. I did not mean specifically Pellencourt, only a place very similar to what I have described, which you tell me is very like your home."

"I see."

He looked like he was processing this information for a minute. I hoped he would accept my explanation and not expect me to tell him why I have such a vivid impression of a place I have never been.

"I suppose what you say is not so astonishing," he continued after a minute. "Had I never visited Pellencourt myself – if I lived somewhere else, for example – I believe I would hold an image in my mind of a like place as my ideal too. Why should I be surprised when others feel the same?"

"You should not be surprised; you have cleverly explained it yourself." I smiled encouragingly, and he seemed to warm to the topic.

"Although that ideal is not universally accepted, I find, Miss Barrett. Some see no beauty in the verdure of the countryside; some only care for the noise and gaiety of London."

"I have often heard such an opinion expressed," I said. "And there is something in it, I suppose. If assemblies and balls are all one cares about, then London has no equal for it, and life in the country may seem very dull indeed."

"But you do not hold to that idea yourself?"

"Not at all, Mr. Cavanaugh. The novelties of town may add a welcome variety from time to time. One cannot dispute the fact that society in the country is not nearly so diverse…"

"Indeed, it must be considered more confined and unvarying."

"…But I regard that fact as no detriment in general, and I would gladly spend most days within the pleasure of my own grounds and house, and most nights very quietly before my own fireside. I have been happy at Laurelwood. If I can continue in that sort of comfort, with family beside me, I will want for little else."

Mr. Cavanaugh made no response other than a nod and what I took to be a look of agreement. He and I then reverted to our earlier silence, which was fine with me. I meant to savor the beauty of the dance and the presence of my partner just as well and as long as possible. It would all be over too soon, I knew, and then Mr. Cavanaugh would be gone forever.

When the music stopped, the whole company applauded – in appreciation of the orchestra and to Mr. Sotheby for providing the evening's delights. Then people began chattering and making preparations to leave. But we stayed where we had come to rest when the dance finished. I felt frozen in place as if that could somehow prevent the night from coming to an end.

After a bit, Mr. Cavanaugh broke the spell, moving first. He came to my side, offering me his arm, and began walking me towards the exit. "Thank you for the dance, Miss Barrett," he said. "I enjoyed it more than I can say – the dance and our conversation. We now part on good terms, I hope."

"We do, Mr. Cavanaugh, and I wish you well."

He handed me over to my father, bowed, and walked away. He disappeared through the door and I didn't see him again.

"Such an agreeable fellow," said Papa as we watched him go. "Do not you think so, Kate?"

"Yes. I did not at first, but now I do. I daresay he will be sadly missed by the residents of Carding."

"I believe he will be, my dear. Mr. Fitch may find he has to work a little harder to measure up."

Our whole family collected to wait for our carriage with Lucy the last to join us. Mr. Sotheby delivered her and lingered with us several minutes longer. I should say that he lingered with Lucy, for he clearly had eyes for her alone. We tried to thank him for the ball and compliment him on what a success it had been, but I don't think he was listening. It really would have been quite rude if he hadn't had the excuse of being in love with my sister. Like Lizzy Bennet observed, general incivility is the essence of love. If anyone had doubted the sincerity of his affection before, here was positive proof.

Lucy was floating on cloud nine or ten. After Mr. Sotheby finally tore himself from her side, she exclaimed, "What a glorious night! I hope you enjoyed it as much as I did, Kate."

"Oh, yes! It was like something out of a dream."

Lucy couldn't have known how long I'd literally been dreaming of a night just like this – the ideal setting, the historically correct music, the authentic food, and dancing period dances with handsome men in cravats. It was as close to perfect as I could have asked for. The ball was easily the pinnacle of my Regency experience up to that point. I suppose that fact almost guaranteed it would be pretty much all downhill from there.

The next day opened a new scene at Longbourn. Mr. Collins made his declaration in form. (Pride and Prejudice, chapter 19)

Chapter 24
Anticlimax

Maybe if I had been able to refer back to *Pride and Prejudice* for what happens next, the day after the big ball at the neighboring gentleman's estate, I wouldn't have been taken off my guard when someone came to call on me late that afternoon, asking to speak to me alone. It wasn't Mr. Collins, thank God, but George Galloway.

Although I had never been proposed to before, in the nineteenth or any other century, I recognized the symptoms right away. George was looking very nervous and speaking very formally when he made his request of my mother for a private interview with me. Mama knew instantly what it meant too, of course, and before leaving the room she gave me a stern look, although I wasn't sure if it meant she wanted me to accept George or to say no.

I flew into a bit of a panic, doing exactly what Lizzy had under the same circumstances: pretending not to understand and pleading for my mother or one of my sisters to stay. "Surely, Mr. Galloway can have nothing to say that is unfit for you to hear," I said to their retreating backs.

And then I was alone with George. I turned to face him and fell under his painfully earnest gaze.

"Miss Barrett... Kathleen," he began, with a tremor in his voice.

He then paused so long that I wondered if he had forgotten what he came for or had changed his mind. I really hoped he had, because I didn't feel ready for this. I had pictured the scene where I accepted the proposal of the man I was crazy about. I had rehearsed *that* in my head a hundred times, but not how to kindly refuse an unwanted proposal. Once again, I felt like my preparations for Regency life had fallen short, although maybe there wasn't any perfect way to handle this situation in any time zone.

"Forgive me," George said. "Perhaps you would prefer to be seated before I... uh, before I proceed."

"No," I said, just as awkwardly. "No, I don't think so, not unless you plan to carry on for a long time. Oh! I didn't mean that the way it sounded. I imagine you will get it over with as soon as possible."

Egad! How could I have said such a thing? It had to be nerves. I suppose I should have attempted another apology, but I didn't dare. I suddenly felt like I might burst out laughing if I opened my mouth again, even though there was nothing funny about the situation. So I just bit my lip and shook my head at my own clumsiness.

George looked a little bewildered, but he pushed ahead anyway. "Forgive me if my visit was unexpected, Miss Kathleen, but I simply could not stay away – not after dancing with you again last night, after hearing you play and sing. You must know in what high esteem I hold your family and, more particularly, how sincerely I admire you. I could not succeed in hiding my affection if I tried. But I do not *wish* to conceal it, from you or from anybody; I wish to declare it to the whole world, this love I feel for you. Dearest Kate, will you do me the great honor of consenting to be my wife?"

I didn't feel like laughing anymore. My eyes were filling with tears instead. "That was beautiful," I said because that's what I was thinking. "But I do not deserve it."

"Do you mean...?"

"I mean that I do not deserve your love because I cannot return it, at least not in the measure required to make such an important commitment. I am dreadfully sorry, dear George, but I cannot accept your lovely proposal."

He took a deep breath and said, stoically, "There is someone else. I should have known; you must be admired wherever you go. Is it Mr. Kingsley? Or Mr. Cavanaugh?"

"No, certainly not! There is no one else, I swear. Do not torture yourself with such thoughts. In truth, I have no intention of marrying anybody at present."

He brightened at this. "Then there is still reason for optimism. You implied you feel at least *some* affection for me."

"Yes, certainly, but..."

"If there is no one else to come between us, it is possible that your affection for me will grow in time. That hope will be enough; it must be. I will not take your answer as a definite refusal, just your honest confession that you are not yet ready for marriage. You are young, and I am patient, Kate. I will show you by my constancy that you can entrust your future to me. Only promise that I may continue to see you and continue to hope."

I probably should have been firm, but I just couldn't bring myself to snuff out his optimism, to squash his little kernel of hope as if it were a crunchy beetle underfoot. Besides...

"Anything is possible, George."

George seized on this tidbit like a hungry dog thrown a T-bone steak, and he went away just as happy, saying that I should consider his offer open for whenever I found myself able to accept it. I didn't want him to be left feeling obligated to me, but nothing I said could change his mind. And really, when I thought about it later, it didn't seem so unreasonable. I did like George, very much in fact, and my affection for him increased a little every time I saw him. So I believed it was at least possible I would grow to love him in time, just as I'd told him.

As for my family, I had to tell them something too. I said, yes, that Mr. Galloway had proposed, and that I'd promised I would consider it.

"Very shrewd, Kate," said Mama. "Yes, very shrewd indeed. You mustn't toy with the young man's affections, for I would not have you put our relations with his family at risk, but it is only fair that you be given time to consider your position. Although Mr. Cavanaugh has flown off again, Frederick Kingsley may yet produce an offer of his own, you know, and no one would fault you for accepting him instead."

Later, I told Lucy, "Mama has it all wrong. I am not weighing George's offer against other possibilities, for I wouldn't accept Frederick Kingsley if he should ask me."

"I do not blame you for that, Kate. I am convinced I could not really esteem him either. But does the same hold true for Mr. Cavanaugh? Would you refuse him just as quickly?"

I sighed. And then I sighed a second time, more deeply. I just couldn't help it because a picture of Mr. Fitzwilliam Cavanaugh on one knee before me had popped into my head.

"But he will not ask me, Lucy, so there is no point in thinking about it. He is gone away, and I will likely never see him again."

~~*~~

Lucy and Arthur Sotheby were married on a Wednesday morning three weeks later. It was a very low-key affair compared to what I was used to and especially compared to the elaborate display of the ball – just a simple ceremony at the local parish church followed by the legendary 'wedding breakfast' at Laurelwood. And then the newlyweds took off on an extended honeymoon.

I was over the moon with happiness for Lucy. I really was. At the same time, I knew I would miss her terribly while she was gone. She would be living only a mile away when she returned, though, and had promised to write faithfully in the meantime. Still, it made a big change to our household to lose Lucy. And there was a very natural letdown after the excitement of the ball and the wedding.

A month went by with nothing of much significance happening. There were visits to and from our local friends, calls from George Galloway, frequent excursions into Carding, and one small assembly in the coaching town beyond it. Otherwise, it was the quiet of home and village life, day after day. I didn't mind at all, though. It was the life I had chosen, and I filled my time with things I enjoyed: reading and music when the weather kept us indoors, walking and riding when it was fair.

More importantly, I had my family – most of it. A hundred parties and fancy balls could never equal the value of that. Looking back, I see those weeks as some of my happiest. Yes, I missed Lucy, but because she was away, I spent more time with the others, learning to treasure each one every bit as much.

Carmen had taken to mooning over Shakespeare's sonnets, and then one day she confided in me that she was "in love" with the new curate of the parish. I still remembered all the wonderfully tragic feelings of my first crush when I was about her age – Joe Hendricks, a bookish college man who lived down the block. I converted him to his Regency equivalent and shared the story with Carmen, swearing her to secrecy. We became fast friends over it.

Matilda decided to forgive me for my newly discovered musical ability, partly, I think, because she found a way to turn it to her advantage. It seems she had always wanted to play duets but never found a suitable partner. Now she finally had one in me. We spent hours happily collaborating at the pianoforte, often racing faster and faster, until our fingers couldn't keep up and we collapsed into laughter.

With Lucy away, Mama began to turn to me instead, telling me her all her plans, taking me with her on her errands, and asking my opinions on this, that, and the other thing. Although she could be a little silly and overly dramatic, like Mrs. Bennet, mostly I found her ways endearing, and it was a treat to spend some one-on-one time with her.

The same thing happened with my father: more one-on-one time. Although I believe Kathleen always had a special place in his heart as something of a favorite, this was my opportunity to experience it for myself. I looked for chances for the two of us to do things together – riding with him when Papa did his weekly tour of the tenant farms, assisting him with his bookkeeping chores, and asking him about his reading. While this was a pleasure, I did have other reasons. I always had in mind Mr. Cavanaugh's charge that I should watch over Papa's health too.

Lucy was faithful to write, just as she had promised, and the arrival of a letter from "Mrs. Sotheby" was the highlight of every week. The newlyweds had gone to Bath first and from there continued to work their way west to Wales, with Ireland their ultimate destination. Lucy filled her letters to the family with colorful descriptions of all the places they had seen and the people they met along the way. I cared more about the things she *didn't* discuss; I wanted to know if she was happy and how she was adjusting to the trials (and pleasures) of married life. But these were the kind of intimate details a Regency lady simply didn't mention, at least not on paper where her parents and baby sister would read it. I intended to get more information out of her in person, though, when she finally returned.

About this time, Mama received another letter, one from her cousin in Staffordshire.

"Oh dear, oh dear," Mama said as she read it over breakfast that morning. "It sounds as if Rosamund is very ill indeed this time." She shook her head with a tsk, tsk as she continued to scan down the page. "Listen to this part, Kate.

"'Some days I am so weak that I can hardly stand, and I have very little suitable help. Jonathan is some comfort to me but Alex is nearly always from home, and Sir Alexander is constantly distracted by business. Men are generally useless to an invalid in any case, and servants have no true sympathy. Oh, for a female companion to ease my misery! One needs a daughter for such a time as this. Alas, I have none, as you know. But if only you could see your way clear to come to me, Anne, dear – you and Kathleen perhaps – I am sure it would do me a world of good.'"

As she read this excerpt, it brought images up in my mind – pictures of Rosamund herself and of her fine house. Sir Alexander was obviously her husband, and the other two mentioned would be her sons, my second cousins. Yes, the blanks were beginning to fill in. Bentley was their last name.

When she finished, Mama turned to her husband and asked, "What do you think of that, Mr. Barrett?"

"Which part? The bit about daughters being a blessing or that men are generally useless? I suppose, on the whole, I must agree with both assertions."

"No, not that! About Rosamund wanting me to come to her."

"Oh, now I see," Papa said, winking at me. "Well, perhaps you should accept the invitation, my dear. And take Kate with you if she wants to go. It would give you both something to do. It seems to me you have been at loose ends ever since the wedding."

"But could you manage here on your own with only Matilda and Carmen?"

"Doubtless it would be a severe hardship, but we shall endeavor to bear it as best we can. Right, girls?"

Here, Matilda jumped in with her opinion. "We are not infants, Mama. I am perfectly capable of filling your place while you are away, and Carmen will help me."

"Oh, yes!" said my youngest sister. "It is time I learnt what to do. I will have a home of my own one day, you know."

"What about you, Kate?" Mama asked. "Would you be willing to accompany me north?"

I considered the idea before answering. "It is a lengthy journey, but I really have no disinclination for the idea if we can be back when Lucy returns. How long would we be obliged to stay, do you think, Mama?"

159

"There is no telling how long Cousin Rosamund may have in mind, but I would not promise her anything above two months. Ten weeks at the most. We would be home by Christmas, and we may hope Mr. and Mrs. Sotheby will as well. We need not decide at once, however, and even then, it will be a week or two before I could possibly be ready for such an extended absence from Laurelwood. In any case, I daresay there is no hurry for fear of being too late to tend on Rosamund's illness. By her own account, it has been waxing and waning these several years, and I daresay it means to carry on a while longer until we come to cure her."

The more I thought about it, the more pleased with the plan I grew. Papa was right; I'd been a little at loose ends, and this trip would give me something different to do until Lucy returned from her honeymoon. It would be sort of an adventure, exploring country that was new to me and a part of Kathleen's life I hadn't opened yet. Through her, I remembered Cousin Rosamund fondly, despite some peculiarities. It was assumed that her illness kept her inactive, which may have been the truth. But I remember wondering if it was possibly the other way around – that she often felt ill and listless because she was perpetually inactive.

In any case, she was easy to please and claimed to do 'a great deal better' when I was with her, which made me feel good. Plus, it would be interesting to see Alex and Jonathan again, to see how they had turned out now that they must be completely grown up.

Mama warmed to the idea too and began making preparations for our departure.

We *did* eventually go to Cousin Rosamund in Staffordshire, but not as soon or for the same reasons as originally planned. Due to a drastic an unexpected change in circumstances, Mama and I were not the ones providing consolation; we were unexpectedly the ones in desperate need of it.

Mr. Bennet's property consisted almost entirely in an estate of two thousand a year, which, unfortunately for his daughters, was entailed, in default of heirs male, on a distant relation... (Pride and Prejudice, chapter 7)

Chapter 25
The Other Shoe

I considered the Coleswold ball the best day of my new Regency life. *This* was definitely the worst.

It was early October and I had been Kathleen Barrett for about five months. I was generally so happy in my new life that I would never have considered going back if I could have. Then the unthinkable happened.

I had been uneasy all morning, although I couldn't really say why. Since I'd grown up in hurricane country, I'd experienced the feeling of dread that hangs over your head when a category four storm is predicted. You knew it was coming, but you didn't know exactly when or where it would strike. It made you want to close up the shutters and hunker down at home.

I felt much the same that morning, so I wasn't happy when Mama insisted I drive with her into Carding on errands. Then, when we were just coming out of Grimstock's and Mr. Smith was about to hand us back into the carriage, we all three saw him at the same time. It was Mr. Smith's son Roger running towards us. My heart dropped into my belly and I just knew.

"It's the master," Roger blurted out, trying to catch his breath.

Even now, I cannot bear to dwell on the details. It seems Papa had collapsed while doing some work in the stable yard – moving heavy fence posts, which he never should have tried in his condition. Seeing what had happened, Roger ran to tell my sisters and then rode as fast as he could to get Mr. Fitch, even giving the doctor the use of his horse so he could be on his way to Laurelwood without delay. Then Roger came looking for us.

Papa was still alive when we arrived home, but barely. Mr. Fitch said there was nothing he could do. We should say our farewells and prepare ourselves for the worst. So that's what we did, although there is truly no way to be prepared for the loss of a loved one. Another hour and Papa was gone.

I cried for days. We were all pretty inconsolable – Mama, Matilda, Carmen, and I. Only Lucy was spared, because she was away and didn't know. Not yet. A letter with the news would eventually find her, though, and then it would be up to her new husband to comfort her.

In my grief, I tortured myself with the inevitable "what ifs" and "if onlys." What if I hadn't gone to Carding that day? If I'd stayed home, I might have been able to prevent Papa from attempting work that was too strenuous for his heart. If only I had been more vigilant. Mr. Cavanaugh had assigned me to watch over my father, and I had failed. But then, what if Mr. Cavanaugh had remained in Carding? Would he have been able to persuade Papa to be more careful? Would he have been able to save him in the end if he came instead of Mr. Fitch? I even wondered what would have happened if I'd never come to take Kathleen's place. Mama had wanted my father to go with her on her errands that day. He might have done so too, rather than moving heavy fence posts, if I hadn't been there to provide a handy substitute. Then he might still be alive today.

It was really hard to believe it had happened again; I'd lost another parent. (Two should be the maximum for anyone!) And it was no less painful for having had a lot less time to become attached, which would have seemed logical. Or maybe these losses of mine, when piled up one on top of the other like they had been, multiplied in weight. Anyway, it didn't feel like I'd loved Papa Barrett for only a few months. I think that by inheriting Kathleen's memories, I'd at the same time inherited her years of history and connection with her dad. Whatever the case, my second father had managed to burrow as deeply into my heart as the first, and it left another awful hole when he too was ripped away from me.

When I look back, though, I can see there were reasons to be thankful, even in the face of this disaster. Help came right away, so at least I knew everything that could be done by nineteenth-century medicine had been done. Papa did not suffer long and he died surrounded by his loving family. I could picture him at peace in heaven now, free of pain and sorrow.

Unfortunately, the same could not be said for those of us left behind. Black bombazine and crepe soon came to drape us all. Matilda took to playing mournful requiems and dirges on the pianoforte, and Carmen, to hiding all day in her bedroom. Mama cried and cried. And she fretted constantly, with good reason, about what would become of us now, expecting the other shoe to drop at any minute.

We didn't have to wait long. We had barely got through Papa's funeral when the letter came from his cousin, announcing that he would be arriving at Laurelwood within the week. Clarence Barrett, as it turned out, was the beneficiary of the entail. He wrote:

My Dear Mrs. Barrett,

Allow me to express my most sincere condolences to you and to your family on this most melancholy occasion. My cousin was a good man, and his passing must be counted as a grievous loss to us all. That goes without saying.

I do not wish to be indelicate, but I know you will be wondering about my plans for Laurelwood. Let me first reassure you that I do not anticipate any need for you and your daughters to vacate the premises immediately. I will be arriving in a few days with my wife and young son, but I believe the house is large enough to comfortably accommodate us all together for a time while you make other arrangements.

Perhaps you would be so kind as to ready two of the best rooms for our use and to make a few other necessary preparations for our arrival. I am thinking chiefly of space for our horses and servants, and ordering in some good cuts of meat. We will, of course, be bringing our own cook with us.

I think everything else can reasonably wait until after we arrive, for I know that my dear Fanny will want to supervise any improvements or alterations herself. She has such a sharp eye for detail and cleverness for how things should best be done. So please do not go to any excessive trouble on our account.

Again, my heartfelt condolences, Mrs. Barrett, to you and your daughters. Your humble servant,

Clarence Barrett

"Oh, that horrid man!" Mama wailed when I finished reading the letter to her.

"I do not remember him," I said, touching the back of my head in case I needed an excuse. I kept expecting some picture or recollection of Cousin Clarence to pop into my head, but it didn't. "Is he really all that horrid?"

"I have only set eyes on him once in my life, years ago, before you were born," she answered, which explained the persistent blank I was drawing. "I only said that because it seems he cannot wait to take control of his property, when your father is barely cold in his grave. And do you hear the way he talks of Laurelwood? It is as if he considers it a rundown sort of place that needs improvements of every kind, as if it will fail to meet his standards or his wife's in all respects. Oh, Kate, I am so distressed." And she started crying again.

With Papa dead and Lucy gone, the role of serving as my mother's primary support fell to me. Taking her hand, I said, "We must try to be composed, Mama. There is nothing too surprising in what our cousin has written, after all." Tactless, maybe, but not surprising. "We always knew it might come to this. We just never imagined it could be so soon. Let us think calmly and rationally about what we are to do next."

But I really had no idea what our options were, now that we were all, apparently, about to be homeless.

It suddenly occurred to me that I was no longer living *Pride and Prejudice*; this was feeling much more like *Sense and Sensibility* now, and we were being evicted from Norland by John and Fanny Dashwood. Well, Clarence and Fanny, anyway. And I had to play the role of the strong, sensible Elinor, when I would have been much more comfortable as Marianne. I wondered idly if Fanny Barrett had a brother named Edward.

"I suppose we must find somewhere inexpensive to live," I said, not knowing what our income was, only that it would be dramatically reduced. "I will begin making inquiries for something suitable at once. Perhaps a cottage," I suggested. Why had I said that? I

164

didn't have a clue how to begin making inquiries! For a cottage or otherwise. Fortunately, Mama didn't take me up on my offer.

"No, let us delay," she said. "It may come to that in the end, but there is no rush."

"Surely you will not wish to remain at Norland... I mean, at Laurelwood, once Cousin Clarence and his family arrive, regardless what he says."

"We have no choice. It is impossible that we should be ready to leave within a few days. And consider, my dear Kate, that we have nowhere to go. Now, if only your sister were come back from her wedding trip we might be saved. Surely she and Mr. Sotheby would offer to do something for us. Thank the Lord Lucy is settled so well and that it was accomplished before this calamity occurred! Otherwise there would be a whole year of mourning to wait through before they could marry. Now I could wish that you had accepted George Galloway at once for the same reason. Then I would at least have had two of you safely off my hands."

Dear George. He had been very kind to me and to my family since Papa passed away, coming to call and offering to do this and that – things that required a man's hand. But I had not yet thought of what this event could mean for him. He said he was patient, but a whole year was a long time to wait for an uncertain outcome (for I still didn't know if I could love him enough to marry him). I would need to insist on releasing him from any obligation to me. If he were still available when I finally shed my black bombazine, then we would see.

~~*~~

Cousin Clarence and his entourage arrived, and we were mortified. It wasn't because they were horrible monsters like the ones conjured up by my imagination, images spawned by *Sense and Sensibility*. They actually seemed perfectly pleasant. But I would have felt mortified (another excellent Regency word) by anyone who came to take Laurelwood and reduce us to the state of visitors in our own home.

Here again, I was surprised how quickly and how thoroughly I had taken complete ownership of my new home and family. I guess you never know how much you love a place or a person until you're faced with losing them.

Despite the awkwardness of our situation, we all managed to be civil to one another for the next three weeks. More than civil, actually. And one very positive thing came out of having our cousins in the house. Carmen, who had made herself a virtual prisoner in her own room since Papa died, was finally enticed out by her curiosity to see the newcomers, especially the little boy. Felix, who was seven, attached himself to her almost immediately, and luckily the feeling was mutual. Every day, Carmen would take Felix on some great "explore" throughout Laurelwood Park, or they might sit together on the floor with his toys and games, playing for hours. I have to assume the boy benefited equally, but I *know* Carmen was transformed. We all noticed it, including Fanny.

"Carmen is a dear girl," she told my mother one day as they were both watching the unlikely playmates out the window. "And so good with Felix, too. It pleases me to see how they have helped each other – Felix with his adjustment to a new place and your daughter in emerging from her shroud of sadness. Yes, it is a very good thing."

I thought it was a handsome sentiment... and well expressed too. This Fanny had much more kindness about her than that other one. I really couldn't bring myself to hate her even a little bit. The entail wasn't her fault, after all, or her husband's. For them, it had come along exactly at the right time too, when they'd been forced to leave their former residence and were in need of a place to live. That, as it turns out, was why they had come so soon.

But it wasn't a completely comfortable situation, crowded together as we were, and we couldn't stay on as their guests forever. So we started making plans for leaving Laurelwood. Mama still believed that the temporary arrangements we came to would only need to tide us over until the Sothebys finally returned from Ireland. All her hopes were pinned on them rescuing us and giving us a home at Coleswold.

Personally, I didn't think that was very reasonable. Lucy and Arthur would never let us starve, but it wouldn't be fair for the four of us to move in on them forever, lock, stock, and barrel. Besides, as I understood it, we weren't penniless. We should be able to afford something modest – perhaps a little house in Carding, where we could all be together, close to Lucy and our other friends.

But, at least for the time being, we were going to be flung apart in all directions. Mama and I were going to accept Cousin Rosamund's summons to Staffordshire for at least a couple of months.

Mrs. Abernathy had invited Matilda to stay with her. "I'm tired of rattling around in that big old house by myself," she'd said when she came to propose the idea. "And I cannot bear the thought of *all* my girls moving away. Matilda can keep me company, at least until you and Kate return."

Although Mrs. Abernathy would have taken Carmen too, my youngest sister had another offer. Since Carmen had made herself indispensable to Felix, and therefore to his parents too, she alone would be staying on at Laurelwood at their insistence. Carmen liked the idea, and Mama had by this time admitted that Clarence was not a 'horrid man' after all. So that was settled.

None of us would be exactly alone. Lucy had Arthur. Matilda and Carmen were going to be within easy walking distance and could visit back and forth as much as they liked. And Mama and I would be together. But Papa was gone forever and the rest of us split off in pairs. And I was moving… again. What had happened to the large, close-knit, rooted-in-one-place family I thought I had adopted? In less than six months, it had nearly disintegrated.

My other optimistic ideas for my new life had fizzled too. No Mr. Darcy, no Pemberley, and no chance meeting with Jane Austen herself. Now I would be leaving Hampshire and the home I'd come to love, not knowing if or when I would ever return.

Had Cora and Poindexter known what was coming and let me walk straight into it anyway? Shouldn't they have warned me instead of letting me get my heart broken all over again? Thinking of Crossroads made me wonder about some of the people I'd met there and what had become of them, especially Karen Altman. Was she still trying to decide what to do, or had she finally made the leap and started her second chance? And what about Ben Lewis? Did he make his baseball dreams come true? More importantly, did he ever hook up with Abby again?

Cora said she'd help him if she could. She had also said she'd keep an eye out for me, like a kind of guardian angel. I hadn't seen her or noticed any help from Crossroads, but then maybe I wouldn't.

167

Maybe that "little nudge in the right direction here and there" would be invisible to me – totally behind the scenes stuff.

The night before Mama and I left for Staffordshire, I gave myself a good long talking to. I was feeling a little sorry for myself and that had to stop. I'd started over before and I could do it again. What had I told Karen when she was worried about the choice I'd made to come here? I'd said something like, "I'd rather go for broke than play it safe. If things don't work out exactly as I planned, I'll just have to make the best of it."

That's what I'd done: gone for broke. And now I practically was... broke, that is. And yet I was glad I hadn't played it safe. Despite the heartache and setbacks, I still believed it was worth the risk I'd taken. This new life had already been one amazing adventure, and the detour to Staffordshire was simply another chapter in the book.

SECOND INTERMISSION

"There!" Poindexter victoriously proclaimed as Cora came into the room. "Didn't I tell you she would bounce back?"

"Who?" Cora asked, scooting herself onto the edge of his desk, where he had been sitting with eyes trained on the monitor screen.

"Miss O'Neil, of course. She was down for a moment, but she's already rebounding from Mr. Barrett's death. I knew the ship would right itself, given a little time. There *is* a long way to go, though, and the difficulties are real enough. Still, she has my every confidence."

"Ah, so you've been watching Hope's progress reports again. Don't tell me you've gotten attached, Dex."

"Don't be absurd," he said in a huff. "I am simply doing my job. You know as well as I that there must be some follow up with our clients."

"Some, yes, but aren't you the one who's always warning me about hovering too closely? Oh, let me guess. This is a 'special case,' requiring your personal attention." Pleased that her teasing was getting under his skin just a little, Cora jumped to her feet again, hands on hips and adopting a shocked expression. "Don't tell me you've been interfering too!"

"Certainly not!"

"Dex?"

"Well, uh, perhaps just a bit... Nothing outside the guidelines, you understand. I thought it was important that Hope – Kate, I suppose I should say – that she have a chance for some closure with Mr. Cavanaugh."

"Oh? So what did you do, then?" Cora asked, warily.

He shrugged, nonchalantly. "Nothing much. I simply contrived to send Mr. Cavanaugh on an errand of business; he did the rest.

Apparently, he only required opportunity – and no encouragement from me – to drop in at the Coleswold ball and see Kate again. Just a nudge in the right direction, as you are so fond of terming it."

"Hmm. Yes, well, all I can say is that you'd better remember this next time you're tempted to call one of *my* nudges interference."

"I will," he promised, rising to face Cora. "I will. Now, don't be angry. I cannot bear to see a beautiful woman unhappy, especially you, my pet." When he tried to pull her close, he felt Cora's resistance. She didn't pull away, but she didn't relax into the embrace either. "Stunning outfit, by the way," he added. "What do you call it?"

"Are you trying to change the subject?"

"Yes. Please."

"Very well, then. I call this one *Atlantic Crossing*. It's my interpretation of what a very stylish lady might have worn on the maiden voyage of the Titanic."

"Then I hope it's waterproof."

Cora laughed in spite of herself.

"There," said Poindexter, smiling back at her. "That's much better. Now, what do you have to tell me about Karen Altman's departure? That *is* why you came in, isn't it?"

"Do I need a special reason? Maybe I just wanted to see you."

"Even better."

Cora collected her reward for saying exactly the right thing. Then, after savoring Poindexter's amorous attentions for a few minutes, she confessed. "Mmm. I would have stopped by just for that, believe me, but I had a second, less important reason too."

"Karen."

"That's right."

"Did she cancel again?"

"It was touch and go there for a minute, but she actually went through with it this time, back to try making something better from her life. I hope she succeeds."

"I'm sure it will all work out for the best. Remember how worried you were about Ben Lewis when he left us, and look how well he's doing now, despite the disciplinary action we were forced to take. Interesting case, though. I can't remember another one quite like it."

"They're all unique. Each person has a different story, different circumstances that brought them here. We get to help them with their choices and see what they make of their new lives. I never get tired of it. In fact, I'd say we have just about the best jobs in the world, Dex."

"Or out of the world. Excellent fringe benefits, too," he said, leaning in for another kiss.

The first part of their journey was performed in too melancholy a disposition to be otherwise than tedious and unpleasant. But as they drew towards the end of it, their interest in the appearance of a country which they were to inhabit overcame their dejection...
(Sense and Sensibility, chapter 6)

Chapter 26
A Change of Scene

Mama was still prone to long periods of silent weeping. I couldn't help shedding a few tears myself when the carriage pulled away from Laurelwood, Carmen and our cousins waving us on our way. And then I shed a few more when we dropped Matilda off at Mrs. Abernathy's. But once we were beyond the borders of Carding and any familiar sights that I would miss thereafter, my mood improved. I was truly torn between my sadness at leaving my home and sisters and my excitement for what lay ahead.

I was sure the journey itself would be enjoyable. There was the scenery, of course – the beauty of the English countryside I had always longed to see – and more quality time to spend with my mother. But when we ran out of conversation or she dozed off, I entertained myself by sometimes thinking about Jane Austen's heroines and their travels. It seems to me that Jane must have enjoyed traveling herself because she gave her characters a positive attitude towards it too.

Lizzie Bennet went to Hunsford to see Charlotte, of course, and then later to Derbyshire with her aunt and uncle, in absolute raptures over the promise of seeing 'rocks and mountains.' Catherine Morland was just as thrilled at the chance for adventure in Bath and Northanger. And Anne Elliot is famous for saying how she had traveled so little that any fresh place would be interesting to her. But this trip of mine and Mama's felt most like when the Dashwood females had to leave their beloved Norland for an unknown future in

Devonshire. They were leaving against their wills and forever. Lizzy could return to Longbourn, but we couldn't ever go back to live at Laurelwood again.

I didn't mean to let that thought get the better of me, though. I still pictured myself as the heroine of my own Austen-worthy story. And like what Jane wrote about Catherine Morland, I believed that something must and would happen to throw a hero in my way. If not in Carding, then maybe in Staffordshire.

Our specific destination was Kantwell, the ancestral home of the Bentley family into which Mama's cousin Rosamund had married, making her the wife of a baronet. As we drew closer, things started to look more familiar, especially the park and house itself.

"Everything is just the same," said Mama as we both peered out the windows at the fine lawn, sprinkled with fallen leaves, and the stone façade of the great house. "Oh, how glad I will be to get out of this carriage and warm myself in front of a good fire!" she exclaimed as we pulled to a stop in front of the door.

I felt the same. No matter how charming a carriage ride had seemed to me before, it definitely lost some of its romance after being bounced around on rough roads for a couple of days. More than once I'd thought longingly of the sporty little SUV I had driven at home and imagined how this same journey would have been made much more quickly and comfortably in my car. I missed my bucket seats. I missed my state-of-the-art shock absorbers! Most of all, though, I missed the heater. It was November, and only a mountain of lap rugs and throws had kept us from freezing to death.

"Good afternoon, Madam, Miss," said the butler when he let us into the house. "It is good to see you again. You will find Lady Bentley in the drawing room. This way, please."

"Thank you, Wilkes," Mama answered.

A maid took our coats, and then we followed the butler in to see Cousin Rosamund, who was reclined on a settee. She didn't rise when we entered, but she did make the effort to upright herself.

"Oh, you poor things," she said languidly, stretching her arms out to receive an embrace from each of us. "How do you do? This long journey on top of your other troubles. You must be nearly done in." She and Mama had a tearful moment, and then Rosamund turned to me. "And Kate, let me have a look at you. I see you are all grown up now, and you appear tolerably well, despite everything that has happened – your fall and now your father, God rest his soul. We shall cheer each other up, agreed? I am so glad you and your mother are come." This long speech seemed to have thoroughly exhausted her. She reclined again and invited her little pug dog back onto her lap, adding to us, "And you two are to do exactly as you like while you are at Kantwell. For a start, you must get warm by the fire."

Mama had already headed in that direction. "Thank you, Cousin Rosamund," I said. "I believe we shall do just that."

"You must not feel obligated to entertain me every minute. I will like your company very much, I assure you, but I am not so selfish as to think only of my own suffering."

With this, Rosamund's eyes slipped closed and soon her hand, which had been petting the pug, came to a rest. She was asleep.

"Shall we leave her?" I whispered to my mother.

Before she could answer, though, another woman – a particularly lean lady of about forty – bustled into the room. She spoke softly (in consideration of the sleeping Rosamund) but firmly, saying, "I am Mrs. Morris, the housekeeper. Please follow me."

The housekeeper. In Regency terms, I knew that meant this Mrs. Morris was pretty much the boss of the place, the highest ranking female servant, equal to the butler and answerable only to the master and mistress. She must have the trust and respect of the family and authority over a host of other household servants in a mansion of this size.

We followed her out of the drawing room and towards the grand staircase, quickening our steps to keep up with her.

"I will show you to your rooms now," the housekeeper said, starting up the stairs.

Mama asked, "How long have you been with the family, Mrs. Morris? I do not recall you from our last visit to Kantwell three years ago."

"No, Ma'am," she answered. "I should imagine you are thinking of Mrs. Beasley. She was housekeeper before me. I came a little above two years ago now. With the mistress so much indisposed, they needed someone who could take a firmer hand with the household staff."

"I see," said Mama. "Then Lady Bentley is lucky to have you looking out for her interests."

174

"You flatter me, Ma'am, but I believe you have spoken nothing but the truth. I take it as a sacred duty to manage this house efficiently and step in where the mistress is not able. You will find me hard working, fiercely loyal and protective of my lady, and ever sensible of the trust placed in me by virtue of my position of elevated responsibility."

What could we say to this speech? It was too soon to either agree with or challenge Mrs. Morris's claims. I hoped, for the family's sake, though, that they might all be true. Rosamund clearly could not have managed things on her own at this point. According to the little we'd seen so far, she seemed to have deteriorated from what I remembered of her through Kathleen.

Mrs. Morris continued, saying, "I trust that I may depend on your cooperation while you are with us. Lady Bentley is not a well woman; peace and orderliness must be maintained for her sake."

"Naturally," said Mama.

"Here we are," Mrs. Morris was saying as we stopped in the upstairs hallway. She opened a door. "I have given you this room, Mrs. Barrett, and the next one further along the passageway is for the young lady. I believe you will find everything you require and that your trunks are already inside. The rooms adjoin. I thought that might be most comfortable for you. Dinner is at six sharp. You will see the master then. We are scrupulous about meal times, so do be prompt."

"Of course," I said. "Will we see Alex and Jonathan then as well?"

"Mr. Jonathan is expected, Miss, but we are not necessarily advised of Mr. Alex's comings and goings in advance. There is always a place set for him at the table, though, out of respect to the heir. Well, now, if there is nothing else, I will be on my way. My duties keep me very busy, and the family depends on me so."

"Thank you, Mrs. Morris," Mama said. "We will not keep you."

She nodded curtly and went back the way we had come.

I walked through Mama's room to find my own. Both the rooms were pleasant and neat as a pin, and, as predicted, our trunks had arrived ahead of us. We had more than an hour until dinner, so there was no rush to change. Besides, the delight of 'dressing for dinner' had vanished, now that all I could do was take off the black gown I was wearing to put on another the same color. This was one Re-

175

gency convention that I really didn't admire. To me, it seemed cruel to require someone who was already desperately sad to wear such depressing clothing on top of everything else. Wouldn't it be kinder to encourage them to put on a cheerful polka dot dress or colorful calico?

I came back into my mother's room and plopped down on her bed. "What do you think of Cousin Rosamund, Mama?" I asked. "I thought she did not look well at all. She could barely keep her eyes open for five minutes, though it is the middle of the day. That did not seem right to me. And what about Mrs. Morris? It appears she runs this house like an efficient military operation. I wonder that we were not required to salute her."

"Kate! I am surprised at you."

"I meant it as a compliment, Mama. Well, mostly. Efficiency is something to be admired, so long as it does not overrule heart and common sense."

Mama paused to consider this. "Yes, well, as to Rosamund, I must admit that she looks worse than I had expected. I suppose it was selfish of me, but I had hoped seeing her would cheer me. It seems unlikely now. Oh, Kate, I hope we have not made a dreadful mistake by coming here. I fear now you will have the task to raise the spirits of not only your mother but your cousin also." She sat down on the bed beside me, adding, "Can you bear it?"

I put my arm around her and let her rest her head on my shoulder. I couldn't hear it, but I knew from how she was shaking that she was crying again.

~~*~~

Sir Alexander welcomed us when we came down to dinner – politely but formally, saying everything that was proper but nothing that really warmed my heart. He offered condolences for our loss. He thanked us for our kindness in coming to them. He invited us to make ourselves at home. And he hoped the visit might do both us and his wife a great deal of good. Fine words, and if I'd seen genuine concern and tenderness shining in his eyes when he said them, I would truly have been touched. Instead, it all fell a little flat. Still, I tried to cut him some slack. I'm sure he was doing the best he could. Some people – men especially, it seemed like – just didn't

176

have the capacity to connect with others emotionally. If that was Alexander's plight, I felt sorry for him… and for his wife and sons too.

Jonathan was much friendlier, and between the two of us, we had to carry the bulk of the conversation over dinner. There were only five of us at the table. Mama was still pretty subdued after her recent crying spell. Sir Alexander remained mostly a quiet and careful observer as he ate. Rosamund smiled placidly, picking at her food and occasionally adding something general and passive. "Oh, yes, by all means," or "Very true." Alex's place remained empty.

So, if not for Jonathan, it would have been a very dull group. Fortunately, he was not of an *unsocial, taciturn disposition*. I didn't need a Mr. Darcy type right then; I needed 'good company' – Anne Elliot's idea of good company, that is: at least one *clever, well-informed person with a great deal of conversation*. Jonathan and I (by which I mean Kathleen) hadn't seen each other in three years, so we had a lot of catching up to do. We did it with an audience of the three others, though, which was a little awkward.

After the initial greetings and standard pleasantries, I said, "I believe I remember from one of your mother's letters that you are to be a clergyman, Mr. Bentley."

"Oh, please do call me Jonathan," he said. "We are cousins, after all, and it will make things so much simpler. But you are correct. I will be taking orders very shortly and assuming the living in my father's gift, here at Kantwell, Miss Barrett."

"Kate, please. You must be looking forward to beginning your career."

"Yes, although I cannot forget that it only comes so soon because of the loss of another man: our good Mr. Kelleher."

"Very true," said Rosamund, morosely.

"I am sorry," I said in concern. "Did he…"

"Oh, no," Jonathan cut in, understanding where my thoughts had carried me. "Nothing like that. We will miss him, but it was actually a happy event that took him from us. He was called to serve in the bishop's office."

"Ah, a promotion. I see." Then I was looking for a new subject, after a minute, trying this. "I shall be happy to become reacquainted with your brother as soon as may be."

"So will I!" said Jonathan, laughing. "We see so little of him here at Kantwell that I sometimes nearly forget I have a brother..." This drew what I took to be a warning glare from Sir Alexander. "...except, of course, I cannot forget. Alex has many interests that take him out into the world, that is all. He returns to his family whenever he can. I daresay we will all have the pleasure of his company again before long," Jonathan finished, giving me a smile and a wink nobody else could see.

I smiled back and said, "I shall anticipate it with pleasure." But I was thinking there was more to that story than first met the eye, more than anybody was telling at the moment.

"Perhaps in the meantime, Kate," Jonathan said presently, "I can reacquaint you with Kantwell. You as well, of course, Cousin Anne, if you would like. Weather permitting, tomorrow I could take you both round the park in an open carriage."

I waited for Mama's response.

"That is very kind of you, Jonathan," she said. "But I remember the park very well, and I am loathe to set foot in a carriage of any sort so soon again, especially in such cold weather. Go with Kate, though, by all means."

"Yes, by all means," echoed Rosamund.

"What do you say, then, Kate? Can I tempt you out of doors tomorrow for a tour of the park?"

"I should be delighted, but could we not go on horseback instead?" I asked, thinking that would make the scheme even better.

"Of course! Forgive me, but I thought perhaps you did not care to ride anymore."

"Not so, I assure you, Jonathan. Although I thank you for your scruples on my account, I returned to the saddle a few weeks after my accident. I only wish I had Horatio here with me now. He is such an excellent creature. No other horse is his match."

Sir Alexander took exception to this, saying very firmly, "No doubt an equally suitable mount can be found for you in *our* stables."

So I had to back up a little and do some damage control. "Yes, sir," I agreed. "I do not doubt it for a moment. I only meant that I have been used to and fond of Horatio until now. But that should not keep us from appreciating new things when they come in our way."

"Very true," Rosamund agreed.

"I think Cleopatra might do very well for you," Jonathan said thoughtfully. "She is a sweet little bay mare – lively but well behaved. Yes, it is decided; Cleopatra shall be known as your horse, Kate, for as long as you want her."

"That is very kind, Cousin, but I deserve no such special attention."

"Nonsense. You must have some exercise while you are with us, mustn't you?"

I glanced at Sir Alexander to see if I could read his opinion of Jonathan's idea, but he looked as if he hadn't even been paying attention. "Well," I said, "if you are sure, I thank you."

We saw nothing more of Sir Alexander or Jonathan after dinner. Mama and I kept Rosamund company for an hour or so longer, until Mrs. Morris came into the drawing room to recommend that her mistress retire. We went upstairs soon afterward; it had been a long day, and I could see that Mama was weary and probably needing to get to sleep.

That night, I lay in my comfortable bed, thinking over what I'd discovered about Kantwell and its inhabitants so far. It was an impressive sort of place – much bigger and grander than Laurelwood – but not necessarily a happy place. The master seemed kind of remote and forbidding. Although the younger son was perfectly pleasant, even considerate, the heir was often absent – possibly off getting into trouble or at least neglecting his duties? Poor Lady Bentley, with her bad health. She could barely sit up long enough to get through dinner, and her favorite companion seemed to be her little pug dog. Then there was the bossy Mrs. Morris...

Why did this all seem so familiar? Kathleen had been here before, and I had inherited some memories from her, of course. But that wasn't the explanation. No, there was something else about the situation, and it kept niggling at my brain. Then suddenly I knew what it was. Could it be I had landed in the middle of *Mansfield Park*?

Fanny Price was just ten years old, and though there might not be much in her first appearance to captivate, there was, at least, nothing to disgust her relations. (Mansfield Park, chapter 2)

Chapter 27
Beautiful Grounds

If this was *Mansfield Park*, did that make me Fanny Price? Oh, dear! I wasn't sure I could pull that one off. Meek and shy I definitely was not!

Plus, there was another problem with the idea, and that was I didn't know the story very well. Unlike Jane Austen's other five novels, which I felt like I had half memorized, I'd only read *Mansfield Park* once, years ago. I hadn't warmed up to it the first time through – not like the others, at least – and so never felt like reading it again, or even watching the movies. Now I really wished I had.

There was a lot of wisdom packed between the pages of Austen's novels – the different way people talked in Regency England, examples of how to behave and not behave, lessons learned, sometimes the hard way. It was valuable material, especially for somebody like me who was new to the era. How could I have ignored one whole book full of advice and experience?

I sure would have liked to have gotten my hands on a copy of *Mansfield Park* right then, to see what I had missed and how it might apply to my situation. For one crazy moment, I had the idea I should check to see to see if the Bentleys had a copy in their library or try to find my way to a book store to buy one of my own. But of course, that really *was* crazy, because the book hadn't been published yet in 1809!

Although maybe my stay at Kantwell wasn't going to be so much like *Mansfield Park* after all. From what I could remember, there were as many differences as similarities. I wasn't ten, for one thing, and I'd brought my mother with me instead of leaving her behind. And weren't there supposed to be two daughters in the family (Was it the Burdicks? No, the Bertrams.) as well as the two sons? Plus, nobody had made me feel like I was a poor relation, not yet anyway. And there had been something about putting on a play too. That's what I remembered from the book, but that was about all.

By morning, I had mostly forgotten any thoughts of Mansfield and the Bertrams. The sun was out, so I knew I had a tour of Kantwell Park with Jonathan to look forward to instead, and that was about as much pleasure and excitement as I could probably expect while I was in mourning. Unfortunately, though, I didn't have a proper riding habit in my mourning wardrobe, and that was all I'd brought with me. This made me wonder if I should have stuck with the open carriage idea Jonathan had first proposed.

It was probably too late to change the plan, though, so I dressed in the black gown I thought would most easily work in a saddle, prepared to make the best of it. Mama wasn't ready yet, and she encouraged me to go down to breakfast without her.

Jonathan was the only one there. He looked up and smiled when I came in. "Good morning, Kate," he said. "We have a fine day for our outing."

"Good morning, Jonathan. Yes, we do, indeed." I filled a plate from the sideboard and sat down across from him.

"You have a hearty appetite," he said, when he saw the pile of food I'd taken – ham, kippers, two eggs, bread, and fruit – "which is good to see. I could wish that my mother did as well."

"Will she be down for breakfast, do you think?"

"No. She sleeps late and Mrs. Morris takes a tray up to her. We never see her before at least two o'clock. So I thought we could go out for our tour of the park this morning and be back before then. Will that suit you?"

"Oh, yes. It sounds delightful. My first object is to be of use to your mother, but if you are certain I won't be missed…"

"Quite certain."

"Very well."

Mama came in then, taking Jonathan's attention away from me for the moment. It gave me a chance to study him unobserved. I'd noticed yesterday that he was above average height – taller than when I'd seen him before, and broader in the shoulders. His face

181

had matured nicely as well. I still wouldn't call him especially hand-some, but there was something attractive in his honest, open looks. More like a George Galloway than a Mr. Cavanaugh, it occurred to me.

But I had no business comparing Jonathan to anybody else. He deserved to be appreciated for himself, for his own merits, which were many, it seemed. He certainly had been sweet as could be to me.

Had Fanny Price ended up with the younger brother in *Mansfield Park*? I couldn't remember. It seemed like the younger brother had been very nice, like Jonathan, but then some other guy came into the picture, and I honestly couldn't be sure how it had all turned out. At any rate, I was glad Jonathan was only my second cousin and not my first, in case there was a chance of something developing between us. Of course I knew that in this time period nobody batted one little eyelash at even first cousins marrying. In fact, it was considered a super way to keep family money in the family – one reason it was the *favorite wish* of Lady Catherine and her sister that their kids should hook up. But I didn't think I could get over my modern-day ideas about it.

Anyway, it was a glorious morning, and by the end of it I was half in love – with Kantwell, if not with Jonathan. Now, if Jonathan had been the heir, as Mr. Darcy was of Pemberley, my opinion of him might have benefited that much more. I understood more than I ever had before what Lizzy meant when she told her sister Jane that she could date her falling for Darcy to when she first saw his beautiful grounds at Pemberley. I know she was mostly joking, but still, picturing a man as master of a beautiful and prosperous estate *does* make him that much more attractive.

It was the wrong model to use in this case, though, since Jonathan was *not* the heir. I realized I should be thinking more like Catherine Morland when she was shown the parsonage that would be Henry Tilney's home.

After riding to the outer reaches of the park, through lovely stretches of woods and past acres and acres of farmland and or-chards, Jonathan showed me the parish church and the parsonage where he would spend most of his time in the future. I thought the old stone house was particularly charming.

"How pretty!" I said when we rode up to it.

"Do you really think so?" Jonathan asked.

"Oh, yes. You cannot imagine how charming it looks to me compared to what I am used to." I was thinking of modern housing developments and apartment buildings, most of which had so little character.

"That is a fine compliment, Kate, coming from you. I admit that I am highly partial to my little house," which really wasn't small at all. "But I do not necessarily expect others to appreciate the modest beauty in it. Would you like to see inside the place?"

"I would, indeed."

Jonathan slid down from his horse and then helped me off Cleopatra, who I enjoyed riding very much, as it turned out. She was lively and yet well-behaved, just as Jonathan had told me.

Opening the door, Jonathan said, "It cannot compare to Kantwell House or to Laurelwood, I know, and perhaps it may admit of some improvements. I claim no eye for such things myself; that I suppose to require a lady's taste." Then he looked embarrassed, as if he had implied too much.

I pretended not to notice.

We didn't go upstairs but we toured a generously sized drawing room on the main floor, a fine dining parlor, a well-stocked library, the kitchen, and a cozy little sitting room, all fitted out for genteel living. Jonathan made comments and explanations to me along the way – what he liked, what things he had a mind to change. I thought it all looked extremely pleasant, especially with the sunlight spilling in through the large windows. I was afraid to be too lavish in my praise, though, in case Jonathan would think I was forming designs on the place (or on him) for myself.

"It is a fine house, Cousin," I said after I had seen it all. "One can only imagine how comfortable you will be here."

I hoped that sounded the right note. He seemed satisfied, and we moved on. After circling the house once to view the gardens, we remounted our horses, walking them back towards the great house. It was almost one o'clock and time to put an end to our expedition. I knew I'd have to say something soon if I wanted to speak to Jonathan while we were still alone. So I dove right in.

"You mentioned before that your brother has interests that frequently take him away from Kantwell. I cannot help being curious to know what you meant, unless of course it is a private matter not to be spoken of."

"Ahhhhh, yes," he said slowly. "Alex's wanderings. My father is a little sensitive on the subject, but it is no secret. I daresay everybody in the region and many beyond know of my brother's exploits, by reputation if not by observation, so there is no reason you may not as well."

"Has he done something very bad, then?" I asked.

"Oh, no, nothing so very bad, unless idleness and dissipation are to condemn a man. Alex merely prefers London to Staffordshire, the company of his friends to his family, and the occupation of wagering on horses or cards to the business of managing an estate, even one he will inherit. There is no true harm in him except the damage that may be done by carelessness."

"I believe carelessness often causes a *great deal* of damage, Cousin. Cannot your father do something, if he disapproves?"

"He tries, threatening to cut off Alex's allowance and so forth. But it does little good. My brother knows he is perfectly safe. His inheritance is secure, and my father will pay off whatever debts he runs up in the meantime. So you see, as the eldest son, Alex is free to do as he wishes. He may be neglectful and lackadaisical if he chooses. It is difficult to even dislike him for it, for he really is an artless, charming sort of fellow, which you will discover for yourself whenever he deigns to grace us with his presence."

"I wonder that you can speak of his behavior so mildly. In your place, I should not have half so much forbearance. He is off enjoying himself and has left you... left you with all the home duties." I wanted to say 'holding the bag' but I was pretty sure that wasn't a period-correct expression.

"My temperament is suited for home and for a country life, so I have no complaints. Whatever his faults, Kate, I love my brother. And he has not injured me. If anyone, he has injured himself, for the estate he begins to impoverish is his own." He was silent for a minute, lost in thought, it seemed. Then he added, "If I am to fault Alex for anything, it would be for neglect of his mother. Since I am convinced her illness is as much of mind as body, I cannot help thinking Mama would find consolation, and possibly even improved health, were she to have benefit of the attention of *both* her sons and not only the one less preferred."

184

It pained me to learn that Jonathan believed his mother favored Alex over himself. I tried to remember what Rosamund had said about her two sons in her letter. "You may be wrong to think she prefers your brother," I suggested. "In her letter to my mother, she mentioned you with praise and what sounded to me like great affection. All she said of Alex was that he was no comfort because he was usually away from home." It was a bit of an exaggeration as to what cousin Rosamund had actually spelled out to us, but I had every reason to believe it was true nonetheless.

"You are kind, Kate, but you mistake my meaning. I am not jealous of Alex – his inheritance, his freedom, or even the place he occupies in my mother's heart. It is simply that I want Mama to be well and happy, and that depends more on my brother than on myself. Try though I might, there is nothing I can do that will adequately fill the place left empty by his absence."

"I am afraid the same will be true of my mother and me; perhaps nothing we can do will make the slightest difference either."

"Not to fill Alex's place, perhaps, but in other ways. You must believe me when I say you have already cheered her. As soon as she knew you were definitely coming, I could see the effect. It gave her new hope, and that is as important as anything."

"I am glad, but how would you advise me, Jonathan? What specifically can we do that would be the most helpful?"

"She wants kindness and female companionship, which you will render best by following your own instincts. Beyond that, there is only one thing I would mention. I could wish someone were able to persuade Mama to take less laudanum."

"So that is why she sleeps so much." One mystery solved. The poor woman was regularly drugged!

"Primarily, yes. The apothecary prescribes it, and Mrs. Morris, who has Mama's ear, believes in its beneficial properties. It may dull pain and have a calming effect, but I do not like to see my mother so dull and spiritless."

I was really pleased that Jonathan had confided so much in me so soon, and yet I wasn't all that surprised. We had some past history but, more importantly, I felt like we were *simpatico*. I instinctively knew I could trust Jonathan, and I'm guessing he felt the same about me. His trust in me wasn't misplaced, either. I intended to do everything I could to help his mother and his family.

"Thank you for telling me these things, Jonathan," I said. "Now let us get back to your mother." I gave Cleopatra a little nudge with my boot and she sprang into action, breaking for the stables. Jonathan was right behind me.

*Fanny had no share in the festivities of the season; but she en-
joyed being avowedly useful as her aunt's companion... She talked
to her, listened to her, read to her... (Mansfield Park, chapter 4)*

Chapter 28
Being Useful

I made myself indispensable.

It had been my goal to be useful – to cure Cousin Rosamund if I
could or at least improve her spirits – but in hindsight, I see where
my enthusiasm may have carried me too far and worked to my own
disadvantage.

At first, Mama equally shared responsibility as Rosamund's
other companion. One or both of us would be there by her side
during the hours she was awake and downstairs, just keeping her
company and doing little things. It might be writing a letter she
dictated, interesting her in a needlework project, or encouraging her
to take a turn about the room and then being that steadying arm
while she did. Rosamund especially liked it when I played the
pianoforte and when I read to her from Shakespeare's sonnets or
some other book.

Mrs. Morris was soon giving me little assignments and errands
on Rosamund's behalf, too, which I was more than happy to do. As
I figured out early on, the housekeeper was definitely top dog, and
Sir Alexander deferred to her judgment and efficiency in nearly
everything concerning his wife or the running of the household.
Rosamund did too, although I was able to make at least one change.

When Rosamund's personal maid came with the regular dose of
laudanum, I could sometimes convince her to take less or none at
all. "I cannot imagine you need any of *that* kind of assistance,
Cousin Rosamund," I might say, "so well as you are looking this
afternoon. It will only make you sleepy, and then how will you finish what you have started? Look what fine progress you have made

on netting your pretty new reticule! No, if your nerves need settling, I will read to you instead. Will you have Shakespeare or Mrs. Radcliffe today?"

That might be all it took. She would smile sheepishly and send the medicine away. "Dear Kate, how did I ever get along without you?" she would say.

I saw definite signs of improvement in Rosamund within the first couple of weeks, and I was pleased as punch. She was more alert and active, more engaged and positive. "Bless my soul!" I told her one morning. "Look who is up in time for breakfast, all bright-eyed and bushy tailed!" She got a real kick out of that.

Mama and I hadn't done anything magical, though. We'd simply given kindness and companionship. And it was good therapy for me too. To focus on helping somebody else kept me from feeling too sorry for myself. It kept me from thinking about poor Papa and how much I missed Laurelwood and all my sisters. I even missed Mr. Cavanaugh, when I stopped to consider it, which I didn't allow myself to do very often.

I could have wished things were different – that Papa was still alive and all of us together – but I wasn't really unhappy. I still had my mother with me (which was more than I'd had in my former life). Sir Alexander and I didn't have much contact, but I'd grown very fond of Rosamund and Jonathan, and I hoped to see Alex again soon. Plus, my duties at Kantwell kept me cheerfully busy with just enough leisure time leftover. I was basically content, and the weeks passed comfortably enough.

Unfortunately, the change of scene and society didn't appear to be doing Mama the good I had hoped or that she herself had predicted. Her spirits were still low. Even the occasional letter from Matilda or Carmen didn't cheer her up for long. The pleasure of hearing from them soon turned into a reminder of their absence, and homesickness set in all over again. Then we finally received a letter from Lucy, which I read out loud to Mama so we could hear it at the same time.

My dear Mama and Sister,

How long since I have seen you both and how very much has changed during that interval. Little did I expect – did anyone expect – that, when I went away so happy, I would never see my father again. And now I return to find the rest of my family dispersed as well.

Arthur is a darling, and he has been such a comfort to me during this affliction. We had a safe and interesting wedding trip, which, under better circumstances, I would have been able to call heavenly. But all pleasure was at an end once the dreadful news reached us while we were sojourning in Ireland. How I longed to fly home that instant to be with you all! Alas, the distance was too great and, as you said in your letter, all would be over before I could possibly arrive.

I know you can easily comprehend the grief and despair I felt. It was not only for myself, however, but even more so for you, Mama – for your loss and what I knew it would mean for your future comfort. I cannot bear the idea that you were forced to give up your home so soon. I have now met our cousins. They seem a very good sort of people, and I make no doubt they will care for Laurelwood well enough. Still, it seems wrong to see them there and to think of another family taking the place of our own within its walls.

Carmen and Matilda are well. I have seen them both. Naturally, I made it clear that they will be welcome to Coles-wold as soon as we are settled, but they both claim to be content where they are and not desirous of any immediate change to their situations. I wonder if the same is true for the two of you at Kantwell. If so, I will not beg you to quit it at once, although for my own part, I could wish you would. I miss you both terribly, and Arthur agrees with me that you are to have a home with us as long as you might need or wish it.

Mama, I will be wanting your attendance before many more months have elapsed in any case. I have been feeling a little unwell, which I am certain you will attribute to the proper cause, now that I am a married woman. I must have my mother with me when the time comes.

Please give my best wishes to all our relations there, and do come to us as soon as Cousin Rosamund can spare you.

Love, etc.
Lucy Sotheby

The change in Mama was astounding. Her face lit up like someone had flipped a switch, and she began to flap and flutter about like
a mother hen.

"Good heavens!" she exclaimed. "Do you hear what your sister
says, Kate? My baby! I can scarce believe it; she is to be made a
mother herself before too long. Oh, I must certainly go to her at
once! Lucy is too modest to demand it, but anybody can hear how
much she needs me by what she *does* say. What could be more
fitting than that a young wife should have her mother with her at
such a time? And her sisters too, of course. No one could think there
is anything strange in that. Oh, I am so happy! I knew how it would
be, that good, kind Mr. Sotheby would invite us all to stay at
Coleswold. If we cannot have Laurelwood, it is the next best thing.
We must make plans for our departure without delay!"

I was nearly as excited as Mama. I almost jumped for joy at the
thought of being reunited with all my dear sisters again, especially
to see Lucy home, married, and pregnant. I closed my eyes to
visualize the wonderfully, tearful scene. And we could make it
happen within a few days if we began preparations right away.

Then I remembered Rosamund. How could I – how could we –
possibly abandon her when we'd seen the good we were doing? She
was better, yes, but she had a long way to go before she would be
out of danger. Or so it seemed to me. Without further encouragement and care, she might very well slide back into the depths again,
perhaps ending up worse off than before. I couldn't live with my
conscience if that happened. And yet I wanted Mama to be happy
too.

"…We will need to send word to have the carriage and horses
made ready," Mama was saying as she paced back and forth in ener-
getic concentration. "And then there is the packing of our trunks. I
suppose it is too late to expect to start out today; I daresay we could
not hope to make much progress before dark. Tomorrow, then, just
after breakfast. That will have to be soon enough."

"You go, Mama," I said, coming to a decision.

She stopped. "What is that you said, Kate?"

"You go ahead, Mama. Go home to Carding, tomorrow if you
like. See Lucy and the girls. I must remain here at Kantwell for the

190

time being, though. Cousin Rosamund still needs me… more than Lucy does, anyway. And I must not be selfish."

"You mean to remain behind? Can that be your intention, Kate?"

"Yes, Mama. As much as I long for home, for the moment, my clear duty is to Rosamund. As I said, she still needs me, but not both of us. If I stay, then you are free to go to Lucy. It is the best solution."

Although I couldn't think of a clear parallel to my situation in Jane Austen, I was sure she would have approved. Both Anne Elliot and Elinor Dashwood often put the needs of others above their own. But, surprisingly enough, Emma Woodhouse was probably the best example of self-sacrifice on behalf of a parent. She catered to all her father's little whims and eccentricities for years, apparently without complaint. Then, she was willing to delay marrying the delicious Mr. Knightley indefinitely so that she could spare her father the trauma of her leaving him. That was truly above and beyond the call of duty!

All I was doing was putting off my reunion with my sisters a little while for the sake of a dear lady, an adopted extra mother, who needed me.

Mama took a little more convincing. "But how will you get home later if I take the carriage now?" she asked. "It will be a long and costly journey."

It was a good question, one I hadn't had the chance to consider yet. "Sir Alexander must occasionally have business that takes him to London," I suggested. "Perhaps he can transport me when the time is right. Or Alex. You are not to worry, Mama. We will manage it. Now, let us get your things packed and ready to go."

Over dinner, Mama informed the family of her change in plans, and Sir Alexander vouched for his willingness to manage the business of seeing me safely home later. That seemed to take care of her last objection.

It was hard to watch her drive off the next morning without me, although I tried not to let it show. Jonathan had joined me on the front porch to wave as she left, despite the cold.

"It is a selfless thing you do by staying, Kate," he said, his breath making puffs of condensation in the air as the carriage pulled away. "I know how much you must have wished to go home with your mother."

I couldn't lie to him by denying it. "Yes," I agreed, "but home is not the same for me." I meant not only that I'd lost Laurelwood but so many other places I had lived and loved. "I believe I can learn to be content almost anywhere, Jonathan, anywhere I have friends and a purpose. I must. So for now, Kantwell is my home."

I could feel him looking at me, but I kept my eyes fixed on Mama's carriage, nearly gone from sight now.

"Nevertheless," he said when he turned away. "I want you to know that, of your friends here, at least one has seen your sacrifice and honors you for it."

It was well for her that she was naturally cheerful, for the change had been such as might have plunged weak spirits in despondence. (The Watsons)

Chapter 29
Bleak House

I knew that with Mama's departure I had lost any chance of making it home to my family for Christmas. I thought I remembered that not much fuss was made over the holiday in Austen's time, but that wasn't the point. It had always been special to me, and now this would make two Christmases in a row that I'd be spending with no closer relative than an aunt or a cousin. Now that I was separated from every last cotton-picking member of my new family, I did find my thoughts turning back to my family of origin more often. Maybe the picture in my mind of my momma and daddy had dimmed a little, but it wasn't gone. I tried to dwell only on the good memories of them, and most of the time I succeeded. Sometimes, though... Well, once in a while even the most determined optimist can trip up and accidentally slip a toe into a puddle of self-pity.

The weeks leading up to Christmas were especially bleak for two reasons. The weather was awful, and Jonathan was away. He'd gone to 'take orders' or be ordained, so that he could begin serving as rector of the Kantwell parish church, the living his father had reserved for him. He would be back in time to conduct Christmas services. That was the good news. At the same time, though, he would officially move from the manor house into the parsonage, so we would probably see less of him.

The morning before he left, he had taken me aside. "Poor Kate," he said. "Now I must desert you as well. But I have a surprise for you. Call it an early Christmas present, if you like. We have heard from my brother Alex, and he is coming in the new year. That must cheer you, for I know how you have been desiring to see him again.

And he writes that he is bringing friends with him, so we shall be a very merry party."

"This is good news about Alex coming," I agreed. "I am especially glad for your mother. Who are these friends of his? People you and your parents know as well?"

"Not at all. We have never met them. But I think it a good sign. With friends here at Kantwell, Alex may be more content and in less of a hurry to quit us for London again. The friends are a brother and sister, it seems. Cranford is their name. And another gentleman: a Mr. Keats, I believe. So you see, in just a short time, the house will be full of young people and liveliness. You shall like that, I think."

"I expect to, yes, but one cannot know for certain. Although I feel quite sure of liking your brother, my liking the others equally well may depend on them being equally agreeable."

Jonathan laughed. "Of course. You have expressed yourself well, my little cousin, with the clear intention of being happy and yet with just that bit of hesitation that speaks of a very proper reserve. That is so like you, Kate," he said taking my hand for a moment before releasing it again. "Well, I must be off. Wish me luck and that I might not make a fool of myself over my first sermon when I return."

I watched out the window as he swung up onto his horse and rode away.

I missed Jonathan when he was gone, probably more than I had expected. I still spent the largest share of my time with Rosamund as before, which was pleasant enough. But now there were no more morning rides with my cousin to look forward to, no more chance meetings with him to brighten my days, and only three of us to keep the conversation going at the dinner table. That became a world-class struggle. I felt like we used up all our resources that first night, discussing the contents of Alex's letter. After that, it was like trying to pick lint off a rock to find something to talk about.

Consequently, I did look forward to more people in the house. But something about the news had been bothering me too. It was the business about the brother and sister. It seemed so familiar, and yet for the longest time I couldn't figure out why. Then one morning, when I was out walking by myself, a flash bulb went off in my head. I realized my uneasy feeling had to do with *Mansfield Park*.

Ever since I had noticed the similarities between my current situation and what I could recall about that novel, I had kept wishing I could read it again. But it suddenly seemed much more urgent, because now I remembered that the arrival of a brother and sister at Mansfield Park had stirred up some kind of trouble for Fanny. I knew that much but no more, which meant I knew nothing at all useful. I wanted to be prepared for whatever mischief these Cranfords might bring, and I was convinced that the wisdom and information I so desperately needed could only be found in the pages of the one Jane Austen novel I had foolishly neglected!

I needed help. I needed advice. Then it occurred to me that what I really needed, short of a copy of *Mansfield Park*, was a really big and not so subtle *nudge in the right direction*.

"Cora!" I hollered out into the cold December air.

Mrs. Morris had sent me on an errand to fetch something from the parsonage, and I had chosen to use the time alone to exasperate myself as much as possible about the unfairness of my current circumstances. I hadn't just slipped a little toe in the self-pity puddle this time; I had marched right in with both feet, stomping and tromping around to be sure I'd be soaked through to the skin and as miserable as possible.

I stated my case aloud to anybody who could hear me – in other words, no one at all.

"Grievance number one: alone again." And lonely. It was the very thing my second chance was meant to ensure against. Hadn't I specifically stated that my top priority was to be surrounded by a close and stable family?

"Grievance number two: black bombazine." Cora and Poindexter had known full well – heck, everybody at Crossroads knew it – that I was taking pains to avoid mourning all over again. Yet here I was, up to my neck in black, this time literally as well as figuratively.

"Grievance number three: no romance." Okay, I admit I was on shakier ground here. No one had promised me a Mr. Darcy. Still, the implication everywhere I looked was that it could happen for me too. Circumstances had paralleled *Pride and Prejudice* so closely at first that how could I miss? Everybody understood that, whatever else might go wrong, Lizzy Bennet must get her Mr. Darcy in the end. And I was Lizzy Bennet, or at least I had been before the rug got pulled out from under my feet. Now I didn't know who I was. If I was supposed to be Fanny Price, I was really up the creek without an oar... or a guidebook. It's not like I had any rule against finding romance at Mansfield Park instead of Pemberley, except how was I supposed to navigate my way through that unfamiliar territory without a map?

"Cora!" I hollered again. "You've got to help me!"

No answer. I don't really know what I was expecting. Maybe not that she would magically appear before me, although that would have been nice. But something, anything to show that the universe heard my pain and was prepared to direct my path. How about a shaft of sunlight breaking through the clouds to illuminate the spot where the solution to all my problems lay?

The sun *was* actually shining on the roof of the parsonage when I arrived. Did that mean Jonathan was the answer? I had no idea.

I sighed once, found what I had come for, and then turned to start back. The whole way, I muttered and whined about how nothing had turned out as it should have. At the same time, though, I promised I would jettison my lousy attitude the moment I crossed the threshold of the manor house again.

Somebody somewhere must have heard me after all, because a sort of miracle did occur, making it much easier to keep my promise of ditching my bad attitude.

That evening I returned to my room about the usual time. I was still feeling restless, though, and not tired enough for sleep. So I brought the book I had been attempting to read with me to bed. But when I rearranged the pillows so that I could sit up better, I found something under one of them. It was a package wrapped in brown paper and tied up with a string. "For Hope," it said on it.

That gave me a real jolt. No one in 1809 knew me as Hope. Even *I* had stopped thinking of myself by that name. My fingers were shaking, I noticed, when I reached to pick up the parcel. With such an unmistakable stamp of otherworldliness on it, I was almost afraid to touch it, as if it might blow up in my hand – matter coming in contact with antimatter or whatever.

Nothing happened, though, and when I turned it over I found a sealed envelope tucked under the string. I set the package down again to open the note first. This is what it said:

Dear, Hope –

    I know I should probably call you Kate or Kathleen, but you will always be Hope O'Neil to me. I'm sorry we could not spare you the troubles you have been through, but I trust this little gift will assure you that you are far from forgotten.

Best wishes,
Andrew Poindexter

Poindexter? You could have knocked me over with a feather. If I heard from anybody at Crossroads, I would have bet my right arm it would be Cora. I dropped the letter on the bed and ripped the string and paper from the package, desperately curious to see what was inside. I could hardly believe my eyes when the last of the wrappings fell away. It was a paperback copy of *Mansfield Park*.

"I hope she will prove a well-disposed girl," continued Mrs. Norris, "and be sensible of her uncommon good fortune in having such friends." (Mansfield Park, chapter 1)

Chapter 30
Reader's Digest

A copy of *Mansfield Park*! My prayer had been answered! Except it had been more of a rant than a prayer and Poindexter wasn't God. At least I didn't think he was.

Written inside the front cover, I discovered another note.

I hope you find this helpful. Guard it carefully and, as with my letter, destroy it when you have finished. For obvious reasons, these things must not be seen by anyone in your present time. A.P.

Good, kind Mr. Poindexter.

I hugged my treasure to my chest and spun around in circles until I had dissipated enough energy to be able to sit quietly and read… and read… and read.

Tossing my other book aside, I started *Mansfield Park* at the beginning, racing through it as fast as I could, devouring the story chapter after chapter like potato chips too good to eat just one. I read about poor little Fanny arriving alone and fearful, looked down on by her rich relations and treated much like a servant, with Edmund her only true friend.

I couldn't understand why I hadn't liked the book the first time, because on this second reading I was spellbound. Probably the difference was that now it seemed so much more relevant. Now, I was living in Fanny's time, in the world where her story took place. Now, the people she knew and events she experienced seemed like they might have a direct bearing on my own life.

I all but ignored Maria and Julia, quickly deciding they had no counterparts at Kantwell. But we *did* have the rather distant and intimidating baronet; his sickly and languid wife (complete with pug dog); the older brother, the heir, who was a little reckless with his life, or at least his money; and the younger brother, kind and principled, who was destined to be a clergyman. I laughed when I discovered Mrs. Norris, seeing some similarity, even beyond the name, to our drill sergeant Mrs. Morris.

And then I found the brother and sister pair I had been trying to remember: Mary and Henry Crawford. Yes, of course. Fanny was wary of them from the start, with their jaded sophistication, and I was inclined to trust her judgment. But it could turn out she was wrong. Or it could be that under her good influence and Edmund's, they would improve. The worst part for Fanny, though, was Edmund's fascination with the beautiful Mary Crawford. It looked like she was influencing him more than he was her, and Fanny was forgotten.

On and on I read, late into the night. There was the silliness over visiting Mr. Rushworth's estate, and then the disaster of the play. I didn't like the way Henry Crawford kept flirting with Maria, who was engaged, and stirring up jealousy between the sisters. But Maria married Mr. Rushworth anyway and they left on their honeymoon... all three of them, since Julia went along as the bride's companion. How odd, but maybe not back then.

It felt good to see how Fanny's importance seemed to increase after her female cousins were gone. People were noticing her more and inviting her places, and Mrs. Norris couldn't stand it. Ha! I liked Sir Thomas for finally sticking up for his niece and giving Fanny her due. Better late than never, I suppose.

I had just begun chapter twenty-four – the part where Henry Crawford decides to amuse himself by making Fanny fall in love with him – when my candle sputtered and burned out. I was plunged into darkness and had to give up for the night. It reminded me of when I was a kid and I would read under the covers with a flashlight so my parents wouldn't know. I wanted to finish my book so desperately – mostly horse stories when I was younger and then later Nancy Drew. It almost never worked, though. It was only a question of which would conk out first – me or the flashlight batteries.

In this case, I was just halfway through when the lights went out, and I was not exactly comfortable with where things were headed. I certainly had been right in thinking that the brother and sister pair brought trouble. Mary was bad enough, the way she was trying to get Edmund to give up the church for a more metropolitan lifestyle. But Henry was worse, sporting with the affections of the Bertram sisters first and now Fanny! If the Cranfords were anything like the Crawfords, I'd have to watch out.

I was hoping to wake up at first light. Then, if I skipped breakfast and read fast, I figured I might have time to finish the story before I was needed downstairs. No such luck. I overslept, only waking up with a knock at my door.

"Excuse me, Miss," I heard when the door opened. It was Pittkins, Cousin Rosamund's trusty lady's maid. "I am sorry to disturb you, Miss, but my lady is asking for you. She says if you could come to her chamber as soon as possible, please, she would be very much obliged."

"Yes, of course," I said, trying to prop my eyes open and get moving. I felt a little sluggish after staying up so late and then sleeping heavily. According to the clock, it was only ten – early for Rosamund, who had never summoned me to her room before. Wondering what it could mean, I asked, "Is she unwell?"

"No, Miss," Pittkins replied. Then she left without further explanation.

I quickly got up, splashed water on my face, and then I remembered Poindexter's warning. I had slid my illicit copy of *Mansfield Park* under my pillow when my light went out the night before, but that wouldn't be a safe long-term hiding place. I needed somewhere the chambermaid wouldn't stumble across it when she did up my room. So I opened the wardrobe and tucked my prized book deep inside one of my bags at the bottom. No one would disturb it there.

That done, I pulled the call cord for some assistance getting dressed. Since Mama's maid, who had served for us both, had gone away with her, I now made do with whoever happened to be available for the parts of my toilette that I couldn't manage on my own – stays, buttons, hair styling. Even after all these months, I still hadn't quite gotten used to that part of a Regency lady's life, being as helpless as a two-year-old when it came to dressing and undressing herself.

Rosamund was fully clothed, and Pittkins was just finishing her hair when I arrived. "You wanted to see me, Cousin?" I asked.

"Oh, yes, dear. Come and sit by me. You know me so very well, and I depend upon you. I could not decide what was best without asking your opinion in the matter."

"What is it?" I asked, sitting down, my back to the mirror, in the space she made for me on the bench of her dressing table.

"Sir Alexander desires that I should accompany him to church today..."

Of course. It was Sunday. With all my excitement yesterday, I had completely forgotten.

"...He says that, especially since Jonathan is to take orders and preside as parish rector, I should make more of an effort to come, and that I should not wait until Christmas to begin..."

Church attendance was taken as a matter of course here; I had discovered that early on, and I didn't mind a bit. However, Rosamund, with her low energy and low spirits, had found the exertion too daunting. She virtually never left the house for anything at all.

"...The question is, do you suppose am I strong enough? I would like to go, but I would not like to swoon or fall asleep or otherwise embarrass myself or my family. What do *you* think, Kate?"

"I believe Sir Alexander is correct, that it is the right thing for you to do. More to the point, though, I believe you are well ready and able to do it. Consider how much stronger you are now! Every day, we are walking farther together, are we not? I daresay the distance from the carriage to your place in church can be no farther than the ten turns around the drawing room you have got used to doing."

"I suppose that is true enough."

"With me on one side and your husband on the other, there can be no question of your stumbling or swooning. And as for your falling asleep, my lady, it will be the curate's fault in giving a boring sermon if that should happen, for you have had no laudanum in nearly a week. Is that not so?"

"Indeed. Why, Kate, you begin to make me feel as if I can do it after all."

"Of course you can. We will do it together – today for practice so you are more confident at Christmas. Think how proud Jonathan will be to see you there when he begins his first service."

It was a huge step forward for Rosamund, and everything went fine. People were kind and seemed encouraged (and very curious) to have the first lady of the parish back with them. Rosamund was pretty tired afterward, but I think she was also darned pleased with herself. So was I. I wanted to see her fully recovered – the sooner, the better – and not just so I would be free to return to Carding someday. I wanted her well for her own sake and her family's.

It was a good day, but I didn't get back to my book until evening. I made sure to have extra candles standing by this time, so I wouldn't have my reading cut short again.

Beginning where I had left off, I was appalled to discover that things went rapidly from bad to worse for poor Fanny Price. First Henry tortures her with attentions she doesn't want. Then, when she refuses to marry him, she's sent away from the home she loves at Mansfield Park (I could relate to this part especially) by her uncle, as a punishment. On top of that, he about breaks her heart by accusing her of ingratitude, the farthest thing from the truth, if he only knew. Badly done, Sir Thomas! Badly done!

And Edmund is no help. He still has his rose-colored glasses on about the Crawfords from being under Mary's spell.

I raced on, worried that Fanny would succumb to the pressure of all those she loved and marry Henry Crawford. *I* knew he was a villain. Deep down, Fanny did too, but she seemed to be wavering. In my hurry, I practically blew right past Tom's life-threatening illness. Fanny missed it too, and other developments at Mansfield Park, since she was still exiled in Portsmouth.

I shouldn't have worried about Fanny, though. The Crawfords showed their true colors in the end; I suppose they couldn't help it. Fanny and Edmund escaped their clutches unscathed – suffering shock, painful distress, and heartache, but no permanent harm. The same can't be said for Maria Rushworth, however. And then Julia ran off with Mr. Yates! Kind of racy stuff, actually. I'd forgotten.

Ah, but then it was finally time to put guilt and misery to bed. Hooray! Just as Jane Austen writes in the opening of the last chapter, I'm always relieved to 'quit such odious subjects' and get to the happy ending. Fanny is brought home to Mansfield and restored, acknowledged by all (except Mrs. Norris) as the wisest and best almost-daughter of the house, and the only child but Edmund who didn't bring disgrace on it.

Ultimately, Julia, now Mrs. Yates, begs forgiveness and is welcomed back into the family. Tom is reformed and becomes a dutiful son. Maria is packed away to an obscure existence with Mrs. Norris as her caretaker. And the Crawfords are never heard of again. Edmund is miserable for a time – over Mary's bad character and his own bad judgment – but he soon learns to judge better. He is not inconsolable, as it turns out, and he finds his true consolation right under his nose in Fanny Price.

So Fanny – the humble, the timid, the good, and the deserving – got the prize and her happy ending, just as she should. After all the abuse she had endured, who wouldn't be glad to see her rewarded for her steadfastness in the end? By the time I finished reading her story, she had won me over. I started to think that if I *had* been cast in her role in this version of *Mansfield Park* (*Kantwell Park*?), it might not be so impossible a fit after all. I might not be timid or even particularly humble, but I flattered myself (as Mr. Collins might say) that Fanny and I had other good traits in common. I considered myself a very loyal person and quite capable of standing up against pressure for what I believed was right, as she had done. I hoped that meant I'd get my happy ending too.

But was my happy ending supposed to be with Jonathan? Is that what *Mansfield Park* was telling me? I didn't feel like I was in love with him, at least not yet. I liked him a lot and considered him a good friend, but that's as far as it went for now.

I wondered when Fanny's feelings for Edmund changed from friendship, or a kind of sisterly affection, into romantic love. Did she recognize it right away, that he was the one, I mean? Did it hit her in a flash of revelation or did it sneak up on her? I decided I would need to read the book again to catch the subtleties. I also decided that I should reexamine my feelings when I saw Jonathan again.

"It was our darling wish that you might be attached to each other, and we were persuaded that it was so…" (Emma, chapter 46)

Chapter 31
Points of Attachment

In the last week leading up to Christmas, I read *Mansfield Park* through twice more – looking for the subtleties, looking for what Jane Austen might be trying to tell me between the lines. But other than proving through Fanny that there can be strength even in meekness, I'm not sure I discovered anything insightful or revolutionary. I certainly knew the story well enough by then, though, that I expected to be able to put the knowledge to good use if similar situations cropped up in my own life.

The Bentley family didn't have any big plans for Christmas other than a bit of a to-do over Jonathan's ordination and first sermon. There would be church in the morning, of course, then special things to eat that night at dinner, and a bowl of punch for the servants. As far as I knew, that was about it. No decorations or cards or shopping or presents, apparently. I guess all that hoopla hadn't been invented yet. Christmas was still more of a simple holy day than the holiday extravaganza it became in the twentieth century.

I missed *some* parts of the hoopla I was used to, like having a tree. But without electric twinkle lights, I suppose it wouldn't have been the same anyway. Mostly I missed the people, though, all my absent family and friends in every time and place.

I can't say I truly missed Alex Bentley, since I hadn't had a chance to get reacquainted with him yet. I thought at first, though, that it was too bad he and his friends wouldn't arrive at Kantwell in time for Christmas, which might have made it seem more festive – having my host family complete and a few extra people in the house besides. The more I considered, though, the more I could see it was better this way. Jonathan deserved his moment in the sun without his brother stealing the spotlight from him.

He came home on Christmas Eve, Jonathan, that is. Since reading *Mansfield Park*, I had been full of anticipation for seeing him again, and wondering if I would feel different in light of what I now knew about Fanny and Edmund. I confess I *did* feel a little thrill of excitement when I first heard his voice in the foyer. Almost immediately, though, that little jolt of juice shorted out and died, giving way to the more standard warm and friendly feelings I had associated with Jonathan before. I concluded that I was clearly NOT in love with him just yet. But I was perfectly willing to be. And gazing up at him in the pulpit the next day, I thought it wouldn't be that difficult.

Jonathan, as far as I know, did a pretty good job on his sermon. Of course, he had the tried-and-true story of the first Christmas to work with, which must have been an advantage on his inaugural voyage. Sure, there were some minor stumbles and stutters (to be expected in a newbie), and Jonathan spent more time focusing on his notes than making eye contact with the congregation.

He did look at me pretty often, though, and I looked right back. His light blue eyes had a translucency that made a person feel like he could have nothing to hide. That was a good thing in a clergy-man. And, to quote Mrs. Gardiner, *there was something pleasing about his mouth when he spoke*, which I spent quite a bit of time noticing. I also started noticing something else. Not a twitch, ex-actly, because that sounds unattractive and this wasn't. It was more like a little tic he had with his left eye, when he was trying to get a certain word out. It seemed almost like a wink, and when I imagined it was for my benefit alone, I found it quite charming.

I imagined that and a lot more during the hour or so in church. Some of my thoughts might even have been considered a little irrev-erent. Consequently, I had difficulty answering Jonathan's questions later that day.

"So what do you think, Kate?" he asked. "How did I do? Was my sermon any good?"

Even though I had given him my full and undivided attention throughout the service, I'd spent much more time studying the man than his message, wondering about the implications for my domes-tic happiness instead of for my soul. I could feel myself blushing, and my tongue seemed tied in knots. I was so worried he'd guess the truth that I couldn't get a coherent word out.

"I understand," he said, crestfallen after seeing my reaction. "No good, then. Well, I'll try to do better next time. I have years to practice."

"No! No, that's not what I meant at all, Jonathan," I finally managed. "I thought you did very well indeed. It is only that I was so anxious for your sake – wanting you to do well and thinking how nervous I should be in your place – that I found it difficult to concentrate. I am ashamed to say that my mind wandered. Forgive me."

His face brightened up again right away. He said, "Of course. Next time, I will be more comfortable, and you may be more comfortable for me. I shall look forward to your appraisal of my second sermon, then. I value your opinion so."

"Thank you. I trust I will do better at listening next time too."

"For today, your solicitude on my behalf is more than enough. It was reassuring to know, as I stood by myself, looking out over the congregation, that I had a friend, somebody who would always judge me through charitable eyes. Am I right to think of you in this way, Kate?"

"Yes, Jonathan, I am that, but surely I am not the only one. After all, I have heard both your parents praise your efforts today."

"True," he said. Then he dropped his eyes. "But I believe I covet your approbation even more than theirs. Kate, I…"

He stopped when a servant came into the room, announcing dinner. I waited, sensing that Jonathan had been on the verge of saying something important to me, maybe even asking me an important question. But he didn't finish whatever it was.

"Well," he said instead, "shall we go in?"

I debated later if I was disappointed or relieved that Jonathan had been interrupted. The fanatical romantic in me thinks there can't be anything more wonderful than a proposal. However, as I had already found out with George Galloway, unless I was ready to accept the proposal, things could get awkward.

And I wasn't, I realized. I wasn't ready to accept a proposal from Jonathan yet, any more than I had been from George. If that's really what Jonathan had in mind, it wouldn't necessarily be a bad idea, just premature maybe. Like when Darcy proposed to Lizzy at Hunsford. It wasn't the wrong guy; it was the wrong time. She

206

couldn't accept him then. She didn't love Darcy yet – or at least she didn't know it – and she certainly didn't understand him. Their story needed time to play out, their relationship to develop in all its shades and colors. It took Darcy's letter and then his heroic actions rescuing Lydia for that. Then, when he offered again, Lizzy was ready and could return his love without reservation.

I sighed every time I thought of it. Lizzy hadn't 'settled' and neither had Fanny Price! She didn't take Henry Crawford when she really wanted Edmund. I didn't want to settle either – not too soon or for less than I believed was possible. I wanted it all, and until somebody sent tingles right down to the tips of my toenails and made me feel like I was glowing brighter than a shooting star, I had no business getting married.

So, I had to keep my head straight, to balance out my rampaging sensibilities with some good sense. No getting carried away with romantic ideas of a Regency proposal… another Regency proposal, that is. No being run away with by my feelings, as Mr. Collins would say. No jumping the gun, literally or figuratively. (Hadn't I learned that lesson in track?)

I needed to be patient and let my story play out too. After all, I'd only been living this new life of mine for about six months. What was the rush? I wouldn't want all the excitement over too soon, would I? The man of my destiny was worth waiting for a little while longer. I was sure of that much. Only time would tell whether he would turn out to be a Mr. Darcy or an Edmund Bertram.

The weeks after Christmas were lonely ones again as I continued to miss my family. I still enjoyed Rosamund's company, but I saw very little of Jonathan, even though he was back in the area. He spent most of each day at the parsonage now, saying he was much occupied with organizing his household and learning his new duties as rector. He did come up to the manor house nearly every evening for dinner, though, which gave me some time to get to know him and my feelings for him better.

I took deliberate note of his good attributes, instead of just taking them for granted as I probably had done before. He was very kind to his mother always, I noticed, respectful of his father, and polite to the servants too. He had an air of self-confidence about him without being arrogant. That was a refreshing change over a lot of the young men I had known, in both past and present lives. Even his looks were growing on me. I observed, I admired, and I nurtured any tender feelings for him that I noticed sprouting up. A little water here, a little fertilizer there. After all, nothing good grows in either the heart or the garden without at least a little encouragement.

Day by day, I was more convinced by how Jonathan behaved towards me that he held me in some special affection. How much, I couldn't be sure, but I wanted to be able to return that affection honestly, if and when the time came.

I longed for news from my family. Mama had sent me a brief note to let me know she had arrived in Carding safely, but nothing since. So I was thrilled, when Hawthorn was delivering the letters one day on his silver tray, that the last one was for me.

"It is from my sister Lucy," I told Rosamund when I recognized the handwriting on the outside. I had been sitting with her that afternoon, as I almost always did, and we were playing cribbage, which she had taught me.

"How nice," she said. "You will, of course, wish to read your letter at once. Go right ahead, dear. Our game will wait. I will just close my eyes and rest a bit until you are finished."

"Thank you, Cousin Rosamund. I believe I shall. Lucy writes in a very tight hand, though, and sometimes crosses her lines to make the best use of the paper. It is often difficult to make the words out. I will just take this over to the window where the light is better."

That was true enough, but my real reason for moving away was for a little privacy. I knew I wasn't very good at hiding my emotions, and lately even the thought of a letter from home had been enough to reduce me to tears.

My dearest Kate,

I hope that you are in every way well, and our cousins at Kantwell too. Mama has asked that you give them all her compliments.

Be assured, we are also well. Carmen and Matilda continue where they are for the time being, joining us for a dinner at Coleswold about once a week. Matilda and Mrs. Abernathy, who both send their love to you, are getting on famously. Matilda has decided that she was meant to teach piano, and Mrs. Abernathy, who never learnt, has been given the honor of being her first pupil! Are you not amazed? Meanwhile, Carmen has all but been adopted by our cousins at Laurelwood. She now has the brother she has always wanted and a perfect excuse to play at cricket and other boys' games. As for my mother, Mr. Sotheby (he is so good to us!) has undertaken to new furnish the dower house for her use. Until it is ready, however, she is very happily settled in with us at the main house.

Miss Sotheby continues here with us as well. I had expected that, once we returned from out wedding trip and I took her place as mistress of the house, she would prefer to return to London. But it seems she has developed a rather strong attachment to this place, which I believe we must credit to the frequent attentions of Mr. Frederick Kingsley. Although he would not have been my choice, his style seems to suit her. She is as giddy as a school girl when he is expected, and no one can deny it would be an excellent match for her as to situation and fortune. So perhaps she will not be staying with us that long after all.

Whether Miss Sotheby stays or goes, however, there will always be room for you here at Coleswold, my dearest sister. You must know that your absence is always felt very deeply and especially so today, at Christmas. It is very hard to think of the two empty places at our table this year – yours and Papa's – and how much worse for you, all alone and far from home. And yet I know your optimistic nature, Kate. I daresay you are far too cheerful and sensible to spend much time feeling sorry for yourself.

I depend on it. As you yourself have told me many times before, we are always happiest when we stop to count our blessings. Well then, I am thankful today for the Christ child of Christmas. I am also grateful for my darling husband, our comfortable home, and for our own little one coming in a few months. It is a personal joy for me, and I believe it is what will prove to be the saving of my mother as well. The burden of her heart seems to lighten day by day in her anticipation of this addition to our family. That is the natural order of things, and we must accept it, I suppose; the old make way for the young.

You see, I am determined to take up your philosophy and console myself with the new blessings God, in His goodness, has chosen to send my way. However, on no account will I consent to parting with you, Kate – not for much longer and certainly not forever. Promise me you will be home in the spring. My joy will not be complete without you.

Write soon with all your news from Kantwell.

Yours, etc., Lucy

Rosamund didn't stir when I got up to leave the room, sobbing almost uncontrollably, so I hoped she had fallen asleep and would not notice I was gone for a while. I hurried up to my own room and closed the door behind me until I could recover.

The letter I expected to cheer me up had the opposite effect instead. What was the matter with me? News of my loved ones, all well and happy, should have given my mood a huge boost; I freely admit it. On one level, it did give me comfort, but mostly I was thinking how I was missing out, how I should be there to share these moments with them, how exciting things were happening even for Miss Sotheby but not for me. Lucy had obviously given me way too much credit. Lately, I'd spent a lot more time feeling sorry for myself than counting my blessings.

I put it down to homesickness… homesickness times two. I'd had the ordinary, garden variety before – every time we had moved while I was a kid and when I went away to summer camp. This was different, though. When we moved, I got to take my parents with me. When I was away at summer camp, I knew it was only for a couple of weeks. This time, I had left behind everything I'd ever known to make this leap, and I could never go back. Still, it was what I had chosen, and I'd been happy… until, one by one, each of my new supports had been washed away too. Lucy left me first, which was supposed to be for only about a month, and then Papa forever. I'd lost Carmen and Matilda when I came north, and finally Mama.

After about another bucket of tears, I shook myself and looked hard to see if I could find any trace of that cheerful, sensible, optimistic person Lucy had mentioned. Nope. She was totally M.I.A.

Fanny had just reached her eighteenth year, when the society of the village received an addition in the brother and sister of Mrs. Grant, a Mr. and Miss Crawford... (Mansfield Park, chapter 4)

Chapter 32
Arrivals and Rivals

It took a full forty-eight hours for this most recent low to pass, before I was able to see that my glass, even if it wasn't quite half full, it wasn't completely empty either.

I had my health, for starters. Kantwell wasn't a bad place. It was certainly comfortable and I was treated well – much better than Fanny had been. Mrs. Morris could be bossy, but she didn't pick on me like the runt of the litter and make my life a living hell. Sir Alexander didn't terrify me either. I had a good relationship with Rosamund and the satisfaction of knowing I was helping her in an important way. Then there was my friendship with Jonathan. That was something good and it might turn into more. Alex and his friends were due to arrive any time, which was bound to add interest to our day-to-day existence. And, if all else failed, I could look forward to when Rosamund was well enough that I could go home to my family again. Whatever the disadvantages of my current situation, it wouldn't last forever.

There. I had taken what was apparently my own advice and counted the positive things in my life. And I did feel better. I even got up a little early the next day to take a ride before Rosamund would need me.

Cleopatra nickered softly when she was led out, as if she were happy to see me. I still missed Horatio, but Jonathan had been smart (and generous) in choosing Cleopatra for my use, I reminded myself. She was always at my disposal. What a luxury! And another blessing.

Off we went, just the two of us, into the cold, crisp morning air. I'd promised the groom that I would keep to the gardens near the house, so he wouldn't feel obliged to accompany me. And that's what I did, at least at first. Then I couldn't resist a long gallop down the tree-lined avenue. It was positively invigorating and got my blood moving again to where, by the time I got back, I was simply glad to be alive.

As I approached the stables, I could see a lot of extra activity there. An unfamiliar carriage stood out front, empty, and extra horses too. A man with his back to me seemed to be directing the servants what to do. He turned then and saw me.

"Well, well," he said, smiling, "can this be my little cousin Kate? How you have grown since last we met. Here, do permit me to help you down."

"Good to see you again, Alex," I said, allowing him to ease me to the ground, where I could fully appreciate how tall he was.

"How comes it that you are out all alone, Cousin? Where is that brother of mine? If he had any chivalry or any sense, he would not waste the chance to accompany such a fine young lady on a morning's ride."

"Jonathan does often accompany me," I pointed out, trying to ignore the rest. "In fact, it is to him that I owe the loan of Cleopatra, here. He knew nothing of my plans for this morning, though. It was quite an impulse of the moment."

"An excellent impulse too, it seems, for it has put a very becoming smile on your lips and roses in your cheeks. Now, come into the house and meet my friends. We must rescue them from an awkward silence, I fear, for I had to abandon them at once to see to the horses. Only my father is there, and I am sure none of them can be easy about that." He laughed, took my gloved hand, pulling it through to rest on his arm, and we started toward the house.

"We have all been looking forward to your arrival," I said, "you and your friends. But we did not know exactly when to expect you. I suppose your mother is still in her room. Does Jonathan know you are here?"

"Someone was sent to fetch him, I believe. Ah! And here he comes."

I followed Alex's line of sight and saw Jonathan hurrying across the lawn towards us. Alex quickened his pace, and I matched it so that in another minute the three of us converged near the front steps. Alex released me to briefly embrace his brother. Then they were both laughing and vigorously shaking hands.

"I see you have already become reacquainted with Kate," Jonathan said. "Does not she look well? And she has worked wonders with our mother."

Alex turned to study me again, saying, "Yes, she is indeed a treasure. I perceived it at once. I hope you have been taking proper care of her, Brother. But now I am here, I shall be glad to assist you."

Fortunately, I only had to put up with this nonsense for about thirty seconds before Alex turned his attention to his brother again. The two of them joked back and forth and threw barbs at each other as we entered the house. It did my heart good to see it. And I knew just that quickly that Jonathan's prediction was right; it was going to be impossible for me to truly dislike Alex. He was charming as all get out and appealing in a slightly larger-than-life way.

Rosamund was just descending the stairs when we came in. Her whole face lit up when she caught sight of Alex, as if the sun rose and set only because of him. He went up the steps to meet his mother, and she fell into his arms, tears of joy slipping down her cheeks. "Alex, Alex," she said, as if in prayer, "you are come back to me at last."

I turned away to avoid intruding any longer on their private moment. Jonathan looked at me and whispered, "You see how it is. Did not I tell you he was her favorite?"

"Perhaps. It is only natural, however, that she should make more of a fuss over someone she has not seen for a long time."

Jonathan only smiled, but a bit sadly, I thought.

We went into the drawing room then, where we found the others. Sir Alexander already knew the newcomers by this time, but Rosamund, Jonathan, and I had never set eyes on them before. Alex made the introductions.

Miss Delora Cranford was not just moderately attractive; she was downright beautiful. There was no denying it. She was at least two inches taller than I, and blonde – more like my former self, in fact. Smartly dressed too, although with her figure, she would have made an old flour sack look mighty good. I was not the only one who noticed either. Jonathan could barely take his eyes off her long enough to be polite to the rest of us.

There was eye candy for me too, though. The brother, Harris, was almost as beautiful in a virile, entirely masculine expression of the same set of genes. I could appreciate without staring, though. In that respect, I felt like I behaved better than Jonathan. And, forewarned as I was, I was determined not to be taken in by a handsome face or fancy manners. Henry Crawford had looked pretty good on the outside too.

Mr. James Keats had the misfortune of being the only truly plain one in the room, which maybe, as with Mary Bennet, caused him to work harder to impress in other ways. He was certainly the most gregarious from the start. After we were all seated, he chattered away almost non-stop about the little trials experienced on their trip from London and how delighted they all were at seeing Kantwell.

No one seemed to mind. Sir Alexander was not a great conversationalist. Rosamund looked content to sit by Alex's side, holding his hand and often gazing up at him affectionately. With no demands on me, I was free to sit back and observe while Mr. Keats talked on with only occasional contributions from one of the others.

"Cease and desist, old boy," Mr. Cranford finally told his friend in a mild tone. "No one doubts that your stories are worth listening to, but you must pace yourself. Save a little something for tomorrow and the day after. I am interested in hearing somebody else talk for a change. Miss Barrett..."

I jumped at hearing my name called so unexpectedly and by Harris Cranford.

"...Miss Barrett, I am interested in hearing from you, and so will my sister be. Your cousin has told us only enough about you to raise our curiosity. You must now satisfy our thirst for knowledge."

"Yes, please do, Miss Barrett," said Miss Cranford in a voice that reminded me of maple syrup – flowing slowly and sticky sweet.

"Very well, but I am quite an ordinary girl," I said. "I doubt anything I can tell you will prove worthy of so much curiosity..." unless, of course, I was to mention my time-traveling experiences, which probably wouldn't be wise. "What is it you wish to know?"

"To begin with, are you musical?" asked Miss Cranford.

"I play the pianoforte and sing a little," I answered.

Then I was surprised to hear Sir Alexander pipe up, saying, "Miss Barrett is being modest, Miss Cranford. She is an excellent musician in every respect."

"Yes, yes," agreed Rosamund. "I enjoy her playing above almost anything else in this world."

"Then I hope you will consent to play for us tonight," Alex said.

I nodded, gratified but a little embarrassed by the praise.

"Very good," said Harris Cranford. "It is established by these reliable witnesses that you are highly musical, Miss Barrett. Is it also true that you to have lived all your life in the country? In Hampshire?"

Again, what shocking stories I could have told! But I said that yes, it was true.

"Then I suppose you have the usual country accomplishments, by which I mean you know how to ride tolerably well."

"Tolerably well, yes."

"Excellent. Here is another point on which my sister will be envious. Like most other girls brought up in town, she never learnt to know one end of a horse from the other."

"For shame, Harris," Delora complained. "You exaggerate my ignorance, although it is quite true that I never learnt to ride and now I sincerely wish I had."

"*I* can teach you, Miss Cranford," Jonathan quickly volunteered. "It is not so very difficult, and I would be honored if you would allow me to instruct you."

Delora rewarded him with a radiant smile. "Would you really, Mr. Bentley? That is very kind. I daresay you will find me a terribly stupid pupil."

"Terribly stupid," repeated Harris, shaking his head.

"I cannot image that to be true, Miss Cranford," said Jonathan.

"Very well, Mr. Bentley," she said. "After having received fair warning, if you still insist, I am yours to direct. Shall we begin tomorrow?"

"By all means, if the weather permits. I will look forward to it." Then he turned to me, as if suddenly remembering I existed. "Kate, you will not mind if Miss Cranford borrows Cleopatra, will you? I think she would be the best mount for a beginner. Unless of course you mean to ride her yourself. In that case, I will ask Miss Cranford to put off her first lesson until another day."

215

Everybody was looking at me. What could I say? I said that *of course* I wouldn't mind, that I had never any intention at all of riding tomorrow myself, and that I would be prodigiously pleased to have Miss Cranford borrow Cleopatra, who was, after all, only mine by his kindness anyway. (I hoped any feelings to the contrary didn't show.)

Wow! That hadn't taken long. Now I knew exactly how Fanny felt – forgotten when the new beauty hit the scene and even her horse borrowed right out from under her for the sake of the other. There was no longer any doubt in my mind. I was living in *Mansfield Park*, and I had just met my rival.

That idea drew me up short. If I considered Miss Cranford a rival, then that must mean I wanted Jonathan after all. Or was it just generalized jealousy? No woman likes to feel she's being thrown over for someone else, even by a guy she didn't care *three straws* about the day before, as Lydia might express it. On the other hand, maybe this was exactly what I needed to make me know my own mind.

As many times as I'd read *Mansfield Park* by this time, I still wasn't sure when exactly Fanny fell in love with Edmund. Maybe it was only when Mary Crawford threatened to take him from her that Fanny woke up and admitted her true feelings. That's the way it was in *Emma* too. Until Emma thought she might lose him to Harriet, she hadn't realized that she was in love with Mr. Knightley and couldn't possibly live without him. Jealousy is a powerful force. But what a painful way to discover the truth!

I did at least have the satisfaction of outperforming my rival on the pianoforte that evening. With Matilda out of earshot, I had no reason to hold back. After Delora had already played – competently but not brilliantly – I let her have it with both barrels. It sort of backfired on me though, at least with Jonathan. I received my compliments from the listeners, Harris being the most vocal among them, and then Delora commenced her sad song of self-deprecation.

"My goodness, that was wonderful, Miss Barrett," she told me in her honeyed tones. Then, turning immediately to Jonathan, she sighed and added, "Now you see me for the poor pupil I really am, Mr. Bentley. I daresay the money spent on my music lessons was all thrown away, for clever Miss Barrett has far eclipsed me even without an expensive London master to instruct her. How you expect to teach me anything about riding, I do not know."

Jonathan eagerly rushed in, heroically saving poor Delora from thinking so badly of herself, saying, "Now, now, Miss Cranford, you mustn't say such things, even though Miss Barrett does play so well. Although your playing was not perhaps quite as accomplished in a technical sense, interpretation is where you excel. You play with superior expression. I am convinced that is something that cannot be taught. It comes from inside, from the heart. I expect it will be the same with riding. You will take to it naturally, and I will have very little to do."

"I thank you, kind sir," she said with a little bow of her head. "You have gallantly saved me from the fate of mediocrity. I cannot bear to be only average in anything, you know. I would much rather not try at all. But I will remember what you said and not be afraid next time."

Ugh! What drivel! I could barely stop myself from rolling my eyes and gagging. How long would I have to listen to these two carry on in such a nauseating way? She was bad enough; I had run into her type before. She had obviously made an art form out of bending men around her pinky finger. But Jonathan! How it pained me to watch someone I cared for reduced to lapdog status, slobbering all over himself and groveling at her feet like Mr. Collins with Lady Catherine, especially when I wasn't sure she really liked him. After purring contentedly for Jonathan, the next minute Delora turned around and flirted just as outrageously with Alex and even some with Mr. Keats.

She was Mary Crawford all over again, only worse. How could Jonathan be so blind? Did he actually prefer that conniving female to me? That was the more important question.

I really had to talk myself down off the ledge that night... and several times more after that. No matter what happened, I couldn't allow Jonathan's ridiculous crush to derail me. Hadn't I sworn to let the story play out, to trust that all would come right in the end? Well, maybe this uncomfortable exercise was a necessary part of that process. Maybe Jonathan needed to sow some wild hay seeds with Delora before he could settle down with me. He might need this experience to mature him, and he might appreciate me more in the long run because of it. What was that line in *Mansfield Park* that I liked so much? I had to go look it up again.

When it was quite natural that it should be so, and not a week earlier, Edmund did cease to care about Miss Crawford, and became as anxious to marry Fanny as Fanny herself could desire.

That was the key; when it was quite natural, or in other words, when the time was exactly right. Not a week, a day, or even a minute before. I just had to be patient. Jonathan would eventually come to his senses... I hoped.

After a short pause, however, the subject still continued, and was discussed with unabated eagerness, every one's inclination increasing by the discussion, and a knowledge of the inclination of the rest. (Mansfield Park, chapter 13)

Chapter 33
A Different Diversion

"Well, Kate, what do you think of her? Is not she the most charming creature you have ever come across?"

This was Jonathan's question when we happened to be alone the next morning at breakfast. Unbelievable. I decided to play dumb. "Who?" I asked.

"Miss Cranford, of course! I do not know when, if ever, I have seen her equal for beauty, countenance, and grace."

"She is beautiful, I grant you." I probably should have left it at that, but I couldn't help myself. I ran on with some of the rest I was thinking. "Are you certain, though, that she is what she appears? Are you certain that you know the level of acquaintance between herself and your brother? Alex knew her first and may consider he has some sort of prior claim. You must not risk offending him, or risk your own heart, by trespassing with unwanted attentions to Miss Cranford."

Jonathan tossed his head back and laughed as if I had just told the most hilarious joke he had ever heard. "Oh, Kate, you are too amusing, speaking of 'claims' and 'trespassing' as if Miss Cranford were a diamond mine in India or somewhere. I only meant to admire her and hear your opinion."

"Forgive me if I have been too presumptuous, Jonathan, but you did seem as if you had taken a very particular interest in Miss Cranford."

"Of course! How could I help it? We do not get many visitors of her quality here at Kantwell. I like her brother and Mr. Keats just as much, but I do not intend to marry one of them either. As for your kind concern for *my* brother's feelings, though, I can set your mind at ease there. Alex has told me that no special understanding exists between them – at least not yet – so never fear."

I chewed on this piece of news for a minute. "Am I to understand that Alex volunteered this information to you out of a clear blue sky?"

"No. I was curious, so I asked him how things stood."

"You asked just out of curiosity."

"Well, yes, and to avoid any possibility of a misunderstanding, I suppose. One never knows where things might lead to, and it is best to be prepared."

"To avoid a misunderstanding like the sort I cautioned you about a moment ago, do you mean?"

"Exactly."

"Then perhaps what I said was not so ridiculous after all."

"I never said it was. I was only amused by how a woman's mind seems to jump very rapidly from simple admiration to love, and from love to marriage. I met Miss Cranford only yesterday, you know."

"Yes, I know."

I was *not* reassured. Hadn't Mr. Darcy said something remarkably similar when Caroline teased him about his admiring Elizabeth's fine eyes? Well, Caroline had been right to worry, and maybe I was too.

~~*~~

Although they said their plans were not yet 'firmly fixed,' it looked like Alex and his friends would be staying at Kantwell for at least a month – plenty of time for things to develop for better or for worse.

Jonathan continued to fawn all over Delora, I'm sorry to say. And it seemed to me that Harris was giving me a lot of attention too, although I decided it probably meant nothing at all. If he was a confirmed flirt, like Henry Crawford, he didn't have much choice; other than his sister, I was currently the only girl around.

The next truly significant development, though, was Sir Alexander's announcement that he was leaving to tend to some business affairs – something to do with his investments in Cornwall – which he said would probably keep him away for about a fortnight.

I shouldn't have been surprised. According to the *Mansfield Park* script, the cat had to go away so that the mice could begin to play. Next, I fully expected one of the mice would propose exactly that: a play. But it was something else instead.

After a week at Kantwell, and with Sir Alexander gone only a day or two, I noticed a certain restlessness among our metropolitan visitors. Although they had at first raved about the beauty of the country and the pleasures it afforded, I think the novelty was already wearing off. They had been for walks. They had been for rides, with Delora catching on quickly and excelling at it (as I suspected she would). The men had twice been out to shoot. But that was only when the weather permitted, which in January wasn't every day.

One evening, after being trapped indoors too long by unrelenting rain, they reached their breaking point. Rosamund had gone to bed early, so it was only we six young people sitting around in the drawing room. Alex paced like a caged tiger. I was behind the pianoforte, lazily tinkling the keys in a half-hearted effort to compose a new tune. Jonathan, Harris, Delora, and James Keats were playing cards.

"Ha!" Jonathan exclaimed. "I win."

Harris dropped his cards and came right up out of his chair, saying, "Who cares? You win or I do – what does any of it matter? It is all such a bore."

"Shall we play again?" asked James Keats. "If Harris is in no fit mood to continue, perhaps Miss Barrett will consent to take his place."

"I have had enough as well," Delora remarked, tossing her cards in the middle of the table and covering a yawn with her fan. "There must be something else we can do."

"You could try a book," suggested Jonathan. "We have a very fine library here. I would be happy to show you."

"Thank you, no. I couldn't possibly settle down to a book, at least not so early in the day. Why, when I am in London, there is always a party or a ball or a soiree. I am never home before one or two and rarely abed before three or four. Is not that so, Harris?"

"I will verify the fact," he answered, "and the same could be said for any one of us."

"But we have none of that here," Alex said with a heavy sigh. "Here in the country, if we are to have entertainment, we must make it for ourselves."

No one had any answer to that, not at first. Then Harris said, "Well, let us begin, then."

"Begin what," asked Keats.

"Begin making our own entertainment. We have six good minds between us. Surely we can come up with some scheme for amusement."

"Could we give a ball?" Delora asked excitedly, looking at Alex.

He shook his head. "Not one of any size or style. Not without my father's sponsorship, at least. Too expensive, and where would we get a quality orchestra so far from London? Besides, Kate is in mourning and could not dance."

It was good of him to remember me. I smiled my thanks in his direction.

"Perhaps some sort of an evening party, then," Keats suggested, "with music, cards, and just a light supper. There would not be too much trouble or expense in that, surely. How many people could we entice to come, do you suppose, Jonathan?"

Before Jonathan could answer, though, Harris jumped in.

"Where is the novelty in such a scheme? What is it we have been doing every night since we arrived if not eating, playing cards, and listening to music? No, we must find a fresh idea, bring some imagination to bear."

"Let us put on a proper gambling hell, then," said Alex, "like those found in the clubs of London where the stakes are high. I daresay our neighbors will find that more exhilarating than a stodgy Whist party where one risks nothing beyond boredom."

"That is a famous idea!" said Delora, and the enthusiasm built from there.

"Perhaps we could lay our hands on a proper Faro box or two," Keats proposed, "and a number of round tables for Speculation."

Harris quickly added his suggestions. "And to do the scheme justice, we must offer Ecarte and require minimum bids for every game."

The idea had caught like a wildfire, starting from one tiny spark and building to an all-consuming conflagration faster than green grass goes through a goose. Everybody was talking at the same time, one outrageous thought piling up on top of another in and out-of-control way. I watched in horror from my safe spot behind the pianoforte without having a single clue what to do about it. I wanted to put four fingers in my mouth, give an ear-splitting whistle, and then tell them, "Hold your horses just a cotton-picking minute!" If it had been my house, maybe I would have. But I knew it wasn't my place to say or do anything. Instead, I stared daggers at Jonathan's head. He'd just been sitting there like a useless bump on a log with a sort of dazed expression on his face. I guess my message got through to him. Anyway, something finally roused him to action.

"Wait!" he said loudly, getting to his feet. "Let us think this through before we get carried too far down the wrong road. Alex, you know as well as I do that your father would not approve of turning his house into a gambling parlor for neighbors and strangers. Can you deny it?"

"Calm yourself, dear Brother. What I propose is nothing so shocking as all that. I am not suggesting we pattern ourselves on some underhanded back-alley operation. It would be done very tastefully and above board. I know you have little experience in such things, but I assure you that some of the most elegant establish-ments in London offer gambling as a harmless amusement. No one need be ashamed to participate. Why, some of the highest ranking nobles in the land have proudly won and lost vast fortunes in such places." He tossed the last line off as a joke with a blasé smile. His friends saw the humor and laughed. "If we find it cannot be done in a respectable manner, we may give up the scheme in the end. In the meantime, though, we shall have had the diversion of planning and preparing. Where is the harm in that? However, you need not take part if you do not like it."

I didn't like it; it looked like nothing but trouble to me, especial-ly in light of what I'd learned from *Mansfield Park*. Maybe I should explain to the others how badly something similar had turned out for a family I knew of. I wouldn't have to say it was from a book, one that wasn't even written yet. But nobody asked my opinion. And there was no reason they should listen to me anyway. I had no authority. I had no official standing in the household. I was only a temporary guest, a distant relation. So I hung my hopes on Jonathan doing the right thing.

Before he could impartially weigh the two sides of the question, though, Delora tipped the scales. In fact, she plumb knocked them over sideways.

"Come now, Jonathan," she said. "I know you would not wish to spoil everybody's pleasure. It is only a little harmless diversion we are after. Stay and help. Please. For me? With you advising us, we cannot go far astray."

Jonathan's resistance quickly melted under Delora's sunny smile. It turned from rock to clay to pea soup in about three seconds. So the planning of Kantwell's very own gambling night went ahead without further protest. I was, thankfully, excused from any direct involvement because of all the time I spent with Rosamund.

"What do you suppose the young people are so deep in conversation about?" she asked me the next afternoon. They had their heads together at the other end of the drawing room, with Jonathan sitting a little apart from the rest.

"I believe they are amusing themselves by planning some sort of an evening party," I hedged, wishing I could tell her the whole truth and not just the half of it. Once again, though, it wasn't my place.

"With cards and so forth?" Rosamund asked.

"Yes, something like that, I think."

"How delightful. The house is so much more cheerful when it is full of young people. I only wish they would not always go away again, especially when Alex stays gone so long."

Her shoulders slumped at this, and I looked for something encouraging to say. The last thing I wanted was for Rosamund's improvement to vanish the moment Alex left Kantwell again. She had to be able to weather that storm or we hadn't really accomplished a thing.

"It is perfectly natural that you should miss your children when they go away," I said. "But consider how equally natural it is for them to wish to go, to spread their wings a little. Birds must leave the nest when they are grown. *It is a truth universally acknowledged.* Would not you agree?"

"I suppose so," she said reluctantly.

"It is a brave thing that mothers do in letting their children fly when the time comes. But you are luckier than many mothers, Cousin Rosamund, for your sons have not gone to some far off place like

224

America or Australia, possibly never to return. Your sons are close by. Why, you see Jonathan nearly every day! And Kantwell will always be Alex's permanent home as well. In time, I daresay their wives and children will bring so much noise into this house that you will begin to think fondly of these quiet days again. Perhaps you should enjoy them while you can!"

"Grandchildren! Do you really think so, Kate?"

"Of course, but there will be no grandchildren if your sons do not leave the nest to find wives first. You cannot keep them at home and expect suitable wives to simply come to them."

"No, no, I suppose you are right. They must be allowed to go, and I must have courage enough to let them. Is that what you mean?"

"Precisely. It is the natural way of things and for your own good in the end."

Rosamund grew quiet, and I did not interrupt the silence, hoping she was thinking seriously about what I'd said. I was thinking about it too. I was thinking that I might not have told the absolute truth, at least concerning Jonathan. He had not needed to go anywhere; suitable wife candidates *had* walked right in the front door – first I did and then Delora.

"Her looks say, 'I will not like you, I am determined not to like you'; and I say she shall." (Mansfield Park, chapter 24)

Chapter 34
Mr. Cranford Revisited

That evening, as the others continued making their plans for a gambling night at Kantwell, I stayed away, sitting apart with a book in my hand. I can't say I was actually reading, because I was way too distracted for that.

"We will need a dealer for each of the Faro tables," I heard Delora say. "A couple of footmen would do perfectly well."

"Do you think your mother will mind if we were to borrow them?" Harris asked.

Alex said, "I shouldn't think so. I will be careful how I present it to her, so that she understands. And then I am sure she will want to see me have my own way."

"The real question is how soon it can all be arranged," stated James Keats. "There is much to do."

I had hoped that the whole idea would fizzle out like a firecracker with a bad fuse, that they would have figured out pretty quickly that they shouldn't attempt to go through with it. But, no. They still sounded determined, and the first frenzy of excitement had merely settled into a serious discussion about logistics. It didn't seem there was a question of 'if' anymore, only when and how they should carry it off. Even Jonathan was joining in now.

After a while, I saw out of the corner of my eye that someone had broken from the group and was coming my way. I expected Jonathan, but when I looked up from my book, it was Harris instead. I was surprised …and wary.

"May I?" he asked, indicating the seat next to me.

I shrugged, saying indifferently, "Suit yourself."

"In that case, I will sit down with you, because that will suit me very well. What is that you are reading, Miss Barrett? What keeps you so seriously occupied that you have no time for your companions?"

"It is only a book of verse," I said, not wanting to encourage him. "And not even a very good one," I added.

"I should not know the difference between good verse and bad. You will think me very uncouth, I daresay, but I will not lie to you, Miss Barrett. I have never learnt to love poetry. It neither informs nor entertains me. Now you know the truth. Do you despise me for it?"

"Not for failing to love poetry, certainly." If I were to despise him at all, it wouldn't be for that. "These things are a matter of personal taste, not of absolute right and wrong. There is no moral principle at stake. I much prefer novels myself, but I try to take some poetry along with my prose to be fair-minded and better educated. I am perfectly willing to love what I did not at first if I discover I was wrong about it, if I should find some example of poetry that truly inspires me."

"That is very generous, Miss Barrett. May I hope that you apply the same principle to other things as well as poetry? People, for example. Is your bad opinion implacable, or are you willing to revise it if sufficiently inspired?"

I wasn't sure how much to read into this comment, but we were definitely not talking about poetry anymore. Finally, I admitted, "First impressions are not always correct. Should I find my opinion has been mistaken, I am happy to revise it."

"Then I shall not lose heart. But I hate to see you sitting by yourself, Miss Barrett. If, as you say, your book is not so very entertaining, cannot you put it aside for now? Will you allow me to convince you to join us instead? You are clever, I think, and I would like to hear your ideas for bringing this scheme of ours about."

I closed my book. "I very much doubt that, Mr. Cranford. I doubt you would like anything I have to say on the subject."

"I cannot imagine that to be true, unless perhaps you disapprove of the scheme altogether."

"It is not my place to approve or disapprove what goes on in Sir Alexander's house. Others have that responsibility."

"Ah, and you worry they are not wielding that responsibility wisely."

I said nothing.

"In that case, there *is* a moral principle at stake – a son's duty to his father. Yes, I see." He was silent for a minute, looking as if he were deep in thought. Then he said, "You must forgive me and my companions, Miss Barrett. We have been used to a freer, more metropolitan way of life, and I fear it may have clouded our judgment. Perhaps we have forgot that what is taken as a matter of course in London may not be considered proper elsewhere. You are thinking particularly of what Sir Alexander's scruples might be."

I nodded.

"You are thinking that he would not like his house and his sons implicated in such an enterprise in full view of all his neighbors, even if no harm was intended."

"When something is ill judged, Mr. Cranford, harm is very often done where none is intended."

"Quite true."

Just then, Delora called out, "Harris, what do you do there for so long? We need your help, and bring Miss Barrett with you."

"Pray, excuse me," he called back to her, without taking his eyes from me. "I have had enough talk of gambling for one day. Miss Barrett has my mind more agreeably engaged at present. She is teaching me to love poetry and to judge better between right and wrong." Dropping his voice, for my ears only, he added, "Is not that so?"

I couldn't answer.

"Never mind, Miss Barrett," he continued. "You need not say a word. I perfectly understand your wishes, and I make myself your bondservant in this matter. Allow me to show myself worthy of some improvement in your opinion. This frivolous scheme we have been playing at will never come to pass; that is my solemn pledge to you. So have no fear."

I was amazed by what he said – amazed, skeptical, and at least a little bit hopeful. "You will... You will take a stand against your sister and your friend?"

"For your comfort and for the honor of Sir Alexander's name, I would do that and much more. Do not think me heroic, however, or that I sacrifice a great deal. It was always the planning – the exercise of mind and imagination – that I found most pleasurable. I could never go through with the thing now that you have convinced me it would be wrong. Whatever you may think, Miss Barrett, I am not such a rogue. My judgment may sometime err, but I hope my principles do not."

I had mistrusted him from the beginning – both he and his sister – mostly because of *Mansfield Park*. But I hadn't realized I was so obvious about it. I felt a little guilty. I had probably been rude without meaning to be… and perhaps without good reason. After all, Harris had never been anything but pleasant and gentlemanly to me. I remembered the first day we met and how he had gone out of his way to include me in the conversation. As for this business of putting on a 'gambling hell' at Kantwell, that had been Alex's idea and he deserved the greater share of blame for it, since he knew best what his father would think.

I might be just as guilty of misjudging as the others, I realized, and of doing harm where none was intended. Maybe I'd pushed the *Mansfield Park* parallel too far. This was real life, not a book, and I had no business allowing what I'd read in a novel to shape my opinion of Harris Cranford or anybody else. It was one thing to be cautious; it was another to be stubbornly prejudiced.

As I thought over these things later that night, I decided I should give Harris – and maybe even his sister – a fresh start. To throw out my unjustified bias against him and be more fair-minded. If poetry deserved every chance to make a good impression on me, then shouldn't I grant a living, breathing (and very attractive) young man the same courtesy?

Yes! Absolutely! It didn't mean I had to throw out my common sense or let down my guard completely, just be willing to give Harris the benefit of the doubt for the time being – the same as I would want somebody to do for me.

When I saw how Harris behaved the next morning, I knew I had been right. As soon as talk started up about the gambling party again, he immediately cut in.

"Let us talk no more of this dull stuff at present. It might have been an acceptable diversion while it rained, but today it would only waste the outdoors. Look, the weather is finally cleared. I am for a walk or a ride in carriages. Surely there is more to be seen in this glorious county than what we have canvassed so far. Let us all have a long explore. Perhaps we could even take a picnic."

"A picnic? In February?" Delora cried. "Do be serious, Harris."

"Very well," he answered. "If a picnic is too adventurous for you, then perhaps we could take tea at an inn somewhere. Let such a place be our destination. Jonathan, Alex, you will know how to guide us."

His enthusiasm was infectious. The subject of the gambling party was forgotten and an outing in carriages taken up instead. Once the others were off and running, Harris stepped back, looking very pleased with himself. He caught my eye and winked.

I mouthed the words "thank you" back at him. He was making good on his promise to me, not by a direct confrontation – at least not today – but by distraction. How easily he had managed it, too! I couldn't help being impressed as well as grateful.

"I believe it would be generally thought the favourite seat. There can be no comparison as to one's view of the country. Probably Miss Crawford will choose the barouche-box herself." (Mansfield Park, chapter 8)

Chapter 35
A Carriage Outing

Harris had been right; it was a fine day for an outing, and it would have been a waste of the good weather to have stayed inside. We decided that one carriage, a barouche-landau, would do instead of two. Since none of the gentlemen was averse to driving, two of us could be accommodated on the box and the other four inside. But when the carriage was brought around to the front door, there was a whole lot of maneuvering to figure out who was going to sit where.

"I fancy a ride on the box," Delora said, "if you will drive, Alex."

"Actually, Keats wants to drive," Jonathan said, "with Alex or myself pointing out the way. So that puts you, your brother, and Kate inside."

"Fine by me," said Harris. "I have no objection to sitting with Miss Barrett. But who is to sit with my sister?"

"I shall," both Jonathan and Alex said at the same time. The two looked at each other, and then Alex explained that, since Miss Cranford had asked for his company on the box, surely she would still want his company even off it. Jonathan disagreed with his brother's logic, saying it was just as likely that the box and not Alex had been what Delora preferred. Finally, Delora pointed out that she was right there and could speak for herself.

"I will be glad to have one of you accompany me going and the other coming back."

After some further debate, Delora awarded Jonathan the prime seat beside her for the first leg of the journey. Then there was still the question of who would ride facing forward and who backwards. It's a wonder we ever got under way!

I kept my mouth shut and let the others decide for me, which got me to wondering if I was becoming timid like Fanny Price after all. But really, if I had minded, I would have said something. As it was, though, I was perfectly okay with the arrangement. I didn't mind riding backwards, and I was happy to spend more time getting to know Harris in my new post-prejudice state of mind.

I was impressed with him again that day, with his manners and with the more respectful, conservative tone he had adopted since our recent talk. I was definitely *not* impressed with his sister, however. Even though I had sworn to give her the benefit of the doubt also, I didn't see much room for any doubt in her case.

From my front-row seat, I had a good view of the whole thing. Delora was sweet as could be to Jonathan while he was at her side. So much so that I was almost convinced that she really cared for him. She snuggled up close to him 'because of the cold,' looping her arm through his. She laughed and smiled at everything he said, even if it wasn't funny. She was as encouraging to him as she de- cently could be.

Since she obviously now returned Jonathan's affection, I was thinking during our tea at the inn how I had better be prepared to give him up to her... that is until she carried on exactly the same way with Alex on the return trip. I'm sure each of the brothers ended the day by thinking he was Delora's favorite. This was going to end badly for one or both of them; I just knew it! And I didn't want to see either Alex or Jonathan hurt.

"What is your sister playing at?" I asked Harris in a whisper when we had arrived back at Kantwell and we stood a little apart from the others.

"What do you mean?"

"You must have seen, as I did, how she flirted with each of my cousins in turn. It seems wrong that she should be encouraging them both."

"Oh, that," he said dismissively. "I daresay she is quite unaware that she is doing so, Miss Barrett. My sister is perfectly artless, but she could no more refrain from flirting with young men than she could stop breathing."

"So you mean to say that she should be forgiven because she cannot help herself?" I was thinking of Mary Crawford's audacious claim that selfishness must always be forgiven because there isn't any hope of a cure.

"Something like that. And also that the gentlemen must take care to guard their own hearts." Here he paused and looked me very earnestly in the eyes. "Although I must admit that is a difficult task for any man when confronted with exceptional beauty and charm."

I had to abandon Jonathan and Alex to watch out for themselves, as Harris recommended. I was much too busy to do it for them. From that time on, every minute I could spare from looking after Rosamund, I spent in the company of Harris Cranford. I don't mean to say that the others weren't around, because they were, but ever since the day of our carriage outing, Harris's attentions to me... Well, I guess I would have to say he began seriously courting me. That was surprising enough but, more remarkable, I discovered I didn't mind. In fact, instead of minding, I liked it. I liked the attention, and there was a certain satisfaction in knowing Jonathan would see that another man found me desirable.

Harris was attractive; there was no denying it. Despite everything I knew from *Mansfield Park*, I started to wonder if he might be 'the one' after all. To tell the truth, the lingering idea that Harris was a bit of a Henry-Crawford-style 'bad boy' added a little extra excitement to the mix. Anyway, I was thoroughly enjoying myself, and our relationship progressed day by day.

Another good thing was that the spell of the proposed gambling night seemed to be broken. Harris told me that he had called in a favor from his sister, who reluctantly agreed to join him in opposing the idea if necessary. Between the two of them, they successfully managed to discourage, delay, and distract when anyone tried to revive the plan.

Harris and the others had been at Kantwell for three weeks by this time, and because of them, Jonathan had spent nearly every day at the manor house as well, probably in neglect of his parish duties. But it would all be over soon, I expected, since the visit had been intended for only about a month. One week left. Then maybe Harris would ride away and I would never see him again. I wasn't sure how I felt about him yet except I knew I didn't want him to go. We needed more time, at least I did.

~~*~~

If I had thought that the next week would slip by in some un-remarkable way, though, I would have been wrong.

First, Alex announced that he intended to take himself off to the Sebring horse races for a few days. Mr. Keats accepted Alex's invitation to go with him, but Harris decided to pass and stay at Kantwell... with me. At least I guessed I had a lot to do with why he remained, and that was later confirmed.

I had more free time to spend with him, because Rosamund didn't need me so much anymore. She had continued getting stronger, both emotionally and physically. She was up earlier and usually came down to breakfast instead of always wanting a tray brought up. Then she went to her morning room to take care of her correspondence and consult with Mrs. Morris about household affairs. She was completely free of laudanum and its effects now, and she rarely complained of the vague and mysterious pains that had marked her illness before.

Her doctor, who I don't think had ever really been able to explain the illness in the first place, likewise could not explain her recovery. Personally, I was convinced that exercise and a more positive attitude were what had done the most good. I couldn't take full credit for her attitude. I'm sure my mother's visit and then Alex's coming home had helped as much or more. But I guess the exercise program had been all me. I had been pretty bossy and pretty insistent about that, starting with small goals and building up from there. At the beginning, Rosamund could barely do one circuit around the drawing room, hanging heavily on my arm. Soon, though, we had outgrown the drawing room and were walking the full length of the house, and then upstairs as well as downstairs. Occasionally, when the winter weather allowed, we even ventured outside. And although Rosamund still usually took my arm, it was more in affection than because she needed my support.

Things were going so well now that I expected I wouldn't be needed at Kantwell much longer. If Rosamund remained stable and weathered Alex's departure all right, I would start looking for a way to get back home to Carding. Meanwhile, though, I had a few more days to spend with Harris... but only a few.

Why couldn't people just stay put long enough to get to know each other properly, I wondered? I would have expected this to be more of a problem in the fast-paced, highly mobile society I had come from. But ever since I had arrived in Regency England, it had been one short-term relationship after another, interesting potential always curtailed by a premature parting. First Fitzwilliam Cavanaugh, then George Galloway, and soon both Harris Cranford and Jonathan Bentley would slip out of my life. It didn't seem fair or reasonable that I should have to make up my mind about anybody so quickly. Of course, it wasn't like each and every one of these guys could have been mine for the asking! George was the only one who had actually proposed… that is until Harris did it too.

It happened the second day after Alex and Mr. Keats left for the races at Sebring. Rosamund, Delora, Harris, and I had all been eating breakfast together. I noticed that Harris was uncharacteristically quiet that morning, barely opening his mouth… except to eat, that is. Then, he lingered after he was obviously finished with his meal.

When the rest of us had finished too, Delora cleared her throat and said, "Lady Bentley, I wonder if I might ask a great favor of you. I have seen your excellent picture gallery already, but I should very much like to know whose faces I am looking at, whose eyes are peering back at me so solemnly. If it would not be too much trouble, would you be so kind as to show me?"

"Why, certainly, Miss Cranford," Rosamund answered, looking surprised but pleased by the request. "I should be delighted. So kind of you to take an interest, and my correspondence can easily wait an hour."

As the two ladies exited the room, Delora looked back over her shoulder and winked at her brother. I distinctly saw her do it.

"Why does your sister wink at you?" I asked Harris.

"Did she? I did not notice." He suddenly shot to his feet, saying, "Miss Barrett, will you walk with me? I would suggest the out of doors but, as you no doubt have seen, the horrid rain of yesterday continues. Instead, I thought we might try the north wing. I have not yet seen the full extent of that part of the house."

I couldn't help being puzzled by both Miss and Mr. Cranford's sudden interest in exploring the house. I didn't have any better ideas, though, so I agreed. I knew we would have the place to ourselves, since Rosamund and Delora's destination was in the opposite direction. That fact plus the wink should have given me a clue, but it didn't.

Jonathan had taken me on a full tour shortly after I arrived at Kantwell, otherwise I wouldn't have been qualified to guide anybody else, because none of the rooms of the north wing had been used by the family during the months of my stay. Jonathan said that they preferred the main branch of the house and the south wing because the light was better, especially in the dark months of winter

"These rooms are only used in the summer months," I told Harris as we made our way from a small parlor into another drawing room at the far end of the north wing. Since I'd only been there once before, I had a look around the room again myself. I tried to imagine it in summer, with light pouring in all the tall windows. "I expect this room will be bright and pleasant six months hence, but it is cold and rather cheerless now," I said, shivering a little and pulling my shawl tighter. "Do not you think so, Mr. Cranford?"

I turned and was startled to find him standing only a breath away. He was not looking at the room he had been so interested to see; he was looking deep into my eyes instead. Then he took both my hands and held them tightly together in his own, just below our chins, only the thickness of our folded arms between us.

"In truth, Miss Barrett," he said very earnestly. "I care nothing for this room or any of the others. I care only for you and for getting you alone to tell you so. I hope I have shown by my actions how sincere my love and my devotion are. Now, allow my words to remove any remaining doubt."

"Wait, Mr. Cranford," I said uneasily. But he didn't wait.

"…Most excellent creature, the moment I saw you, I was fairly smitten – bewitched by your beauty, your character, your grace. The more indifferent you were to me, the more under your power I fell. Your every look and word, they have been my instructors for what is right and how to behave. I only trust my own judgment so far as it tells me to look to yours."

I tried again. "Please allow me to…"

"…Your goodness has inspired me to be a better man, and now I hope you will secure my future happiness by pledging your faithfulness as well. Kathleen, Kate, will you do me the great honor of agreeing to become my wife?"

"Mr. Cranford!" I exclaimed, finally getting his attention. I tried to step back.

He held me fast, saying, "Please, do call me Harris."

"Mr. Cranford, I do not know you well enough yet to address you by your Christian name... much less to accept an offer of marriage from you! I know nothing of your family beyond your sister, or your situation, or your goals and aspirations. And you are just as ignorant about me. Therefore, you cannot be serious."

"Indeed, I am in earnest. None of these details you mention worry me in the least. The answers will come in time. For now, it only matters what we feel."

To demonstrate his point, I suppose, he kissed me. How odd that it should have had the exact opposite effect on me as the one he clearly intended. Up until that moment, I had thought of him as attractive and sort of intriguing. I had, admittedly, even been trying on some romantic ideas about him for size. But that one kiss pretty much killed it all.

I had been kissed before in my former life, so I had a little something to compare it with. Let's just say Harris's technique was not exactly up to par. That could have been overcome with enough practice. What couldn't was the total lack of chemistry. I have no idea what he experienced when he kissed me, but I felt nothing except discomfort. A really good kiss can be wonderful; a bad one sticks in your throat like a hair in a biscuit.

I pushed away, more forcefully this time.

"Do not be angry, my darling," he said at once. "I should not have done that, I know. I was carried away by my feelings; that must be my excuse. Say you will forgive me."

I forgave him... gladly. In fact, I was grateful he had done it, so that I could stop wasting time thinking about him in a romantic way. That possibility was at an end, as far as I was concerned. "I shall not say a word about this to anyone, sir. Just promise me you will never attempt such a thing again. I would also be much obliged if you would put aside any ambitions you have in regards to me and look to someone more compatible for a wife."

"Here is a young man wishing to pay his addresses to you, with every thing to recommend him..." (Mansfield Park, chapter 32)

Chapter 36
Returns and Arrivals

Harris Cranford promised he wouldn't try to kiss me again against my will. He did *not* promise to give up hope of gaining my affection, though. He also said he intended to extend his stay at Kantwell, if possible, and he would not hesitate to tell Sir Alexander why.

"Perhaps you are right, Miss Barrett. We do not know each other as well as we ought. I trust that with the application of a little more time, my proposals will not fail being acceptable to you."

I told him it would do no good. I begged him not to stay only to torment himself... and me.

If I believed he was truly and deeply in love with me, I would have pitied him, but that seemed impossible. I wasn't any particular prize – no fortune or family connections to speak of – and I couldn't believe that my beauty and charm were irresistible enough to have Harris bewitched in so short a time. No, it had to be more of an infatuation or a passing fancy. Or maybe he didn't care for me at all. Maybe I was only a challenge, and he had set out to prove he could make me fall in love with him, that he could put a little hole in my heart, as Henry Crawford had tried with Fanny Price. If that were the case, though, he had taken an awful chance by proposing to me. I might have said yes, and then he would have been stuck.

Anyway, I did my best to stay clear of Harris after that, which wasn't easy with so few of us in the house. But then, all of a sudden, the house seemed full again, and the atmosphere changed completely. As Jane Bennet wrote to Elizabeth, *something occurred of a most unexpected and serious nature.*

Sir Alexander returned first, heard Mr. Cranford's suit, extended the invitation for him to stay longer if he chose, and then talked to me about what a good match it would make.

"Since you have no father or brother to look after you, it was perfectly proper that Mr. Cranford should have spoken to me. He told me of his circumstances and what he could provide you by way of security and a handsome situation. He has a comfortable income of over four thousand a year, you know, and a house in town as well as a country estate in Sussex. It is unlikely, my dear, that you will be able to do better, so I strongly urge you to consider accepting Mr. Cranford's offer."

I was luckier than Fanny. Sir Alexander only "strongly urged." He did not insist. He didn't call me obstinate or ungrateful or bring any other painful pressure to bear. He did not threaten to send me away. Jonathan was better behaved about it than Edmund had been too.

"Do you like the man?" he asked me.

"Yes, as a friend, but I do not think I can like him well enough to marry."

"Then you were right to refuse him. Never mind what my father or anybody else may say. You should not allow money to cloud your view or convince you to marry without true affection. To my way of thinking, Mr. Cranford is not for you, Kate."

"No?"

"No. There is something not quite right about him. You are so kind and trusting – all goodness and innocence – you cannot know what men can be. It would not be proper for me to go into particulars; I will only say that I should hate to see you, of all people, shackled for life to a man who is less than what you truly deserve."

"I am surprised to hear you speak so, Jonathan. How long have you had such an ill opinion of Mr. Cranford?"

"I cannot say that my opinion of him has much changed over time. My idea of his character was formed early on by what I observed and what I heard from Alex. It is only the current situation that puts a different complexion on the matter. One may find a man acceptable as a guest in one's home without wishing to see him married to a favorite sister or cousin."

I felt a little flush of pleasure at this, to think that Jonathan considered me a "favorite." Still, I wasn't his *only* favorite, and he probably wouldn't describe Miss Cranford in sisterly or cousinly terms. I dared to poke my nose into that subject next.

"True," I said. "And does your assessment of Mr. Cranford's questionable character extend also to his sister?"

Jonathan didn't answer right away, and when he did, he seemed unsure, or at least uncomfortable, with the topic. "I... I can hardly tell you, Kate. I do see that not all of Miss Cranford's ideas and actions are exactly what they should be. I am sure you have noticed this too. But rather than a proof of questionable character, I believe the flaw to be in her upbringing, which was spent altogether too much in town and under the influence of the wrong sort of people. We do not look to our great cities for examples of the best morality, you must agree. Wrong ideas and behavior can be corrected, however, and it would be uncharitable to judge a person too harshly for what she cannot help." *Besides, Miss Cranford is very charming and beautiful and I hope to marry her one day.*

No, he didn't actually say the last part, but I couldn't help thinking those facts influenced Jonathan's reasoning more than they should have. Otherwise, why was the sister being forgiven for the very same sort of things (and worse, if he only knew) that were still held against the brother?

~~*~~

The business of Harris's proposal was completely forgotten the next day, however. That's when, toward evening, Mr. Keats returned to Kantwell with Alex, who was so sick he had to be practically carried in. He was groaning, filthy, and he had a black eye and a bloody lip. That was all I could tell was wrong with him as Jonathan and Mr. Keats hauled him through and up to bed.

At first, the alarm wasn't too great. Once Alex was settled in his room, with his mother there beside him and a maid to help her wash and undress him, the rest of us gathered downstairs to hear the story. According to Mr. Keats, Alex had got into a fistfight with some man at the races over a bet. They had gone at it pretty evenly at first, inflicting superficial damage on each other without ever deciding a winner.

"...But since he sees he isn't getting anywhere," continued Mr. Keats, "the scoundrel slips a knife from his boot and starts slashing away, nicking Alex full in the belly. With blood spilling every-where, the coward runs off through the crowd with the money, and then somebody else sends for help. They keep a surgeon on the premises, you know, to stitch up whatever man or beast comes to harm, so that is how it was handled. The surgeon said the wound was not serious and that he expected Alex to be right as rain in a couple of days. A little brandy for the pain would do the job. On our way home, however, the fever set in. I am no apothecary, Sir Alex-ander, but I believe your son may have developed an infection."

There was a universal sharp uptake of breath upon hearing that last word, and I had to remind myself that I now lived in a time before the dawn of the antibiotic age. You couldn't just pop into the local urgent care clinic, pick up a prescription for penicillin, and know everything would be fine in a few days. This was serious, possibly even life-threatening, just like Tom Bertram's illness in *Mansfield Park*.

"May we not send for some medical advice?" I suggested, still not sure about the title of the proper person for the job.

"Yes, at once," Sir Alexander answered decisively. "Jonathan, go for Mr. Billings."

I recognized the name as the same medical man who attended Rosamund through her illness, without result. So I wasn't all that confident in his ability to help Alex either. Still, I doubted there were any other options or that my opinion would carry much weight.

Jonathan left at once, and it was a long, tense hour and a quarter until he returned. While the others remained in the drawing room, Sir Alexander and I came to meet Jonathan at the door. He ran into the house alone at first, soaked from the rain he had obviously ridden through.

Out of breath, he gasped, "I could not get Mr. Billings."

"What do you mean?" his father demanded in some agitation.

"I mean that he is gone and unavailable. Some personal business has taken him from Staffordshire, apparently. There is another man come in his place though. He rode right behind me."

Jonathan returned to the door and swung it wide. At that mo-ment, Mr. Cavanaugh topped the steps and strode in out of the dark night air.

"Mr. Cavanaugh!" I exclaimed involuntarily as my heart did a giant trampoline flip inside my chest. He saw me, then, and he looked just as astonished as I felt.

"Miss Barrett," he stated with a slight, uncertain smile.

"Do you know this man, Kate?" Sir Alexander asked.

"Yes, sir. He happened to be in Carding and attended me after my accident. I believe you can rely on him. Mr. Cavanaugh is a knowledgeable and conscientious medical man."

Mr. Cavanaugh bowed in appreciation.

"Very well. Thank you for coming, Mr. Cavanaugh," Sir Alexander said, shaking his hand. "Come with me."

Jonathan followed them.

Partway up the stairs, Mr. Cavanaugh turned and looked back at me. "Miss Barrett," he said, "will you accompany us. I may need your assistance."

It was the invitation I had been hoping for. I didn't hesitate; I scampered to catch up. I wanted to be doing something to help if I could. Beyond that, though, I was extremely curious as to why Mr. Cavanaugh had turned up at Kantwell, of all places. There was no time to ask him, though. He went straight in to examine Alex, sending Rosamund out to await his findings with the rest of us in the passageway.

Rosamund grabbed my hand. "My dear Kate," she said. "I am so distressed! I am afraid Alex is very ill indeed. How shall I bear it?"

"Six months ago, perhaps you could not," I said, "but you are equal to anything now. This is just one of those times a mother must be strong for her child, as we talked about before. And I know this Mr. Cavanaugh. He is a very clever medical man, I believe. He will be able to help your son; I am sure of it."

It was probably only ten minutes before Mr. Cavanaugh e-merged again, although it seemed like thirty. Addressing Sir Alexander and Rosamund, he said, "The source of your son's trouble is the wound in his belly. His other injuries are insignificant. The belly wound, however, has become putrid. If nothing is done about it, the infection could spread throughout the body with dire consequences. What it means is that I must operate. I must surgically open the wound, clean it, and stitch it up again, this time with the proper materials. Then, I think there is a very good chance it will begin to heal properly."

Rosamund gave a little cry and turned into her husband's shoulder for support. Sir Alexander was silent a minute, considering what Mr. Cavanaugh had told him, no doubt. Finally, he said, "Do what is necessary, sir. What do you need from us?"

"Candles, please, as many as you can spare, hot water, a shallow basin, clean towels, and strong spirits to dull your son's pain. I have brought everything else with me. Oh, and I need someone to assist me in my work."

Sir Alexander stammered his response. "I... I should be glad... That is to say... or possibly my wife..."

Rosamund wailed at this.

Mr. Cavanaugh cut in. "In my experience, sir, the best person for the job is one who is not so close to the patient. I thought perhaps Miss Barrett." Turning to me, he added, "If you feel up to the task. I hope you do not swoon easily."

"No," I said. "Never in all my life." That was true of me in my former life, at least, although I did wonder about Kathleen's history and if it was more *her* constitution I should be worrying about. "I would be happy to assist you, Mr. Cavanaugh – to help my cousin Alex, that is."

Jonathan took his mother downstairs. Sir Alexander went for the strong drink and began pouring it down Alex's throat. The maid left in search of the other necessary articles. Thus, Mr. Cavanaugh and I had a moment alone. I had so many questions for him, but I didn't have any idea where to start. He looked flummoxed too.

"I did not know you were in this neighborhood," I said after an awkward silence.

"Nor I you." Another silence, then he said, "I was deeply grieved to hear about your father, Miss Barrett, and sorry to be right in his case."

"Thank you. How did you learn of it?"

"From one of Mr. Fitch's communications."

"Oh, of course. It has been difficult, especially for my mother."

"Naturally. And now you are come to Kantwell. You said young Mr. Bentley is your cousin?"

"Yes. Is he really going to recover, Mr. Cavanaugh?"

"It is difficult to say. I will do what I can, and the body must do the rest. Your cousin is young and strong, which gives him the very best chance. You must prepare yourself for what you will soon see, Miss Barrett... and what you will smell. There is a collection of blood and putrefaction fluid that must be drained. It will be unpleasant, perhaps shockingly so to someone uninitiated. I did not care to speak so plainly in front of the parents, but now I must, so that you may change your mind if you wish. No one will think the worse of you for it. I could ask the maid or the brother to stand in your place."

"That will not be necessary."

"I honor your courage, Miss Barrett. I hope you will not come to blame me for putting you through this ordeal."

"I would do anything to help my cousin, Mr. Cavanaugh. This family has become very dear to me."

"Miss Barrett, I..."

Sir Alexander joined us. "I believe you will find my son adequately sedated now," he said.

"Very good, sir. Then we shall begin."

Without any particular affection for her eldest cousin, her tenderness of heart made her feel that she could not spare him; and the purity of her principles added yet a keener solicitude… (Mans-field Park, chapter 44)

Chapter 37
Man at Work

The surgery went as well as could be expected, according to Mr. Cavanaugh. He opened the infected wound, drained it, flushed it out with clean water, sprinkled some kind of powder inside and out, and then neatly stitched up and bandaged it again. My job was to respond to simple instructions: hold this, give me that, press here, blot there, etc. As long as I had something to do, I was fine. It was only when I was left idle for a minute or when I thought too much about what was happening that I started to feel the teensiest bit queasy.

Mostly, I was fascinated. It was a glimpse of something so completely foreign to me. Of all the careers I had considered in my former life, medicine hadn't been among them. Now I wondered why.

I was also fascinated to watch Mr. Cavanaugh work. His hands were skilled and efficient and his demeanor so calm. I have to say I was impressed, although I couldn't help thinking his talents were somewhat wasted in this age. How much more a man like him could have accomplished with modern knowledge, drugs, and facilities! The people of the nineteenth century were lucky to have him, though. Alex and the whole Bentley family were lucky to have him.

I sat quietly, surreptitiously watching Mr. Cavanaugh as he finished bandaging the wound, cleaned up, and then began putting his clothing back in order (for he had removed his jacket and cravat and rolled up his sleeves). Considering the anything-goes culture I had come from, it was surprising how much a man's shirt gaping open at the neck and the glimpse of the dark hair of his lower arms affected me. Not to mention his hands. Hmm. I hadn't been free to notice while we were working, but afterwards... Afterwards, my mind and my eyes were at liberty to wander.

Probably I'm building mountains in my mind out of molehills again, but I had never been through anything like that before – working in close quarters and an intense situation, being made so aware of the human body's beauty and frailty, doing a job that potentially made a life-or-death difference. And to go through that kind of experience with someone else... I know it sounds weird, but it seemed like it established some sort of intimacy between the two of us. I wondered if Mr. Cavanaugh felt it too. Probably not. After all, it wasn't *his* first time.

"Would you be so good as to sit with your cousin a bit longer, Miss Barrett?" he said, calling me out of my reverie. "The family will be anxious to hear my report."

I nodded and said, "Of course."

When he came back twenty minutes later, I expected to be dismissed. Instead, he sat back down where he had been before, saying he meant to stay another half of an hour at least. He seemed to accept, even assume, that I would remain as well. At first, we sat in companionable silence, watching the semi-conscious Alex breathe in and out. But eventually my curiosity got the better of me. Also, I didn't want to waste a valuable opportunity. Who knew when I might have another chance to talk to Mr. Cavanaugh?

"I admit I was very surprised to see you arrive today," I said. "How is it that you happened to be in this vicinity, if you do not mind my asking? I had thought you returned into Derbyshire."

"I did for a time, yes, but then I was summoned by Mr. Billings to lend a hand."

"The same as you did in Carding for Mr. Fitch?"

"Exactly. It is my chosen way to carry on my profession, to fill the place of other medical men when they are ailing themselves or must be away."

"You have no practice of your own, then?"

"No. My other responsibilities make it wholly impracticable. There would be little point in establishing a settled medical practice somewhere when I would only have to abandon it – from time to time while my father lives and permanently when he is gone – for my duties at home. Instead, I volunteer my services wherever I am needed. Each time, I see a new place and I have useful employment to fill my days until I am needed at home again. It works out quite well."

"It seemed like a very sensible arrangement," I said. And then I had another thought. "You say you volunteer your services, Mr. Cavanaugh. Forgive me, but does that mean you receive no compensation for your time and effort? You need not answer, though, if you think my question impertinent."

"Inquisitiveness shows that you have a thinking mind, Miss Barrett..."

Well, that was putting a generous spin on it. I more expected the curiosity-killed-the-cat warning from him.

"...and I see no reason not to explain. I receive my reward in knowing I have been of use to people at a difficult time. I do not need or want their money. If those I attend can afford to pay, then the funds go to the medical practice where I am employed. These doctors have ongoing expenses and most of them can ill afford to be entirely without income while they are away."

I thought this over a bit. "So..." I continued, wanting to answer the question (and that old accusation) once and for all. "So, you would never refuse to attend somebody just because they have no money, since you are not being paid anyway."

"Your conclusion is both logical and correct, Miss Barrett. But conscience would forbid doing so in any case."

"Of course."

So much for the last spindly leg on which my former prejudices against Mr. Cavanaugh had balanced. How unreasonable they seemed now. I had started with a kernel of bias and a block of misinformation and cleverly built every other possible circumstance up on top of them into a grand but false edifice. Every piece had since come tumbling down, and I hoped no one else, especially Mr. Cavanaugh, would remember it ever existed. *I* deserved to remember every nasty word and thought to prevent me from making the same kind of mistake again.

Despite all my knowledge of Jane Austen and all my confidence that I had learned valuable lessons from her, in the end I fell into the same trap as Lizzy Bennet. Toward Mr. Cavanaugh, I had been equally *blind, partial, prejudiced, and absurd*. Yet he didn't seem to resent me for it. In fact, I thought he had actually looked kind of happy to see me again. The truth is, I had been real happy to see him too… and not just for Alex's sake.

Alex remained feverish and in and out of consciousness for about forty-eight hours more, with everyone in the house feeling tense on his account. Mr. Cavanaugh came twice a day to monitor his progress, and Rosamund, Sir Alexander, Jonathan, and I all took turns keeping watch at the patient's bedside.

I was proud of Rosamund, for how strong she was through it all. Once the first shock was over, she held her own and didn't shrink from doing her part. In fact, she sort of took charge, overruling even Mrs. Morris for how Alex's care should be managed and directing who could sit with him and for how long.

It seemed wrong somehow to have outsiders in the house at such a time, by which I mean Mr. and Miss Cranford, and Mr. Keats. I can't speak for the rest of the family, but I would have wished them gone. I knew that they had originally planned to all return to London together, Alex included. But it seemed to me that the polite thing under the circumstances would have been to discreetly excuse themselves and go. A family in crisis doesn't want relative strangers hanging around.

They showed no signs of leaving, however. Mr. Keats stayed out of the way, at least. But Harris! He glued himself to me like flypaper… although I'm not sure if I was the fly in that scenario or he was. Either way, it was exasperating. Despite my hints that I wasn't interested, he kept trying. He seemed to be using the situation to show how attentive and supportive he could be. It only annoyed me, though, and then I felt bad for being annoyed, when it was at least possible that his motives were as pure as the driven snow.

On the third day after Alex's surgery, he turned the corner. The fever broke and he was more in his right mind again. When Mr. Cavanaugh gave the official word that Alex was out of danger, I think we all heaved a collective sigh of relief. I was at least on cloud nine at the news, and I felt like busting out in song.

Soon the whole house was filled with cheerful noise and activity again. Music and laughter no longer seemed out of place, and we were all allowed to enjoy our meals without feeling guilty that Alex wasn't able to. He continued to improve day by day, and I no longer minded having the Cranfords and Mr. Keats in the house. Nothing at all could destroy my good mood, not with the Bentley family safe again.

With all the happenings at Kantwell, I had plenty to fill my letters to my family at home in Carding. I received regular responses from them too.

Carmen wrote of our cousins Clarence, Fanny, and especially Felix, of all their comings and goings and doings at Laurelwood. I was reassured, primarily on Mama's account, to hear they had made very few changes to the house since taking it over, although it did sound as if they had various "improvements" planned for the gardens once spring arrived. I just hoped they wouldn't disturb Mama's roses. Carmen also updated me on the romantic front. She told me she was definitely *not* in love with the new curate after all, especially since he had engaged himself to somebody else. I thought that was very sensible of her.

Matilda, from her ideal vantage point in Mrs. Abernathy's house, observed and related everything that went on in Carding and all the village gossip. I could hear her voice in the way she told the stories, complete with her dry sense of humor that reminded me so much of Papa's. She also said she was pleased to report she now had three young girls taking piano lessons from her, making a total of four students with Mrs. Abernathy. As a music student, however, it seemed Mrs. Abernathy was turning out to be a bit of a disappointment. Matilda wrote, "Her interest began to wane as soon as it became clear to her that her abilities could not keep pace with her ambitions."

It was a joy to receive Mama's letters because I could tell by them that her spirits were high again, which relieved my mind. She was very excited about Lucy's pregnancy, naturally, but also about the progress being made in the dower house at Coleswold. It sounded like the remodeling project was coming along just fine. "Mr. Sotheby has fitted everything up so snug," she wrote. "When it is done and I can have my girls back with me again, I shall be the happiest creature in the world."

I had been most candid about my feelings – my homesickness and my confusion over various men – in my letters to Lucy, and so her letters back tended to be more personal too. After relating the recent dramatic events to her, I was desperate to hear her response. Thankfully, I didn't have to wait long.

Dearest Kate,

All your news has quite overwhelmed me. Another proposal of marriage, our cousin's illness, and Mr. Cavanaugh's unexpected appearance! I am all amazement, and I scarcely know where to begin this letter.

I suppose I must start by assuring you that we all continue very well here. Then, I shall move immediately on to more interesting subjects, such as the love-struck Mr. Cranford. Lately, your letters spoke more favorably of him, but I must say I never expected anything like this. I should not be surprised by anyone's admiring you, but this seems to have come about so quickly. Although, when I consider how precipitously Mr. Sotheby came to the point, I suppose it is all of a piece. Young men can be very determined and impatient. I am sorry, though, that he should have treated you in an overly forward manner, and with the result being less than auspicious too.

From what you say, his is a very eligible offer as to fortune, and his constancy, even after being refused, must be credited in his favor as well. But if you cannot love him, that overrides all. You must by no means feel obliged to accept him out of kindness or pity, and I would counsel you not to accept him only to secure a comfortable home either (for my advantageous marriage makes any such desperate measures unnecessary for my sisters). I know you would not do so, though, otherwise you would have accepted George Galloway, which would at least have held the advantage of being settled near your family.

George still asks after you, by the by, so I do not think he has given up on his attachment to you either. And what of our cousin Jonathan? You did not mention him this time. Will you soon be adding him to your list of conquests?

I am glad to hear that Alex came through his crisis so well, and I am grateful you did not write of his illness until it was over. It would have been a dreadful suspense for us otherwise, especially for Mama. But the most extraordinary part of the story is that Mr. Cavanaugh should have been the one to come to his aid! I know you did not like him at first, and yet he seemed to improve on you later. In fact, I believe you had developed a certain fondness for him by the time he went away. I can only imagine your surprise at seeing him again! To what, if anything, will this reunion lead, I wonder?

For my part, I always thought well of him – so handsome and gentlemanly without being overly fine. I also esteem him for finding something useful to do instead of frittering away his time and money, waiting for his father to die, as so many young heirs seem to. He did you a good service after your accident, and now I think his part in securing our cousin's recovery must raise his value still higher in everybody's eyes.

Do send word of any developments as soon as may be. I wish we were together, so there would not always be this delay of conversation between us. But perhaps you do not desire yourself removed from Kantwell just yet.

All my love, etc.

Lucy

What Lucy said about the business with Mr. Cranford was exactly what I wanted to hear. It gave me confidence that my feelings and actions couldn't be very far out of line. I was pleased with what she said about Mr. Cavanaugh too. Yes, his value in my eyes had risen up pretty darned high, especially considering the down-in-the-dumper place it had started. And my sister wasn't the only one wondering if our reunion might lead somewhere – wondering and even hoping. As she suspected, I wasn't in so much of a hurry to leave Kantwell now.

There was comfort also in Tom, who gradually regained his health, without regaining the thoughtlessness and selfishness of his previous habits. He was better for ever for his illness. (Mansfield Park, chapter 48)

Chapter 38
Travel Plans

Mr. Cavanaugh's visits to Kantwell dropped from twice a day to once, and then there really wasn't any medical need for him to continue coming even that often. Alex was back on his feet and had begun to resume all but the most strenuous of normal activities.

I couldn't be one bit sad that Alex was doing so well except that it meant not seeing Mr. Cavanaugh so often. In the two weeks since his arrival, I had begun to look forward to his visits as the highlight of my days. Not that we ever spent much time together or were ever close to being alone again as we had been that first day while attending to Alex. But he always seemed to have a warm greeting and a smile for me – well, for everybody, I guess. Maybe I just happened to be in the room too. Sometimes, after he had seen Alex and if he had no other pressing business, he would accept Rosamund's invitation to sit with us for a while.

That was the situation on this last call. Alex had rejoined his friends grouped at one end of the drawing room, and Mr. Cavanaugh sat down with Rosamund and me at the other. Rosamund had just finished thanking him – probably for the hundredth time – for saving her son's life, and he was in the process of fending off her copious compliments as best he could.

"No, truly, Mr. Cavanaugh," Rosamund continued. "We are forever in your debt, and I for one shall be very sorry to see you go."

"I am happy to have been of service, Lady Bentley, I assure you. And if anything else should arise, I am sure Mr. Billings will serve your family quite ably."

"When does Mr. Billings return?" I asked, suddenly hoping the man was on an incredibly lengthy voyage, preferably lost at sea.

"In point of fact, Miss Barrett," he said, looking a little sheepish, "he has already returned. As I had nowhere else I needed to be and I wished to see this case through, I stayed on longer than was strictly necessary. Now, though, I really have no more excuse for delaying my departure or for continuing to impose on Mr. Billings's hospitality. I leave the day after tomorrow."

I struggled to keep my composure, to avoid showing everything I felt at this upsetting news. He was going away again. Probably forever... again. Again, I had to face parting with a guy who interested me, before anything wonderful that might have developed had a chance to develop. Was this always going to be my fate? It was unbelievable. It was maddening. It was déjà vu all over again!

"So soon?" Rosamund said. "How unlucky. But if you will not impose on Mr. Billings's hospitality any longer, than I entreat you to take advantage of ours, sir. After what you have done for us, you are welcome to stay at Kantwell as long as you like."

Bless you, Cousin Rosamund! You go, girl!

"You are too kind, madam," he said, "but I could not possibly accept your offer."

Sure, you could! You could at least try.

"It would be no imposition at all," Rosamund encouraged, but then she relented. "Or at least say you will dine with us tomorrow."

He gave a nod of his head. "Very well. I will and I thank you."

It was something, although one dinner compared to an as-long-as-you-like stay felt like a huge disappointment.

"Good," said Rosamund, "but now that I think of it, come and spend the afternoon too. You have never been here for a proper social call, and this will be our last chance to have you with us. Kate, dear, perhaps you will give Mr. Cavanaugh a tour of the house, for I daresay you know it nearly as well as anybody else by now. The gardens too, if the weather is not unfriendly."

"I should like that very much," Mr. Cavanaugh said. He glanced at me, and for a moment, our eyes held.

"Then... by all means," I managed to say. "I would be delighted." This time, his answering, lazy smile was definitely for me.

So, I would be giving another house tour to another handsome and eligible bachelor. My imagination went into overdrive as I thought about it that night while getting ready for bed. Hopefully, it meant we would be alone together, as I had been with Harris Cranford under the same circumstances, with plenty of time to talk. There was so much I still wanted to know about Mr. Cavanaugh, like where he was headed next or if he would be returning to his home in Derbyshire. Speaking of Pellencourt, I certainly wanted to hear more about that too, and about the parents who lived there. If Mr. Cavanaugh was my Mr. Darcy, then his youngest sister, still at home, was obviously the Georgiana character. I bet she would be sweet and painfully shy.

It occurred to me that I would acquire more sisters and another set of parents if Fitzwilliam and I married. But that was getting carried away. It was probably too much to hope for that Mr. Cavanaugh intended to propose as well. I doubted there would be a lack of chemistry between us if he did, though. When I pictured myself in his arms, the hands I had studied holding me tightly against his body... Well, let's just say something pretty stimulating – chemistry or gravity or electricity – kicked in. There had been hints of it even in the past but stronger since Mr. Cavanaugh arrived at Kantwell. I felt it every time he came within ten feet of me now. Actually, I felt it pretty much whenever I saw or thought about him. Unless that really was just my imagination too. I had been wrong about Mr. Cranford, after all.

Whatever happened the next day would tell the tale one way or the other. If *nothing* happened, that would be it. I couldn't expect the man to keep popping up in my life again and again, could I?

~~*~~

I fell asleep thinking of Mr. Cavanaugh, woke up the same way, and I could barely contain my excitement for him coming that afternoon.

To fill time and burn off some of my excess energy, I took a long ride on Cleopatra. In early March, temperatures could still drop pretty low overnight. In fact, it had snowed a little only the week before. But, dressed warmly and with the sun out that morning, it was pleasant enough. I thought again about how kind Jonathan had been in providing me a horse to ride. Although I did still sometimes have to share with Delora, her initial enthusiasm for riding had quickly waned. The novelty of Delora herself also seemed to have worn off, for Jonathan didn't spend nearly so much time with her anymore. Nowadays, if he came up to the manor house from the parsonage, it was usually to visit his brother. I was glad of that, for the brothers more than for myself. I no longer worried over Delora as a rival, but I would have hated to see her come between Jonathan and Alex.

When I approached the house again, some movement in the knot garden caught my eye. Rosamund waved to me and, as soon as I could dismount and turn Cleopatra over to a groom, I joined her among the boxwood hedges. At first glance, a person would have thought nothing else grew there. But when you looked closer, you could see that the spaces between weren't empty. The rose bushes weren't dead; they were only dormant, with their stems already beginning to swell and form buds for new growth. Lots of bulbs and perennials had started pushing their way up from the earth. They had been encouraged to poke their heads out by the warmth of lengthening days, same as we house-dwellers. That's what delighted me most, the sight of Lady Bentley taking some outdoor air and exercise of her own free will, and so early in the day besides.

"I just adore spring," she declared with a contented sigh when I came near. "Soon we will have flowers blooming everywhere we look. Nothing could be more cheerful. Do not you agree, Kate?"

"I do," I told her truthfully. Spring had always been my favorite season, and for a moment I thought of the magnolia trees on my old college campus – one of the last sights I'd enjoyed before leaving that life. "I hope you are dressed warmly enough, Cousin," I continued. "You have always told me that you are particularly susceptible to taking a chill."

"Now you sound like Pittkins. Had she been given her way, she would have seen me stay safe indoors by a roaring fire. But when I told her I was quite determined to dress and go out, she helped me on with my warmest things. Be assured, Kate, I am perfectly comfortable."

I smiled at the enormous change in her from only a few months before. We fell into step together, and I asked, "Have you seen Alex this morning?"

"I have. We breakfasted together, as a matter of fact. He is doing so very well; every day brings another sign of his return to health. This morning he spoke of expecting to soon feel strong enough to endure the long trip back to London. I gather his friends, who have been patiently waiting, are become a little restless with country life."

After checking her face for signs of distress, I said, "You speak of Alex's going so calmly. Are you now truly resigned to it?"

"Birds must leave the nest when they grow up. Is not that what we talked about before? Besides, I am less fearful for him than at our former partings. I have seen a fundamental change in him. I believe this misadventure he has so recently come through will have a durable and properly sobering effect. It will teach him what was wrong in his former judgments and habits, and serve as some protection against wildness and imprudence in the future. He is not without sense, you know."

"Of course not. Alex has many excellent qualities. I daresay he will turn out exactly what a young man in his position should be: steady, thoughtful, a great help and comfort to his parents."

Rosamund looked sharply at me and said, "It occurs to me that you have just described Jonathan instead…"

She was right. I supposed I had been unconsciously thinking of Jonathan as that sort of ideal son.

"…Although he is my younger son, I must admit he has always surpassed his brother in good character. Perhaps I have not always esteemed him for it as I ought to have done," she finished, dropping her head and her voice a little.

I knew it was true, that it was Alex, not Jonathan, who had always been Rosamund's favorite. But I had no desire to see her punished for it, especially now when she had repented of the fault herself. After thinking a minute, I told her, "If a person has more than one child, I think it must be almost impossible to love them all just the same, because they are themselves not the same as each other. One does not love a son more or less than his brother, only perhaps in a little different style due to his unique virtues and character traits. That is the way it is for me with my sisters. I love all three of them, but for different reasons."

"You are too kind, Kate, but you must allow me to own where I have been in the wrong. I am not afraid of being overpowered by the impression, and I will yet endeavor to put the situation right so far as I am able. I shall let Alex go on his way without bemoaning him to the rest of the world, and I shall be sure to make Jonathan see how much he is loved and valued. This is my resolution. It is a very good one, I think; and you, Kate, shall be the judge of how well I keep it."

I thought it was a good resolution too, and I looked forward to seeing it put into practice. It was one more proof that Rosamund was now strong enough to stand on her own two feet – emotionally as well as physically. She might still like my company (much as I liked hers), but she didn't really need me anymore. When the time came, I would be able to leave her without feeling guilty.

I wasn't exactly sure when that would be, though. Mr. Cavanaugh was definitely going away. Mr. Cranford also, from what it sounded like. One, I would regret; the other, I wouldn't. That left only Jonathan, and I didn't really think I had a future with him. So, very soon there would be no more reason for staying at Kantwell and every reason to go home to Carding. Sometimes – in quiet moments with nothing to distract me – I missed my family so much I could hardly stand it. And I was determined to be home before Lucy's baby was born.

Transportation would be the tricky part. Sending a private carriage for me alone would be terribly expensive, what with having to hire horses for each successive stage of the journey, both ways. And I wouldn't be allowed to travel alone; I would probably have to take at least one maid and one footman with me in addition to the coachman to drive. What a bother! Carriages had seemed very romantic to me once upon a time, but now I would have been very glad for a bus or train ticket.

Then I had another idea – practical if unappealing. I wondered if space could be made for me in Mr. Cranford's carriage when it headed south with his sister and Alex. It would be a perfectly proper means of travel with my cousin and a female companion as chaperones, and it wouldn't put anyone to extra trouble. But I had looked forward to being rid of Harris Cranford – his presence and his unwanted attentions. Could I endure so many more hours with him in close quarters? Would he wear me down and wear me down, mile after mile, until my resistance was gone, until I had no more will to survive? I might eventually agree to marry him just for some peace!

No, that would never happen, and it was in every other way so logical a solution to the problem that I thought I should at least offer the suggestion to Sir Alexander.

"I have been making the tour of the park," he replied, "as I generally do every year, and intend to close it with a call at the Parsonage." (Pride and Prejudice, chapter 34)

Chapter 39
Raised Expectations

Rosamund had sanctioned the idea of my giving a tour to Mr. Cavanaugh when he came, but still I could imagine that, once he arrived, one or more of the others might invite themselves along for some reason, unaware I wanted to be alone with him or unwilling to let me. I had a difficult time evading Harris Cranford under any circumstances, so he wasn't likely to give me up to the unchaperoned company of another man without a fight.

I thought my best chance would be to intercept the good doctor as soon as he arrived. Half an hour before he was expected, I slipped away from the others, put my coat on, and used a back door to let myself outside again.

Luckily, Mr. Cavanaugh rode directly to the stables instead of the front door. I heard the hoof beats approach and managed to be nearby when he dismounted. At least I think it was hoof beats I heard; it was hard to tell above the pounding bass drum of my own heart. It wasn't just the way I had snuck out of the house like some escaped felon that had my blood pumping; it was the thought of being alone with Fitzwilliam Cavanaugh and what might happen.

As he left the stables, he was looking down at first, brushing off and straightening his clothes, so he didn't notice me right away. I had the advantage over him there, and I didn't waste the chance to openly admire what I saw. I thought he had never seemed more attractive – tall, well-built, and every inch the gentleman. If clothes make the man, then his were working overtime that day, from his black Hessian boots and buff-colored breeches up to his hunter-green coat and immaculate cravat. I'd never seen him looking more the quintessential Mr. Darcy... and Mr. Darcy was supposed to marry me and carry me back to Pemberley...

"Stop it!" I muttered under my breath, ashamed that I still hadn't broken the habit of thinking in fairy-tale terms about this Regency life of mine. No matter how devoted I was to Jane Austen or how many intriguing similarities to her books I noticed, this was not a novel; this was real life. This was *my* real life! I had to keep reminding myself of that fact. I was Kate Barrett, formerly Hope O'Neil. I wasn't Elizabeth Bennet or even Fanny Price. Although it was fun to play at their parts, to picture myself in their shoes, even to borrow some of their words from time to time, when it came down to the important stuff – like deciding to marry somebody – I needed to make sure I was thinking straight. Marriage was forever, at least in *my* plan, so I had to get it right the first time. I had no more second chances coming to me.

"Miss Barrett!" he said when he was nearly on top of me. "Excuse me for not looking where I was going. I nearly ran you over, I fear."

"Not at all, sir. I could have easily stepped aside."

"Ha! That would say little for my gallantry if you were only spared being trampled by your alertly getting out of my way. Were you going to the stables for a ride?"

"No, I rode earlier... but it was such a fine day that I could not resist a walk also."

"May I join you? We could just as well begin the outdoor portion of that tour you promised me at once, if you are not too tired."

"Tired? Oh, no. I am perfectly ready to carry out my promise. In fact, I have been looking forward to it. Shall we start with the stables, since we are so near to it already?"

He nodded his assent and we headed in that direction. I introduced him to Cleopatra and some of the other horsier members of the family in the boxes that flanked either side of a central walkway. Then we emerged back out into the sunlight at the far end of the stable block. From there I took him to see some of the other outbuildings before the orchards and fields. My goal was to conduct him as far from the house as possible for as long as possible, so that I could keep him to myself without anybody getting a chance to spoil it.

"Is it much like Pellencourt?" I asked Mr. Cavanaugh half an hour into our tour.

"In some respects," he said, looking amused. "Everything you have shown me is handsomely built and well maintained, but then I have often observed that one dairy or poultry barn is much like another."

"True. I have not yet shown you anything really beautiful or entirely unique. We are coming to a view that I like particularly well, though. Perhaps that will make a more distinct impression on you."

"If you like it, then I am sure to as well." We walked on. "Ah, I see what you mean," he said when we arrived at the spot a minute later. He took time to properly admire the scene – how the ground fell away to a small lake below and some wooded hills beyond – before turning his attention back to me. "It is a beautiful prospect, indeed," he said. There was a thoughtful pause as he continued to look at me. Then, finally noticing the bench I had cleverly brought us to, he said, "I see we are not the first ones to admire the view from here. Shall we sit down and linger a little?"

"By all means," I answered. That was exactly what I had in mind, after all.

"You are not too cold, I hope."

I thought about saying I was, imagining him putting his arms around me to keep me warm, but I didn't want to give any reason for him to cut short our walking tour. "Not at all," I said.

"Good, for there are a few things I most particularly wish to say to you, Miss Barrett."

That got my heart pounding all over again. We sat down – close but not too close to remain respectable – and I smiled encouragingly at him. "You wanted to tell me something?"

"Yes. It is difficult to know where to begin, though. First, allow me to thank you for agreeing to show me Kantwell. I hope sometime to be able to return the favor. Perhaps you will allow me to give you a tour of Pellencourt one day."

Wondering if this meant what I thought it meant, I said, "I can think of nothing I would like better."

"I am glad to hear it," he said, and the most adorable crinkles broke out at the corners of his eyes as he smiled back at me. "I also wanted to tell you again how much I enjoyed our dance at the

Coleswold ball and our discussion there. I have often thought of it since."

He waited, but I didn't know what to say. I just nodded and let him continue.

"Upon further reflection, I sincerely regretted not being able to stay on in Carding. The more I thought about that night, the more I wished for some way to continue our friendship. Do you understand me, Miss Barrett?"

I didn't want to over-presume here. "I think so. I have often felt the same way when circumstances have separated me from a friend. Consider my current state, away from all my family."

"Yes, well, I endeavored to remedy the situation by writing to your father with hopes of securing a connection back to you. Unfortunately, my letter went unanswered, and then I learned from Mr. Fitch the reason. 'What has become of the family,' I asked him by return post. He told me your elder sister was on her wedding journey somewhere, that he thought your younger sisters were staying with friends in Carding, but that you and your mother had gone away and he knew not where. Although I never gave up hope, I could find out nothing more of you for the time being. Imagine my astonishment, then, when I came to Kantwell and discovered you here."

"I do not need to imagine, Mr. Cavanaugh. Your surprise could have been no greater than my own at seeing you again so unexpectedly."

"I was surprised, yes... and delighted," he said, taking my gloved hand in his and looking intently into my eyes.

Oh, my goodness! This is it! He was about to tell me he loved me, and suddenly I knew I felt the same way. My heart was swelling up inside my chest to the size of a birthday party balloon, ready to burst. My spirit was belting out a tune – something operatic, I think – for sheer joy. It wasn't Mr. Darcy I loved after all; he had just been a stand-in, holding the place for Mr. Cavanaugh! Now he only needed to declare himself. On one knee preferably, but that didn't really matter. Once he said the words, I would be justified to fall into his arms and claim the kiss that would confirm the chemistry I already knew existed between us. My lips were humming in anticipation. I just needed to hear the words. He opened his mouth and...

Then there was a noise on the path and he closed it again. *Drat!* Mr. Cavanaugh also let go of my hand and drew back a little. Someone was coming. Of all the lousy bad luck! Just when things had been getting good, too… really good.

It was Jonathan, walking over from the parsonage.

Mr. Cavanaugh stood to shake his hand and exchange awkward greetings. "Your cousin has just been showing me the grounds," he said. "We only sat down to rest for a few minutes and enjoy the view."

"I see," Jonathan said cheerfully. "Well, I hope Kantwell meets with your approval, sir."

"Very much so, although I have not seen all of it yet."

"If your fair companion is sufficiently refreshed, perhaps we three can continue on together. I would be happy to guide you. I do not doubt that my cousin has done an admirable job so far, but I daresay I can tell you more of the details and history of the place." Turning to me, he said, "Come, take my arm, Kate."

I had never been more put out with poor Jonathan than at that moment. He seemed to be totally clueless that he had interrupted anything at all, and his assumption that I would be glad to have him join us was understandable. Any other time, I *would* have been. Any other time at all, but why today?

So much for privacy. So much for my chance to be alone with Mr. Cavanaugh. We continued around the park and finally ended at the house, Jonathan talking most of the time, communicating what seemed to me very tedious information about the landscaping, the acreage in cultivation, a recent drainage project, and finally the dates various additions were made to the house. I'm sure Mr. Cavanaugh was absolutely mesmerized! Actually, he was heroically patient and gave no reason for Jonathan to suspect his interruption and information were unwelcome. Of course, there was always the possibility that the interruption *wasn't* unwelcome, that I had misunderstood Mr. Cavanaugh's intentions or that he was relieved for a chance to change his mind. I might never know.

My worst fears for the rest of the day were realized. Once we entered the house, we were surrounded by people every single minute – before dinner and certainly during dinner. Then afterwards, when Rosamund renewed the idea of my giving Mr. Cavanaugh a tour of the house, both of the Cranfords as well as John Keats invited themselves along. What could I do? When we got to the north drawing room (where Mr. Cranford had ambushed me and where I'd had half a mind before to do the same to Mr. Cavanaugh), the only thing flirtatious that happened was a wink and a significant look from Harris!

I was already picturing how the night would end. No doubt Mr. Cavanaugh would mount his horse and, with one backward glance and perhaps a small twinge of regret, he would ride away into the darkness. The next day, he would leave for Derbyshire without me, and that would be that.

I couldn't have been more wrong, though. That's not what happened at all.

"No. I thank you," she replied, endeavoring to recover herself. "There is nothing the matter with me. I am quite well. I am only distressed by some dreadful news which I have just received from Longbourn." (Pride and Prejudice, chapter 46)

Chapter 40
Distressing News

When we all returned to the drawing room, I could tell right away that something was up. Rosamund hurried over to me with what looked like a letter in her hand, saying, "Kate, dear, we were about to send someone to find you. This just arrived by express."

I was instantly alarmed, since I figured no *good* news would come this way. "It is from my sister Lucy," I told the others, who were all sitting or standing at attention, waiting for me to tell them what the matter was. I opened and silently read the brief letter, feeling myself sway a little by the time I got to the end. Mr. Cavanaugh immediately caught my elbow and helped me to a sofa.

"What is it, Miss Barrett?" he asked gently. "Some unhappy news from home? Take your time."

I did take a minute to reread the note and try to compose myself. But it was no use; I was shaking and crying already. "It is my mother…" That's all I could say. With my mind already leaping ahead to envision the worst, I handed the letter to Mr. Cavanaugh.

He quickly scanned through it and then told the others in a grave tone, "Apparently, Mrs. Barrett is very ill – some serious digestive complaint. Mrs. Sotheby writes that the doctor is advising the family to gather round at once."

I began to sob at this, hearing it said aloud.

Rosamund came to sit beside me. She put her arm around my shoulders, saying, "There, there, Kate, take heart. It may not be so very bad after all, but of course you will want to go to your mother at once."

There were similar murmurings from the others. After a minute, I remembered the question of transportation. "I'm sorry, but I have no carriage," I said.

"You will take one of ours, of course," said Sir Alexander, "and a maid and a footman. There can be no question of your traveling post at such a time."

"You are very kind, sir," I replied.

"Yes," agreed Mr. Cavanaugh, "but excuse me, *I* will take Miss Barrett to Carding. Perhaps my medical training may be of some use when we arrive."

"Oh, I could not trouble you to do that!" I said. "You must have other responsibilities."

He stooped to speak softly to me. "Nothing important, Miss Barrett. You must allow me to assist you. I could not save your father; I wish to do what I can for your mother."

"I daresay that is very generous of you, sir," said Mr. Cranford, pulling himself up to his full height and getting in Mr. Cavanaugh's face. "But it would hardly be proper, the two of you traveling alone together."

Mr. Cavanaugh held his ground. "I am sure we can borrow a maid from Kantwell, as Sir Alexander has already offered. That should make it respectable enough, especially if Miss Barrett and I are engaged to be married."

I did a double take at that, wondering if I could possibly have heard right. "Engaged?" I said, echoed by some of the others.

"Are you engaged to this gentleman, Kate?" asked Sir Alexander in a very parental tone.

"No!" I said, "at least I do not think so." I looked up at Mr. Cavanaugh for an explanation.

Amazingly, he dropped to one knee beside me so that he looked me straight in the eye. "Surely you know that I was about to ask you this afternoon when we were interrupted. I'm sorry for the less appropriate setting now, but will you marry me, Kate?"

"Now just a minute!" Mr. Cranford protested. "I was there ahead of you, sir. I asked Miss Barrett to marry me two weeks ago, and I am still hopeful of a favorable reply."

Mr. Cavanaugh smiled calmly and looked back to me. "Then I gather she has not accepted you yet, sir."

Mr. Cranford sputtered a little before answering, "Nevertheless, a gentleman would respect my claims and not interfere."

Mr. Cavanaugh gave up his proposal position then – I couldn't blame him – rising to face the persistent challenger. "I was unaware that you considered Miss Barrett your personal property, sir, and I will not believe it until I hear it from her own lips. Let us have no more of this bickering, though. Miss Barrett need not decide anything now. All that is important at the moment is getting her home to her mother."

"Very well," agreed Mr. Cranford, "but you are not the only one who wishes to be of service. I and my carriage are at her disposal as well. If you are going with Miss Barrett to Carding, I am certainly going too."

"And I!" said Jonathan, getting to his feet. "I feel some responsibility, as representing my family, to lend our cousin my support and protection. After all she has done for us, I shall surely accompany her to Carding."

The discussion continued back and forth with no one prepared to give in. All three of the guys insisted on going, and both the Mr. Cs intended to take their own carriages, Mr. Cavanaugh because he wasn't returning to Kantwell and Mr. Cranford because he was. Also, they didn't like each other very much right then. Fortunately, Jonathan was sort of like Switzerland – neutral territory, a friend to both – or there might have been three carriages making the trip.

Still, I felt like I was watching a tennis match (or maybe it was a game of ping-pong). The men volleyed back and forth contesting for custody of me! If I hadn't been so worried about my mother, it might have been funny. If I'd had my wits about me, I might have spoken up and settled the question myself, right then and there. But I was too shocked by my mother's illness and by Mr. Cavanaugh's abrupt proposal to say anything. Besides, at that moment I didn't care whose carriage I rode in or who felt the need to protect me from whom. I just wanted to get home as soon as possible. That was the only thing everybody could agree on, that preparations should begin at once so that I could be on my way first thing in the morning.

This was not the way I expected to leave Kantwell – rushed and under duress. The place as well as the whole Bentley family had grown very dear to me. We all deserved an unhurried take-leave ceremony after the months I had spent with them, but it wasn't in the cards.

I took care of some of the good-byes that evening – Alex, Mr. Keats, and Delora Cranford – not wanting or expecting them to leave their beds early in the morning just to wave at my departing carriage (correction: carriages, plural). Rosamund and Sir Alexander both insisted on seeing me off in the morning, which I appreciated, even though it meant more tears – on both sides, as it turned out.

Sir Alexander's eyes were glistening when he wished me safe travel and that I would find my mother well after all. He also thanked me for coming and ventured to hope "that your time at Kantwell has not been spent unpleasantly." I kissed him on the cheek and said that it certainly had not been, which was mostly true. Except for my homesickness, I had been happy there.

Rosamund was even more painful to part with. I'm afraid I blubbered and wailed about how much I would miss her, and she did the same for me. It seemed like there was more that needed to be said than what we could find words for. Finally, we both promised to write and then I turned quickly away.

There they were, waiting for me: two carriages and three men at the ready. But I couldn't please them all, not at the same time, at least. I would obviously have to take turns who I rode with. That was the only fair solution. Judging that Harris Cranford would likely be more unpleasant about being skipped over, I decided to go with him for the first leg of the journey. Also, to get it over with. My assigned maid, Jenny, came with me and Jonathan went with Mr. Cavanaugh.

Although I was glad when we were finally underway, the journey itself I would have to describe as difficult. First, I had to watch Kantwell – its beloved people, then the house, and finally the grounds – slip past my window and out of sight, wondering if or when I would ever see them again. Then, there was Harris Cranford to deal with. To be fair, he wasn't that obnoxious. He didn't spend the whole time trying to win me over with his charm or killing me with ultra-kindness either. He was smart enough to know that wouldn't impress me.

I wondered what Mr. Cavanaugh would say to me when I took my turn riding in his carriage, but he hardly spoke, at least while Jenny was with us. That night at the inn, though, he did pull me aside for a brief one-on-one as the others went ahead of us into the private dining parlor arranged for our use.

"I believe I owe you an apology, Miss Barrett, for being so silent in your presence today. There were things I wanted to say but they were for your ears only. Still, you must think me very rude."

"Not at all," I said. "I was in no mood for talking. Quiet companionship was all I wanted."

"It is kind of you to say so. I was not entirely idle, however. I was contemplating your mother's complaint – what the problem might be as well as what might be done for her. Mr. Fitch may well have the situation fully under control by the time we arrive. Otherwise, another head and another pair of eyes may be just what is needed. Would that I could do something to ease your distress in the meantime, Miss Barrett. I know it will do no good to advise you not to worry. When it comes to people we care about, we cannot help ourselves."

"Very true."

"I care about *you*, Kate. May I call you that?"

I nodded.

"Thank you. I have no intention of demanding an answer from you now, but I do wish to assure you that despite the awkward business I made of it, I was perfectly serious in my proposal to you. It was not the impulse of the moment either, as it may have appeared. It is something I have been thinking about for a long time, nearly since the first day I met you, in fact. As I said, I meant to ask you earlier, and I would have while we were admiring that fine prospect yesterday afternoon – how long ago that seems now! – if it had not been for Mr. Jonathan Bentley's interruption."

"I hardly know what to say, Mr. Cavanaugh."

"Fitzwilliam, please. And you need say nothing at all. Indeed, I do not wish you to answer now. That conversation is for another time, after the current crisis has passed."

Jonathan was equally kind and undemanding, but no one could speed up the trip for me beyond ten or eleven miles per hour. That was the real rub. Every minute of suspense, not knowing my mother's condition, was a misery. I couldn't help yearning for one little modern convenience. If only I could have gotten my hands on a motorcycle with a full tank of gas... That would have made quite a picture: me in my long, black, mourning gown, hunched over a

Harley Davidson and flying down the road to the amazement of every farmer, milkmaid, and tradesman I rumbled by.

But, even without the help of an internal combustion engine, I and my entourage did eventually make it to our destination. We drove through Carding, past Laurelwood, and then turned down the lane to Coleswold. As we approached the house, I was half agony, half hope (never had Captain Wentworth's famous phrase seemed more appropriate), not knowing what I would find when we entered. Mama might be better or she might still be dangerously ill. I didn't want to think about any worse possibility.

I had a fleeting thought of *Sense and Sensibility*, the part where Maryanne seems near death's door and Colonel Brandon goes to fetch Mrs. Dashwood to her bedside. I could only pray the news that awaited me was as good as what greeted Mrs. Dashwood.

Elinor... waiting neither for salutation nor inquiry, instantly gave the joyful relief; and her mother... was in a moment as much overcome by her happiness as she had been before by her fears. (Sense and Sensibility, chapter 45)

Chapter 41
Complications

I hurried into the house and found Lucy coming to meet me as quickly as her noticeably pregnant body would carry her.

"All is well, Kate," she cried out. "Have no more fear. Mama is out of danger."

I couldn't speak. I just threw myself into her arms and sobbed in relief. It was *so* good to be home and to know that Mama was well. It was so good to see my sister again too.

While I was still clinging to Lucy's embrace, she said over my shoulder, "Why, Mr. Cavanaugh, what do you do here?"

"I happened to be with your sister at Kantwell when your message arrived," he answered. "I thought perhaps I could be of some service. The same applies for these other friends – your cousin Mr. Jonathan Bentley, and this is Mr. Cranford. Did I hear you say that Mrs. Barrett is out of danger?"

"Yes, she is quite safe, sir. Mr. Fitch can tell you more about it. You and your friends will excuse me now, though. I must take Kate up to see her mother."

"Of course."

Before heading upstairs, I gave one backward glance at my three gallant escorts, a look that I hoped conveyed some of my gratitude. After that, I vaguely remember hearing the butler invite the men to make themselves comfortable in the drawing room and directing footmen to see to the luggage. I couldn't think of that, though; I could only celebrate that my mother wasn't dying and that I would be with her again in just a minute!

Mama looked remarkably well, especially compared to what I had imagined ever since I got Lucy's letter. She was a little pale and drawn, lying there in bed, but she opened her eyes when I came in and then her face brightened. I went to her at once and hugged her as best I could without crushing her. I was still too choked up to speak, though.

"Hush, hush," she said in my ear. "You mustn't cry any more. I will be well, Kate. I will be perfectly well very soon."

We didn't have much conversation; not much was necessary. We each just needed to see and hear enough to reassure ourselves after the long separation. But I could tell Mama was tired, and soon her eyelids drifted shut.

"We should let her sleep," Lucy said, gently touching my arm.

"Yes, of course," I agreed, yet I was reluctant to leave the bedside. I just needed another minute.

Lucy then led me out the door and to her own dressing room. "I know we have guests below," she said, "but I must have you to myself for at least a few minutes first. Oh, Kate, I have missed you so!"

We embraced again and then sat down together. It had been six months; it seemed even longer, though. And next to my mother doing well, the sight of Lucy in the bloom of health was the very best medicine for me. "You are well? And the baby and Mr. Sotheby?" I asked her. "Well and happy?"

"Very. Now that you are here and Mama is on the mend, I have nothing whatsoever to distress me."

I had a whole passel of questions for my sister, things I had long wanted to know about her life as a married woman, but it didn't seem the right moment. Instead, I asked, "What more can you tell me about this illness of Mama's?"

"It came on very suddenly, as I wrote. Pain in this area," Lucy said, indicating the lower right side of her belly. "And a high fever. Mr. Fitch was quite alarmed, and so I sent for you."

"What was the cause? Was it ever determined?"

"Something digestive. Bile, Mr. Fitch calls it, although I am not quite convinced he knew exactly what the trouble was, which makes it all the more remarkable that Mama has come through it safely."

"Mr. Cavanaugh came prepared to confer on the case if it was needed."

271

"So I gathered. How very kind of him. But then perhaps his service to you is not completely disinterested." She looked at me suspiciously. "And your Mr. Cranford is here as well, and Jonathan! You certainly have a devoted following, my dear sister. Will one of these gentlemen win your heart in the end?"

"I don't know. My mind has been too full of worry for Mama to think of it. They insisted on accompanying me, though, *all* of them. Nothing else would do."

"Are all three your suitors, then?"

"Not Jonathan. He came only as a friend and to represent the family in seeing me safely home. Mr. Cranford, you know about already, and he has refused to go away gracefully, especially once Mr. Cavanaugh proposed."

"He proposed?"

"Yes, right there in front of God, Mr. Cranford, and everybody else. He thought it would be more proper for us to travel together if we were engaged, although he says that is not the only reason. Oh, Lucy, my head is in such a muddle! What am I to do?"

"If you are not sure what the right thing to do is, then you must wait. Make no answer. Give yourself time to consider once your mind is fully composed about Mama again. There are plenty of rooms here to accommodate the gentlemen in the meantime, and Mr. Sotheby will be delighted to have so much company."

I figured I had at least a day or two before anybody would make demands on me. Boy, was I wrong! Actually, my situation was about to get even more complicated... a lot more complicated.

~~*~~

More happy reunions followed the next day when Carmen and Matilda both visited Coleswold. Mr. Fitch came as well, examining his patient and then renewing his acquaintance with Mr. Cavanaugh. I spent as much time with Mama and my sisters as possible without being totally uncivil to the others.

That afternoon, though, I checked the drawing room and was relieved to see only Jonathan there. I knew Mr. Cavanaugh was still with Mr. Fitch, and Jonathan explained that Mr. Sotheby had interested Mr. Cranford in inspecting his hounds.

"Thank heavens," I said, sitting down near him. "I know I should be flattered by Mr. Cranford's enduring devotion, especially since it persists without encouragement, but I am too worn out to be polite."

"You are still firmly decided against him, then?"

"I hardly know what to think anymore. These last few days have been a whirlwind."

Jonathan was oddly silent, and when I glanced up at him, he had the look of a man with something particular on his mind.

"What is it?" I asked. "Do you have anything new to say on the subject of Mr. Cranford?"

"Mr. Cranford? Oh, no. My opinion of him has not changed. I still maintain that he is not deserving of you."

I didn't know how to react to that except by making a joke out of it. "Then what about Mr. Cavanaugh?" I said flippantly. "Does he better deserve your wonderful, virtuous, darling cousin? He did save your brother's life, after all."

"I see you can hardly bear a compliment, Kate, but you must know how highly I think of you. As for Mr. Cavanaugh, yes, he is no doubt more deserving of you. But I want to give you one more thing to consider before you make such an important decision."

I had no clue where he was headed, so the next words out of his mouth came as a complete shock.

"I wish you would consider marrying *me* instead."

I couldn't believe it. Had Jonathan just asked me to marry him? At one time, that had been exactly what I had lived in hope of, but I had since given up and moved on.

"Now, hear me out," Jonathan continued. "I know I cannot offer you the fortune either of the others can. I am very comfortably situated but I will never be rich. I have something they do not, however. I have a family connection that I would venture to say you value more than money. Kate, you have endeared yourself not only to me but to my whole family, and you have given every reason for me to believe you feel much the same about us. As my wife, you would live always at Kantwell instead of among strangers. By agreeing to marry me, you will not only be giving a most excellent gift to myself but to my mother and father as well. I have lately come to see it is exactly the right and best thing for everyone." He then slipped from his chair and onto one knee. "So I ask you now, Kate, will you marry me?"

I had no chance to answer (not that I was prepared to anyway) because I could hear somebody approaching. It was Harris Cranford. He appeared in the doorway before Jonathan could quite get to his feet.

Harris stopped abruptly and said, "What's this, Bentley? You sly dog. Have you been skulking around, waiting for a chance to cut in on my territory?"

"Well," Jonathan answered, straightening his waistcoat, "I would hardly characterize the situation in that way, sir. You are certainly not entitled to know all my nearest concerns, and Miss Barrett is still a free agent. That makes what just passed between us none of your business."

At that moment, Mr. Cavanaugh happened to walk in too, which I could hardly believe. He looked around and must have been able to tell by our faces that he had just interrupted something. "Please excuse the intrusion," he said. He was bowing out when Mr. Cranford called him back.

"No, no, you might at well stay, Cavanaugh. This concerns you too. It seems our boy Jonathan, here, has just officially thrown his hat into the ring."

"Pardon me? I do not understand you, sir."

"Young Bentley, here. If I am not very much mistaken, he has now joined our little club by proposing marriage to Miss Barrett."

Mr. Cavanaugh, Fitzwilliam, looked doubtfully at Jonathan and then at me. It was too much. I groaned, dropped my head, and covered my face with my hands. I earnestly prayed the floor underneath me would open up and swallow me whole like a bigmouth bass would an unlucky horsefly who ventured within reach.

"Oh, very well. I have nothing to hide," Jonathan declared. "Anyone may know of my high regard for Miss Barrett."

"Aha!" said Harris. "So it *is* true!"

"I have said so," Jonathan confirmed.

It was too ridiculous, and since the whole disappearing-through-the-floor thing didn't seem to be working out for me, I had a good mind to stand up and give those guys what for. I would have enjoyed it, too. With my temper warmed, vestiges of my long-neglected southern vocabulary strained to be set loose on them. I felt like hollering, "Y'all hush your mouths and cool your jets just a darned minute!" I wonder what they would have thought if I had. Probably that one of my oars wasn't all the way in the water.

Mr. Cavanaugh saved me from embarrassing myself by suggesting a more dignified solution. "I would be the last man to fault anybody for admiring Miss Barrett, but cannot you see how distressed she is by this business? It has been a trying few days for her, and her true friends must wish more than anything to see her calm and well-rested. So let us have done, gentlemen, and not raise the subject again. Let us allow the lady to withdraw in peace and answer our questions in her own good time."

From between my fingers, I could see his feet approaching.

"Kate?" he said.

Mr. Cranford laughed indignantly. "'Kate,' he calls her. Did you hear that, Bentley? He feels himself entitled to address her by her Christian name."

Ignoring the remark, I glanced up to see Fitzwilliam's extended hand. It looked like a mighty welcome lifeline to me, a way to escape what surely qualified as my most embarrassing moment to date. Well, one of them, at least. I had gotten myself into some pretty awkward situations in the past. What a relief to know this one was about over... or so I thought. I had accepted Fitzwilliam's escort and was halfway to the door when the butler cleared his throat and addressed me.

"Mr. George Galloway, Miss."

I dropped Mr. Cavanaugh's hand and prepared to greet George as he came into the room. *Oh, Lord*, I was thinking. *Could it get any worse?*

"Who is this fellow?" Harris demanded, looking at me.

Poor George. It wasn't his fault. He had no idea what he had walked into. "This is Mr. George Galloway," I repeated for Mr. Cranford's benefit. "He is a neighbor and a dear friend." I hoped we could leave it at that. I held out my hand for him to shake, saying, "How good to see you again, George."

He kissed my hand instead and said, clear as a bell, "Perhaps, Kate, you should inform these gentlemen that I am also the man who hopes to marry you."

It was a very awkward moment; and the countenance of each shewed that it was so. They all looked exceedingly foolish; and Edward seemed to have as great an inclination to walk out of the room again, as to advance further into it. (Sense and Sensibility, chapter 35)

Chapter 42
Too Many Suitors

So the Kate's-Matrimonial-Prospects Club had officially convened with everybody present and accounted for. But they'd have to hold their meeting without me. I knew I would owe George a huge apology, but I just had to get out of there. I zipped up the stairs to my bedroom as fast as a hot knife cuts through butter. If I could have bolted the door behind me, I would have.

Four offers of marriage? Good lord! It was crazy! Ironic too, considering that I was technically still in mourning and not supposed to marry anybody for months. It made me think of that saying, *Be careful what you wish for.* When I chose my new life, hadn't this been more or less what I'd asked for? – handsome suitors and lots of romance? Hadn't I envisioned proposals more than once? Somehow, though, it had never looked like this! I'd never considered that the dream could turn into a nightmare by having too much of a good thing.

There were at least two mysteries I couldn't figure out. First, what did any of these guys see in me that made them so keen on marriage? And second, what on earth was I supposed to do about it?

Normally, I would expect to find some wisdom or at least some viable options from consulting Jane Austen, but there was absolutely no precedent established in any of her books for multiple, simultaneous marriage offers. Both Elizabeth and Emma had received two proposals, true, but the first for each of them was unthinkable and flatly turned down long before the right one came along. No contest there. Anne Elliot technically received three (Captain Wentworth, Charles Musgrove, and then eventually Captain Wentworth again), but nobody had four. And besides the excessive number of suitors, I had the added problem that none of mine could be thrown out on the basis of being ineligible or positively revolting. Even Mr. Cranford's suit had merit.

Only the men themselves would be able to clue me in on my first question – why on earth they wanted to marry me. I didn't feel like I had much idea about any of them. It seemed ages ago since George had addressed me, and his feelings might have changed some since then. Both Jonathan and Fitzwilliam had been interrupted before full explanations could be made, and yet I could believe each had *some* affection for me. Harris was the biggest question mark. He had claimed to be in love with me, but I didn't really buy it. We didn't even seem very compatible.

Without more information, it would be like trying to order a meal from a menu in a foreign language; no telling if I'd like what ended up on my plate. Only I'd have to live with this particular entrée for the rest of my life. Or, just as scary, I might go hungry forever if I chose the wrong one or passed on all four. How could I make that kind of decision without all the facts, without hearing what each of the guys had to say for himself?

When I thought about it, I decided that might not be a bad way to proceed. Why not interview each of them as if they had applied for a job – in this case, the job of being my husband? Maybe that would be too demeaning. Okay, so it wasn't really a job interview; it would simply be a chance for us to get to understand each other better. There was a lot at stake here, and not just on my side. Every one of these guys should know what he might be getting himself into and have a chance to change his mind before things went too far.

I suppose it was unfair of me, though, to expect them to explain themselves, to give me some clear and logical reason they each wanted to marry me, when I couldn't begin to do the same. At this point, I didn't know what (or who) I wanted. I still considered Harris a long shot, but I had feelings for the other three, and I hated to disappoint any of them.

~~*~~

I pleaded a headache (not much of a stretch) to avoid going down to dinner, so I could only imagine the awkward scene there. Mercifully, George had gone home, but the others were stuck eating together since they'd accepted the Sothebys' hospitality for as long as they remained in the area. I had by this time updated my sister on the multiple-suitors situation so that she could try to head off any trouble. Her husband's amiable nature would go a long way towards keeping the peace, too, I expected.

"They were perfectly well behaved," Lucy reported back to me afterward. "I hardly know what you expected, Kate. They are all gentlemen, in any case."

"If you had witnessed what happened in the drawing room earlier, you would understand. Barbs and veiled insults flew back and forth over my head so furiously that I thought surely fur would be next."

"Fur?"

"Oh, never mind. I am just pleased there were no open hostilities in the dining room. That is all."

"I see your dilemma, though. I like all three of them, actually, and George too of course, each one in his own way. I am glad I never faced such a challenge as deciding between them. When I met Arthur, he was head and shoulders above anybody else I had ever seen. His proposing made me the happiest girl in England. No questions plagued me; no doubts; no confusion."

"Yes, you were the lucky one."

I checked on my mother next and was glad to find her not only awake but sitting up. "Can I talk to you a minute?" I asked.

"Of course, my dear," she said, patting a place on the bed beside her. "What is the trouble?"

I laid it all out for her, step by step, suitor by suitor, and proposal by proposal. I wasn't sure she would believe me; it sounded pretty far fetched even to my ears.

"…I simply cannot understand it," I said to wrap up my story. "I mean, it's not like I'm an heiress or something that men should fall all over themselves to marry me, is it?"

"You have a respectable dowry, my dear, but you are no heiress. That is true. How nice to know that, whatever else, it is not money that your suitors are after. As your mother, I may be prejudiced, but

I do not find it so surprising that four men should admire you. Go to my dressing table and look in the mirror, child."

"Mama, that is not necessary," I complained.

"I think it is. Now, go."

I reluctantly did as I was told. There I saw a pretty, petite young woman with a clear complexion, shiny dark hair, and bright eyes. I had finally grown used to that reflection, and it no longer shocked me as it had at first. I would have been shocked to see anybody else's face looking back at me now. In fact, it was hard to believe that had ever been the case.

"Now you see one reason men admire you," Mama said. "They are only human, and they cannot help being drawn to your beauty. But there are other reasons. You know that there are."

I came back to sit by her, still feeling kind of sulky. "I play the pianoforte tolerably well, I suppose," I said with a sigh.

She laughed. "Better than tolerably well. And you have a good mind and a sweet spirit. There is a certain spark about you, too, that tends to light up a room. No, I am not puzzled by four men admiring you. I am only a little surprised that four should have become at- tached at once. But you need not marry any of them unless you are sure. Do you really not have any preference?"

Of course I did, I admitted to myself. At Mama's question, one face and one face only popped up in my mind. It was Fitzwilliam Cavanaugh's. When I thought of nothing but the man himself, he was the one I wanted. He was the one who made my heart sing and my imagination bloom with daisies and possibilities. But there was more to this decision. What I wanted just as much was to stay close to my family. Only George Galloway could offer me that. Jonathan would take me away, but at least I would be settled near other people I loved. I would know no one at all at Pellencourt. As often as I had dreamt of a fine estate in Derbyshire in the past, living there would now mean extended separations from everybody else I cared for. Could I bear that? Would being married to the man who could make my insides do somersaults and my spirit tap dance, simply by saying my name, be enough to compensate for losing so much? Plus, I wasn't completely convinced Fitzwilliam loved me. He still had never said so.

"They each have their good qualities and their disadvantages, Mama," I told her. "I am not ready to decide anything yet."

Elizabeth, however astonished, was at least more prepared for an interview than before, and resolved to appear and speak with calmness... (Pride and Prejudice, chapter 44)

Chapter 43
Interviews

The next day, when I told Lucy that I needed a place where I could meet privately with each of the four candidates, she gave a small parlor over to my use. It was sunny and cheerful, which I hoped would set the right tone for what I had in mind. I didn't want dark melodrama or even smoky romance. I just wanted to keep a clear head while gathering whatever information would help me with my decision.

I sent a message inviting George Galloway to call on me, and in the meantime, I discreetly asked Harris Cranford to come in. This was starting with the easiest, since I wasn't nearly so emotionally involved with him, and I suspected he really cared no more than three fiddlesticks about me.

At first, when I asked him why he wished to marry me, he maintained what he'd said before: he loved me passionately and that was all that mattered to him. When I pressed him a little more, though, he finally admitted he was under uncomfortable pressure from his father to find a suitable wife.

"'...a gentlewoman of good family and good fortune,' the old pater says to me, 'a lady suited to a country life, one who gives herself no fancy airs.' His list was an excellent start, but I stipulated for something additional. She must be handsome and mild tempered as well, I thought. Imagine how I blessed my lucky stars when I met with you so unexpectedly! Here was my chance to make both my parent and myself happy, for you fulfilled all these requirements and more. And I daresay you will be very happy too, Miss Barrett. Once we are married, it shall be my life's work to make you so."

Where he got the idea that I possessed what could reasonably be described as a 'good fortune,' I still am not sure. It must have been something somebody said that he misinterpreted. Anyway, I soon straightened him out on that detail.

"Oh… I see," he said. There was a long silence before he could think how to go on. "Well, that does put a different complexion on things, Miss Barrett. As much as I admire and respect you, as much as I would sincerely like to marry you, I am afraid it would be inadvisable. Impossible, really. We would never receive my father's blessing, and without it we would have very little to live on. I hope you will forgive me if I reconsider my offer to you. It seems I was too hasty in making it."

I did forgive him, and I wished him better luck next time.

He rose to leave but then stopped. "Under the circumstances, you would probably prefer me gone. However, I fear I must impose on your forbearance and the Sothebys' hospitality a little longer."

"Why is that, Mr. Cranford?"

"It is because of your cousin Jonathan. He expects to travel back to Kantwell with me, and I daresay he will not care to go until he knows his fate. Will you be long deciding about him, do you think?"

"No, not very long."

Once he left the room, I heaved a sigh of relief. The interview had turned out better than I could have hoped; Harris had withdrawn his proposal of his own free will. Oddly enough, I believed him when he said he really wanted to marry me, and yet I also believed he wouldn't suffer much for having to give me up. Perhaps he wasn't the sort who felt anything very deeply.

One down; three to go.

Mr. Galloway arrived a little while later. I invited him into the parlor and closed the door. "Thank you for coming, George," I told him. "Please, do sit down. God only knows what you must be thinking after that royal fiasco yesterday… I mean that awful scene. Can you forgive me for abandoning you?"

"Of course, Kate. You were obviously much distressed, and it was at least partly my fault. I should not have said what I did. I only meant to pay my respects to you and enquire after your mother. Then, when I saw you surrounded by those other men, I suppose I went a little mad. I wanted them to know you were spoken for, or at least I hoped you considered yourself so. But I was later informed that the others feel the same way."

"Not Mr. Cranford," I said, trying to offer him something. "He has since withdrawn. And I want you to know that I have not accepted anyone yet. You were the first to speak, and I owe you a definite answer."

He seemed to brace himself. "Than I am ready to hear it."

"I wish I were ready to give it, George. That is the problem; I have no answer for you yet. Honestly, I'm having the hardest time understanding my sudden popularity. I think it might help if I could hear why you wish to marry me."

"Very well, but there is nothing sudden about my admiring you. I have known since we were all children together that I should one day become a permanent part of this family, that I would marry one of the Barrett sisters when we all grew up. I think most people considered Lucy the handsomest, but I always preferred you, Kate – your looks as well as your manner. It was only a question of waiting until you were old enough to ask."

"I had no idea," I said in true amazement.

"There was no reason you should have until the time was right. I thought that time had almost come, but then your accident intervened. You seemed rather changed afterward, too."

"Did I? And yet you still wished to marry me?"

"Of course. As I have told you, it is something I settled on long ago, and I did not love you less for nearly losing you. If anything, I loved you more. When you were recovered, I could wait no longer. Perhaps it was still too early, though, since you did not seem inclined to marry when I asked you. Now, however, I hope my patience will be rewarded. You know I care for you, Kate, for you and all your family, and I will provide for you well. You can depend on it."

"Yes, George, I do know it, but you must be patient with me yet a little while longer."

When he had gone away again, I sat for a long time thinking about what George had told me and what it meant. Something about it seemed familiar – familiar and touching. I had never put it into words before, but I agreed with what he said; it seemed like he belonged to our family, and marrying me would obviously seal the deal. I couldn't decide if his explanation should make me more inclined to marry him or less. I supposed loving me for my family was at least as legitimate as loving me for something superficial like looks. Maybe not as flattering, though. One thing was for sure: the interview certainly hadn't ended with a neat, clear-cut answer like the previous one. That would probably have been too much to hope for.

Jonathan was next. I asked the butler to locate him and send him in to me if possible. He arrived ten minutes later with a hopeful look on his face.

"You wished to see me, Kate?"

"I do. Please, sit with me for a few minutes, Jonathan. I hoped to finish our conversation from yesterday. You honored me with a proposal of marriage, but I was not quite certain you had finished when Mr. Cranford interrupted. I wondered if there was anything else you wished to say on the subject."

He considered a moment. "No, no, I do not think so. I said all I meant to. Now I merely await your answer, which I hope will be in the affirmative."

"I see. Then perhaps you will answer a question for me. Why did not you offer for Miss Cranford instead? That is more what I expected since you seemed to show more positive symptoms of love for her than for me. I am not offended, you understand; I am simply trying to comprehend this unexpected turn of events."

Jonathan looked down at his hands for a bit before answering. "It is a fair question," he began. "I admit that Miss Cranford's beauty and charm did rather bewitch me at first, but there was nothing serious in it on her side... except when Alex fell ill. I did not tell you, Kate, for I did not want to prejudice your opinion against her. But when it looked as if Alex might die, Miss Cranford spoke to me of how it would not be a tragedy for *everyone*, that I might come to regard it as a blessing in disguise, for then I would inherit Kantwell and the baronetcy, 'and who should be more deserving and better suited to the position?' Her implication was clear. She could not be interested in marrying an ordinary Mr. Bentley, but it would be different if I were the heir and the future 'Sir Jonathan Bentley.' I was ashamed for her, Kate, and of course her favor vanished as soon as Alex recovered.

"And yet, it is not the loss of herself that distresses me so much as the loss of my good opinion of her. If I could still believe her character as irreproachable as I once fooled myself into thinking it was, I would have fewer regrets.

"It struck me then that it was a very different sort of woman who would suit me best, one upon whose goodness of character I could absolutely rely. And when I looked about myself for such a woman, there you were, Kate – you who had already engaged my affection and whose smiles and ways had become so dear to me. I knew I should never be disappointed in you, and I should be very fortunate indeed if you would agree to be my wife."

This made perfect sense; it was exactly the conclusion Edmund Bertram had come to in *Mansfield Park*. But one more question remained. "And yet you do not love me, Jonathan, nor I you, at least not in the way a man would desire that his wife should. Does not that worry you?"

He shook his head. "Not in the least. We should be no different from the majority of other couples at the outset. And where there is a foundation of true affection to build upon, love will follow in time. I have faith in that."

He was probably right, and yet I wasn't sure I wanted to bet my entire future on it. I thanked Jonathan for his candor and promised I would carefully consider everything he had said, which of course I would. Until I had come to some definite decision, how could I think of anything else?

Now only Fitzwilliam Cavanaugh remained. I'd saved him for last, sort of like dessert, I suppose. But what kind of dessert would he turn out to be, I wondered? Cold, like ice cream? I hoped not, although ice cream did melt in the mouth. Hmm. Cake started out warm but cooled over time, much like many doomed relationships. That wasn't a promising analogy. I was rooting for crème brûlée: a little crusty and unapproachable at first, but sweet, rich, and oh-so-yummy once you take the trouble to break the shell and dig in. I never got tired of it, and I always ate it with a spoon so as not to miss one tasty bit.

After lingering on that mental image a minute or two, I went in search of Mr. Crème Brûlée.

"Am I the last?" he asked when I found him in the library.

"The last for what?" I said, pretending not to understand.

He laid aside his book and stood. "The last of your suitors to be interviewed. Have no fear, Miss Barrett. I do not mean the question as a criticism; in fact, I admire your approach to this... this unusual situation. It is very fair-minded of you, I daresay."

"Considering how this has come about, I thought it only right to allow each of the gentlemen to speak his peace. And yes, you are the last," *just like dessert.*

"Are you finding the exercise enlightening?"

"Very."

"The others have set the mark pretty high, then. I only hope I will not prove a disappointment."

"I hope that as well, Mr. Cavanaugh. If you would come with me, I have use of a room where we can speak without being disturbed."

"I would prefer the out of doors, if you don't mind. The weather is very fine, I believe."

I supposed the fresh air might do me good, maybe help me keep a clear head, which was sometimes difficult where Fitzwilliam Cavanaugh was concerned. I'd had powerful reactions to him from the very beginning. That hadn't changed. Although my sentiments for him had done a complete one-eighty, I still couldn't be near him without feeling kind of discombobulated. And I needed to be completely combobulated now, if that was even a word. After all, I was trying to sort this problem out logically.

"As you wish," I said. "Let me just run and get my shawl." It might be a sunny afternoon, but it was only March.

When I returned, we struck out into the back gardens. There was a large, gravel semi-circular area fanning out from the house, with a tiered fountain in the center. We strolled around the perimeter, which was framed out in low boxwood hedges and other manicured plantings. I'd never really had much chance to explore Coleswold's grounds since I left the vicinity before it became my sister's home. That gave us an excuse for something else to talk about, postponing the need to dive into the stated purpose of our little walk together. I commented on the pleasing symmetrical design of the garden and a couple of plants I recognized. He pointed out a few of the herbs that had medicinal value and explained their uses. But finally, we exhausted those topics.

"Shall we?" Fitzwilliam said, gesturing to the pathway that took off from the gravel expanse and jutted straight out from the house, sloping gently uphill toward a distant gazebo-looking structure.

I nodded and fell into step beside him. Clearly, it was time to get down to business, but still we stalled, walking on together in silence. Unlike with the others, I had no idea how start. The whole exercise suddenly seemed ridiculous, as if I'd decided to sponsor an essay contest with myself as the prize. The best entry titled *Why I Want to Marry Kate Barrett* wins.

Maybe he could read my mind, because he said, "I do wish to marry you, Kate, but I cannot make speeches. If that is what you expect from me, you should know that I will not try to persuade you against your will or win you by excessive flattery."

"No, of course not. That is not at all what I desire. I only meant to allow you a chance to say anything you might have wished to before, to finish what you had begun... or not. You *were* interrupted after all."

"That is true. And then I made a clumsy business of finishing it later..."

"...which I understood completely. But now..."

"...now we have an opportunity to set things right. Is that it?"

"Yes, to set things right, one way or the other. I am very sensible of the honor of your proposal, Mr. Cavanaugh – indeed, it amazes me – but I will not hold you to it, considering the circumstances under which you made it. You see, I would endure anything rather than to marry without true affection. If there is none or insufficient on your side, I beg you would say so now and withdraw."

"Withdraw?" he said, sounding rather perturbed. "Why would I do that? I'm in love with you!"

I stared at him. "You are?"

"Yes, of course! Did I not say so before?"

I shook my head. "I listened quite attentively."

"Well, I am saying it now, and I speak nothing but the truth. I would never have asked you to marry me if I did not love you."

"I thought that... that..."

"That what?"

"That you might have felt under some obligation."

"Only to my heart."

"I have no fortune to speak of."

"If you think I care one whit for that, you do not know me."

"I just wanted to be sure you were not mistaken in that idea, like Mr. Cranford was."

"Is that why he retired from the field?"

"Yes, but I did not mind. I did not wish to marry him."

"And the other two?"

"I like them both much better, and there is some advantage to each."

"You 'like' them. I noticed you did not say 'love.' *I* listened quite attentively too."

I smiled. "That is correct; I did not."

"Then perhaps I still have some chance?"

By this time, we had arrived at the gazebo and gone on in. I turned towards Fitzwilliam and looked up into his handsome face, now become so dear to me. On the way to those mesmerizing eyes of his, my gaze slid over his warm, full lips. I imagined what it would be like to be kissed by them. "You do have a chance," I told him. "A very good one."

He grinned and took a step closer. There was less than a foot between us now, and I swear I could hear electricity snapping and sizzling across the gap. With him so near, it was impossible to think clearly. It didn't matter; I had officially tossed out the idea of making a *logical* decision as soon as he'd said he loved me.

"Is there anything I can do to convince you in my favor?" he asked with a provocative double lift of his eyebrows.

My only excuse for what I did then is that I simply couldn't bear the suspense any longer.

Elizabeth's spirits soon rising to playfulness again, she wanted Mr. Darcy to account for his having ever fallen in love with her. (Pride and Prejudice, chapter 60)

Chapter 44
The Cherry on Top

It's true; I more or less threw myself at Mr. Cavanaugh and kissed him. Fortunately, he recovered from the shock in a split second and thoroughly kissed me back, otherwise I would have been mighty embarrassed.

It was a kiss like no other. He wrapped me up in his arms and lifted me off my feet. Chills tingled and pinged through my chest and shoulders at the same time the delicious warmth of his body nearly swallowed me up. I couldn't feel my toes anymore, and I was pretty darned sure my legs had turned to Jell-O. I wouldn't have been surprised to see fireworks either when I finally opened my eyes.

"Does this mean I have convinced you?" he asked, still holding me tightly with our faces only inches apart.

I just smiled at him, and then I went back in for another kiss. I was convinced, all right. The chemistry I suspected before was there in spades… plus the love. Nothing else seemed important – not the obstacle of living at a distance and not the inevitable disappointment of the other guys. I couldn't be worried for them at that moment. I loved Fitzwilliam and he loved me. We belonged together; it was as simple as that. We'd deal with the rest as it came along.

One surprise, though: Mr. Cavanaugh wasn't exactly crème brûlée after all, but something even better. More like a premium version of my favorite chocolate bar, the kind with a pinch of chili pepper added – sweet, satisfying, with a spicy little kick to keep things interesting, made to be savored slowly as it melts on your tongue, and leaving behind a warm glow to remember it by. Just about the most perfect flavor ever invented.

I'm not sure how long we lingered at the gazebo (a place we would always consider "ours" afterward), but we finally came up for air. "I suppose we had better be getting back," I said reluctantly.

"Must we?" he asked with a groan.

"We will have been missed by now, and soon they will send out the search party."

"Very well, but it really is too cruel. Now that I have tasted a sample of what I have to look forward to, I never want to let you go."

Likewise. "There is one thing even crueler," I told him. I looked down at how I was dressed, now modified to 'partial mourning,' and held my arms out helplessly. "According to custom, we must wait to marry until October, when my year is up. But I'm sure Papa would have wanted us to be happy together as soon as possible."

He tucked a stray lock of hair behind my ear, saying, "We will speak to your mother and follow her advice in the matter." My arm tucked through his, we started back to the house. "Do you think she will be pleased about us?" he continued.

I laughed. "Pleased? Are you kidding, uh, I mean joking? It was practically her idea! She had the match made while I was still in my sick bed, recommending to me that I mind my tongue and make myself agreeable to you. But of course, I did not like you then, so I did not bother being civil."

"How well I remember," he said dryly.

"And yet you fell in love with me anyway. Remarkable." Then I felt myself lapsing into my Lizzy Bennet role again. I thought it might be almost my last chance too, since her story didn't go beyond the wedding into married life. I'd be on my own soon, with no more help from Jane Austen, but I thought I was ready. Playfully, I asked Mr. Cavanaugh, "How do you account for it? – falling in love with me, I mean? Oh, I can comprehend your going along very charmingly when once you had begun, but what set you off in the first place?"

"I hardly know. Perhaps it was your impertinence. It was something new for me, and it set me a challenge to win you over. Then I found myself firmly caught instead."

"You may well call my conduct impertinence or at least incivility; it was nothing less. In the beginning, I never saw you without rather wishing to laugh at you or give you pain. Had you not been really amiable, you would have hated me for it. But you showed by your behavior that you did not. I suppose that was my first clue that I was wrong about you, that you were perfectly noble and good. How lucky for me to have discovered it in time."

"How lucky for *me* that you changed your mind and were not too proud to admit it."

I smiled to myself. "Let us just say that I had not enough pride to maintain my early prejudice against you, although I had solemnly sworn I would. Holding a grudge is very hard work, though; falling in love with you was much easier in the end." Now Mr. Darcy's words came to me. I just *had* to borrow a version of them too. I was sure he wouldn't mind. "I cannot tell you how it happened or fix on the hour, the look, or the words which laid the foundation. I was in the middle before I knew I had begun."

He paused our walk and turned me around to face him. "So you do love me, little one?"

"I do, and I offer you this solid proof. I know that by marrying you I will be moving away from all my dear family. I would not do that for anybody I did not love quite extravagantly." Just one more quote… "But the wife of Mr. Cavanaugh must have such extraordinary sources of happiness necessarily attached to her situation that she could, upon the whole, have no cause to repine."

"That is a handsome sentiment, Kate, but I believe your love and loyalty may not be put to such a test, at least not in the near future."

"Why? What do you mean?"

"I was speaking to Mr. Fitch the last time he came to attend your mother, and he proposed an interesting idea to me. He is not a young man anymore, as you know, and he finds the needs of this growing community often outstrip his ability to respond to them. He asked if I might consider returning to the practice long term. There is plenty of work for both of us, he says. My help would allow him to lighten his load considerably; his continued presence would allow me to travel home to Pellencourt when I need to. It seems a very sensible arrangement. I was thinking we could take a house in

Carding, where you would be near your family. Would that be agreeable to you?"

"You would do that for me?" I asked in total amazement. It reminded me of Mr. Knightley's selfless offer to move to Hartfield when he married Emma, so that she wouldn't have to abandon her father.

"Of course. Some things must change when a man marries. I could not expect my wife to follow me about the countryside in my former nomadic style. Since we must settle somewhere, what better place could there be than here, where you will be happiest?"

I threw my arms around his neck and nearly squealed with delight. I didn't care who might see it from the house. I was busting with joy, and it just had to overflow somehow. "Thank you, thank you!" I cried.

~~*~~

Fitzwilliam discreetly disappeared as soon as we reentered the house, knowing I had a piece of delicate business to attend to. I needed to speak to Jonathan as soon as possible. As it happened, Jonathan had seen enough from the window to guess what was coming, and he made it very easy for me.

"No apology necessary, Kate, really," he said after I had used the word 'sorry' at least six times. "You must go where your heart leads you. I will miss you, though, as will the rest of my family, and it may be a long time indeed before I find anybody charming enough to take your place in my affections. Mr. Cavanaugh is a very lucky man. You must both come to visit us at Kantwell as often as you can."

Thoughtful and generous to the end. I should have expected nothing less of Jonathan.

I meant to find Lucy next, which I did... or she found me. She was lurking nearby when I finished speaking to Jonathan. She knew I would have something to tell her after all my interviews. I think she had pretty much figured out *what* by the look on my face. She pulled me into the empty library and shut the door.

"Well?" she said with hushed excitement.

"Oh, Lucy! I am so happy," I cried, throwing myself into her arms. (I'd sure been doing a lot of that lately – throwing myself at people.) We hugged and cried; cried and hugged some more.

"It's Mr. Cavanaugh that you love, then?" she asked presently.

"Oh, yes. And he loves me too!"

"Of course he does. So he will marry you and spirit you away to his fine estate in Derbyshire, where you will, no doubt, live happily ever after. I am so pleased for you both, but oh, how I shall miss you, Kate!"

I then got to fill Lucy in on the other part of my good news – the cherry on top of my happiness – that we would be staying in Carding for the time being. "...We will often travel to Pellencourt, but while the senior Mr. Cavanaugh is alive and well, there is no need for Fitzwilliam to be always there too. But I must go to Mama now. Is she strong enough for such important news, do you think? I have not seen her since early this morning."

"Oh, yes, and good news is the best medicine. She is out of bed and fully dressed today. I believe you will find her in the sitting room adjoining her bedchamber."

And so we did, Fitzwilliam and I. I knocked softly and then slipped in ahead of him. "Mama, I have a surprise for you," I said. "Here is your future son-in-law."

Mama's reaction was everything I could have hoped for. Afterward, though, I had to face a disappointment. In the hallway outside Mama's room, Fitzwilliam told me, "I must leave you for a time, my darling."

"Why? Where are you going?"

"Well, it strikes me that it would not do to expect my former rivals to sit down to dinner and keep polite conversation with the man who has ruined all their hopes."

"I had not thought of that," I admitted, "but of course you are right." I didn't want to pain Jonathan any further or even Harris Cranford. And I had sent a message to George Galloway asking him to come the next morning.

"I think it would be kindest if I took myself out of the way for at least a day or two, availing myself of Mr. Fitch's standing invitation. We have many things to discuss, he and I, now that we will be working together. Besides," he added, drawing me close, "it would

292

be too much temptation staying in the same house with you day and night."

Right again. *Way* too much temptation.

~~*~~

What an amazing, life-changing day it had been! When I had gotten out of bed that morning, I'd had no idea how things would turn out – what my suitors would tell me, what I would decide, or even if I would be able to decide anything at all. Now, as I climbed back into bed, it was all settled; I was going to marry Mr. Fitzwilliam Cavanaugh as soon as my year of mourning was up, and we were going to live in Carding. The best of all possible outcomes!

I was so happy that I wanted to tell everybody, or at least my two younger sisters, who were still in the dark. But George deserved to know first, before the news spread any further. That was the only thing that dampened my parade a little, the fact that I would have to hurt someone I liked so much.

I was quite sure neither of the other two had actually been in love with me, but George might be. He might suffer quite a bit when I told him I wouldn't marry him. I hoped not, or at least that his pain would be of *short duration*.

As I lay there in bed thinking about how I should break the news to him, I realized why what he had told me of his feelings sounded touchingly familiar. It reminded me of Laurie in *Little Women* (although I couldn't remember if this part was in the book or only the movie). Laurie had 'always known' that he should be part of the March family, but he settled on the wrong sister at first, wanting to marry Jo and then later falling in love with Amy. How awesome would that be if George could do the same – recover from his infatuation with me and discover true happiness with Matilda or Carmen a few years down the road? That was an intriguing possibility.

I wanted *everybody* to be as happy as I was, but I have to admit my thoughts were mostly self-centered. I pondered at length how wonderful Fitzwilliam was, how amazing that he loved me, and how divinely happy we would be together forever. Such yummy brainwaves made for some pretty delicious dreams that night... and many more to follow.

But now suppose as much as you chuse; give a loose to your fancy, indulge your imagination in every possible flight which the subject will afford, and unless you believe me actually married, you cannot greatly err. (Pride and Prejudice, chapter 60)

Chapter 45
Anticipation

I expected the months before my wedding would drag by as slowly and painfully as hospital tape being peeled off my arm, one hair at a time. It wasn't so bad, though. Part of the pleasure of a happy event is in the anticipation, after all, in looking forward to it. I did a lot of that in those months – looking forward, and also some looking back.

Yes, it was hard to wait, but we were all very busy, including Fitzwilliam. He started taking medical calls right away and also looking for a suitable house to buy or lease where we would live together once we were married. In the meantime, he stayed nights at Mr. Fitch's (to avoid temptation) and spent at least some part of every day with me (which was temptation enough for both of us). Week by week, I got to know my future husband better. That only made me love him more and confirmed that I had made the right choice. He is truly my own Mr. Darcy... and Mr. Knightley, and Colonel Brandon, and Captain Wentworth rolled into one, because it seems to me like the best virtues of all of Austen's heroes have been joined in this one amazing man. Of course, I freely admit I might be prejudiced... again... but in his favor this time.

In April, Mr. Sotheby momentously announced that the improvements to the dower house were complete, which meant that Mama would have a place of her own again where her daughters could live with her. We all moved in – Mama, Matilda, Carmen, and I – and we thanked Mr. Sotheby for his generosity. Sometimes, though, I think we might have saved ourselves a lot of trouble if we hadn't bothered moving. I *know* we would have saved a lot of walking to and fro, along with some major wear and tear on the lawn. We ran back and forth between the two houses so much that we soon wore a new path.

The traffic only increased after Lucy's baby – a sweet little boy, named Edward after my father – was born in early June. Mama, especially, couldn't tolerate being away from him, her first grand-child, for any time at all. Plus, she insisted that Lucy, as a first-time mom, needed lots of guidance from the voice of experience. Mama's experienced voice (along with the rest of her) ended up staying the night so often at the great house "to help out" that her old room was once again given over to her exclusive use. No one seemed to mind the arrangement. That's the nice thing about a big mansion; there's plenty of space to get away when you need to, even without leaving the house.

July was glorious with beautiful weather, giving plenty of chances for Fitzwilliam and me to get away on our own. We walked, rode, and went by carriage to any and every place worth seeing in the area. Or no place in particular at all. It didn't matter, just as long as we could be together.

Our biggest excursion that summer (and most exciting destina-tion) was our trip to Pellencourt. I had been desperately curious to see the place that would one day be my home, and also to meet Fitzwilliam's family. I'm sure they were just as curious about me, the lady their son and brother planned to marry. We asked Matilda if she would like to go with us as a chaperone and then decided to take Carmen too. We really were a very merry party along the way.

As we traveled north, I tried my best to lower my expectations for Pellencourt from where I had let them soar to before, thinking it was going to be as grand as Pemberley is always pictured in the movies. I really shouldn't have worried, though; I wasn't in any danger of being let down, as it turned out. The place was positively magnificent. Not that everything was super ornate and gold-plated. (I would never be comfortable living in or even sitting on the sofas in a house that felt like a museum.) Pellencourt, I soon discovered, simply operated on a much larger scale than I was used to – house, rooms, servants, stables, gardens, the overall size of the park – and yet it still didn't feel like showing off to me, because it was just so tastefully done.

The aspect of the house I liked most on that first trip was that there were so many windows, making the views the feature instead of the furnishings. I felt like I'd never get anything done, though, if... (I mean *when)* I came to live there; I'd probably be always staring out the windows or waiting for a break in the weather to get outside, because the grounds were so beautiful. Lush lawns, and trees, and hills, and a lake. *Natural* beauty, for the most part. I was delighted, as Lizzy was with Pemberley, that nobody had deemed it necessary to awkwardly 'improve' on something already so perfect by planting silly topiaries or Greek statues everywhere you looked.

I said my favorite part was all the windows, but that isn't exactly true. The best part of our visit was touring the estate with Fitzwilliam – seeing him there where he had grown up, and hearing the pride in his voice as he told me a little piece of the history or some funny anecdote from his childhood. I think it helped me more than anything else would have to really understand the man I'd fallen in love with. His parents and sister could not have been nicer either. I'm sure over time they will grow very dear to me, like my own family.

But moving to Pellencourt is somewhere in the future. My next move will be into the fine house that Fitzwilliam bought for us after we returned from our travels. It's called the Grady-Louis House – a stately brick place just outside Carding and not far from Mrs. Abernathy's. I'd seen and admired the house before, but I'd never been inside it. That hasn't changed.

When Fitzwilliam first brought me there and told me he'd purchased the house for us, I was literally jumping up and down with excitement. "Oh, Fitzwilliam, it's perfect!" I enthused. "Let's go in. I want to see everything!"

He held me back, though, saying, "No, wait. You can only look at the outside of the box for now. It is to be my wedding present to you, Kate, so you cannot see what is inside until that day. Besides, there is work to be done first to make it ready and worthy for Mrs. Cavanaugh to enter."

"Is your mother coming to see it?" I stupidly asked. *Duh!*

He laughed. "No, my pet. I meant you: Mrs. Fitzwilliam Cavanaugh, for so you shall be by the time you cross the threshold."

How strange that sounded to me – *Mrs. Fitzwilliam Cavanaugh* – strange and wonderful. I've been trying to get used to it ever since. I even practiced writing my new signature, attempting to give it a little flair, as if I was an author preparing for a book signing. It took a while before I didn't feel like an impostor any more, but I think I can finally believe it. I'd gone through the same sort of thing with my first name change. This is just the next step in my trans-formation – the last one. I went from Hope O'Neil to Kate Barrett, and soon I will be Mrs. Cavanaugh.

Even though sometimes it felt like the waiting would never end, it finally has. Tomorrow, I will become Fitzwilliam's wife! The idea thrills me right down to my toes... and a few other important places along the way.

I can hardly believe my dreams are about to come true – everything I hoped for when I made the leap to Regency England. And that's probably the hardest thing of all to believe: that I ever was a different person living elsewhere... and else-when. It all seems so long ago and kind of hazy when I think about it now.

My past in the future is fading, but letting go is easier because I've got my whole heart and soul invested in *this* life now. When I set out on my second chance, I was hoping to find family, love, and a little adventure. As far as I can tell, I got everything I asked for. I don't know what I could have done to deserve it or how I got so lucky, but I'll always be grateful.

Actually, come to think of it, there is *one* thing I wanted and didn't get, at least not yet. I haven't gotten to meet Jane Austen, although I'm not quite sure what I would say to her if I did. I would want to gush and tell her how much her books have meant to me, how they have inspired me and enriched my life – both lives. But I couldn't do any of that without her thinking I'd dropped a loop somewhere.

Instead, I plan to do something tonight I should probably have done a long time ago; I'm going to cut my only tangible link back to Jane and to Crossroads too. It will be difficult, but here goes.

I look around to be sure no one is watching, which *is* a little crazy since I'm alone in my room at the Coleswold dower house. Convinced the coast is clear, I pull out my copy of *Mansfield Park* that I've kept carefully hidden ever since I received it. It's my most treasured possession, but it has to go; I can't risk Fitzwilliam find-ing it when I and my things move in with him. I plan to have no secrets from my husband... with the tiny exception of my entire past life in a different century.

So I take one last look at the precious novel, stroke the cover one final time, hug it to my chest for a moment, and then toss it into the fireplace before I can change my mind. The flames from the paper burning brighten the room and warm my face for a while, and then it's gone. I'm not going to cry over the loss, though. I have already decided that's not necessary for at least three reasons.

For one thing, I have parts of *Mansfield Park* (and all the other Austen novels) already committed to memory. Secondly, if I'm not mistaken about the publication dates, I don't have long to wait until I can start a new and legitimate collection of her books in this time zone. And they'll all be first editions! But most importantly, if it's a contest between a novel (even a Jane Austen novel) and Mr. Fitzwilliam Cavanaugh, it's *no* contest. Who would want a hero on paper only instead of holding the real, flesh-and-blood man in your arms? I have my own Austen-style life now, and I wouldn't trade my Mr. Cavanaugh for the world.

POSTLUDE

"Good girl!" Poindexter said, smiling at the monitor before him.

"What is it?" Cora asked from across the room.

"Miss O'Neil-Barrett-soon-to-be-Cavanaugh. As instructed, she has destroyed the book I sent her. I had no business worrying after all. Did I tell you she's getting married tomorrow?"

"Only about a half dozen times. I believe you're rather sorry you can't be there to give the bride away."

"What a first-rate thought! Hmm. She hasn't got a father, you know."

"Dex! Don't you dare! I'm sure there is an uncle who can do the job very nicely. Or maybe her brother-in-law, Mr. what's-his-name."

"Sotheby. Arthur Sotheby."

"Right. In any case, it's probably about time to close Hope's case, don't you think? I know she's *special* to you, but it's been almost a year and a half now. And you've told me yourself how well she's settled in. She doesn't need the memories of her former life and Jane Austen anymore. Slowly or all at once, they have to go. It's policy; you know that. Besides, every client, including Hope, agrees to it ahead of time."

Cora assumed the matter was settled when Poindexter didn't say anything more. He seemed to have returned his attention back to his work, so she did likewise. Actually, she wasn't working at all but playing the digital game she was currently addicted to. Dex didn't need to know that, though. Then, just when she was about to score a new personal best, there was another distraction. Tick, tick, tick, tick. Dex was unconsciously tapping a pen on his clipboard again, like he always did when he had something worrisome on his mind... but not only then. It was an annoying habit. When she couldn't get him to break it, Cora had tried, for her own sanity's sake, to learn how to tune the sound out – tried and failed, obviously. She gave up her game and quietly sauntered over to him, snatching away the blasted pen before he saw what was coming.

Poindexter looked as offended as if Cora had uncivilly struck him across the face with a glove, thereby challenging him to a duel with pistols at dawn. "What was that for?" he demanded.

"You were doing it again," she said, tapping the pen in mid-air to demonstrate.

"I'm sorry, my dear. I didn't realize. It's this business with Hope that's bothering me. I do so dislike this part of the process. It seems like a punishment to steal a client's memories away."

"You didn't seem to mind when it was Ben Lewis's memories you were stealing," she pointed out. "In fact you voted to take them away early, long before he was ready, and you urged the rest of the council to vote the same."

"Ah, but that was different. That *was* punishment. Ben had very clearly violated his contract. Hope has done nothing wrong at all. I know she won't miss the memories once they're gone, but many people find the sensation disconcerting. They feel things slipping away, like somebody punched a hole in the base of the hourglass and they're helpless to stop their memories running out the bottom. I'd like to spare Hope even that temporary distress."

"Then there's only one way, although I'm not sure it's any kinder. If it could be done while she was sleeping, that would be ideal, but we've tried that before…"

"…and it doesn't work. Yes, yes, I remember. Well, let's put off anything of that sort until after the wedding. I'll give the matter further consideration and see if I can come up with an appropriate solution. These things take a little style and finesse to do properly, you know." He stuck his hand out, palm up. "My pen, if you please." When Cora hesitated, he added, "I'll be good, I promise."

Cora gave him one more stern look and then dropped the pen into his hand. Nobody was perfect, but Dex was pretty close.

I have just filled the last page of my diary, which is entirely fitting since I am closing one chapter of my life and beginning another. (For Myself Alone, by Shannon Winslow, chapter 43)

Epilogue

As a general rule, the weather in England is not severe, not when compared to some other places one might name. There are no violent extremes of heat or cold, no tornados, and few tempests of hurricane proportion. Yet every rule is made to be broken... at least once.

Afterward, there would be endless conjecture over exactly what happened that day. People from beyond that isolated region of Hampshire where it occurred often scoffed at the story. But residents of Carding talk about the freak storm of 1810 to this day.

Really, considering how severe it was – brief, but severe – it is quite remarkable, perhaps even miraculous, that there was only the one casualty among man and beast. And even that one victim suffered no real harm.

It was an ordinary November afternoon with people going about their normal business, when a raging wind came out of nowhere. By the time anybody could look to the heavens and call out "God help us!" the sky immediately overhead had turned black and opened up. Instead of the more usual and expected rain, hail pelted down – hail larger than any ever seen in that part of the country before or since. Everybody who happened to be out in it scurried for shelter, nearly all successfully.

But Mrs. Cavanaugh, the young doctor's new wife, was not so fortunate. Having just completed her errands in the village, she had begun the short walk home, thinking once again how lucky she was to have had a second chance at life and that it had turned out so well. When the onslaught occurred, she was caught betwixt and between with nowhere to hide. First, her pretty pink bonnet blew off. And then she looked up, her attention drawn by a howling sound overhead. Mr. Gibson, who was sheltering nearby, swears he heard the lady utter the words, "Not again!" just before the giant hailstone struck her down.

The freak storm was over and gone in a matter of minutes, leaving behind shattered nerves and exactly three broken window panes. But most upsetting was the sight of Mrs. Cavanaugh lying unconscious in the street. Onlookers rushed to her aid, and Mr. Cavanaugh himself was at his wife's side by the time her eyes fluttered open again.

"What has happened, Fitzwilliam?" Mrs. Cavanaugh asked when she awoke and sat up, apparently unharmed.

"They say you were hit by this large hailstone, my dear," explained Mr. Cavanaugh, holding up the icy projectile for her inspection. "It was all over before I arrived, though, and I can find very little evidence of it. Are you well?"

Her hand went to the back of her head to check for herself. "Quite well," she said. "How odd."

Mrs. Cavanaugh suffered no lasting consequences from the incident... at least none she is aware of. When asked what she had meant by her enigmatic utterance, "Not again," Mrs. Cavanaugh said she had neither any idea nor, indeed, any recollection of saying it.

Thus, Hope O'Neil's assimilation into Regency life was officially completed. Occasionally, a stray, colorful expression will still pop out of Kate's mouth, words which no one including she herself can really account for. But that only adds to her charm. So say all her friends, of which she has many. There are no lingering memories of another time, another place, or another family to trouble her. With little else to vex her either, she is quite content. And why not? She has everything a reasonable person requires for true happiness: good health, the benefits of an exceedingly comfortable income, a fine house near her family, and a husband she adores.

She does sometimes wonder how life will change when the time inevitably comes to leave her snug home in Carding for parts further north. Even this prospect holds no terror for her, however. Visits to Pellencourt have had their due effect. Mrs. Cavanaugh now concedes that being obliged to live as mistress of one of the finest estates in Derbyshire cannot rightly be considered a hardship, especially when there will be no impediment to traveling back to

Hampshire to see her family just as often as she likes. No, she intends to submit to her fate gracefully when the time comes.

The time, in fact, will not come for years, and by then, Mr. and Mrs. Cavanaugh will have begun to assemble a new little family of their own, one which they can take with them to Pellencourt.

Looking a little ahead, we see that their first child will be a girl, whom Mrs. Cavanaugh shall insist be christened Hope for no more particular reason than, "I have always liked the name. It seems comfortable and familiar somehow. One cannot imagine, with such an appellation, that our daughter will ever be anything but cheerful and optimistic."

Mr. Cavanaugh will not object. Nor will he object when his wife wants to call the two children that follow, twins, Faith and Charity. He will only complain that neither of them can reasonably be called Henry after his father.

"Girls are all very well, but am I never to have a son?" he shall ask sometime thereafter.

Since he so obviously dotes on all his daughters, Mrs. Cavanaugh knows her husband's remonstrations are not terribly serious. Therefore, she will answer very composedly. "The word 'never' has such an air of finality about it, and persistence is often rewarded. I trust, my dear, that you are not yet to the point of giving up the idea of fathering a son."

"Giving up? I should say not! The end result is not the only thing that matters. I believe, madam, that oftentimes at least half the satisfaction can be found in the endeavor itself."

His wife shares his opinion. Accordingly, Mr. and Mrs. Cavanaugh will continue to industriously *endeavor* and, at last, after only one more girl, their persistence will indeed be rewarded. Mrs. Cavanaugh will then have the joy of fulfilling her husband's only previously unfulfilled wish by presenting him with an heir… and then a year later a spare, thus ensuring by her large family that she will never be alone again and that her progeny and his will carry on at Pellencourt for generations to come.

Throughout her long life, literature will continue to hold a special place in Mrs. Cavanaugh's heart. Expense being no obstacle, she never misses an opportunity to add another book or two to her collection. If she and her husband travel to London or any other sizable town, she is always on the lookout for a new bookshop to investigate or an old favorite to revisit. This is a habit that begins very early in her marriage.

In the autumn of 1813 as they pass through one such town in Hampshire, it happens again. Without warning, Mrs. Cavanaugh raps her knuckles on the roof of the carriage and shouts out, "Stop the coach!"

Somewhat alarmed at the sudden outcry, Mr. Cavanaugh demands to know what the trouble is.

"Look there," says his wife, pointing excitedly.

"Ah, I should have known – a bookshop. Surely you have stopped at this one before, so often as we have passed this way."

"It must be new, for I have never seen it. Would you mind terribly, my love? I shall only be a few minutes."

"Ha! Do you take me for a fool, woman? If you are gone less than half an hour, I will suspect you of being an impostor when you return, and I shall insist on knowing what you have done with my wife."

"Very well," she says lightly. "Have it your own way. I shall make free to take as much time as I like lest I leave myself open to any such slanderous accusations."

"Now *that* is much more like the Kate Cavanaugh I know and love." He sends her off with a kiss, one meant to make a favorable and lasting impression, to stay with her and ensure she will not wish to be away from him *too* long. Then, smiling to himself as she goes, he slides his hat down over his eyes and puts his feet up, intending to have a short nap while he awaits her return.

Inside the shop, Mrs. Cavanaugh peruses the shelves for something appealing. At length, when she cannot make up her mind, she looks about for some help. The proprietor is nowhere to be seen.

"Can I be of any assistance?" offers a lady Mrs. Cavanaugh has not noticed before, a woman with a pleasant, round face who appears to be nearing forty.

"Good morning," says Mrs. Cavanaugh. "I was looking for the shopkeeper. I thought perhaps he could advise me. My husband and I were passing by when I saw this place and had to stop. I am excessively fond of books, you see – novels in particular."

"As am I," says the other lady, "and I know this shop very well indeed."

"Then… Then would *you* be so kind as to recommend something for me? Perhaps you have a favorite author."

The woman smiles as if pondering some secret delight. "I do, in fact. Come with me," she says, leading the way. Finding what she wants, she pulls a three-volume novel off a shelf and offers it to Mrs. Cavanaugh. "Here. Of all the books I have ever read, I do believe this is my very favorite. If I had written it, I would call it my darling child."

"High praise, indeed," says Mrs. Cavanaugh glancing at the title: *Pride and Prejudice*. "Thank you very much. But who is the author? It says only 'a lady.' How mysterious."

"She is too modest to want to see her name in print, I should think."

"Yes, that must be it. I am Mrs. Cavanaugh from Carding, by the way," she says, extending her free hand.

Briefly clasping it, Mrs. Cavanaugh's new acquaintance comments, "Ah, then we are almost neighbors. I reside in Chawton. I am Miss Austen, Miss Jane Austen. Perhaps we will meet again."

"Perhaps so."

Fate has determined that they will *not* meet again. But Mrs. Cavanaugh will never forget the lady from the bookshop as one might soon expect to do after such a fleeting encounter. She will not forget because Miss Austen's favorite book soon becomes her own favorite. Upon purchasing it that day, Mrs. Cavanaugh reads it nearly straight through… and then a second time and a third until all the characters who populate the pages become quite well known to her, like old friends.

In truth, however, some of the people and events of *Pride and Prejudice* (and the other novels by the same author that Mrs. Cavanaugh collects over the years) seem familiar to her even on the very *first* reading. But she supposes that is only because she sees herself as living out a similar sort of fairy tale life, the heroine of a grand romance. In her eyes, her own husband is every bit as splendid as Mr. Darcy and she, as fortunate as Elizabeth Bennet.

The End

Thank you for reading

Leap of Hope
Chance at an Austen Kind of Life

If you enjoyed this book, please look for Book 1 of
Shannon Winslow's Crossroads Collection:

Leap of Faith
Second Chance at the Dream

featuring Ben Lewis,
whom you met in chapter 3-5 of this book

Shannon Winslow's other novels:

The Darcys of Pemberley
Return to Longbourn
Miss Georgiana Darcy of Pemberley
For Myself Alone
The Persuasion of Miss Jane Austen

Learn more at
www.shannonwinslow.com